CATCH *My* FALL

MICHAELA WRIGHT

DEDICATION

To Mum,

Who told me to do the thing I was meant to do and stopped me from going into finance when I had a quarter life crisis.

Thanks for letting me mooch for so long. I promise I'll pay off your mortgage someday.

ACKNOWLEDGMENTS

A shout out to my writers' group - Lianne DeRosier,
Persephone Valentine, Marcie Gerard.
To my first readers - Claire Bridgewater and Carol Roege
Crockett.
To Billy Idol for all those bitchin jams I cranked while
writing this book.
And to Alexander Skarsgard, whose face settled into my
psyche when I tried to bring Stellan to life in my mind.

CHAPTER ONE

How do you identify a girl by a picture of her hoohah? I'm serious – is it even possible? If you were mugged by three naked women, all straddling you as they robbed you blind, do you believe you could identify them in a lineup? Could you pick them out of a book of cooter mug shots? I'm pretty sure I couldn't. I'll tell you though, I was trying my damnedest. Standing on that cold tile floor with a cell phone inches from my face in an attempt to proclaim, yay or nay, that this offending crotch shot was in fact a picture of my crotch.

You're mocking me, aren't you?

Fine, I should probably bring you up to speed before I embarrass myself further.

My name is Faye, and I don't spend a lot of time inspecting ladies' nether regions. Personal choice, really. Yet, I'd woken up that morning beside my boyfriend, Cole, elated to be in just such a situation. It was getting light outside, and I snuck out of bed to head home. Might sound cold to you, but we'd agreed on it the night before. Ever since the company I worked for went bankrupt, and I lost my job (and in the resulting four months of destroying my savings while looking for another, lost my condo) I've been living back at home with my mother. That miserable fact resulted in my spending almost every weekend curled up in this bed – Cole's bed - pretending I'm not an utter failure. The arrangement worked, but he said he found it impossible to get out of bed when he had the warmth of my company next to him. Not a problem on the weekend, but on a workday? In our three years together I'd never woken next to him on a weekday. This was an exception. This was a step in the right direction, I'd thought. Still, the only way he agreed to my spending the night was my offer to be out of the apartment before his alarm went off.

Like the miracle of a girlfriend I am, I rose with the sun, silently gathered my things and slipped into the bathroom to get dressed without disturbing him. Feeling a wee bit frisky that morning, I decided to leave him a present for later that day. I snuck back out into the bedroom and took his ancient cell phone from the nightstand. Then I slipped back into the bathroom to take a risqué picture. I unbuttoned my shirt, pressed the camera button, aimed the thing at my tits and clicked away. No shutter sound. I posed again, making a face somewhat reminiscent of a duck. I pressed again. Nada. I finally turned the bastard around to see what was wrong, and the aforementioned twat shot offended my eyes.

Now I don't know why it popped up when I pressed the camera button, I wasn't going snooping through his phone, if that's what you're thinking. And no, I don't know what kind of phone it is – it flips open, it has buttons and it takes cripplingly high resolution pictures of Labia. If I knew the brand I'm sure you'd run right out and buy one, wouldn't you?

Cole hasn't exactly updated his cell phone in a while. Pretty sure they don't even make the thing anymore. Joke's on you.

So there I was in his pristine bathroom trying to convince myself that this was my hoohah, and I had somehow gotten so severely drunk that I'd let him take it and forgotten. Kind of pathetic when you consider that the offending Vagina was pierced. No amount of alcohol will magically put a metal rod through my clitoris.

I stood frozen for longer than I care to admit, buttoned my shirt, texted the picture to myself, and slipped back out into the bedroom. I stared down at Cole's dark hair, imagining the sound his cell phone would make if I chucked it full force at the back of his head. I imagined it would be very satisfying, but I didn't do it. Instead, I propped the open phone with picture up onto my pillow beside him. When he woke, it would be there – a picture of the little man in a boat floating in a white sea of bamboo sheets

I carried my shoes to the front door before putting them on, still taking care not to wake him and left his apartment. I made it all the way to my car before the tears came.

Now you might envision me careening down the road sobbing, but I didn't drive for a while. I sat there in the parking lot of that tired, three story brick apartment building, and I wailed. Didn't even start my car to cool it down. I just sat there keening until snot was dripping into my lap. I didn't stop until my phone buzzed. I snatched it up and found Cole's text.

Good morning, baby.

I laughed, and I sounded batshit insane. And you might be thinking, what the hell is he doing texting you like nothing has happened? Well, let me just tell you, that's how he rolls.

Cole's Magic Get Out of Trouble Card (patent

pending) – pretend nothing happened.

I had a feeling he might do exactly that – find a way to explain the shot or simply pretend it didn't exist and that I was crazy. I'd been on the receiving end of these tactics before, and I hated them. Unlike every other time, I wasn't going to put up with it that day. I quickly went from a sobbing, snotty mess to a tempest of rage. I pulled up the twat shot and texted it to him. No words, no text acronyms and emoticons – the picture could speak for itself.

You were wondering why I texted the twat shot to myself, weren't you? I plan ahead, ladies and gentlemen. I don't fuck around.

Once it was sent, I chucked my phone onto the floor of the passenger's side to keep myself from reading his response and drove my ass home.

I pulled up outside my mother's house. I had angry break up songs blaring so loud, I'm sure I announced my arrival to the entire neighborhood and if that didn't alert them to my presence, the sound of me swearing as I slammed my car door on the seat belt might have done the trick.

I parked in front of my mother's house and paused before storming inside. I didn't want my mother to see me like this. I stood at the bottom of the steps and pretended to inspect the plants.

My mother's house was one of the nicer houses in the neighborhood - not because it was larger or better landscaped, but because it was memorable. Let's be honest, there's probably more weed than there is rosebush by now, but it still doesn't deter from the appeal. My grandmother planted the vines at the base of the porch in several different spots. We, of course, left the things to grow like fungus after she passed, and Ivy and Clematis peppered the columns and rails of the porch like some floral apocalypse.

I stood on the sidewalk, blowing each breath through tightly pursed lips as I tried to calm the tears. I looked up at the farmer's porch, and didn't move.

Still wasn't ready.

There were Adirondack chairs on the porch, and I considered plopping down in one and rocking like a mental patient until I got it out of my system.

I hovered, hoping my mother wasn't about to see me hovering like some creeper. Once, if I wanted to go home and throw things while flash dancing in the living room, I could do so. Now, if I attempted such a thing, my mother would appear and ask what was wrong or for me to turn the music down. I felt a moment's relief when I realized it was early Monday morning. My mother was already on her way to work. I trudged up the steps and opened the front door. The house was quiet. If I'd been thinking straight, I could have parked in the damn driveway.

After texting my misery to my three closest friends, I spent my morning in the shower or in bed, listening to 80's music. I punched my mattress to the angry songs and wailed into my pillow to the emotional songs – if you can call Billy Idol emotional. I assure you, on that morning, I could.

That's the problem with music – it just fucking knows. For example, I would like to take this opportunity to say "Fuck you, Journey." I would punch the song 'Separate Ways' in the face, if I could.

About halfway into the keyboard intro of Corey Hart's "I Wear My Sunglasses At Night," I heard the doorbell. I glanced at the clock – 11:30.

I stumbled out of bed in my penguin pajama pants

and a sweatshirt cut to match that of Jennifer Beals in "Flashdance." Yes, I may be more than a little fixated on the 80's, but god damn it, that sweatshirt makes my collar bone look like hot sex. I padded down the stairs and spotted Meghan through the window. She'd come, and knowing her, it was probably her lunch break. The iced coffee from dunks only further hinted at her rushed tripped over.

She wrapped her arms around me and squeezed. "Oh, honey! That bastard is gonna feel this one."

Meghan Trotsky was, by far, the sexiest big woman I'd ever known. Actually, she's probably the sexiest woman, at any size. She might be a big girl, but she knows how to work it, and she takes her time every day to look like a catalogue model. Today she was wearing a navy sweater with a belt just under bust and the most flattering pair of jeans on the planet. Her hair was perfect, with a curl at the end of her highlighted blond hair. Meghan has long eyelashes and crystalline blue eyes. She's also been on a 'diet' the entire time I've known her.

She dragged me to the couch, demanding I tell her everything, only to have the doorbell ring again around noon. This time it was Jackie Antunes, or Jacinta Antunes if you wanted to get punched. She joined us on the couch, and I was forced to retell the whole thing. The two of them listened and hemmed and hawed, riling me up and getting me righteously indignant. They brought up every little shit thing Cole had ever done, every time he'd been an asshole, swore they'd never liked him, and began regaling me with how stunning and special I was and how instantaneously I'd be swept off my feet by some roguish Highlander. Their company felt good, and I needed them desperately.

Finally, the moment came - the undeniable and somewhat relished moment when Meghan, my go to girl for inappropriate curiosity, finally asked. "Did you delete the picture yet?"

I paused. "No."

Both of their eyes lit up, though Jackie tried to hide it. Meghan demanded my phone, and I handed it over. The thought of the rest of town seeing this girl's shebang appealed to me. Judge if you must.

"Oh, Christ! What a skank!" Meghan said.

"Let me see!" Jackie snatched the phone from her and made a sound that was a mix between a gurgle and a cough, covering her mouth while she gazed up the offending vulva.

Meghan shook her head, her lips pursed. "Seriously, what a skank! If you're going to let a man take a picture of your pussy, at least require that it be classy. And did you see that landing strip? It's the sloppiest wax job I've ever seen."

"I bet she has Chlamydia," Jackie said, throwing wood on Meghan's fire.

"Hell yeah, she has Chlamydia! And if she doesn't, she still has a fucking amateur for a waxer."

Jackie nodded. "It is a little ragged."

"And for Christ's sake, what kind of foul slut gets her Clitoris pierced? I mean seriously." Meghan directed her question to both of us, and I nodded. Listening to them fight for nasty things to say about this complete stranger was better than contemplating what about this 'foul slut' surpassed me, and why.

I was ready to join in when I noticed Jackie's face. She was blushing.

Meghan spotted it too. "Oh no! You're kidding

me?"

Jackie shrugged. "It was a spur of the moment thing!"

"Wait, you have your hoohah pierced?" I asked, and believe me I was truly shocked. Jackie Antunes was a light skinned, half-Latina with freckles. She wears glasses when she reads, enjoys watching Jeopardy with her grandmother, spends most of her time baking and living the life of a feminist housewife, and apparently having a perfect stranger handle and stab her girly bits. I was flabbergasted.

Meghan was at the ready with her thoughts. "No, stopping for a latte is a spur of the moment thing. Getting your clit pierced is-"

"Hey, at least my landing strip is clean," Jackie said.

Meghan held up a hand. "Damn straight it is!"

They immediately high fived, and Jackie went on to explain the intricacies of just how 'not so bad' getting pierced was. We listened, but stopped her before certain details. Hearing your friend describe the 'most excruciating pain you'll ever feel' in reference to that region was well off my list of things to learn more about.

Meghan shook her head, tossing her curls over her shoulder. "Seriously though, what kind of dirty slut would let a guy like Cole take a picture of her pierced hoohah?"

"He doesn't have any of yours, does he?" Jackie asked.

I shook my head. "No! Never!"

Meghan hummed her approval. "See, cause you're not a dirty fucking skank."

I thought about it for a moment.

"Well -" When I was trying to convince myself it

was my uncleanly waxed and pierced toonana I was looking at, I wasn't startled so much by the idea of having posed for it. "I can't say I would never let someone take such a picture. If he were the right guy - "

Jackie made a face. "And you'd had a few."

Yes, Jackie knew me well.

Meghan shook her head. "Honey. No matter who the guy is, if you let the bastard take a picture of your pussy, you best expect that somebody else is gonna see it."

"Not necessarily," Jackie said, and I sensed she'd taken part in a few of her own erotic photo shoots. I hurt when I thought of Jackie and her devoted husband, Kevin. There was no question in my mind that if Kevin had such a picture of Jackie, he'd be dead before it saw the light of day. There was also no question in my mind that if Kevin asked, Jackie would be bare-assed with her feet behind her head before Kevin could get his phone out of his pocket.

"No, I'm sorry. You have to assume that if a guy wants a trophy like that, he's probably got a trophy case somewhere," Meghan said, snatching up her iced coffee to take a sip.

That bothered me. If there was one, what if there were more? It must've played on my face, because both women were soon holding my hands and consoling me yet again. A little before one, heavy footsteps echoed down the hall from the kitchen just as Meghan collected her keys.

The footsteps startled me. Stellan had come.

Why after all these years was I surprised?

Meghan greeted Stellan as he came in from the kitchen, then apologized for leaving. She offered to take me shopping for something sexy that evening. I wasn't ready to feel sexy.

Stellan plopped down on the couch beside me, cracking a can of root beer he'd snagged from the fridge. He turned on the TV as Jackie collected her coat to head out as well. We exchanged a few more agitated words – *he's a schmuck, you're too good for him, if I see him on the street I'll run him down*. She and Stellan smiled at each other.

"I'm a phone call away," Jackie said. With that she slipped out the front door.

I sat next to Stellan watching as he flipped through channels - soap operas, news casts, and cartoons all bled together as my eyes grew heavy.

Stellan glanced my way, and I fought to keep my expression still. Then, he shifted and turned off the TV. A second later, he wrapped his arm around my shoulders and the next thing I knew, I was pulled into his chest, and I was sobbing.

I leaned on the counter as Stellan made himself a sandwich. He'd asked for permission to raid the fridge, since I was standing right there. Most occasions, he wouldn't bother asking. You might think such a cavalier attitude toward manners is rude, but Stellan spent so much of his free time at my house during our friendship, my mother finally demanded he simply stop asking and treat our house as his own. Even though I'd been living in Arlington, and Stellan and I rarely saw each other for years, the minute I came home, we picked up where we left off. Easy enough when he lives less than a quarter mile down the street. Stellan comes by, keeps me company, takes what he wants from the fridge and despite my mother's protests, delivers groceries to the house every few weeks to replenish the stock.

Stellan Odegard is a monster of a man – 6'5" or so, though I've never bothered to measure him and he doesn't seem to care. He's a black belt with a blond mullet that he's maintained since high school despite everyone nagging him to cut it, and an inappropriate humor that simply ruins me. His father, Lennart, is a Swedish immigrant who married his American mother, Linda, after learning English from her when he first went to business school in Sweden. Despite Lennart's stoic nature, Stellan was raised in the most disgustingly loving household ever. He still happily lives in his parent's basement a few blocks from my house. Stellan was Swedish born, but only by a few months. His parents moved him to Concord, Massachusetts before his first birthday. Despite growing up an American, Stellan spoke Swedish and still had most of his conversations with his father in the man's native language. I'd loved listening to them when we were growing up. It is a lot easier to listen to a father and son rip each other's heads off when you can't understand a word they're saying.

I met Stellan in middle school. He was swearing at a computer in Swedish when it failed to keep up with him. There wasn't much on earth that could. I'd initially thought he was an exchange student and felt compelled to befriend him. He hadn't hit his growth spurt by then. After a bullying incident in fifth grade, Linda put Stell in martial arts in hopes he wouldn't be bullied again. By junior year of high school, Stellan was a lumbering giant who could sneak up and kill you with your own finger. Almost twenty years later, Stellan taught at the same Ninjutsu school where he'd been taught as a kid. Despite my thinking he's a raging jackass, he is one hell of a teacher.

He had one motto that seemed to remind his students of just who they were dealing with.

Stellan's #1 Rule - 'You raise your hand in anger, I break it.'

Oddly enough, no parents have ever complained.

Interesting choice of job for an MIT drop out, wouldn't you say?

He teaches Ninjitsu in West Concord, and when he isn't playing video games, he's programming iPhone applications on his five thousand dollar laptop, or he's here - eating my food.

He pulled out the ingredients for two sandwiches, and I declined before he could make the second. He raised an eyebrow. I couldn't help but laugh. The second sandwich wasn't intended for me.

"Though, now that you mention it, have you eaten anything today?" Stellan asked.

I shook my head. We both glanced at the clock. It was two thirty. I was about to get reprimanded if I didn't eat something. I didn't care. My stomach was in knots. I was anxious as though some terrible event were about to take place. Then I'd remember it already had.

Stellan didn't push eating as I'd expected, but he did offer me a bite. I took one. It felt like eating paste. Stellan pushed a second bite, but I declined. We sat on the couch watching taped episodes of America's Funniest Home Videos despite his having made fun of me for loving them for years. Apparently today it was ok to laugh at people falling down. And I did, I laughed every chance I could.

Stellan and I spent the afternoon together until

Meghan returned around six. The three of us sat there, Meghan doing most of the talking, but when she again offered to take me out for some girl time and shopping – anything to distract me - I just wasn't ready. Those penguin pajamas were really comfortable and stupid television felt miraculous. She hung out for a little while, then left. Stellan followed shortly thereafter, having blown off a day's worth of work to be with me. It took a few minutes to convince him it was alright to go. I collected myself from the living room couch and went upstairs. My mother was still out, Monday night being her standing dinner date with someone from the Museum.

I had the house to myself. Rather than blare some Billy Idol or sing loudly while cooking myself dinner, I simply crawled into my bed. On the bedside table, my cell phone sat silent where I left it that morning. I'd wanted to avoid hearing Cole's ringtone when he texted or called. Yet after a day with friends, I was ready to face whatever pathetic attempts he'd made to excuse himself.

There were texts from Meghan, Jackie, and a message from Stellan to let him know if I needed him to come back to the house.

Nothing from Cole. He hadn't called to fix things. He hadn't chased me down to explain this pain away.

He'd done nothing.

I cried harder then than I had all day.

***

There is healing power in sleep. I don't know if it's the therapy of dreams, the passage of time, but no matter how miserable you are when you fall asleep, you wake up feeling just a little lighter.

Well, today wasn't one of those days.

I woke up with the feeling of a vice clamped onto my temples and a wolverine in my stomach. I managed to get out of bed with one simple purpose – take Tylenol - then go back to bed.

Too lazy to rub the gunk out of my eyes, I found my mother topless, sitting lotus style in the center of the living room floor with her morning coffee steaming away in a nearby mug.

My mother, Pamela Jensen, was an eccentric. She was an art curator, a painter, a poet, a nude yoga practitioner (and teacher), spoke three languages, and let her salt and pepper hair grow wild and long. It was pinned up in a bun at the top of her head, letting the power of 'tits out yoga' work its full magic.

I stopped dead in my tracks.

Damn it, Faye. You grew up with the 'naked time' behavior, why are you so startled now?

Maybe because I've lived on my own for almost ten years and have kept my 'Mom's tits' quota to an absolute minimum?

I took a deep breath. I should have known, given the ambient spa music oozing from the downstairs stereo. I tried to pass by her without disturbing her, but she glanced my way.

I smiled and hurried by, praying she wouldn't try to have a conversation with me until *after* she put a shirt on.

She smiled at me, but the jovial look was fleeting. I'd betrayed my mood, and I was practically half asleep.

Shit, shit, shit! Half naked meaningful talk incoming! Please don't hug me, Mom. I'm too fragile for Mom boobs right now!

"You alright, sweetheart?"

Should've stayed in bed.

"Yeah, just a headache."

"Well, let's take care of that," she said and was off the floor in a heartbeat, gliding down the kitchen hallway in her baggy yoga pants toward the medicine cabinet, her breasts tanned and undulating as mammaries are wont to do.

She popped a couple of pills from the bottle and handed them over. When I received my bounty it included a multi-vitamin and a St. John's Wort. Ah, the pleasures of having a crunchy mother.

I didn't complain. I didn't want her efforts to feel unwelcome. She offered me coffee or orange juice. Standing before the open fridge, tits still out. I chose water and downed the pills. She stood leaning against the counter, silent, crossing her arms over her chest as she watched me. She knew I would open up if there was something to tell. I told my mother everything that went on in my life. When my company went under, she was the first person I called. She spent ten minutes assuring me that some other company would snatch me up in a heartbeat and be more than happy to match my just over six figure salary. When I realized I was going to lose the condo, she took a half hour explaining why such an event was a blessing in disguise and that my bedroom was always ready if I ever needed it. Yet, despite those moments of unadulterated positivity, on that morning, I felt allergic to her sunshine.

I was especially allergic to topless sunshine. Sure, I grew up with her nudity, but having lived on my own for so long, coming home to it felt odd.

I drank the rest of my water and wished her a good day at work, then turned back for my warm bed and the serenity of not being conscious.

"I'll leave the mat out for you? A little yoga might be just the thing to settle your mind."

I grumbled my approval as I hunched up the stairs. "Sure. That sounds great."

Mom stood at the bottom of the stairs, watching me as I escaped back into my bedroom.

I listened to her get ready for work, then relished the sound of her car pulling down the road.

I spent the day lying there replaying each moment I'd spent with Cole – each kiss, each gift he'd bought me, each Valentine's Day, each sexual encounter. I tried to recover from those memories with the terrible and miserable ones that had come in between, but I couldn't help but miss him. I hated myself for it.

I didn't go back downstairs.

I didn't do any yoga.

I didn't change out of those penguin pajamas for three weeks.

***

"Honey?" My mother called from outside my door one morning. I murmured for her to come in. "I made some eggs. Scrambled with ham and cheese, do you want to come down, or should I bring it up here?"

"I'm not really hungry. Thank you, though."

She stood at the door a moment. I could almost hear her fretting. Finally, she delivered the eggs to my bedside table and headed off to work.

I didn't eat a bite.

This was another infuriating part of living with your parents – not only to do they like nudity a little too much for your tastes, they have the audacity to care about you.

I tried not to feel guilty for causing my mother worry. It wasn't working.

When noon rolled around, I heard heavy footsteps across the downstairs floor. My brow furrowed and I turned to watch as my door swung open, slamming against my bedside table. Stellan appeared in the doorway and jumped on the bed. He knelt beside me, bouncing up and down, chanting "Wakey wakey, eggs and bakey!"

I slammed my pillow into his face and returned to my prone position. He had me by the ankles in a millisecond.

"Let go of me!"

"God, you fucking stink."

I kicked at him, pulling feet from his grasp. "Oh, and you smell like roses?"

Stellan grabbed my wrist, hoisted me up off the bed and over his shoulder. I screamed, but it was no use. When he wanted you to move, you had no choice.

Stellan shifted me on his shoulder. "What can I say? Some days, I sweat awesome. You on the other hand are just festering. I'm doing everyone a fucking favor."

"Fuck you!"

"You wish."

I kicked and pushed against him, but he simply ducked himself through the doorjambs and carried me to the linen closet. He set me on my feet, pulled out a couple towels, and pressed them to my chest.

I glared up at him. He'd been my best friend for

most of my life, but damn it, I've lived on my own – a grownup – for almost ten years. Suddenly I'm back home and he's treating me like he did when we were in high school. Who the fuck did this guy think he was? "You suck, you know that right?"

"Hey, it ain't my fault your mom called me."

She did? Oh god, I thought.

He turned me toward the bathroom door. "I should be fucking working, right now. So suck it the fuck up. You're not spending the day in bed."

"I fucking hate you."

Stellan puckered his lips and made kissing sounds as he pushed me toward the shower. "Love you too."

He clomped down the stairs and turned on the TV. I knew if I tried to get back in bed, he'd be back up here in ten minutes, and we would go through this scene all over again, only next time he'd use his big voice.

I went about the bathroom, slamming every door and hinged object I could as I undressed and climbed into the shower. Despite my determination to avoid this very thing, the warm water felt good, like a baptism into a better humor. I washed my hair and face, brushed my teeth – hell, I even flossed, as though the crannies of my molars might hold untold twat shots that had yet to foul up my mood. When I tossed the penguin pajama in the hamper, I felt released – a little. I pulled the sheets off the bed and tossed them in as well, pulled mismatched sheets from the hallway linen closet and made my bed. Once I'd finished, I was ready to properly tear Stellan a new asshole.

My mother's house has the blessing of wall to wall hardwood floors – deathly cold and merciless in the winter, but cool and inviting in the warmer months. It was late August and the central air was whirring away through the vents, a sign that outside was uncomfortably hot. For a split second, I forgot the shame of living with Mom, and was grateful.

I shuffled down the stairs in my bare feet and made my way to the kitchen. I collected a cup of coffee from the fresh pot bubbling in wait for me. I'd thank Stellan for it if I didn't want to punch him. When I came back to the front room, I kept distance between us, curling up in my grandmother's old club chair by the fireplace. The light from the corner windows poured in there all day long. I pulled a dog-eared book from the small bookcase and cracked it to the last page - read a month earlier - and began to read. The two of us sat in each other's company, content to be together, but separate. It was nice – for about four minutes. That's how long it took for me to remember why I'd left the book for a month. It was terrible.

I joined Stellan on the couch. So much for intellectual relaxation. "Remind me never to buy a book based on its title again."

Stellan didn't look at me. "Never buy a book based on its title again."

"Thanks."

"Anytime."

We sat watching a documentary on the making of a Coen Brothers movie and quietly melted into the couch.

Stellan shifted. "What was the title?"

"Pussy King of the Pirates."

"Well, if you're not going to read it -" he said and went to snatch it out of my hands.

I swatted him away and laughed. "No, I can't in

good conscience let this book out into the wild. It must be destroyed."

"Should I get the blessing salts?"

"No. This must be scoured by fire."

The two of us silently rose from the couch and walked to the fireplace on the other side of the front room, my favorite room. It spanned the width of the entire house with windows on three sides. It was bright and open, separated at the middle by the bottom of the staircase, and along one side of the stairs was the hallway to the kitchen. On the other side of the stairs the front room curved around, leading to the office and dining room. Over the years, my mother had managed to gut the house of all remnants of carpet and seventies wallpaper, leaving it to look like a Home & Garden spread. Someday, I hoped to have my own house, just like it.

We hunched over the fireplace and Stellan started chanting, ominously, holding his hand out for me to hand him the book. I did and joined the chant.

Yet, when Stellan suddenly produced the fireplace lighter I snatched it back from him. "I'm not seriously going to burn this, you jackass!"

He feigned devastation. "Why?"

"I don't know. Something about book burning just doesn't settle right. Call me weird."

"You're weird. And no fun," he said and crossed back to the couch. I tossed the book back onto the bookcase and promised to choose a different book the next time I felt like reading.

We wore divots into the couch for an hour. I hadn't left the house in weeks and a part of me missed the outside world. Then, as evidenced by the embarrassing 'splurf' of my gastrointestinal workings,

I apparently missed food as well. Stellan rolled an eyeball in my direction, and I smacked his arm.

"Don't look at me like that."

He hopped up off the couch, towering over me as he held out a hand. "I gotta get back to work, but come on. Let's get you some grub."

I followed him into the kitchen.

He'd gone a half hour later, and I found myself stewing on my mother's couch. This felt rather pointless, given the battle it took to get me out of bed.

After an hour of soap operas and old game shows, I texted Stellan, Meghan, and Jackie in the hopes that one of them would be free for something – anything to distract me from the passage of time. I'd become dependent on them for human contact. I stood in the middle of my front room, sipping raspberry tea with honey when boredom inspired an unexpected thought.

I went into the office and sat down at the computer. I pulled up a job search website, one I hadn't even considered for a month or more now, and began searching. This act had become tedious over the months after I moved home, and I found myself despondent to the idea the longer I went without luck. I'd managed to find one job during that time, one possible savior onto which I clasped with every ounce of my being. All my hope, my gospel, my self-worth, lay weighted on that one position. Head of Marketing at Endine, a position that offered perks, sixty plus hour work weeks and a comparable pay grade to the job I'd recently lost. I played that interview like a fiddle, regaling my interviewer with 'anything to please the client' talk. I'd retold every extra mile I'd gone, every midnight meal, every last minute flight I'd managed to catch, just in order to please some client who I knew from experience, was just as desperate for business as I – as my firm was. When the bank called a dozen times a day, I sat in front of my computer, willing it to bring good news. I spent my days waiting, praying, assuring the mortgage company that my prospects were looking up and if all went well, I would be able to make my payment.

That miracle didn't happen. They went with 'the other guy.' The bank stopped calling. They foreclosed. I was evicted. My condo sold at auction to some young single guy, perhaps even the guy who'd swooped in and stolen the only job prospect I'd had. What a cosmic glitch that would be.

I stared at the screen, my stomach churning out of habit alone as it saw the lines of job positions in bold purple and pink. This was my exit strategy, my road to reclaim my life. Yet, the life I built overworking myself, smiling through exhaustion - that castle was built on sand. One good wave and it was gone.

I held the cup of tea to my lips, letting the steam warm my face as I tried to focus on something else, something hopeful. I couldn't. I was still mourning.

My resume and info was already programmed into my account so if something caught my eye, I was ready to pass my life along. There were random jobs, some temp work here and there; the same lines of repeated positions that were kept constantly open due to high turnover rate. These positions had been unacceptable to me once, but a few more months of mooching off of my mother and shoveling shit might start looking good. I highlighted a temp job, but something caught my eye. *Marketing Strategist*, the position read.

I took a breath. The position had opened at a firm still located in Concord. I quickly opened the link.

Bachelor's Degree? Check. Previous work of at least five years? Check. Willing to travel? Check.

I stared at the 'Click to Apply' button for five minutes. Somehow, the promise of work, of the same, well paid, busy work that for seven years I busted my ass doing, felt almost ominous. I couldn't decide whether this was Inertia having set in – an ass on the couch is inclined to remain an ass on the couch – or if it was the remains of my dashed hopes the last time I'd applied for something. I thought of the running tab of rent not paid and lunches bought by well-meaning friends and clicked the link. I attached my resume, rewrote my cover letter and a second later it was gone.

I stared at the screen a few moments, sipped the last of my tea, and made a decision. I was going for a walk.

The air was cool and damp from the chilly night before. It was only halfway into September, but the weather was beginning to hint at its intentions, scouring the earth with burning heat for a couple days, then leaving a frost the third night. Today was the first cool day that week. I was content to be out in it.

Autumn in New England is my favorite time of year – the leaves, the breeze, the smell of the air and the familiar whir of tourists sailing by on their mountain bikes. I reached Concord Center, crossed the rotary and headed down Main Street. I passed the Mill Dam that still traveled just under the street. My grandmother had once told me about the scores of musket balls they found when the town dug up the

Mill Dam to lay a parking lot - hundreds of tiny musket balls once dumped there by villagers who refused to let the Red Coats have their munitions. Concord was an interesting town for stories.

I slipped into the Main Street Café for a cannoli and a coffee. Yes, it cost ten dollars – no I wasn't working. Luckily, and much to the chagrin of my pride, I had a very generous mother.

I snacked at one of the corner tables, and listened to the voices around me. Someone had left a newspaper at the table, and I borrowed a pen to do the crossword. When I was stumped by four down, I found myself sketching a nearby child in the borders of the paper. I perused the Police Blotter for any criminals I might know, finding several reports of a quite possibly rabid raccoon roaming the neighborhood one street over from me. Apparently, Monument Street was turning into Wild Kingdom. Stellan and I would walk down that very road to climb trees at the State Park when we were young. Stellan climbed far higher than any non-primate should be able to, only to jump down from an outrageous height when it was time to go. Stellan was once reprimanded by a grandmother for pulling such a stunt.

'You should know better! My grandson thought that was the most spectacular thing he's ever seen. I'm sure it's only a matter of time before he breaks a leg trying to emulate you. You should be a role model at your age, not an idiot!'

She stormed away with her sheepish grandson, and the dare devil side of Stellan almost died. He might be huge, and he might be snarky, but put a screaming grandmother in front of him and Stellan shrinks like cooked plastic.

These memories made me feel drawn toward old haunts, and I found myself heading down Rabid Raccoon way toward the National Park. I stopped on the North Bridge to gaze down at the water, still and glassy today despite the passing kayaks and canoes. My Grandmother Jensen brought me there many times, even before my mother and I moved in. She was proud of her hometown, having grown up with a Historian for a father and a raging bitch for a mother (her words toward the end of her life when she stopped worrying about manners and decorum). To impress her, I'd managed to memorize the inscription on the Monument there.

By the crude bridge that arched the flood,
 to April's breeze their flag unfurled,
here once the embattled farmer stood and
fired the shot heard round the world.

I glanced toward the monument a dozen or so yards away, but couldn't quite make out the inscription. *Oh well,* I thought. *It goes something like that.*

I followed down the path, past the monument. It was the time of year when the fields were overgrown, the stalks of grass long and light, snapping and swaying in waves across the fields. The breeze kicked up, and I leaned my head back. I was growing fond of leaving the house with my hair still wet.

"Is that Faye Jensen?"

I startled, searching for the source of the voice. I met the gaze of a small park ranger with the cutest little button nose I'd ever seen.

"Patricia Hannity?"

She beamed, obviously pleased to be remembered.

Of course I remembered her – she was one of the sweetest girls in school before she transferred to Concord Academy and points beyond. She looked almost exactly the same – tiny little upturned nose, perfectly curled dark hair that never grew past her ears, beauty mark on her right cheekbone. If you can imagine, the Ranger outfit just amplified her cuteness. "Oh my god, you look so great!"

"Oh, thank you! You too!" She said and smiled.

She laughed and it was as though pixies had scampered by. I had never imagined that the button of a little girl I'd once known would have turned into a button of a woman. Somehow, I felt cuteness of this magnitude was probably against nature.

I stuffed my hands in my pockets. "What are you doing around here? Last I heard you moved away?"

"I did. Went to college in Edinburgh."

My stomach tightened. Somehow, whenever anyone mentioned living somewhere exotic and far off, I felt a pang of envy that was nearly overpowering. I'd never so much as seen Canada.

"Wow! That must have been something!"

"Oh yeah! Met my husband Geoffrey there," she said and displayed a hand to me. That pang I mentioned before? Yeah, now it was downright excruciating - a Charlie horse of envy, if you will.

"Are you kidding me? That's amazing!"

She smiled and her perfect, pearly white teeth glistened. My cynical mood of the past few weeks desperately wanted to hate her, but she was just so damn cute. Then the dreaded moment came – the one I'd found myself desperate to dodge in conversations like this for the past five or so months. There's a reason why I don't leave the house.

"So what are you up to?" She asked.

I fumbled for an appropriate response. *Oh, you know – living at home, vegging on Soap Operas and Cheetos, buying my coffee and cannolis with Mom's money or letting my best friend buy me lunch when he isn't holed up in his parent's basement.*

"Well, I got laid off a few months ago, so I've been in between things."

"Oh, I'm sorry to hear that. You home with mom these days?"

That bitch. "I am, actually. Yeah."

She nodded. "Nothing wrong with that. It's been happening to a lot of people, recently. Damn economy, you know?"

"Don't I?"

She smiled again, a pleasant redirection prepared. In the split second that I realized she wasn't going to press further, I fell madly in love with her and decided she needed to be my new best friend.

"So, is there a lucky man in your life?"

I wanted to cut her face. "No. Just me for now."

She puckered her lips in an exaggerated frown. It was so fucking cute I wanted to punch her.

"Well, are you still in touch with Stellan Ødegård? Oh, or Evan! Weren't you friends with him?"

Evan Lambert. The lady had a damn good memory.

Evan Lambert was the third member of Stellan and my trifecta. He was the only son of one of the wealthiest families in Concord, and we'd spent much of high school together. Last I heard from him was three months after he went live with his website, made more money than God, and became a local celebrity.

He wasn't just a local celebrity anymore. Being a

billionaire will do that to you.

"I am, actually. Not Evan, but Stell, yes."

Where are you going with this, you demonic sprite?

"He's a handsome guy. And as I recall, he's always loved you."

"Yeah, not like that though. Besides, I can't imagine myself the den mother of giant, mulleted Swedes."

She laughed, and somewhere a fairy was born. "Doesn't sound so bad. I could totally see you as Mrs. Faye Ødegård? Has a nice ring to it, doesn't it?"

"You know what? It does. I'm going to call him now and demand a ring, now that you mention it."

She laughed and wished me well, heading back to the Visitor's Center. I turned back toward the bridge and Monument Street, silently promising myself that I would become an insane hermit and never leave the house again.

I was halfway back down Monument Street when my phone buzzed in my pocket. It startled me. The most likely culprit had left my company to go 'plow through' some last minute work. I pulled out my phone.

I miss you, baby.

My stomach turned. Three weeks, two days – nothing. Now, on the first day I'm even capable of leaving the house…

I'm pretty sure Cole Blanchard has asshole clairvoyance.

I stood there on the side of the road staring at my phone as cars whizzed past on their leaf peeping day drives. I wasn't ok. Any feeling of relief or joy I had while spending the afternoon with Stellan, or walking through town was gone. It wasn't just fucking gone; it was like it never was. I swallowed and started to walk,

28

watching the ground just inches in front of my feet, oblivious to the oncoming cars. I got home, clenching my hand around my phone, half ready to throw it.

"You all right, honey?"

I startled. "What are you doing home?"

My mom shuffled in from the kitchen and watched me. She was wearing one of her trademark flowing dresses of every color. I didn't know why she was home, but at that moment I'd never been more grateful for her presence. Still, I wasn't going to tell her what was wrong.

"Just not having a great day."

"Did you see Stellan?"

I nodded and quickly ended the conversation by turning on the TV.

Despite my better judgment, I texted Meghan and told her of the new contact.

You are NOT going to respond, right?
I don't know.

She was calling three seconds later.

"Faye! You can't respond!"

I wanted to fight that logic, but deep down, I knew I needed to hear someone say it. "So what? I should just ignore it?"

"He cheated on you!"

"We think. I haven't actually let him explain anything. Maybe -"

"What?!" And that was it; the sound of Meghan's righteous indignation practically splintered the earpiece of my phone. "The fucker has a picture of someone else's va-jay-jay on his phone and you think maybe he came by it innocently? That's bull shit!"

"What if one of his friends texted it to him?"

"Then not only does he hang out with scumbags,

but he kept it! Then – THEN, when you discovered it and clearly assumed the worst, he waited three fucking weeks to make any attempt to talk to you about it – or anything for that matter? Hell no! Fuck him!"

"Maybe he was busy…" I cringed, even with the words only half spoken. God, I sounded pathetic.

"Yeah, even you know that's just not going to fucking fly. Seriously!"

I turned to find my mother standing by the stairs. Shit.

"Sorry Mom."

"Your Mom is there? Can she hear me? Mrs. Jensen! Back me up!"

Mum could hear Meghan. I wouldn't have been surprised if Mr. Hodges across the street could.

"I can't say that I know any better than Faye, but I will say -" Mom stalled a moment almost fearing her next comment would meet with an adverse response. "- he doesn't seem to know your worth, honey. And I don't think he ever did."

She was right to expect a response.

"What does that mean?"

Even I could hear the tension in my voice.

"I just don't think he's ever showed you the kind of consideration he should."

My jaw shifted. "You're just saying that because he never comes by the house."

"Yeah, let's just talk about that!" Meghan said, ready to run with it. "Let's put the poontang pic aside and talk about that. Why *doesn't* he come over?"

"I think he's just uncomfortable with the situation."

"Has he even met your Mom?"

"Yes, of course!" I said.

"Once," my mom said. Then she quietly turned and

headed back into the kitchen. This wasn't helping. I was tense, but what most bothered me was they were right. Believe me, I'd spent three weeks making an inventory of just how big a schmuck he was, but this text somehow managed to scribble over that inventory, like a shopping list that has been half purchased. Maybe there was a reason, an explanation, an exit strategy from this near month long depression I'd been wallowing in. He'd caused it. Maybe he could fix it?

Having my mom leave the room only offered a moment's relief.

Meghan took a deep breath on the other line. "You deserve better, Faye. You know you do."

I sighed. "I do, but what if he is willing to offer -"

"You can't be serious. People don't change, girl."

"That's not true."

"No, it's fact. If you're thinking of talking to him, or worse, fucking getting back together with him, you need to do some serious fucking soul searching. He is what he is, and the woman you were three years ago when you met this asshole would have never, I mean fucking never tolerated half the shit he's done, let alone a twat shot on his fucking phone! Christ!"

I wanted to hang up. I loved Meghan, but I needed to process. She hollered and swore until my mother came in to offer me dinner. I took the opportunity to end the call, and despite not being the slightest bit hungry, I sat with my mother and pushed food around my plate.

An hour later I was in bed, fondling my phone. It buzzed again in my hands and my heart leapt.

I opened it to find a quick text from Stellan.

I'm here if you need.

My brow furrowed, but I smiled. I knew he was. My oldest and best friend always was. No matter how long I'd been gone, too busy to be anyone's friend really, I always knew he was there. Sure, he had a mullet, but otherwise he was the greatest man I'd ever known. Still, his text wasn't what I wanted.

I opened the text from Cole and stared at it.

...I miss you too. I typed.

It was the truth, but I didn't send it.

Two weeks went by. I didn't hear from him again.

CHAPTER TWO

School started up in mid-September, pulling Meghan away for a good amount of the time. At the age of thirty one, Meghan had decided to return to school to become a nurse, and she was halfway through her studies at the local Community College. Her life was entirely dictated by the pursuit, and she'd often suggested I follow in her footsteps whenever we discussed my futile job hunt. After that text incident, and not hearing from Cole again, I spent a bit more time with Jackie. I was ready to go out of the house and despite Stellan being my closest friend, he worked every chance he got – and watching Stellan programming in his basement, be it iPhone apps or for work, was not as exciting as it sounds. When he wasn't working, he was ensconced in the newest installment of *Fallout*, and I was still too depressed to play video games. I needed more distraction than watching him play while swearing in Swedish.

Jackie was married to an old fashioned guy who was content to be the lone breadwinner while his 'little woman' stayed at home and baked cookies all day. He didn't require a housewife by any means, he loved his 'strong, independent woman.' He just also loved baked goods, and Jackie's last job had caused her such crippling depression, Kevin finally one day grabbed her car keys and refused to let her leave the house.

After a couple hours of argument, tears, and Kevin himself calling in to work, Jackie agreed to quit her job. She'd been unemployed – and happy – ever since.

That was enough for him.

She liked that just fine. That's right, a feminist who enjoyed being a housewife. Eat that, Gertrude Stein!

I rolled into Jackie's driveway for lunch and found her fully ensconced in a recipe for lemon cake with raspberry mousse. Despite my new life decision of becoming a svelte and gorgeous version of myself, I was fully prepared to eat that whole cake.

"So have you heard anything more?"

"No. Nothing."

Unlike anyone else in my life, I felt safe telling Jackie I'd thought about responding. Jackie had more patience for love inspired action, given that she actually had the castle and the prince, and she'd gone through hell to get it.

Let's just say, Kevin was a miracle compared to the men that came before him.

"How do you feel about that?" She asked.

"Miserable!"

She nodded.

"I mean, did he text me just to see if I'd respond? What the hell?"

She pursed her lips. Jackie didn't always speak her mind. Probably because when she did, she usually spewed truth, and you usually hated her for it.

"I think you're doing the right thing," she said, spooning lumps of cookie dough onto a sheet of parchment.

"What do you mean?"

"Well, you're taking care of yourself now. Have you texted him back since?"

"No."

"Good. Just focus on you, what makes you happy. You sign up for a gym yet?" Jackie asked.

"No. I've just been exercising at home. Going for walks." I was lying.

"That's great! How are you doing otherwise?"

This was the moment of truth. I didn't feel ashamed to tell Jackie exactly what I was thinking. I was so grateful to have her, despite secretly hating her for having the kind of love I'd yet to find. Well okay, I admit it wasn't so secret. I actively told her I hated her. She seemed to appreciate it.

I paused. There were words poised to be said that I wasn't sure I was ready to hear, let alone say. I'd spent every waking moment regurgitating thoughts of Cole over and over until I was sick to death. Perhaps if I said them out loud, I could purge them. Perhaps.

"Well, I guess I'm scared I won't find someone else who -" I stopped.

Jackie set two slices of cake in front of me. I was literally floating in a sugar cloud from all the baking she was doing. She assured me there was no bake sale coming. Jackie's answer to boredom was confection.

"You're talking about the sex aren't you?"

Jesus, Jackie. Do you read minds? "Yeah, I guess I am."

"Honey, sex doesn't make for a healthy relationship on its own."

"I know that!"

Yet that knowledge didn't change the fact that I was truly worried. I'd been with a few guys before Cole and a couple had managed to get the job done, but it was different with Cole. Cole had succeeded at least twice as often as every man who came before.

That is – when he was ever in the mood to touch me.

Point taken. I'd never really been all that fond of the guys that came before.

Jackie flashed me a smile and returned to the oven.

The counter was strewn with the shrapnel of her baking project. In the center of the counter there was a piping bag filled with a white substance. I wondered if it was frosting, but more importantly, whether she'd be willing to squirt it directly into my mouth.

She reappeared from the oven, apron clad and double fisting a set of apple oven mitts. In her hands she held the source of the amazing smell.

I stared at her. "Cannolis? Are you kidding me? You made fucking cannolis?"

She smiled and removed the shells from the pan. "It's only my second attempt, they might not be all that good."

"Is that my purpose here, to test Operation Cannoli, take two?"

"Yes."

I feigned apprehension. "You're a terrible person."

She took a shell, still warm from the pan and piped in the cream with a steady hand. She dipped each end into chocolate chips before handing the beast to me.

I went at it hard. Warm, crisp shell with the cool burst of cream at its center, then the texture of the chocolate – that first bite was enough to make the earth move. Before I took my second, I moaned as the concoction combined and congealed in my mouth to create this smooth mixture. I licked my face as best I could, assured her that I would be hiring people to kill her, and took another bite.

It was quite possibly the best cannoli I'd ever tasted, which was a big deal, given that I was in a truly foul mood. "My god, it tops the Boathouse by miles."

"Really?"

"Oh, by far."

Her entire house smelled like Christmas. I envied her kitchen savvy. My kitchen prowess seemed to only appear at holidays. Instead, I'd been blessed with more frivolous gifts, like drawing the shapes of shadows and charcoal shading. You wouldn't know that about me anymore, given I hadn't picked up a sketchpad or a pencil in years.

"Well, I think you're doing great. Just keep your focus positive, you know? If he's your soul mate, you'll figure it out, and if he's not… Are you gonna try them?"

I looked down at my two slices of cake. One was Chocolate with salted caramel buttercream, the other was the lemon raspberry. I'd just eaten a cannoli. Today was not a diet kind of day.

I took a bite of the lemon.

I moaned. "Oh goodness."

"You like?"

I nodded. A bite of the chocolate followed. It was sinful, but I soon chose the lemon as my favorite.

Jackie smiled. "Besides, as I've said a thousand times, there's easily a million guys out there who would be overjoyed to have a girl as funny as you."

"Ha!" I said, without any real humor to speak of. "Oh naturally. I know that's what they're all talking about around the locker rooms and water coolers of the world. 'Damn did you see Dale's new lady? Oh, the one with the eyepatch and club foot? Hells yeah! That girl can sure tell a fart joke!'"

Jackie shot her a sideways glance. "You don't have an eyepatch."

"Shut up."

She let me finish my cake, the textures of chocolate and mousse, the hint of salt, or the tart of the lemon - as addictive as Crystal Meth. Not that I have ever partaken in Crystal Meth, I'm speaking in allegory here, but you catch my drift. I pointed at the cake, waggling my eyebrows at her.

"What's with all the cakes?"

Jackie's eyebrows shot up like some startled animal. "Oh, just trying new things. Feeling a little cooped up these days, I guess."

I knew the feeling. "Well, they're spectacular."

She smiled. "Still can't make a pie like you, though."

I scoffed, waving her away. Though I admit, my blueberry pie is pretty life changing.

We both went quiet a moment as she buttered another cake pan. I jutted my chin toward the cakes.

She glared at me. "Tell me you actually want another slice and you can have it, but if you're going to come in my house talking about being svelte, I don't want to be responsible for you feeling bad later because you ate like a steelworker."

I stared at Jackie, part of me grateful for her interference and the other part of me desperate she'd just shut up and be the conductor on my train to fat town. She stared me down as I mulled over my decision. That Lemon and Buttercream was like crack, I swear.

"Ok, one more and then I'll head out for the afternoon. Is that okay?"

"Of course."

My phone buzzed just then as I rubbed my hands together in excited expectation. I startled, pulling the contraption from my pocket to check.

Where you at, fool?

Stellan. Apparently his work load was lightened. I could already envision him slumped on my couch. I sighed just so and let Jackie cut me a generous slice.

I was halfway through it when she leaned onto the counter. "You're doing really well, Faye. I'm proud of you."

"Shut up," I said, in the sweetest, self-deprecating tone I had to offer. I knew she wasn't talking about my dietary choices.

"Why? Because I'm not texting him? Because I was only a little disappointed to see that text wasn't from him?"

Jackie's brow furrowed, and she paused.

"What is it?"

She pinched her lower lip between her teeth. "We saw him the other day."

My heart dropped through the floor. I swallowed. "Where?"

"He was at Vinetti's having dinner."

She spoke in the tone of a priest reading last rites. I took a breath. I didn't want to know the answer to what I was about to ask. Apparently, I'm a masochist. "Was he with someone?"

Jackie dark eyes met mine, and she frowned. Yes, he was.

I took a deep breath. "Ah. Guess I was right to ignore his text."

My mood soured instantly. If it wasn't sour to begin with.

I gave Jackie a hug and headed home, making sure not to crack in her company.

I was fine. I would show the world that I was just fucking fine. Sure, I was still crying myself to sleep at night, I'd only sent my resume to one job offer, and let's just say my brain recoiled at the thought of even trying to have an orgasm. I couldn't help but think of Cole if even the hint of sexual thought crossed my mind. The man that accused me of being obsessed with sex was the reason I was now practically asexual. I wondered if he'd find that ironic.

You can cry when you get home, I thought. Cry all you like when you get home.

Anyone who sees me driving will see a normal person. They don't need to know I am an empty outline of myself, hardly holding it together.

When I arrived home, Stellan's Jeep was outside, and I growled. I'd forgotten his 'where you at?' text. Crying on the floor plans thwarted.

I found him sprawled across the couch.

He looked up at me as I came through the door. "Glad to see you out of the house, babe."

"Yeah, I'm sure. Leaves you free to raid the fridge without disdainful looks."

He smiled, turning back toward the TV. "That was disdain? I thought that was undying love."

"Yeah, I'm pretty sure they're the same thing."

I offered him something to eat, and fled into the kitchen. He accepted, as I knew he would. Stellan never turned down food.

I was standing over the stove, a stew pot filled with water still cold on the burner when Stellan appeared at my shoulder.

"You alright?" He asked.

I shrugged. Much like Cole's Asshole Clairvoyance, Stellan seemed to have his own superpower – Faye's About To Lose It Clairvoyance.

"I'll take that as a 'no,' then." He said.

I shrugged again and felt the tension in my throat return. I didn't want to cry. Damn it, I hate people seeing me cry.

I kept my eyes on the stove as my chin creased. It was coming. I turned back toward the pantry for the box of spaghetti so he wouldn't see my face. He moved as I moved, and when I reached the other side of the kitchen island, he was there. Fucking ninja.

He grabbed me around the shoulders and pulled me into him. I clutched my fingers into the folds of his t-shirt, begging the knot in my throat to dispel. I held it together, my eyes welling with tears, but I didn't crack. I'd reined it the hell in.

Fuck Cole. Fuck him and the girl he took to our restaurant. Fuck that pierced girl who could very well have no idea I even existed – a girl whose only fault was falling for the same guy I fell for *and* having her clit pierced when it happened.

After a long moment, Stell released his hold on me, glancing down at my face. His gaze almost set me off anew. I let my lip tremble.

I could cry alone, but I didn't want to be alone. So trembling chin crease would have to suffice. I headed down the kitchen hallway, knowing full well there was no glass. I just needed a moment.

My phone buzzed in my jeans pocket as I reached the living room. I pulled out my phone and read the message.

I miss your laugh.

Cole.

I stared at it. There was a fleeting instant of joy – relief almost. I was loved. I was missed. I was important and needed and worthwhile and desirable. I'd left a mark that some pierced clit bombshell couldn't completely erase in a matter of weeks.

I wasn't worthless.

I wasn't forgettable.

I wasn't unloved.

These thoughts barreled through my mind, making me painfully aware that this man had managed to convince me otherwise. The fleeting, instinctive rush of hope quickly faded, then splintered and died as I realized the extent of his betrayal. He hadn't just cheated on me. This man had made me believe I didn't deserve love.

"I fucking *hate him*!"

Stellan came in just in time to watch me scream at the top of my lungs and throw my cell phone across the front room, shattering it against the bricks of the fireplace. I took a breath, then dropped to the floor and screamed again. Stellan didn't speak. He sat beside me and grabbed me, and I didn't just bawl; I primal-scream-therapy-style bawled. I was hollering and wailing and slobbering all over this poor bastard, cursing the very air that Cole breathed. Stellan didn't say a word.

He'd been doing this since we were kids. When I was stood up for prom by my closest female friend because she miraculously found a date the night of the dance – Stellan let me slobber my mascara all over his Jane's Addiction t-shirt. When I had to put my cat, Freya, down during sophomore year of college, Stellan was at the house when we got home from the vet. He handled enough snot that day to be patented by Kleenex. And when David Gregory kicked me between the legs in sixth grade and I tried to hide how much it hurt – Stellan pulled me aside during recess and let me cry.

Stellan later punched that kid in the nuts so hard, David Gregory was out of school for three days.

"Why is this happening?" I asked – more of a crying declaration than an actual question. Stellan rubbed my shoulders, fanning out his shirt to dry it when I finally pulled away. I frowned at the mess, but he just rubbed my head and offered to blow his nose on my sweater.

Even Stellan had never seen me lose it like this, but I didn't care. I was a fucking mess to be mopped up by the cleaning lady. If we had a cleaning lady, that is.

He waited for me to look at him.

I met his gaze, but could only hold it for a moment. "I'm sorry."

He grabbed me behind the neck, pulled me into his chest and squeezed. When he let me go, he smiled. "You've seen me worse."

I frowned.

Stellan's tough exterior has crumbled twice since I've known him. Once in a waiting room at Emerson Hospital as his father was wheeled in for surgery. The other was at the hands of a girl.

Stellan met her Junior year of high school. She was one of those girls – you know the ones – they run in packs, all with names like Stacie, and Kylie, and Heather, and Danielle. This one was a Danielle. This one made me hate all Danielles.

It wasn't anything she said, really – I admit I can be a bit judgmental, but thus far, that judgment has never been wrong. It was her laugh. She had one of those awkward, almost vapid laughs - the laugh that means she didn't get the joke, or didn't think it was funny, but would pretend anyway.

It was the only response she had to anything.

She broke Stellan's heart at the end of senior year.

Four days later, Evan and I were in the lunch line, weaving halfway across the cafeteria. The line slowed and stopped us right at Danielle's lunch table. She sat with her girlfriends, all busy with their outfits and diet soda.

I can't guarantee that her volume was intended for Evan and me, or if she simply projected bull shit at all times when she wasn't laughing awkwardly, but we heard every word. She was describing the break up to her girlfriends – that Stellan was curled up in a ball on his then bedroom floor, sobbing, begging her to change her mind. She said she was done, that he played too many video games, that he was a hornball, that he was boring.

My Grandmother would have referred to this as "the small talk of small minds." She would have also prescribed grace and silence. Given the circumstances, I would have disappointed her greatly.

I blew that cafeteria up. I ripped that girl a fiery new asshole the size of Mount St. Helens. I threw the c-word around like beads at Mardi Gras, ladies and gentlemen. I hollered with such abandon, several teachers heard me down the hall, and as they hauled me away, still screaming as Danielle and her friends sat in stunned silence, Evan gave me a slow clap.

I was suspended for a week.

Stellan didn't talk to me for a month.

People from high school still mention that event from time to time, followed by 'never piss off Faye.' I always prided myself on maintaining my calm, but on that day, I couldn't maintain. I couldn't because she was telling the truth.

The day she broke up with him, I sat on Stellan's

bedroom floor with his head in my lap for three hours as he cried so hard he nearly choked.

As far as I was concerned, she had every one of those c-words coming.

She works at the DMV now. I suppose that's karma.

Stellan wiped a tear from the corner of my eye and pinched my chin. "Come on. Let's go for a drive. Put your coat on."

I shook my head and whined, but slipped my arms into their sleeves when he held my coat out for me. "But I don't want to."

He grabbed his sweatshirt off the couch and gently led me out the front door.

The air outside was crisp and calm. Stellan opened the door to the Jeep for me, and I grumbled as I climbed in. I didn't think to ask where we were going. I felt like a complete idiot at that moment – a slobbering, miserable, phoneless idiot, and I was still sniffling every few seconds.

Stellan handed me his iPhone. "Even if it's Shania Twain - if you wanna hear it, it's my favorite song."

I stared at the foreign display screen of Stellan's hacked iPhone. I searched for five minutes, trying not to get worked up at the title of every love song in the contraption. Finally, I found something I thought might ease my mood – AC/DC.

We drove aimlessly. After an hour or more, Stellan stopped at White Hen to buy me a water and himself some snack food. We cracked open our bounty, letting the Jeep idle as we each agreed to eat a whole Devil Dog in one bite. The resulting spray of dry cake product got me laughing again. Stellan won, naturally, and I managed to spray Devil Dog across his windshield with such force that when he attempted to wipe it off, he swore there was some on the outside.

"Oh man, did I tell you about my dream last night?" He asked as we pulled out of the parking lot.

"I don't think so."

Stellan proceeded to regale me with a dream about his demise during zombie apocalypse.

"See, I told you," I said.

"Told me what?"

I took a sip of my water for effect. "You'd never survive Zombie Apocalypse."

Stellan feigned offense. "Who says? And when did you tell me that?"

"I've told you that repeatedly. Many times."

"Bull shit. I'd be a killing machine in Zombie Apocalypse."

"False. You can't even handle a dream about zombies. You're screwed."

Stellan laughed. "Hey, I'm a certified badass -"

"The subconscious doesn't lie, Stell."

"What? You think you know me?" He asked in his best Robert De Niro impression. "And you suppose you're going to somehow thrive when the walking undead hit the streets?"

"Oh, hell yeah. I've already got a plan and everything."

He smirked. "Well, what's your plan?"

"I'm not telling! You'll try to take it."

Stellan went quiet. When I looked at him he was purposefully pouting.

"Oh, fine. I'm gonna take everybody and head up to East Bum, Maine. Live on a peninsula in the middle of nowhere. We're gonna live on Mussels, Lobster, and Moose until the plague passes."

"I'm hurt that I'm not invited."

"Oh, you're invited. You'll just need to declare yourself with some kind of flare to let us know you're cool. No flare? We shoot you."

"Ok, I can handle that," he said, then paused. "Now, do you mean like emergency flare, or like TGI Friday's FLAIR?"

I laughed.

"Or both?"

I imagined him in some red and white striped uniform, covered in pins as he stood on a blown out bridge with an order of nachos and kept laughing.

Stellan cracked open a bag of salt and vinegar chips. "Or emergency TGI Friday's flair, even?"

"As of this moment, I've decided that both are now required."

"Can do."

He drove around for a time and I sporadically burst into laughter for the duration of the drive.

I didn't want to admit that I was still avoiding the world, not just because I was wallowing in misery, but because I honestly feared I might cross paths with Cole somewhere – or more aptly, with Cole and his new paramour. I hadn't so much as brushed my hair in weeks. I wasn't exactly ready to be seen.

"Oh hey! Did I show you my newest one?" He asked, suddenly.

Stellan snatched up his iPhone as we sat at a red light. If there is an Apple product in the world that has been more hacked and rehacked than Stellan's phone, I'd like to see it. He flipped through icons and showed me his prize - "Beer Goggles" it read in happy red letters. It made a bubbling, chugging sound as it loaded.

I gave Stellan a sideways glance. "You have no class."

"Yeah, but look -"

He pointed the phone at himself and took a picture. The application made some inappropriate comment in slurred speech, and suddenly a picture popped up of Matthew McConaughey.

"How *you* doin?" said the "Beer Goggles" voice.

I laughed. "Okay! Do me!"

Stellan smiled and shook his head, putting his phone away. I protested.

"No, you're too pretty to need Beer Goggles. You'll confuse it."

I punched him. He rubbed his arm as though I'd been a mosquito.

I leaned back in my seat, catching sight of my reflection in the passenger side window. I stared at my own face; the slight ski slope of my nose, the curve of my jaw and the hollow under my cheek bones. Despite how terrible I'd been feeling, I didn't think I was all that bad. A sudden flash of 'fantasy twat shot' popped into my head. I'd imagined her short, a perky little height that made it easy for average height Cole to rest his chin on her head when they embraced. I hated short women. Well, I did those days because Twat shot was tiny, and I hated Twat Shot. Ok, fine - Imaginary Twat Shot was tiny and therefore all tiny women were an abomination. I imagined her with bushy dark brown hair and big earrings, maybe even one through her nose to match her Tutu, and she had the slightest, tiniest little waist and she enjoyed long walks on the beach, moonlight serenades, showering together, being on top, and Cole was happy – so elated to give her all those things, and I hated her. I fucking hated her.

"You alright, F-bomb?"

God damn it, how does he fucking do that?

"Yeah -" I started and stopped before I could say *fine*. I wasn't *fine*. Even if I lied, he already knew I was a million miles from *fine*. "I've been better."

"I know," he said and patted my knee. "Wanna vent?"

I laughed. "Naw. I can't go venting to you about this kind of stuff. This shit you berate your girlfriends about, not your guy friends."

"Well, it's not exactly a stag party, babe."

"I know," I said, reluctantly. The thought of telling Stellan about my thoughts - my feelings of female inadequacy, my fears that I would never find someone who could please me sexually, the thought that I'd only ever been serious with one man, and it had blown up in my face – these weren't exactly the stuff of letters you read in GQ. Not that Stellan would ever read GQ, but still...

"Tell me one thing. I know you have an infinite amount on your mind. Vent about just one," he said. I mulled it over a moment, tempted to spill what was running through my mind, as though purging it to him of all people might somehow cure me. I still just couldn't see Stellan taking it easy when I told him I'd found it impossible to masturbate since my break up because Cole had been my only sexual desire for almost four years.

That would be a fun conversation.

"I applied for a job," I said finally.

Stellan glanced at me smiling. "That's good, yeah?"

"I hope so. It'd be nice to get my life back together."

He slowed down to turn onto Strawberry Fields Road, a winding side way through the woods. We were no longer heading anywhere in particular. I didn't protest. I guess supper could wait.

"Your life isn't all that bad, babe."

"I know," I said, and for the first time since I moved home, I actually let myself mean it.

I knew there were people who'd suffered worse than I when the recession hit – people with kids and no support system, people out in the cold. Sure I'd lost my house, but I had a home to come back to. I was warm at night.

I closed my eyes for a moment, and thanked God. "I just feel like there are expectations of me that I'm not meeting."

"Whose expectations are we talking about?"

I thought for a moment. "Mine."

He made a soft 'Ah' sound and turned down another side street. The leaves were bright even in the dark. Autumn in New England was just days from full swing.

"So, what are your expectations?"

"I don't know. If you'd looked at me five years ago, I was one of the most successful people of my graduating class. I'd say, by far the most successful woman, and now…"

I paused.

Stellan watched the road, driving aimlessly into the dark. "Now what?"

"Now I'm not, I guess."

Stellan rolled up to a stop sign, put the Jeep in park, and turned to me. He didn't speak. He just waited for me to go on. I felt exposed suddenly, and without knowing what was coming, I started talking.

"I'm a failure. And worse than that, I'm the one reminding myself most often. Every time my mom offers me cash, every time I fill my gas tank on her dime, or come home and feel agitated that she left a bunch of shit on the kitchen table – who am I to be agitated with her, it's her fucking house? And I'm such an asshole, I shouldn't have said anything about you and your family yesterday, but I did, and I think about you and compare myself in so many ways." I was unloading. One thought led to the next and the next and my filter was just about gone. "When I was doing well, I looked down at your situation. Not at you, but your situation. You can hate me for that, but I did. I thought 'why doesn't he do something with that brilliant mind of his and get out of there,' and now I'm the hypocrite sitting in the same situation – only worse."

"Why is it worse?" He asked, and there was nothing tense about his tone.

"Because -" I said, and for the first time, I actually let it sink in. "You're not unhappy. I am."

The jeep sat on that dark, wooded road like some quiet Golem waiting for passersby.

Stellan stared at the radio, quiet. "I'm going to say something, dove, and I need you to promise me you won't get upset."

My chest tightened. 'Faye, we can't be friends anymore - I'm moving to Argentina, Faye – Faye, I hate your haircut; it looks stupid.' I didn't know what he was going to say, but his tone scared me so completely that I was almost willing to suffer the curiosity and never hear it.

"Okay," I said, finally.

"You weren't happy before, either."

If words can hit like a right hook, these were the ones to do it.

My mind raced toward immediate defense, but he wasn't done.

"When you were 'the most successful woman in your graduating class,' I never saw you. No one saw you. Then if I got lucky, you were exhausted and frustrated, complaining about one thing or another. You were miserable." He paused. "And you dressed like a yuppy, which was the worst part, really."

"Hey -" I said and realized my steam was gone. "- I dressed like a yuppy?"

"When you were all traumatized over losing your job, it was the hardest thing in the world to pretend I wasn't happy. Yeah, I was happy that I'd get to see you for a change, but I was elated you were out of there."

"It was a paycheck. I was successful, I was good at it -"

Stellan leaned back in his chair, propping his hands behind his head. He looked up at the roof, his face serene. "There's a difference between being successful and being -"

He faltered a moment, and I pounced.

"Being what, oh all-knowing Guru?"

"Prosperous? I don't know. I just don't think success is what brings you peace when you're on your death bed, babe. I'm just saying."

I had trouble arguing this point, but it reminded me of the other piece of my puzzle that I'd recently lost. "No, but I thought I had that other part handled, too."

Stellan breathed in softly, and I could hear the apology. Yet, he didn't hide from the conversation.

"That's another thing I haven't really said."

I waited, scared.

He shot me a sideways look, giving a sheepish eyebrow raise. "Good riddance."

I bristled. "Why do you say that?"

"He was a douche bag from jump street, babe."

"Don't say that." My tone was low and warning, but Stellan blew right through it like a fugitive heading for the border.

"No, let's be real here, shall we? You've been with him since you lost your job, yeah?"

"Yes."

"Had he been to your mom's place - even once?"

I paused. "No."

"There you go. I could go on for hours on the guy, but I think that right there will cover it for now."

He set his hands on the wheel and checked the rear view - still no lights in any direction. We had no reason to move.

"He wasn't comfortable. And honestly, I wasn't either. Spending time with your boyfriend while your mom is in the next room -"

"Has he even met your mom?"

"Yes!"

Once. He'd met her once. I didn't inform Stellan of that fact.

"Look. He should have been banging down your door to meet your mom, not avoiding the prospect."

"Not everyone is as comfortable in other peoples' parents' houses, Stell."

"Watch it, babe. Don't make it about me because I'm being honest."

I slumped back into my seat, finding my reflection again in the window. My eyes had gone watery, and I hated myself for it. It's so painful to hear your friends assassinate the character of the man you love. It's exceptionally hard to hear it when they're spewing what you knew and refused to say yourself. We didn't speak again for a few minutes. I was sure Stellan could tell I was getting emotional.

"You deserve better, F-bomb. I just don't think you realize that."

And there we have it - start crying around Stellan time: number three. He rubbed the back of my neck with his right hand for a few moments, then put the car into gear. We drove down the dark roads for a few minutes, Simple Minds playing softly. I started to quietly sing along, half my notes coming through and the other half silent. I didn't want to admit to him that I was afraid there was no better. I didn't want to admit to him that I was sure all the men my age who were worth a damn were taken, as Meghan often complained, with prettier, daintier, more 'successful' women. These were details I share with my girlfriends, these were the details that scared me most. Stellan didn't need to hear that; he didn't need to listen to me cry about penis size and babies and fantasy wedding plans that were destroyed now.

I asked to borrow Stellan's phone and texted Meghan. I needed a woman's ear for these thoughts.

She instantly responded with chagrin that I would text from Stellan's phone, and demand that I get food with her.

"Anybody good?" Stellan asked, shooting me a sideways glance.

I swallowed, unsure how well this proposal might go over. "Meghan says she's hungry, too. Any chance -"

54

I didn't even get the final words out before Stellan had a wicked grin on his face. "Oh, absolutely. But only if you agree to eat in public."

I whined my protest. Why couldn't we just pick up the pizza, bring it home, and never see people ever again? Meghan quickly texted her agreement, and my hands were tied. I was going out in public.

I wasn't happy about it.

Stellan dropped me at the hippy pizza restaurant and shot down the street to 'pick something up.'

"I'll come find you guys! Go order, chill out, won't be more than a few minutes!"

Meghan complained about work and life, being single and being underpaid, all the while looking like she stepped out of a department store catalog. I'd once asked her how long she took to get ready in the morning. The answer made me wonder if she ever slept - and that perhaps I was close friends with the walking undead. Vampires are supposed to be pretty, right?

The two of us were settled at a table by the massive oven, the heat of the flames within traveling throughout the room. She regaled me for some time. When she was done, she crossed her ankles and asked how I was.

It was like a cork from a champagne bottle – I practically exploded. I told her about my complete inability to even think about sex and despite the angry look I received when I mentioned his name, I told her I was afraid Cole was the closest I would ever come to getting it right.

"I don't understand how you can say that, hon?"

"Why?" I asked, trying to keep my voice down.

"Because he wasn't 'right' - in any sense of the word. Were you there? Did you miss that whole ordeal with the cell phone and the vagina and the -"

"No, I know. He sucks. He sucks beyond reason -"

"Do you really believe that? It almost sounds like you're mourning his loss or something."

"Well, I am sometimes. Is that so wrong?"

And she was off. "Faye! The guy is a scumbag! He cheated on you, and kept evidence of it!"

This was a mantra she'd been happy to repeat for over a month now.

"I know that!"

"When you lost your place, did he offer to let you stay with him? No. It 'never came up,' right?" I started to respond, but she was on a roll. "Did he not openly embarrass you in front of all his friends when you lost your job and couldn't afford to pay for your own dinner one night?"

That one stung, and I'd nearly let myself forget it.

"Did you or did you not tell me you dreaded going out to eat with him long before then because the two of you sat in silence most nights because you had nothing to fucking talk about?" God damn it, she knew her shit. "Are you seriously missing him because sometimes he was good in bed?"

"It's not just that," I said, realizing I was about to – no let's be honest – I'd already completely lost the helm of this conversation.

"No, Faye. Think about it. What is it that you really miss?"

She waited. I was surprised to see her slow down, as she usually didn't take even a moment to breathe once she got going. I thought about Cole, looking into the eyes of a friend who actually heard all the troubles he and I were having long before I discovered his cell phone's adventures. I couldn't push aside the bad in order to dwell on the good with her. I remembered that night in the bar when the handsome bartender asked for my number. I remembered the night we first slept together and the days I spent reeling from it. Was there nothing else to dwell on?

Damn it, why do women have to actually feel when it comes to sex? Why can't we just be like men and fuck our merry way to an orgasm, then forget it ever happened? Am I being sexist? I don't fucking care! I wish it was easier. I wish I had a cock shot on *my* phone!

"The intimacy?" I finally said.

"Ah," she said. When she turned to me, I expected another tirade. "Weren't you the one complaining about a lack of just that a few months ago?"

Yes sir, she'd been a good friend for a long time, and she wasn't going to let me forget it.

"I was."

"And why was that? I know, but I think maybe you need to remind yourself."

"What do you want me to say?"

She took a deep breath and tossed her hair with her hands. Her hair fell in perfect ringlets, as always.

"Faye, I'm going to quote you, alright?"

I nodded.

"It was good, yes? Cole was a sexual dynamo, right? Except for the fact that you told me yourself he didn't always take the time to give you an orgasm, yes? Sometimes he just assumed and rolled over. And, then to top it off, he hardly ever put out, am I right?"

Zing. I was beginning to resent her for being a good listener. Didn't she realize I just wanted to wallow in self-pity for a while? Christ.

"He was the best I'd ever been with -"

"Which isn't saying much, hon. Even if he was the greatest lay on the planet, if he refuses to actually put out, it doesn't do you much good, now does it? Especially if that's all he's got going for him."

Fuck me. Hearing her say it brought a tumble of bad memories back to the fore. I remembered lying beside him at night wondering why he didn't want me, feeling disgusting because I'd gained twenty pounds since we first met, and thinking it must be my fault that he didn't find me attractive anymore. Somehow, I'd failed to acknowledge the nagging sense in the back of my mind that maybe I had been the cause of his meandering. If I'd just taken better care of myself, if I'd just gone to the gym more often, if… if only.

Meghan leaned toward me and gave me a hug, softly muttering expletives. Only then did I realize I was tearing up – yes, again. Fuck!

"I can't help but feel like it is my fault."

Her expression went stony and for a split second I thought she might punch me. Still, she let me speak. I began to hear her words in my own mind, and I let myself recite them. "Ok, I know. Don't blame the victim."

She rubbed my shoulder. She'd tried to get me to do this exercise over the past few weeks – remember the bad about the relationship so you can let go of it. Somehow, I'd found that chore impossible.

"He was mean. When we fought, he didn't get agitated or excited, he just walked away like I meant nothing, and I would have to go find him to fix things, even when it was his fault –"

She nodded and gestured for me to go on.

"He never let me keep my stuff at his house. He never let me decide the restaurant when we went to dinner, and we really didn't have anything to talk about when we did. It was like those miserable middle aged couples who should be divorced, but they don't have the balls to admit it -"

"Right? *Right?*"

"He hated children. Said he'd rather die than be a father."

She threw her hands up. "Thank Christ that prick isn't going to procreate!"

"Whenever anyone made a comment about us getting married, he changed the subject, instantly. It was like he was offended by the prospect, I swear."

Meghan scowled. This was the longest she'd ever let me speak in our entire friendship.

"He didn't like my friends." That comment inspired a raised eyebrow from Meghan, but still she didn't speak. "He hated Stellan. We got into so many fights since I moved back home because I was spending time with Stell and – oh God."

Meghan's expression went stern. "What is it?"

I stared at the table, then at my hands. "I almost feel like a bad person for admitting this out loud -"

I stopped.

Meghan gestured for me to go on. "Honey, just say it. You're not betraying the fuck bag, by any means."

I took a deep breath. This memory needed lead in, but the lead in? How could I betray this knowledge to anyone. I felt like I'd somehow become a bad girlfriend, and he'd been the one to cheat and abandon me. "He couldn't always get it up," I said, and exhaled. It felt like release to say it out loud. "And I did everything I could to make him feel better about it, but he would just push me away, tell me I'm obsessed with sex. Then he goes and has no problem fucking some other girl?"

Meghan shook her head like a guest on the Maury Povich show. "Oh honey, no."

"I mean - it makes me think, was it me?"

"No!"

Finally, I was ready. I'd built up to it, letting it out, piece by piece, but now I was ready.

"I was afraid to initiate sex. I was fucking afraid to ask for sex from my fucking boyfriend. I'm the most passionate person I know – no man has ever been able to keep up with me. I thought that made me a fucking treasure, but I would never even try because after we'd been together for just a few days, he decided he 'wasn't in the mood' for the first time, and when I tried to *get* him in the mood, he pushed me away."

"What a cunt."

"He left bruises."

Meghan straightened in her seat, rage so clearly etched on her face, I feared she'd catch fire. "What?!"

"I didn't wear sleeveless shirts for a week after because I didn't want anyone to ask how I got the bruises. It was fucking August."

She stared at me. She hadn't known this fact. No one had. It had embarrassed me so desperately when it happened that I never wanted anyone to know about it. Now, it felt imperative to admit it to someone else. To be made to feel that unwanted – I'd never wish it on anyone.

"You stayed with him." Her tone was soft, almost disbelieving.

"I took it to be my fault."

"I didn't realize Cole was such a delicate flower."

Letting myself rage a moment was fueling something. Words were coming that felt like fire on my tongue. "Stellan's right, I deserve someone who can't keep their hands off me -"

"Stellan's right? What about me?"

"I deserve someone who can't wait to meet my family, who doesn't get angry at the prospect of potentially getting married, or having kids for that fucking matter. I want babies someday damn it!"

"Jesus, how are you two not suffocating from all the Estrogen in here?"

Meghan and I both startled at the voice.

He might be fucking huge, but the man can be light on his feet. Meghan and I turned to find Stellan as he came around the table.

"Fuck you, primate," Meghan said.

"No thanks. I'm not a fan of crabs, oddly enough."

This was their relationship. In private, if you were to ask either of them what their opinion was of the other, their words were only positive – affectionate even. Yet, put them in a room together and they were merciless.

"What do you mean? It would go perfectly with the 'Head up your ass' disease you've always suffered from."

"Hey, I'll take that over your Herpes, anyday."

I hissed at both of them to shut up. I was too emotional to listen to the two of them banter, especially since I'd come so close to actually expunging all of my bull shit in one sitting. Being interrupted felt offensive and a part of me wanted to send Stellan away so I could finish my rant. Somehow, I felt as though I'd been close to some revelation, some epiphany that would have released me to sleep filled nights without the endless bouts of crying and the morning headaches. Now, I just felt deeper in it.

"I can come back later if the two of you want to cry and hug some more."

"You're a fucking asshole," Meghan said and unlike her usual assaults, at that moment, she meant it.

"I know," he said and reached down to rub my knee. I patted his hand and smiled up at him. There was something to his face that looked different, almost pained. I was suddenly mortified. He'd heard. Of all the people I'd considered telling those details too, Stellan was nowhere on the list. Somehow, admitting to him that my boyfriend was appalled by me enough to leave bruises – felt completely humiliating. I squeezed my eyes tight and willed Stellan's sad look out of my mind.

Meghan went back to complaining about work. I was grateful for the noise. Despite her monopoly on the conversation, when Billy Idol's "Flesh for Fantasy" came on over the speakers, she caught the lyrics and had an opinion.

"Wait, did he just say 'You'll see and feel my sex attack?'"

"Yes, yes he did," Stellan said.

"Are you kidding me?"

"I don't think Billy kids when it comes to sex attacks, Trotsky."

She shook her head. "You'll see and feel my sex attack? Really?"

Stellan started singing along, soulfully.

I forced a smile, despite my mood, and looked across the table to Stellan, who was leaning back in his chair, his hands behind his head. When he sat like that, his arms up and on display, the definition of his biceps was apparent. I'd always been curious about Stellan's martial arts training, some part of me in awe. I'd never admit it to him, but I'd always wanted to see him get into a fight. My gaze caught his attention, and he glanced at me, winked, then returned his attention to the roaring oven fire.

My face burned for a moment.

The waitress took our order, her demeanor cool and drowsy, and then went her merry way. Stellan kept his attention to the fire burning high in the oven, watching one of the employees chop wood in a corner.

I listened to Meghan, but my attention was drawn about the room. Every dark haired man, every couple seated at a table near us drew my eye.

My thoughts were traitors. What if he comes here? What if I see him out in the world?

The thought made me feel itchy.

They brought Meghan and I our salads, and I began picking at my food.

Come on, Faye. Your friends are buying your meal, the least you could do is eat it. I took a bite. It was delicious.

Meghan didn't let her full mouth stop her from speaking. "Hey, you considering going to the Lambert Halloween party?"

I held my hand over my lips, cursing the law of the restaurant cosmos that someone must ask you a vital question right as you take a huge bite of your food. They then wait and watch you eat until you answer. I hate to be watched eating, let's just be clear about that.

I swallowed. "I was unaware of such a shindig."

She popped another forkful in her mouth. "You were invited though."

I smiled. "Was I? That was nice of him."

My words were sincere. After high school, Evan Lambert pursued a similar track to Stellan, but unlike Stellan, Evan's father didn't suffer a massive heart attack during his sophomore year at MIT, causing him to leave school to tend to his family. Evan left school for very different reasons. From what I'd heard – several billion reasons.

I glanced at Stellan for a moment in a surge of affection. He was still watching the fire.

Meghan her fork through a massive clump of goat cheese. "Your whole class was invited." Well that deflated me quick. "It's a costume party, which will be fun, and it isn't on Halloween. I know you like to hand out candy."

"That I do. When is it?"

I asked more out of manners than actual interest. I still hadn't quite regained my interpersonal skills. Just the restaurant was practically giving me hives. The thought of going to one of my oldest friend's houses after a decade of no contact, surrounded by every asshole we went to school with – some of whom had made Evan's life hell – sounded almost less appealing than stumbling upon Cole and his Robo-vagina girlfriend.

"It's October 15th - a Friday," Meghan said through a chomp of carrot sticks. She watched me, and I realized I was expected to RSVP at that precise moment. I felt trapped.

"What are you going as, Trotsky?"

She glanced at Stellan, her perfectly tweezed brows raised.

"I haven't decided yet. Was going to find out what Miss Faye was going as and decide then - and don't call me Trotsky."

Oh dear God, she should know better.

"Why not, Trotsky? Whatsamatter?"

It had begun.

Meghan glared. "Don't call me Trotsky."

"Oh, I'm sorry Trotsky, I didn't realize I was."

I stopped chewing and watched.

"How do you stand this asshole?"

"Come now, Trotsky. There's no need to get upset."

"You're obnoxious, you know that?"

"Trotsky -"

"Seriously, if I could cut you -"

"Calm down, Trotsky."

"- make me want to rip that mullet right out of -"

"There's no need to yell, Trotsky?"

She wasn't yelling. I stifled a laugh.

"If we weren't in public right now -"

"Think of the children, Trotsky."

Suddenly the waitress appeared at our table, balancing two pizzas. She managed to catch the end of a nicely colored tirade from Meghan, hissed with serious tenacity. The waitress smiled at Stellan who returned it with that traffic stopping smile of his. The waitress left our food, and Stellan made quick work to snatch a piece.

Meghan took a bite and moaned. "Oh god, I would curse the day you made me come here with this asshole if this weren't so fucking good."

"I know right?"

Stellan's voice got bedroomy. "I tell ya, this pizza's about to see and feel my sex attack."

I coughed through my food, nearly spraying it across the weathered table. Stellan smiled up at me over his pizza, having taken half of the pie onto his plate. Stellan milked my discomfort, seducing his pizza with promises of what he was going to do to it with his mouth. Then he started asking if I needed a fork, a napkin, a glass of water, all in that same husky, sexual tone, with a 'baby' or a 'yeah, like that' here and there. I hissed and shrieked at him with each word. It was only egging him on, but god damn it, I couldn't help it. Stellan is not supposed to be sexy. Never, never, never, never, never.

Meghan actually laughed, only to finish the jovial act with a declaration of Stellan's lack of penis.

The conversation lulled as we finished, Meghan and I ordering a slice of Chocolate Chip Banana Bread for dessert. Stellan just sat and digested. When the act of gorging ourselves lost its allure, Meghan started back in on the Halloween party.

"Come on, Faye. How often do you get out of your mother's house these days?"

I shrugged. "Not often."

"See?"

Meh, just be honest, Faye. "Yeah, and there's a reason for it. I want to avoid exactly the kind of situation you're asking me to get dolled up for."

"You'll love it!"

"Slight exaggeration there, Meg."

"Oh come on! You can dress up like Pat Benetar-,"

Stellan and I made the same expression. I'm not a Benetar fan; he knows this.

"- and I'll go as Cyndi Lauper or some shit."

The thought of dressing up like an 80's pop star did spark something in my psyche. I began to run through ideas - Adam Ant, Freddie Mercury, Billy Idol (naturally), a member of A Flock of Seagulls. Still wasn't particularly interested in this party.

Stellan leaned onto the table. "I tell ya what, babe. If you wanna go, I'll go. We can do Sonny and Cher. I'll be Cher, obviously."

Meghan and I both stared at Stellan a moment, still unsure whether he had actually spoken or not. He seemed disappointed not to get a laugh. I couldn't laugh, I was too startled by his offer.

I blinked. "You're not serious?"

He shrugged. "Why the hell not? I've been told I need socializing with other human beings on more than one occasion." He gave Meghan a gentle knock on the elbow. "You know, maybe I'll evolve."

"I'm not going as Sonny Bono," I said, swallowing.

I just wanted to make that perfectly clear.

"What you're gonna crash it?" Meghan asked.

Stellan gave her the most piteous look I'd ever seen. "No," he said and laughed. "But I might go. I told Evan I'd rather amputate a testicle, but I've changed my mind on bigger things to be sure. And he did ask about you, Faye."

"He did?" Meghan asked in unison with me.

Meghan glared at Stellan and the true nature of her interest in this party became clear. "You know Evan Lambert?"

Evan Lambert, local celebrity and all around rich bastard, was a handsome, single guy, and I could see Meghan practically salivating. I was actually rather pleased with myself that I'd never mentioned him around her.

Stellan shrugged. "Yeah, we're friends. Worked on a couple projects together in school."

He was underselling his lifelong best friend. I understood completely. Despite Evan and I not speaking for almost ten years, people still gave me the third degree at the mere mention of our having been good friends.

A lot of people wanted a slice of Evan Lambert.

Meghan leaned in. "You were at school together -"

I smirked at him. "Why on earth would you go? You hate parties."

"I don't hate parties, I hate people. There's a distinction there, dove."

Stellan loved get-togethers, but get-togethers of that magnitude made up entirely of brown nosing people from our high school? Not by a long shot.

"Well -" He glanced at me. "Let's be honest, you do need to get out of the house."

Meghan hooted her approval and demanded that Stellan high five her, only to have him pull his hand away at the last second, leaving her hanging. She hit him, of course.

I frowned. "Don't say that."

He nodded. "It's not that you're turning into a recluse or anything, babe, but -"

"What? Yes she is! She practically broke out in hives when we got in here! Who has she seen other than you and I for the past -"

Stellan sighed. "Ok, strike that. You're practically a hermit. I keep expecting you to start talking to squirrels and trying to get me to read your manifesto."

I laughed uncomfortably. If he'd been talking about anyone else, I would have found it funny, but this intervention felt like being bullied by Sarah Foley in fifth grade for not shaving my legs. I wanted to get up and storm out, telling them both to screw themselves, but sadly I had a long walk home if I chose such dramatic flair. Damn it, how does a woman in modern society expect to pull classy broad moves without looking ridiculous?

Stellan put his hand over mine. "I'm sorry babe. Don't be mad."

I looked up to find Stellan leaning toward me. Apparently, my thoughts read on my face.

"You promise you'll go with me, and you won't leave me alone with random high school acquaintances?"

He smirked. "You know I'd never let that happen."

"Cause I swear to God, if someone asks me what I'm doing with my life, I'm going to smash a bottle of tequila over their head."

"I support that implicitly," he said.

I glanced at Meghan, who was silently waiting with bated breath. Apparently she knew well enough to let Stellan plead her case. I was her wingman as much as Stellan was offering to be mine. After all, she didn't go to my high school. She wasn't invited.

I nodded.

"Oh man, you'll have so much fun! We can go shopping at the costume store when I get paid; get you all vixened up – it'll be spectacular!"

I let her drone on a moment, losing the ability to pay attention. Stellan sat across from me, glancing between Meghan and myself with silly expressions only I could see. I smiled at them, trying hard to settle my stomach. I hadn't realized just how agoraphobic I had become over the past month. It felt as though being out in the world was walking across a shooting range. Having my reclusive nature declared as stoned waitresses bustled around me made me feel like someone held up a mirror to my haggard face and said, Look.

I did my best not to fidget as we drove home.

I was ready to be by myself. I wasn't waiting to cry myself to sleep or anything – they'd somehow managed to tag team distract me from those thoughts. I did, however, want to sit with my thoughts.

You have a month, Faye. Plenty of time to prepare.

Was I really going to go to a Halloween party at Evan freakin Lambert's house?

Stellan pulled up outside my house and put the jeep in park, then he leaned across me to open the door of the jeep. I climbed out. I waved and mumbled my good bye, still trying to hide my racing thoughts, but he stopped me.

"What're you up to tomorrow?"

I glanced down at my phone, pretending to check my calendar. "Surprisingly, no plans," I said, and if my tone was sarcastic, it was thoroughly intended.

"Want to do something? I kinda had something I want to run by you."

I shrugged, too tired to be curious. Then the date on my phone registered. I checked it again – September 14th, 12:24AM.

September 14th? Oh god.

"Oh my god, Stellan. I'm so sorry."

His eyebrows shot up as I came barreling back toward the jeep.

"What's wrong?"

I reached across to him, wrapping my arms around his shoulders. "I'm the worst friend ever. Jesus, you bought *my* dinner on *your* birthday? Happy Birthday, almost an hour late."

He chuckled and squeezed me. "Honestly, Meghan

paid for your dinner. She refused my money. Don't even worry about it, lady."

But I did. I'd spent the day with him, chased him down, cried to him about all my problems, all the while oblivious to the fact that it was September 13th – my best friend's birthday.

I sucked at life.

"Here. I got these to celebrate." Stellan reached into the back of the jeep and produced a package of chocolate cupcakes.

"You bought yourself cupcakes? I literally hate myself right now."

He just laughed. "Mum made me a cake, but she didn't have any chocolate, so – thought I'd treat myself, damn it."

He handed me one of the cupcakes, and the two of us feasted in the front seat of his jeep, Stellan moaning in sexual ecstasy all over again.

We finished up and he smiled, promising to stop by the next afternoon. I gave him another three hugs, then I sat there a moment, silently wishing he wasn't leaving. I'd spent all day with him, I was sure he must need a break.

"You all right, babe?" He asked.

I nodded. "Yeah, I'm fine."

"You sure?"

His tone sounded open ended, and the urge to ask him in grew near to overpowering.

Come on, Stellan. Come watch craptastic television with Mopey MacGee into the wee hours of the night. You know you want to.

I climbed out onto the sidewalk, but he stopped me before I could shut the door to the jeep.

"And F-Bomb."

"Yeah?"

He jingled his keys, then ran his knuckle over his lips. "It wasn't you."

I stared at him, waiting to understand.

"When that douche bag pushed you away; it wasn't you."

My breath caught in my throat, and I couldn't respond. I felt miniscule.

Stellan smiled at me, but I couldn't meet his gaze.

"Any real man would be up on that for days. Everyday."

I stared at the passenger seat of his jeep, my face flushed. "Shut up," I said, but my smile and my tone made it sound more like 'Shucks.'

He said his goodnight, started up the engine, and waited. I headed up my steps and opened my front door. I knew he wouldn't leave until I was inside. I watched him pull away. Before long I was standing on my sleepy dead end street, listening to the leaves rustle overhead, and I was alone.

I walked inside to find my mother fretting at the fireplace.

"Oh god, you're okay!" She said.

I furrowed my brow. "Of course I am."

She gestured to the fireplace and the bits of cell phone everywhere, her face taut.

I frowned. "Oh…yeah."

"What happened?"

"I lost my temper."

I noticed the dustpan under her arm and demanded them from her, determined to clean up the evidence of my tantrum. I got close enough to see tears in her eyes, and I realized she'd come home to a scene of damage with no way to contact me and had done the

'Mom' thing – assumed I'd been murdered. She asked what had set me off and despite my usual lack of candor, I simply told her. She pursed her lips and set her hands on her hips, staring down at the remnants of my phone.

"I have the afternoon off tomorrow. We can go to the mall and grab a new one."

"No Mom, you don't have to do that. I can make do without -"

"I would feel much better if I knew you had a means to contact someone if you need to."

I attempted to protest again, feeling miniscule, but she simply ignored me, said good night, and stormed off into the kitchen. I tossed the phone shrapnel into the office waste basket and slumped onto the floor. The motherly generosity left me feeling like a twelve year old. My mood soured all the way to bed.

CHAPTER THREE

That night will live forever in infamy.

You might remember that comment about sleep curing what ails you. Well, it seems sleep can do some other magical works, so I found out, because that night I fell madly in love with Stellan. Well, I fell in love with dream Stellan, at least.

I dreamed I'd bought a house with endless rooms I'd yet to explore, and as excited I was to explore my new place, it seemed every member of my extended family was there to check the place out as well. The place had Jacuzzi bathtubs, a dozen bedrooms, holes in the walls and floor, and a ghost of course – this *was* a dream. And then there was Stellan.

He appeared at my side, declaring the find of a lifetime just down the hallway. I followed him down the hall to a grand bedroom, and fell in love - despite the strange holes in the hardwood floor that showed my family members below. Stellan closed the door behind us and grabbed me about the waist, pulling me away from a rather large hole in the floor that had decided to appear when I wasn't looking. I mumbled something about how easy it would be to fix the floor and that the house was well worth the miniscule price I'd paid when I looked up to find Stellan smiling at me. His arms were still around me as he looked at me.

I was undone by it.

No one had ever looked at me the way dream Stellan was looking at me.

Thanks a lot, subconscious.

Have you ever felt love in a dream – the kind of love you imagine exists in the world, but perhaps haven't yet found? Be it with someone you know, your imaginary great aunt's mailman, or Benedict Cumberbatch, it doesn't matter - you feel the warmth of familiarity, of kindness and desire, not just of the sexual nature, but of something far deeper than that. At that moment, I simply wanted to fold into Dream Stellan's arms, even his eyes, and live there in the warmth between us. And because it was a dream, I didn't feel odd, incestuous, or surprised – this was where I belonged, and I pressed my palms against his broad chest to feel his skin beneath his shirt.

The dream quickly descended into a Benny Hill episode where Stellan and I were running from room to room trying to steal a private moment so we could shag, and being interrupted each time by a mad gaggle of family members hell bent on cockblockery in the form of a self-guided house tour.

I was practically homicidal when I woke up.

Homicidal, but smiling. The feeling of affection - of overflowing and reciprocated affection - stayed with me. I wrapped my arms around my pillow and hugged it tightly, letting the untouched coolness of the fabric warm against my cheek.

I heard my mother moving around the house. A moment later, she hollered for me to get up. There was a phone to procure. I lingered in bed, and on the memory of that feeling. After a few moments, I recognized that for the first time in weeks, I hadn't woken up thinking about Cole. I hadn't woken up with that momentary serenity of everything being right with the world, only to have it ripped away in an instant by memory. This time it didn't tear from my fingers. It lingered, as did my smile.

This is interesting, I thought.

My inner workings scolded. Thinking about Dream Stellan was near to sacrilegious, and I should just cut it out, they said. I ignored the inner voice. I felt held by the memory, as though Dream Stellan was still next to me, his arms around me. I felt the sleepy comfort of being in love, or at least what my subconscious had decided was how love should feel. Yet, under that I felt frustration - the aggravation of what I was sure a man might refer to as 'blue balls.' I wanted to hunt each of those dream cock blockers down.

A moment later I felt a warm rush between my legs. My body had responded to the dream as well.

I shifted in bed, fighting the tingling that seemed to be emanating from down below. In my attempts to ignore it, I climbed out of bed and headed down the hall, towel in hand.

I undressed, climbed into the shower and sat down. Despite years of having done this, I still faltered for a moment at the thought of doing this in my mother's house. I wasn't seventeen anymore.

You're alone, I thought. Even if she were to come in, you're in a locked bathroom. I let my fingers begin their work. I thought of that warmth. I thought of the arms around me. I thought of Stellan's eyes.

Stop it! Think of something else.

I thought of the most passionate porn scene I'd ever witnessed. I thought of the second most passionate porn scene I'd ever witnessed. I thought of a handsome Captain named Malcolm, piloting a ship called *Serenity*. I thought of young Val Kilmer as Mad Martigan in *Willow*, of Cary Elwes whispering 'As you wish.' I thought of Stellan towering over me, my fingers curled into his shoulders.

Stop it Faye! God damn it!

Ok, ok. Edward Norton? No. Sam Rockwell? Usually, but no. Stellan's blue eyes and him pinning me up against the porcelain sink whispering in his bedroomy voice?

Oh god yes!

It was innocent enough to just let a dream carry me through, wasn't it? I didn't ask for the dream, but I enjoyed its effects, and I was going to strike while the iron was hot. Oh wow, it was really hot. The voice in my head hissed and booed, but I noticed that as my hands moved, the minute Stellan's image appeared in my mind – his face, his hands, that bedroomy voice of his that always made me squirm – it made the sensations triple in intensity. The heat rose, rose again, and then my fingers and my wrist went nearly limp and useless – a side effect of relying on one's own efforts to achieve orgasm and not having a Garden Bath Tub like I did in my condo to do all the work. I fought against atrophy to maintain, but the orgasm had crested and fallen back, not half the strength it could have been. I would have to be satisfied with that.

I've read that three orgasms a week make women look ten years younger. Well, actually, the article said women should be having sex three times a week – a feat I've never actually managed to maintain for any real duration of time due to lackluster partners, but they said solo trips counted for single ladies. At this rate I probably looked forty something, because my vagina and I haven't been on speaking terms. Previously to that, Meghan wasn't wrong when she mentioned Cole's libido in comparison to mine. I think three times a week is low – far too low. Maybe Cole was right and I really am just obsessed with sex, but damn it, I don't think wanting daily sex makes me 'oversexed.' I remember thinking, in order to be called oversexed, I would need to actually be having sex, but I didn't say that out loud at the time when Cole made the comment.

That morning there was a definite spring in my step as I ventured to the store with my mother.

An hour later, I was the proud owner of a new cell phone.

The new phone was glorious. Given my mother's generosity, and more importantly, her love of gadgets, I had the newest iPhone, and it was a clean slate - no contacts, no old texts. I was happy to be rid of contacts like Stephen, the guy I kept programmed so I knew not to answer if he called; Jamie, the girl from college who told me I should vomit if I wanted to lose weight, then bought me a pack of Ex-Lax; or Janet Tildon, my old boss who broke the news to me that the company was going under, and I would be out of a job two days later. I didn't need these numbers, but they were in the old phone. Starting fresh felt kinda good, and despite knowing the number by heart, being rid of Cole's contact felt liberating. Bittersweet, but liberating.

I rustled around the house for a bit, filling Mom's birdfeeders, wiping down the counters and picking up here and there. Once I'd spent a couple hours simply plodding around the house, I performed my second miracle of the day. I went out for a walk.

The air was cool and crisp. Autumn is New England's season. The trees don't fade into a wintery slumber by any means. They explode. The world was bustling outside. Even the quiet empty streets were in constant movement, the bright orange and red debris swirling across the gray asphalt, leaving it collected along the roadsides, only to be picked up in a gust by the next passing car. The world seemed beautiful. Truly beautiful.

Wow, the wonders of masturbation. Were I attempting a marketing campaign, the catch phrase would be: *Masturbation! Start your day off right.*

I rounded the corner onto Davis Court an hour later and stopped dead as I caught sight of my house. Stellan's jeep was parked outside. I sat there, awkwardly staring at my own house with a knot in my stomach. I nearly turned right around to flee. There was plenty of town I could meander to.

Faye, he isn't going to know you imagined him naked this morning. He isn't going to know you had an orgasm at his expense. Just go inside.

I glanced at my phone. I'd managed to spend eight minutes futzing around at the end of my street. Pathetic, I thought. It still took me a couple minutes to get up my front steps. I actually almost sat down in one of the Adirondack chairs, just to keep the wall and the front door between myself and the sole member of my morning spank tank. He was going to take notice and come out soon.

I opened the front door and went inside. Stellan wasn't on the couch.

"Hello?" I called.

"Hey Ray!"

His voice came from the office. He was muffled, like someone speaking through a blanket. The butterflies in my stomach only quadrupled at the sound of his voice. He was just a few yards away.

Just go say hello, just be cool. Just stop being a jackass. I mean, seriously.

I walked down the hall. I didn't immediately see him when I looked into the office. The room consists of white walls, and built in bookshelves and cabinets surrounding the empty space where I'd once had my drawing table.

Let me rephrase - where my drawing table now stood, two long denim clad legs protruding from beneath. It looked like a dusty angled surface with work boots on its second set of legs. Stellan shifted out from under the table, a screwdriver in his hand.

He sat up, smirking at me. "Whaddaya think? Pretty rad, eh?"

I stood silent.

He seemed to take my shock as a positive thing. "Just a few bits of missing hardware, and it'll be all set."

I wasn't sure which thought to share – how furiously my stomach was turning at the mere presence of him, or how far my stomach sank at the sight of that table; a table I spent hours upon hours at for all of my youth.

Should I say 'thank you?' 'How thoughtful?' Wait, why is it thoughtful? I haven't drawn so much as a comic since college. What the hell was he doing?

Sadly, the most prominent thoughts I had were how handsome he looked with his hair pulled back. The words, 'You fucker, you're not helping!' crossed my mind.

After another minute of silence, he got up off the floor.

"You alright there?"

I nodded and swallowed.

"You're ok with it, yeah?"

"Yeah," I said, and the word stuck in my throat like raw octopus that doesn't want to be eaten. "I just – why did you bring it up?"

I tried my hardest not to let my voice betray – well, any number of thoughts.

He shrugged. "You remember that project I mentioned? The one I needed your help with?"

I swallowed. "Yes."

He gestured to the table. "You're gonna need this. That is, if you say yes. I hope you say yes."

I was going to say yes. No matter how uneasy I felt looking at that table, I knew I'd say yes to anything Stellan asked. So did he.

Jesus, what was I going to agree to?

He nudged my arm and turned to explain the last bits of work that needed to be done to finish the table – a few screws of various sizes, easy things that we could pick up in the hardware store down the street. He put his hand on the corner of the drawing board and shook it. Despite a slight squeak, it was sturdy. I watched Stellan bend down to pick up the little amount of trash he'd created in his project and felt ridiculous. One stupid dream and I've turned into a slack jawed yokel in his company, ogling his bum when he bends over. This is just fucking fantastic. I felt like a wolverine was giving birth in my intestines.

"You're really quiet today," he said after another moment passed.

I nodded, but quickly realized that a silent answer would only further fuel his sense of something being wrong, or worse, a lack of gratitude from me. "I've just had a strange day."

"Oh yeah? What you been up to?"

I replayed the simple, and somewhat pointless pursuits of my afternoon and almost felt embarrassed to share. "Driving around."

He nodded. "It has its place," he said. I caught my breath as he brushed past me and stood there listening to him in the kitchen. However fleeting and pointless the contact was, I hoped it would happen again.

I fought the desire to follow him. This was unreasonable – it's Stellan for Christ's sake!

"You wanna' walk down to the hardware store with me?" He asked from the kitchen. I could hear him cracking the top of a can of soda and despite my inner berating, I was hoping for the sound of his returning footsteps. He wasn't moving.

"You don't have to do that -" I called. He appeared at the dining room doorway. I jumped at the sight of him. He smiled as he always did when he snuck up on me.

 He smelled good today – like clean laundry and soap. Why the hell does he have to smell nice *today*?

"You coming?"

I'd been standing there silent while he waited. God damn it, Faye. Snap out of it! "Yeah, if you want."

He swigged at his root beer, and disappeared into the kitchen. When he returned he had our jackets.

We walked down to the center of town, meandered through the hardware store on Main Street, Stellan scouring the screws and bolts and things and me looking at paint swatches, mentally paint shopping for the house in my dream. Stellan finished his shopping, and I followed him out, only to have him suggest we stop in the Boathouse Café for a cannoli. I love cannoli. Stellan could survive without them, and I knew this, but still he pressed the suggestion.

"I'm trying to avoid that stuff right now," I said, avoiding eye contact like a twelve year old.

He nodded. "Ah, I forgot about that. Do you want coffee instead?"

He seemed quite adamant, so I accepted. It was a few doors down, a bistro style coffee and sandwich shop that made the neighboring alleyway smell of cookies and Italian subs on any given day. He ordered my Salted Caramel coffee and nothing for himself. I did notice, however, that he spent a good few minutes talking to the girl behind the counter. She was mid-twenties, auburn haired and quite lovely in a green hills and leprechauns kind of way. I stood back toward the door while he made her laugh.

I stared at the floor, my stomach churning and my throat tight. It was a fury I wasn't accustomed to and without warning, I turned and walked out. I didn't feel like waiting for Stellan to get some random girl's number. Problem was, I didn't think she was random. Stellan knew full well she would be behind that counter, and I was sure that was why he was so adamant to go.

Well, he can fucking stay all day for all I care, I thought.

"F-Bomb! Wait up!"

I cringed. His footsteps closed in quickly as he came after me. Now I would have to acknowledge that I'd left. How the hell do I explain that I didn't like seeing him chatting up a girl?

"What's up?" He asked as he matched my pace.

I shrugged and kept walking, throwing my coffee in a trash bin as we passed. I regretted it instantly, but I was a whirlwind of spite at that moment, so coffee be damned.

He nudged my arm softly. I pulled away from the touch. That would show him.

We walked back to my house in silence, Stellan a few steps behind me as I walked. I kept my head high, inspecting the leaves overhead as though they were the most interesting thing I'd ever encountered.

I would not acknowledge him.

I would not acknowledge him.

I would not acknowledge him.

Go let Miss MacGillacuddy acknowledge you, fuck bag!

We went inside, and I slumped down on the couch.

Stellan stood in the front room a moment, and I could feel him looking at me. Finally he went for the office and began fumbling around. I took the opportunity to turn on the TV, letting the familiar sounds of *The Price is Right* fill the room. Drew Carey hadn't gotten halfway through revealing the first showcase when I found Stellan standing in front of me, blocking the TV completely. He was a big man, and big men are very hard to ignore.

He lightly kicked the bottom of my shoe. "What's up with you?"

I shrugged.

Suddenly he leaned down over me, his hands on the back of the couch behind my shoulders. I was trapped there between his arms, his face just inches away from mine. There was no escaping the sight of him, or worse the smell of him. *God damn it, just let me fester! It'll go away if you just let me fester!*

"Look at me," he said in a sing song voice. I stared at the rolled up sleeve of his flannel shirt. It wasn't the best spot to choose, given that it made the contours of his forearm all the more prominent.

Damn it, Faye! Stop finding him attractive!

"No," I said, still staring at his arm.

"What did I do?"

"Nothing."

He laughed. "Come on, F-bomb. Why are you mad?"

"Oh, I don't know. Maybe because you dragged me to the Boathouse to schmooze some girl."

His eyebrows went up instantly. "Really?"

"Yeh," I said, curtly. "I think you'd find if you'd asked me to tag along for such an adventure I would have declined."

He sank down to his knees in front of me, searching my face, waiting for me to look at him. When I did, he smiled. Despite all my effort to be angry, his smile cracked me, and I fought not to smile back.

"You jealous?"

"Fuck you," I said, and tried to get off the couch and past him. He wouldn't have it.

I slumped back into the couch as he half tackled me.

"You're jealous!" He said, beaming.

For a quick instant, his hands shifted across the couch and up my legs. The sensation sent a current of electricity through my whole body, and I gave an involuntary shriek. This wasn't my response to being tickled, for that cry is in protest. I was startled by how electrifying just the mere graze of his fingers was. Yet, his true purpose was instantly clear as his hands found my waist and my under arms. I wailed and kicked at him, only driving him on. He launched himself up onto the couch, straddling me and pinning me there as he tortured me. I screamed my undying hatred, pushing and pulling at his hands in an attempt to stop the tickling, but as you may realize, I was up against a giant ninja. It was an exercise in futility.

"I fucking hate you!" I screamed.

"No you don't! You're madly in love with me! I always knew this day would come. You're no match for my masculine charms," he said, still squeezing at my sides. Finally, he dove for my feet, pinning me beneath him as he pried off my shoes. My feet were the most tickling part of my body. I screamed so loud, the glass in the windows shook.

He laughed maniacally as I cried out. I continued to protest until he finally let me free, lifting himself up off the couch to go work in the office. I lied there across the cushions, a frazzled and tortured mess, but the warmth of his body lingered.

I didn't dare move. Something had shifted in me. For the first time in my life, I'd enjoyed being tickled. Damn it, how could this happen?

I listened to him working in the office, still unwilling to get up from the couch as Drew Carey celebrated with a college kid over his brand new trailer. I heard a familiar sound buzzing upstairs and realized I had left my phone on the bedside table.

I headed upstairs and unplugged my phone to check my messages. Meghan had offered lunch, Jackie had asked how I was doing, but it was the other texts that startled me out of the warm euphoria.

I miss you, baby. Please talk to me.
I need to see you. Can I call?

Every little nuance of grief, every night I'd cried myself to sleep, every memory I'd been told to sweep aside – they all came flooding back. These were the messages I'd been waiting for. Yet I was there, floating atop all that grief with a strange serenity. Yes, a part of me still ached and hurt, and I missed being close to someone, but something had shifted in me.

Stellan had shifted in me. He'd worked this strange magic, and he had no idea.

I stared at my phone, took a deep breath, and responded.

No.

I exhaled and pressed send.

"Fayeninator!" Stellan called from downstairs.

I stared at my phone, waiting for the message to read *Sent*, then called back. "Yeah?"

"Shit! You comin down? I got something I need to run by you."

***

I felt like a gelatinous mass that was just waiting to jiggle publicly. Christ, jumping jacks are enough to give me black eyes and bruised knees if I don't have a proper sports bra, which if you're wondering, I do not, but there I stood in the most flattering pair of yoga pants I owned and a t-shirt.

Why did you agree to this?

Ninpo Dojo of West Concord didn't have too many cars outside by the time I arrived. Stellan had begged, pleaded, and cajoled for twenty minutes before I relented.

"Please come to class tonight? I need you!" He'd said.

I'd agreed. I'm sure he knew I would before he dropped to his knee for effect.

I arrived a half hour before class and meandered into the quiet dojo. Stellan's office door was wide open. I crept into the empty front room glancing around for a sign of life.

"Come on in," he said.

I swear the man is a freakin' ninja.

I felt weighted to the spot, my nerves screaming for me to turn around and leave. Still that nagging voice in my head kept chanting, *It's Stellan, It's just Stellan, stop imagining him naked, he's Stellan.* I stepped into the office to find him sitting at his desk, his hair pulled back in such a way that for a split second I thought he'd cut it in the hour and a half since he left my house. He noticed the look of awe.

"What'd I do?"

I smiled. "Nothing. Your hairstyle fooled me for a second."

He smiled back. "Oh, did it?" He pulled the elastic from his hair and gave a Pantene worthy hair flip with limp wrists on both sides. "How can you deny the sheer animal magnetism of my gorgeous mane?"

I stifled a laugh. "Uh. It's a mullet."

"Oh hell yeah! Spite mullet! Business up front, party in the back."

I laughed and tried to ignore the fact that his uniform, which crossed over his chest, was tied loosely and falling open. Seeing Stellan's bare skin would usually go by without incident, but at that moment, we were very close to having an incident.

He restored the elastic in his hair before hopping up. "You ready to get suited up?"

"Would you be offended if I said no?"

He smiled and wrapped his arm around my shoulder, shaking me as he led me down the hall. He showed me to the changing room where he'd laid out a uniform. He whispered another thank you as the first students filtered into the front room. I locked myself away in the women's changing room and held the black drawstring pants before me. Why couldn't I just wear my Yoga pants? They made my butt look fantastic. I slipped into the pants, which were an easy one size fits most kind of deal. Then I tried to pull the Gi top over my head and met with the resistance of my somewhat surplus sized boobs. I twisted, repositioning the girls, but there was nothing to stop them from flying out in the middle of class. No knot in any sailor's repertoire was strong enough to hold this cleavalanche at bay. At least not in this size top. If I wore this, everyone would expect a lap dance. I was pretty sure Stellan wanted the class's full attention, and I was the grand fucking canyon in that thing.

I paused. Now came the devastating reality of my next move – I was going to have to tell Stellan that I needed a bigger size. I hated my life with such implicit fervor that had I the option of Seppuku in that dressing room, I'd have considered it. Let Stellan find my stripper cleavage corpse later.

Sadly, I didn't have a sword.

I cracked the door to the dressing room and hissed. Stellan left his conversation with a younger man I knew as Daniel and reached for the door as he approached.

"Let me see," he said and gave the door a pull. I almost ripped my fingernails off trying to keep hold on the door. He held his hands up, startled.

"I'm not decent!"

I held the shirt out to him, and he raised an eyebrow.

He gave me an eyebrow wiggle and moved toward the door. "Well, F-bomb, now's not the time or place for that, but if we make it quick -"

I swung the shirt at him, satisfied to hear it slap against his bare forearms - his chiseled, masculine forearms – fuck! "It doesn't fit!"

His face softened. "Oh shit! I forgot about that rack of yours. Gimme a sec!"

He bounded back down the hall. I stood there, trying not to blush. He'd mentioned my boobs. Sure, it's just about impossible to miss them, but still, however misplaced the sensation might be, I felt flattered - and if one could call it that, attractive, for a moment. He came back down the hall and handed me another shirt. I prayed silently that large would be big enough to contain the ladies, because if I had to ask for XL, I'd commit Seppuku with my teeth.

The shirt fit. I stepped out into the hallway feeling ridiculous. A few of the familiar guys greeted me. This wasn't my first time at Ninpo Dojo, but I'd never visited as a student before. I scanned the front room and saw Stellan off on the opposite side of the dojo, setting up for class.

A few younger boys were tying their shoes when Thomas O'Ryan spotted me. He knew me to be in cahoots with his sensei, and let's just say, it bought me serious street credit.

"Hey Ms. Jensen!"

"It's Faye, hon."

The dirty blond hair flitting about as he shook his head. "No way. Sensei would kill me if I called you Faye."

"Well, I promise *I* won't kill you."

He laughed and the other young boy introduced

himself as *Mr.* Gregory Federer. He looked about eleven, and reminded me of a once young and slight Stellan. This was a boy lying in wait of his growth spurt by learning how to defend his tiny self. I smiled at the sight of him.

There was a sudden burst of voices in the dojo as the older boys (and one girl, I might add) filtered in.

"Man, I can't wait to be in this class. They get to spar and learn weapons and stuff," Mr. Gregory Federer said.

"Wow, sounds pretty cool," I said, and it was sincere. Martial Arts had always intrigued me, and I had a healthy respect for anyone who mastered it. Well, let's be honest, anyone who stayed in classes longer than a month earned my respect.

"I wanna learn the sword," said Mr. Gregory Federer. He began flailing his arms around and making light saber sounds. Thomas smiled and pretended to clash blades.

A spray of spit flew from Thomas' lips as he made a rather convincing saber clash. "I can't wait until I have to register."

"Oh yeah! Like Dan?" Gregory asked.

"Yeah, and like Sensei Ødegård!"

"What like Sensei?" I asked, glancing into the dojo for a sight of the devil.

Thomas' eyes went wide. "Sensei's a 5th dan! That's like 20th degree black belt or something in Karate."

Thomas' flair for exaggeration was unparalleled.

"Yeah! If he wanted to get any better, he'd have to go train at a Ninja school in Japan like Sensei David."

"Wow," I said, listening intently. The mannerisms of ten year old boys were a wonder to behold. "I didn't know they had Ninja schools in Japan."

Gregory gave me a sad look, like he pitied my limited intelligence. "Oh yeah! They gotta!"

I smiled. "You probably have to be a Ninja to find one!"

"Well, then Sensei's all set, right? Cause he's a Ninja," Thomas said.

"I bet he loves to hear you say that."

"It's true! He had to register with the police as a deadly weapon," he said, his tone hushed. "Dan Hubbard just got his 1st dan, and he had to register. Now, if he gets into a fight, he can go to jail because his fists are deadly weapons."

"Even his feet are deadly weapons," Gregory added.

Thomas shook his head. "Yeah, the police want to know, you know. Which stinks, because now the police know who the Ninjas are."

"Well that defeats the whole purpose, doesn't it?" I asked.

The two boys stiffened, their posture impeccable.

"You boys ready?"

I should have known by the towering shadow across the floor, but Stellan still managed to surprise me as he appeared behind me.

"Yes Sensei," the two boys said in unison.

"You two do your best tonight, and I'll consider letting you move up."

The two boys' eyes widened like the moon in late eclipse, and they were gone, mingling in the dojo with the older students. I turned and met Stellan's gaze. God, he's fucking tall.

I gestured to the girl in class. "Thought you needed me."

He scoffed. "Grace is a baby. I needed a Wo-man!"

He said, and dropped his tone to that bedroomy place, outlining an hourglass with his hands. I swatted at him.

We heard a soft voice behind me, and I turned to meet the woman whose savior I was intended to be.

I extended a hand to the older woman. "Hey there! I'm Faye."

The woman beamed at me, twisting the tie at her waist. We shook hands, and she introduced herself as Candyce. Before we could get too familiar with one another, Stellan hollered something in Japanese, and any stragglers in the front room darted into the dojo, each stopping to bow at the door as they entered. I bowed awkwardly and followed, Candyce shuffling close behind. We lined up before Stellan. He stood a head above the rest of the class, his broad shoulders still pulling the collar of his shirt apart. Candyce nudged me to inform me that I wasn't the only one aware of how sexy our Sensei was. I smiled. It was a relief to have her there, possibly more so for me than it was for her.

We did a warm up and by the end of it, I was cursing the day Stellan was born. I did my best to pretend I wasn't huffing and puffing like a beached Manatee, but let's be honest, it was pathetic. I tried to keep up with everyone. Pushups, run, sit ups, run - Ichi, ni, san, yon, go, ichi, ni, san. I was beginning to feel weightless and disconnected from the rest of my body, but I kept up, repeating each random, unintelligible phrase Stellan hollered to the class until he announced that we were to run around the room again. I sighed and turned to follow. Stellan slid in front of me.

"Hey you," he said.

I almost ran headfirst into his chest. The sudden stop made me dizzy. "Hey."

I attempted to go around him. My head was dense and heavy, as though someone had clamped a concrete vice just above each ear. Before I could pass him, he placed his hands on my shoulders and held me still.

"How bout you sit down for a minute, babe?"

I furrowed my brow. "What? No."

Again I tried to pass him, the sounds of padded feet tromping past us over and over as they ran around the perimeter of the dojo. Even Candyce was keeping a relatively even pace as she passed us. Stellan swooped one of his long arms around my waist and turned me toward the benches.

"Stop it," I said, trying to loose myself from his arm. He let me go, but gently took hold of my hands.

He hunched down to look me in the eye. "Have you eaten today?"

"No?"

"Yeah, I need you to sit down, hon."

He pushed a little more insistently, and I waited for the runners to pass before hissing up at him. "Why are you trying to embarrass me?"

"I'm trying to avoid that. Trust me."

I shoved his hand away again. "No, you're singling me out."

He laughed. "Quit being so stubborn. All the color is drained out of your face, babe. I don't want you doing a face plant into the hardwood. Just sit down for me, okay?"

"I'm fine, Stell. Pick on Candyce or something -"

He leaned down again meeting my gaze just as my head nearly detached from my body and floated away.

"Young lady, while you're in my dojo, I'm Sensei. What I say, goes."

He spoke with the gentle authority of a Geriatric doctor talking to a belligerent dementia patient. I let him sit me down on the bench, given that I felt like I was riding an escalator rather than actually walking across the room. He brought me a cup of water and his voice sounded cloudy, as though I were wearing headphones without any music playing. I glanced around the room, mumbling about how weird it felt and that I couldn't hear him.

He smiled.

I called him a dick.

"I mean, Sensei," I said, snidely. He nudged my leg with his as he squatted down.

"Just sip slow, alright? You can jump back in when you're ready."

He was up, walking backwards to keep an eye on me as though I might launch into a Flash dance style calisthenics number the second he turned his back. When he was sure I wouldn't move, he hollered to the class again to do another round of sit ups and bicycles and leg lifts and – Christ, I don't even know what. I lost track and stared into my water. It was the only thing in the room not spinning. When Stellan finally called over to me, I glanced up and found the rest of the class suiting up with pads and boxing gloves. He waved me over to him, and I took my place next to Candyce.

Stellan approached and spoke quietly. "You look better. You good?"

I nodded. He smiled and handed me a pair of boxing gloves. Candyce had on the mitts, so I turned to her. This looked like it might be fun.

Stellan tugged me aside. "Alright, Candyce, I'm gonna put you with Daniel."

Daniel came by in his usual sweet manner and led her off to another section of the room. I felt something padded nudge me in the side and turned to find Stellan with mitts on his own hands.

"I thought you wanted me to keep her company?"

He smiled. "I did. And you did, and I owe you dinner for that."

"Well, I'm not actually doing anything, am I?"

He held his hands up in front of me and took his stance, gesturing for me to do the same. I obliged, glaring at him.

"You've been a greater help than you know."

"And yet, now she's off with Daniel. Correct me if I'm wrong, but doesn't he belong to the 'sausage party?'"

Stellan smiled and ordered me to hit his left mitt with a right cross. I did.

"That's the whole point. Now that she's here, she can get comfortable with the guys so she won't be afraid to come back. Who better than Daniel to show her that they're all a bunch of harmless dweebs?"

I laughed and hit the mitt for the tenth time. He switched to his left and demanded ten back fists.

"You call your students dweebs? How kind of you."

"Hey, I'm the king of the dweebs. I can say what I want. Come on, you can do better than that."

He held both mitts out now. I was winded, but I was enjoying myself and my head was still attached. When I finished the tenth combination, he ordered me to switch legs and we started over on the other side. I caught him watching me in the midst of my punches, and I knew he was making sure my head wasn't floating away. Embarrassment aside, his concern felt comforting. Despite my state, he didn't make me feel weak. Well, except when he called me a pansy for not hitting harder.

I growled at him. "You suck!"

"Breathe out when you strike. Burst of air – pow! There you go!"

He set up both mitts for the combination again, and I punched through and swung back with a nice rhythm. It was satisfying, and almost relaxing to be pounding the shit out of something. I forgot to worry about the fact that I might look like a glistening pig being hosed down in the sun and just punched away, determined to hit hard enough to appease him. I breathed out on the last back hand, and nailed the mitt. His eyes went wide.

"Hell yeah! Watch out for Faye's south paw," he announced to the class. I felt my face flush. He ordered everyone to trade off mitts and gloves and returned his attention to me. When Stellan struck my mitted hand, there was no question he was holding back.

"And you were calling *me* a weakling?"

He smiled. "Never called you a weakling, babe."

"Well, I'm calling *you* one."

"It's true."

I scoffed as he tapped the back of his fist. I felt a little insulted, as though he didn't think me strong enough to withstand him. It must have been apparent on my face.

"I never hit full strength in class, F-Bomb."

"Why not?"

He shrugged. "Maintain some mystery, I suppose." He bobbed his eyebrows at me.

I shook my head. "No, you're just afraid you'll hurt me."

He stopped punching my mitts and cocked his head to the side. It was the 'Are you serious?' look he gave me whenever he thought I was being ridiculous. "Does that offend you; that I don't want to hurt you?"

"Yes, actually."

He rolled his eyes before hollering to the class to add another ten set to the last combination. "You want me to actually hit you? Want me to rough you up a little, is that how you like it?"

I squirmed. Damn it, Stellan. Stop finding a way to make everything sexual! "No!"

He settled back into his stance and gestured for me to do the same. "Alright, I'll hit a little harder on the last one? Will that appease you, Warrior Princess?"

"Fuck you. And yes, it will."

He smiled.

He hit with ten lackluster left crosses, then his backhands. I held my hand at the ready, returning it quickly after each hit, growing annoyed with the weak impact. He counted them out – 5, 4, 3, 2... and then that last one hit.

Oh my god, I should learn to shut my damn mouth.

I pulled the mitt off quickly and rubbed my hand. He moved toward me, grabbing it as well. "Did I hurt you? I'm sorry."

"No, it's alright, I'm fine."

My hand was burning and limp. I shook it out beside me, hoping the searing pins and needles would stop. He snatched my hand in his and began massaging his thumbs into my palm. I felt a surge of excitement at his touch. I snatched my hand away. He reached for me again, but I held my hurting hand behind my back.

"I'm ok, Stell. Just never let me convince you to do that again."

He forced a smile, but I could see he was upset with himself. He put an arm around me, rubbing the back of my neck for a moment. I tried not to look at him. He turned to the rest of the class.

I felt pathetic. I shouldn't have let him see that it hurt. Still let's be honest, it really freaking hurt. To make it even worse, I could tell he'd still been holding back.

He sent us off in small groups, staff weapons on the far wall, forms at the back of the class. Daniel pulled a big blue pad from the back room and began practicing a form that included a flip and roll. I couldn't even comprehend that he would one day be performing such a thing without that pad to catch him. Damn Ninjas.

Stellan pulled Candyce and I to the front of the room and taught us our first form, then he left to help the advanced students. We lined up to start our third run through of the form when someone made an impressed whooping sound. I turned in time to catch Stellan doing the very flip and roll move that Daniel was attempting moments earlier. Stellan didn't need the pad. He bounded to his feet, gave a couple kicks that were high enough to have easily decapitated Andre the Giant, God rest his soul, then clapped at Daniel in encouragement, sending him off to try again. He turned toward the front of the dojo and caught me staring. He called me a 'looky-lou' and said I owed him another ten forms. I grumbled only for Candyce to hear, and noticed she'd been with me in the gallery of slack jawed 'looky-lous.'

"Oh, I'm definitely coming back," she said, fanning herself. I laughed, and we lined up again.

A few moments before class ended, the phone rang in the office. Stellan hustled by, gesturing for me to follow.

I caught a few words of the conversation – David Callahan. Stellan nodded into the phone, before winking at me. I waited patiently as he finished up.

"Hell yeah, Brutha. Glad to hear it."

David Callahan was Stellan's Sensei and owner of Ninpo Dojo. He'd placed Stellan in charge of the school when he left to study at that fabled Ninja school in Japan. David would be one of the highest ranked Ninjitsu Sensei's in the country when he returned – in a year. Stellan was content to lead the pack in his absence. The students seemed content as well.

Stellan hung up and handed me a set of keys.

"Tell Daniel to lock up the gear for me, will ya?"

I nodded and turned.

"Sensei?"

The young girl, Grace, was standing in the doorway.

Stellan raised his eyebrows at her. "What do you need, dear?"

I searched the girl's face, something about the expression familiar. She wanted to say something, but her cheeks flushed instead.

"I was looking in the bathroom -" She started.

Stellan waited patiently, his eyes soft. She froze again, and it clicked. I knew the look.

I curled my arm around her shoulders and led her back toward the bathroom. Grace was probably around thirteen or so, and held her own in class to some of the older boys. As I led her down the hall, I was sure this wasn't her first, but perhaps it was her first time being caught unawares. I silently thanked whatever God's she might pray to that the Ninjutsu uniforms were black.

"Here ya go, honey," I said, pulling a box of pads out from under the sink. She visibly relaxed, snatching the box from my hands. I pulled out a box of tampons and set them by the sink, as well.

You never know what a woman prefers. You should have both.

I remembered the conversation vividly – explaining to Stellan why he needed to stock just this very thing in the girl's bathroom. He didn't argue, but simply swooshed his hair to the side in the drug store and walked with a limp wrist up to the counter to purchase them. We looked ridiculous – huge mulleted man buying tampons with a lisp, and me laughing to the point of oxygen deprivation.

Despite the difficulty I had going into that CVS thereafter, this moment made it all worth it. I left and found Stellan still in the office. He raised an eyebrow, but I just waved him off. He knew not to press further. A moment later Grace ran back to class. The smile had returned to her face.

I stood talking to Candyce after class. Each of the guys stopped to speak to Stellan on their way out the door. They all had to look up to meet Stellan's gaze, but you could see reverence in their eyes. Many of them had been in classes at this school since they were young and having the same trouble Stellan once had. They started out picked on kids with glasses and bad skin, and they'd grown into these well-mannered

101

men who walked with a comfort, (I won't say confidence, because not a one of them was cocky) that comes from knowing they could protect themselves if they needed to.

I'd heard a story years earlier about Daniel being attacked during high school – four kids decided to beat the shit out of him in front of their girlfriends for no better reason than lunch room boredom. Daniel put two of them in the hospital. As I recall, Stellan wasn't the least bit pleased, and he hollered at him in front of class for using too much force. Still, no one bothered Daniel ever again.

Candyce waited until the rest of the class had filtered out, saying a quick thank you and goodbye to Daniel as he left. She followed Stellan into his office, and I waited patiently outside the door. I didn't want to intrude on the conversation, but I could hear Candyce asking for a schedule and professing a desire to return. Stellan praised her for having kept up with the rest of class and said she was more than welcome. I felt a slight twinge of embarrassment, reminded of my own failings in the whole 'keeping up' department.

She met my gaze as she left the office. "Will you be coming Tuesday nights?"

I floundered a moment, unsure whether I should lie, or if Stellan would be requesting my presence. He stepped out from the office behind her and nodded at me, vehemently.

Guess I could tell Jackie I joined a gym.

"I should be," I said, and Candyce smiled. She grabbed her coat, waved to the two of us, and she was gone. Stellan and I stood there alone a moment. I didn't speak.

Stellan crossed the room toward me and put his

arms around my shoulders, pulling me into his chest. I felt his chin rest on the top of my head a moment and tried not to stifle at the close contact. Despite the complete sweaty disgusting mess I was, he still smelled of soap and laundry detergent.

"You're the best, F-bomb," he said and released me. I couldn't make eye contact. Illogical as it may sound, I was sure if ever anyone were to magically sprout telepathic powers it would be Stellan, and it would be right now.

"I try," I managed to say.

"Well, I owe you dinner."

"You don't have to do that."

"Yes I do," he said and made this almost disgusted face, as if to say, 'what sort of Neanderthal birthed you?'

I shrugged. "I'm kinda disgusting."

"Only kinda?" He braced himself for an attack, but I didn't hit him. Despite not looking at his face, I could tell he was a little disappointed. "Alright, let's get changed. We can order Chinese at your place, yeah?"

Damn, that sounded good. I nodded and collected myself, wandering down the hallway into the women's changing room. He followed, disappearing into the men's. I stood inside the little room, looking up at the wall that separated the two dressing rooms. The wall didn't reach all the way to the ceiling, leaving an open space near the ceiling. Had Stellan the desire, I was sure he could jump up and look over. I stared at the break, listening. I could hear him undressing, hear clothes dropping to the floor, hear his belt as he pulled on his jeans. I imagined the way he must look, imagined standing this close to him as he dressed, but without a wall between us, imagined him letting me see, wanting me to see.

Standing there, I felt further away from him than I ever had before.

"You all set, babe?"

The sound of his voice startled me. I'd made no moves to change whatsoever, and he was done. I tried to kick off my uniform, untying the waist band and dropping the pants as I tugged the shirt up over my head. The combination of movement threw me off balance, and I toppled onto the bench, bare-assed. *What the fuck are you doing, Faye?*

"You alright in there, dove?"

I grumbled back at him. "Yes, I'm fine."

He said he had something to show me and would collect it from his house before heading over. He promised to give me enough time to shower when I got home.

"For the good of mankind," he said.

I was grateful to have the moment to myself. Perhaps I could get that nagging sense of wanting out of my head. I showered, wishing as I sometimes did, that my own private bathroom shower worked. I thought about calling a plumber when I started working again and shell out the cash to have it repaired. I quickly corrected myself.

When you start working again, you won't live here.

I heard movement downstairs and hustled out of the warm cocoon I'd created. I returned to my bedroom in just a towel and fought the thoughts of him miraculously deciding to come upstairs for some unimaginable reason just as I accidentally dropped my towel, displaying my gelatinous womanly wiles for his prying eyes – no, damn it, this is my imagination and in my imagination I'm a hard bodied Victoria's Secret model, and he can't help but take me in his arms and make passionate love to me until the end of our days. Of course, what actually happened was I went into my bedroom, fell over trying to pull my yoga pants on, and Stellan called up to ask if I was okay. Indeed I was, though my yoga pants were somewhat ruffled.

"Come have a seat, I gotta show you something," he said when I finally joined him, his words a little mangled by the object he'd just slammed into his mouth. He'd picked up food on the way over and was breaking into a slab of beef teriyaki. The smell was almost nauseating. I was too nervous in his company to eat. I rejoiced in the thought that even if Stellan was appalled by me sexually, at this rate, at least I'd be skinny as hell when he rejected me.

Rejected you? Shut up Faye, you're never going to actually tell him! You're going to let it pass, because you know it will. Now shut up, sit down, stop picturing him naked and eat a god damned crab rangoon!

I did exactly that, Stellan content to let me eat for a moment before he unveiled whatever mystical item he'd brought to my door. I made it two bites into the Crab Rangoon before my stomach revolted.

Dear God, I'm fucked.

"So I wanna show you this – what's up?" He saw something in my face to betray my uneasiness.

I shrugged it off. "Nothing, just a little nauseous."

Stellan set the back of his hand against my forehead. He held it there a moment, then retracted, seemingly satisfied. I shifted my legs away from the coffee table, hoping to keep the food out of my line of sight. Stellan swiftly collected the bag and hopped up from the couch, disappearing into the kitchen with it. When he came back, he had a glass of water for me.

"Thank you," I said, and drank gratefully.

"You want me to show you some other time? I can go grab you some ginger ale?"

"No, no. I'm really fine. I'll be okay."

He raised an eyebrow at me, but didn't say anything. I knew once he was gone, I'd be able to get something down.

I wriggled into the corner of the couch and stared at the TV. When we spoke, I kept my eyes on something innocent, some third party entity like the wood grain of the coffee table or my feet. He didn't seem to notice, or at least he didn't comment. Suddenly there was a flat white object in my lap, and Stellan was setting up his laptop on the coffee table.

"What's this?" I asked.

He smiled. Stellan had one of those smiles that could light up a room when he wanted to. Though I say again, I did not look directly at it.

He was excited. "It's a drawing tablet."

I stared down at the smooth surface of the device, then glanced up at Stellan, ensconced in his laptop. As soon as he turned back to me, I realized just how interesting the drawing tablet was, or at least that was the impression I was trying to give.

"Pretty nifty," I said.

He chuckled, still working at the laptop. He turned the screen toward me, hunched back into the couch and leaned over.

"All right, draw something."

For a moment, surprise overpowered lusty shame, and I met his gaze. "What, on this?"

"Yeah."

I stared at the doodad, intimidated and somewhat embarrassed. Stellan pulled the pen from its holder and handed it to me.

"I haven't drawn in years, Stell."

"So? Show me some chicken scratch then. I just want you to see what it can do."

I swallowed. "What do you want me to draw?"

"Anything. Doesn't matter."

I took the pen and stared at the tablet. There was no paint, no ink – this was a concoction of science that troubled and bewildered me. I dragged the pen across the surface of the tablet, and I could practically feel his smile. I dragged the pen across it again.

"Look," he said.

I glanced at the laptop and two lines had appeared on the screen.

I gave a flourish and a squiggle. "That's so cool."

"You think so? Here," he said and quickly scrapped the doodle that I'd drawn on the screen. The clean slate appeared, no paper to crumple, no failed detail to hide. "Try to really draw something."

I was on the spot, but curious. I wanted to see if I could. I imagined the hours I could spend relearning any gift I might have once had without having to buy the seventeen sketchpads it would most likely take for me to get there. I fiddled with the pen, instinctively letting it pass beneath my nose as I did with my usual pens. The tinge of disappointment at the stale plastic scent was fleeting. I began whirling the pen about on the tablet. As I moved my hand, lines, shapes, an image began to unfold on the screen. It was a grumpy, slouching man in a suit with a rim of hair around his bald head and a tired notepad in his hand. I gave him two Popeye style hairs sticking out of the top of his head and a couple squiggly lines rising from his shoulders to signify dissatisfaction. Stellan laughed as he appeared on the screen, the unexpected image that had been somehow lying in wait in my psyche. What Stellan didn't know was that I'd been thinking about this guy for a few days – thinking about drawing him, and maybe his exploits. I'd once passed my days drawing comic strips. Ever since Stellan asked for help, I was searching my brain for an inkling of the artist that once resided there. I convinced myself she was gone, but here was Stanley; angry antiques dealer who couldn't understand why his business was going under. I shifted my attention to the scene behind him, a quaint looking storefront and the sign hanging over the door of his Antique Store. I sketched in some words.

Stanley's Antiques: We Sell Old Shit

Stellan laughed. I shaded background, and fiddled until I was done. I signed my name in the lower right hand corner.

F. T. Jensen

Stellan launched himself forward to the laptop, pressed a few buttons, typed a word or two and then turned to me. "And there you go. Saved to file."

"Really?"

"You can come back to it, color it in, edit it, whenever you like."

"Oh no. I wouldn't try to sneak your laptop away from you, are you crazy?"

He took a second to make sure I met his gaze. I felt myself shrinking before him.

"I installed the software on your computer in the office when I was here the other day. It's for you to use."

I looked down at the contraption in my lap and back to Stellan. "I couldn't do that, Stell."

"Do what?"

"I don't want to steal your new toy," I said, and I meant it.

"I bought it for you to use."

My eyes went wide. "What would make you do that?"

He gave me a sheepish look. "Well, I kinda had a favor I wanted to ask you."

I paused, feeling my hand get sweaty around the plastic pen. "What favor?"

Stellan's phone was in his hand a second later, showing me the early endeavors of his newest project.

"Ok, so – I'm working on something right now -"

"When are you not?"

He smiled. "True enough. I've been working on it for a couple weeks now, kinda fine tuning it and testing it out."

This was his hobby – programming apps. Just last week he'd shown me a D&D character generator he'd banged out over the course of one evening. D&D, for you unwashed masses, is Dungeons and Dragons – a role playing game that many a geek delved into hard whilst meandering their way through life. You shake the iPhone and it rolls for attributes. I appreciated his excitement, and let's be honest, what he does over the course of one evening sounds like absolute rocket science to me. Yet, this excitement was different. A project taking him more than a few hours was something to take notice of.

"So what is it?" I asked.

"It's a prototype right now, but it's a kind of strategy game. See -"

A game. Stellan wanted me to illustrate a game.

He pulled it up on his phone. He showed me the details; how to shoot and move. I took it from him, finding the bare screen surreal. He liked flare, big letters and logos and sound effects. This looked like something a twelve year old drew, something he would have been playing on his Atari when we were kids. Still after a few minutes of trying to bring the tower down, I was hooked. When he took it back from me, I was hard pressed to give it up.

"Nicely done, hon," I said, wondering when he was going to get to the point. "Is that your first game?"

"Second. You remember *Tight Corners*?"

I did, and I said so. He'd made his first game about a year ago – an almost hybrid of Tetris and Minesweeper and Mouse Trap. As I recall, it was another mind-numbingly addictive game, and it had sold decently from what he told me. Stellan wasn't one to brag about numbers, so I never knew how much 'decently' translated to in dollars. It was none of my business, as far as I was concerned.

"So when do you go live with this one, then?"

"That depends…" The tone was a dead giveaway, and I was about ready to smack him for avoiding his point. Finally, he sighed. "I was wondering if you would help me animate it."

My stomach was in knots.

I'm pretty sure my jaw dropped.

Stellan wanted me to animate a game?

"Stell, I haven't even sketched in years."

"Bull shit, you doodle constantly."

"Yeah, doodle. That's not animation."

"Whatever, F-Bomb. Your 'doodles' are fucking masterpieces. Say yes!"

I stared at him. "I don't want to disappoint you -"

"What did you originally go to school for?"

I stalled. I felt cornered. "That was only for a year."

"And it was? That's right, Animation."

I paused. "I just drew comics, single panels – nothing like this.

"You lying sack of shit."

I tensed in exasperation. How the hell was I going to say no to this man, but how the hell could I say yes? I was a hack, didn't he see that I was a hack?

"Fine! One five minute cartoon. Once! Once, Stellan."

It was coming up on the twelve year anniversary of the day I had my early mid-life crisis and decided I needed to buckle down and pursue something that would pay bills. I dropped my art classes, changed my major to business and marketing and never looked back. Well, alright – hardly ever looked back.

"You wanted to leave Matt Groening in the dust, as I recall." I stared at him, dumbfounded. The notion that anyone ever paid that close attention to my dreams was almost unheard of. Well, anyone other than my hyper supportive mother.

He smirked, seeing the fight fade in my expression. "That's what I thought."

He handed me the iPhone again. The new game was open and taunting me with its nearly destroyed structures. I wanted to slaughter, rain terror, but I nonchalantly glanced down at the barren screen.

"See, I'm a programmer. That's what I'm good at. Every other app I've made, if I needed design done, I made due with stock. But I'm not like you, I don't have your imagination, and this is too big a project - I need this to be streamlined. I mean, this is only one level of the game -"

"I guess if you tell me what the premise is -"

He frowned. "That's part of the reason why I need you. I don't know."

He looked at me hopefully, and I couldn't keep his gaze. I stared down at my hands, thinking of the years I spent with nearly permanent black smudges on my fingertips from the hours I spent sketching and inking my own work, or of stealing a camera from the art department to take pictures of my stills and running them on a projector for my Art Final. I hadn't even looked through my supplies since I moved back home. I didn't tell Stellan the ancient things were all in the basement, drying out and weathered with time because my mother didn't have the heart to toss them out.

I didn't have the heart to tell him I'd been grieving over the idea of new art supplies just a few hours earlier.

"I don't want to disappoint you, Stell."

He seemed to sense my resolve fading, because he put his arm around me and shook me like I'd already agreed.

"Then say yes!"

"That's not what I -"

"Walt fucking Disney, woman!"

Oh, that dick! That dick! My mantra. My go to response to every single naysayer who told me my dreams were silly when I was a kid. I'd summon up the name of the most successful animator of all time. People usually shut up at that point.

Just like I did at that moment, staring at Stellan as though he'd betrayed everything I loved.

"Besides – I'd love to see you sketching again."

That summoned a smile, though he couldn't see it, given that I was back to staring at my pristine fingertips. I'd agreed to this, internally if not out loud, but he still knew. Without even waiting for verbal affirmation, he slumped back, put his feet up, and turned on the television. I stared at the cartoons that came on the screen, and for the first time in years, acknowledged to myself that I was critiquing the cartoonists work.

He smiled. "Because I know you."

I shook my head. I'd worked under constant pressure for near to a decade in my marketing job, but nothing came close to the way I felt at that moment.

He fidgeted with the phone, averting his eyes. It was so rare to see Stellan shy like this. I almost wanted to give him a hug.

"Alright -" he paused. I knew it was coming. "Will you say yes?"

I pursed my lips. "What if I can't do it anymore -"

"Not fucking possible, dove. I know you could come up with something great. If you need a while to do it, there's no hurry. Even if you just help me brainstorm, sketch some shit up-"

"Don't you have friends who could help? Some of those geniuses at MIT? Christ! Ask Evan!"

He laughed. "Yeah, bunch of regular Picassos, those homos. Not the artsy types, babe."

"But I'm not the artsy type either, Stell. Not anymore."

"What?! You think you can shut that off?" His face brightened. "I remember those comic strips you used to draw, they were fucking hilarious!"

"That was a decade ago, Stell."

"So? Have you somehow stopped being funny?"

My throat grew tight. "I don't even know!"

He paused, watching my face. "Just say you'll try. Please?"

I stared at the pen in my hand.

He clapped his hands together, celebrating my answer before I'd found the words to give it. "You're helping me more than you can imagine, F-Bomb. Call it an investment."

I swallowed, glancing back down at the contraption. Ten minutes later, I'd drawn a blown out bridge with haggard apocalypse survivors on one side, watching as a group of people fired a 'flare' into the air. I then drew a cartoon of the WWE wrestler Rick Flair flying across the sky, his signature 'Whooooooo!' scribbled in a path behind him as he sailed past. Stellan laughed even harder at this one.

He saved it, then reached for the tablet, glancing at me to make sure I was done. When I nodded, he took hold of it, his fingers curling under its edges and grazing my thigh. Pathetic that I felt enlivened by that tiny contact, isn't it?

He settled into his seat, staring at the television as an infomercial for some outrageous exercise program came on. I had absolutely no interest in watching it, but Stellan seemed oblivious to what was on.

"You're thinking of drawing still, aren't you?" He asked.

I stopped my mind from wandering and met his gaze. "What do you mean?"

"Your lips," he said and flattened his lips, pinching them between his teeth. "You always do that when you draw."

I forgot myself for a moment and smiled – the kind of smile where your nose crinkles – the kind of smile you give a man you love. "I do not, do I?"

He smiled back. "Yeah. I'd almost forgotten that, it's been so long. You were drawing good old Stanley there, and your lips pressed together."

I covered my mouth with my hand. My cheeks were burning. "I didn't know I did that."

He stared at me a moment. I had to look away. Stellan and I didn't need to fill silence before, but somehow, the quiet felt electric, charged almost, and I was certain it was entirely my fault. I prayed he didn't notice.

I sat there and imagined myself crawling across the couch to straddle his lap and kiss him until he took me.

Instead, we sat quietly and watched a sweaty man sell exercise.

CHAPTER FOUR

"Morning, hon," my mom said as I entered the kitchen.

It was Saturday morning, several days since Stellan's project proposal. I hadn't worked on it since. Something about it turned my stomach every time I tried to sit down at my old drafting table. I had ideas – I had a million ideas for sketches, but without Stellan there, I half feared the house would burst into flames the second I put a pen to paper. Or plastic pen to doohickey.

I paused in the hallway, watching her sitting at the counter, drinking her coffee, reading her book, or on Sunday's, her morning paper.

She smiled at me. "You put the drawing desk back together, I see."

I yawned. "That was Stellan."

She smiled into her coffee cup. "What a sweet thing. Have you been drawing then?"

I stopped and considered my answer. Telling your mother you've potentially rediscovered an interest in art when she spends her days breathing it – it's just asking for a supportive exchange. She'd always loved finding my comics around the house, pretending to get my obscure humor. When she couldn't make sense of it, she praised my technique or use of color, acting as though she'd discovered the lost Vermeer at every napkin doodle of mine she found.

I shrugged and leaned against the wall. "Stellan asked me to work on some sketches."

She shifted again, and I could see the excitement, like steam rising at the hourly surge of Old Faithful. I slowly faded down the hallway, but there was no dodging my mother when it came to art.

"Can I see what you're working on?"

I pursed my lips. "I haven't really gotten started, honestly."

She frowned, then did her best to hide the once over she gave me. Yes, I was back in my penguin pajama pants. Yes, they were clean.

She left me to my own devices. I was feeling a bit introverted and left my phone in my bedroom. The allure of its mystical 3G powers was simple – I could send and/or receive texts from Stellan. Therein lies my trouble. I'd felt almost teary eyed when he left the night before, like some urgent business had yet to be attended to. It was as though when he was near, the world was as it should be – there were no miserable flashes of Cole berating me for being opinionated or loud, there were no thoughts of naked women in Cole's bed. In fact, when Stellan was near, there was no Cole. Still, my better senses assured me that this magic elixir I found in Stellan was the death knells of a desperate and broken heart. It was easier to remind myself of that when he wasn't around. When he was, I was fucked.

Unplug Faye. Just Unplug, I thought.

Odd that after this well thought out advice, I sought solace on my computer.

I watched the screen come to life and reached for my coffee, tapping it sideways as I swung toward it. I jumped up from my chair, snatching the cup before it had a chance to fully fall to its side. It lost only a tablespoon or so of its contents, but that was enough to give me a heart attack given the object it spilled on. I launched myself out of the office and into the kitchen, grabbing no less than seven paper towels in my panic. I wiped down the Drawing Tablet, as though I'd somehow managed to spill coffee on the baby Jesus. Once I wiped it down with the fourth paper towel and was certain that it was dry, I glanced at the computer screen – fully powered up and ready.

There was only one way to be sure you didn't just completely destroy Stellan's gadget. I turned it on.

There's something about blank paper and pen that begs for marks and doodles. I've found that to be true my whole life – a blank canvas, a sketchpad, a brick wall behind the old Brigham's – these were surfaces that cried out like the dead on the River Styx. I stared at the screen, frowned at my coffee, and took the pen in hand.

I revisited Stanley, now a restaurant manager installing a sign in the kitchen to announce to his waiters the exact moment when a patron has something in their mouth. I drew the light coming on and the first waiter in a line of trained sprinters bounding out the kitchen door and assaulting the chewing patron with the time honored question, "How is everything?"

Drawing the confounded restaurant goer with a mouthful of meatball was the best part.

After a few sketches of the random and mundane, my mind searched for new inspiration, new subjects to draw. Stellan's game, however I tried to avoid it, came to mind. I let myself doodle as I futzed around online, bombarded as always by Facebook friends hilarious cat videos. I was distracted for a split second, laughing at a video of a baboon startling small children by pressing his backside against the window of his enclosure in proud display.

I laughed.

Something sparked deep in my cerebral cortex.

I let myself draw a gorilla. I let myself draw the façade of a jungle painted zoo enclosure, vines and cracks across its bricks.

I let myself draw a chimpanzee throwing shit.

No, actual shit. I drew a brigade of feces throwing apes, and despite myself, I began laughing. I drew a tableau of apes with crazed looks, some of them excited with rage, some of them mad with laughter, all gathered around a chalkboard with calculus equations showing the best trajectory for shit flinging. The notion of what I was drawing or the unmitigated joy on the creatures' faces made me giggle – and judge the shit out of myself.

I was thirty three years old, and I was drawing shit flinging monkeys while laughing to myself.

No wonder I'm still living at home, I thought.

I deleted a few quick sketches, but more and more, I found myself saving them to file. I was actually going to let Stellan see these.

"Faye, honey? Have you eaten?"

I startled at the sound of my mother's voice. I looked at the clock – six. Dear God, I'd been sketching for seven hours.

My mother convinced me to have dinner with her to celebrate an exhibit the museum approved. I started to shut down the computer when I noticed the tiny icon for my work email. I paused. Who the hell was emailing me?

Dear Ms. Jensen,
*   We reviewed your resume and would like to schedule an interview with you. Please call at your earliest convenience so we might set up a time.*

Look forward to speaking with you,
Dennis Shay
Head of Marketing, Chalice Enterprises

I called to my mother in the kitchen. When she arrived, I was freaking out.

I ran upstairs to grab my cell, and when I finally returned to the office, my mother was smiling at me.

"There's no rush, hon. Take your time. I'll be in the living room."

I sat down in the leather seat and took the deepest Lamaze style breath I could. I didn't want to sound winded when I called. I would sound nonchalant, casual. I would apologize for the delay and make it sound as though I'd been off jet setting and changing the world rather than festering in self-pity and penguin pajama pants since the email arrived over a week before.

I finally dialed the number.

A pleasant male voice informed me that I had reached the voicemail of Dennis Shay, and if I would kindly leave a message he would get back to me.

"Hi there Mr. Shay. This is Faye Jensen returning your message. I'm sorry it took me so long to respond to your email, but I would be honored to talk to you further about the Marketing position at Chalice."

I stopped, realizing I had opened with 'Hi there,' and quickly deleted the message, starting over with a far more classy 'Hello.' The second time around I decided to forgo the apologies, hoping that in not mentioning the delay, he wouldn't even realize it had taken me so long to respond to, literally, the first potential job I'd found in five months. That desperate thought slipped into the tone of my voice, and I deleted the message again, starting over with the smoothest and least crazed tone I could muster. I then deleted it a third time because 'least crazed' sounded practically stoned. Finally, I heard my mother milling about in the upstairs hallway and realized perhaps this moment wasn't the best time to leave the message. I started with 'Hello, Mr. Shay,' was sure I sounded like a fourteen year old calling the boy she liked and laughed at how ridiculous it all was.

"This is Faye Jensen, and I'm sure you'd be interested to know this is my fourth attempt at leaving this voicemail and yet again, I sound like I'm reading a script written by a monkey with a typewriter. Spectacular! One would think this would be an easier process, but given that I'm one of the desperately unemployed and that apparently makes me an imbecile with a cell phone, I'm beginning to question why our species gave up Smoke Signals. I'm pretty sure I could come off classy in smoke signals. Maybe not, given that I'd end up setting myself on fire with my luck. Alright, here goes try number five."

I pressed the pound sign and then star and put the receiver to my ear.

"Your message has been sent."

I froze. "Wait. What?"

I stared at the phone, aghast. Had I somehow managed to hit pound twice? Had I somehow managed to send the voice mail message of a lumbering jackass? Was that me? Was I that jackass?

I almost burst into tears. My mother appeared, smiling. She wasn't aware that I had just completely blown that opportunity like a two dollar hooker.

We went out to dinner, downtown. I listened to her stories and her work concerns, but in the back of my mind I was preoccupied. I'd drawn for nigh on seven hours that day. The catastrophic voice mail slipped to the back of my mind and instead of wallowing in self-pity as one might expect, I wanted to go home and continue working.

We enjoyed our meal and walked back as the sun was setting, my mother settled in the front room to read while I returned to the office. I sat down and started planning a quick comic strip I wanted to create before I called it a day.

The email icon at the top of the screen reminded me of my utter failure earlier that evening, but I grit my teeth, determined not to let it deter my focus. I wanted to get this comic out, then if I really needed to, I could wallow in self-loathing til the proverbial cows came home. Or perhaps I could walk away and forget I have an email account at all. Hell, I could borrow some money and go buy sketchbooks instead, grow a beard and train squirrels to do my bidding, and never have to look at another computer screen again. As I was contemplating relocating to the woods and living in a hut built of dung, a tiny number appeared next to the email icon.

Oh shit.

Faye,

Your voicemail was hilarious and completely unexpected. I'd say you'd fit right in here in the office. Though I had a good laugh, you didn't leave a number where I could reach you. Please give me a call tomorrow morning and we can set up your interview.

- Dennis

Oh. My fucking. God. What?

I launched out of my chair and into the front room, bounding around the place as I explained the situation to my mother. I kept my voicemail experience to myself, but now I was almost proud to be such a rampant jackass. Somehow, being a jackass might have led me to success. Who knew you could be yourself and still be appreciated for it?

She smiled, gave me a 'good for you,' and sent me on my way. I tried to sit back down at the desk, but instead I texted everyone, ecstatic to have a prospect to speak of. I was going stir crazy. I needed to get out of the house.

I grabbed a sweater from the hall closet, waved a quick good bye to my mother and headed out.

Linda greeted me with her radiant smile. Lennart was busy watching crime dramas. I waved in to him, hoping not to disturb. He smiled my way and waved back. Before I could head down to Stellan, Linda cornered me in the kitchen – how was my mother, the museum, my life, and so on. I did my best to answer her questions.

Linda was a magnificent example of the female species. She was sixty, if I recall, but she could pass for much younger. She had blonde hair which had once been the same color as Stellan's, but had lightened with age. They shared the same blue eyes, her's a shade darker, but still just as piercing when you were in their sights.

"So how is life with you, young lady? I haven't seen you in – goodness, ages? Where've you been? I hear you're working on something with my boy?"

I nodded. "Just some animation stuff. I'm not even sure he'll be able to use any of it."

"Well, that's wonderful."

I shrugged. Then without warning, words spewed from my lips as though they'd been rigged in a trebuchet. "I actually have an interview coming up for a marketing job."

Linda's eyes lit up just as the basement door opened behind her. Stellan appeared, and I realized in the excitement of my news, my stomach had forgotten to tie itself in knots at the sheer thought of him. His appearance quickly remedied that.

Linda turned. "You're just in time! Faye has wonderful news."

Stellan smiled at me over his mom's shoulder before kissing her on the top of the head. He then went straight for the fridge, which in the Ødegård house was a signal to his mother to go into overdrive.

"You hungry, gullebit?"

He leaned into the fridge, stared a moment, then turned to his mother with an accentuated pout. She gently slapped his hand away from the fridge and began procuring her ingredients from within. She went to work like a conductor preparing for Beethoven's Ninth. Within five minutes there were two huge sandwiches on the counter and a cold can of root beer. Stellan wrapped his arm around her neck in a gesture much like an affectionate choke hold, pulled her toward him and kissed her head again. She smiled and patted his stomach.

"Tack, Ma," he said. She left us and joined Lennart in the living room. Stellan sat down to his supper, happily munching away in silence.

I smiled. It was as it had always been, Stellan doted on and adored by his mother to the point of his father complaining. Seeing him in his thirties and still able to procure his mother's doting with a simple pout was humorous. I thought of him giving me that pout one day in the hopes that I might make him something to eat.

What, are you married now, Faye?

I quickly redirected my thoughts.

"She still calls you gullebit?"

He gave me a mischievous smile. "How could she not?"

'Gullebit' had been his parents' nickname for him when he was a child. It meant "gold piece" or treasure. His father stopped using the term when Stellan began to resemble a man, but apparently his mother was still keen.

"How adorable."

He smirked at me. I laughed, and he threw his crumpled napkin at me before taking his plate to the sink. When he returned I was still smiling.

"Welcome back, gullebit."

"Tack så mycket, sötnos."

Something shifted in my very psyche and those words – words I'd heard a thousand times, words that were probably a wiseass comment if I knew him at all - suddenly felt warm and hypnotic. Their every syllable played me like a cello, my frame reverberating with each note. This wasn't good. If I was going to start feeling googly-eyed every time Stellan spoke Swedish, I'd never be able to set foot in his house again. I openly shook my head, as though denouncing some silent declaration.

Stellan eyed me a moment and smiled. "You all right? Sure you're not hungry?"

"Oh I'm sure. Just had dinner with Mom." *(And you speaking Swedish makes me want to stick my tongue down your throat.)*

He sat across from me at the kitchen island, resting his weight on his elbows, his white button down shirt open, its sleeves rolled to his elbows over a Bruins t-shirt. His hair was wilder than usual, having most likely reached this stage when he rolled out of bed and never cared to tame it. He was staring at me.

"You seem happy today," he said, suddenly.

"Do I?"

"Yeah, you do. You're very smiley. What have you been up to?"

I smiled and covered my face. He'd seen it and chuckled. The sudden accusation made me painfully aware of just how much I was smiling in his presence. Christ, I felt like I was in fifth period study hall with Joe Mullen all over again.

"Actually, I spent a good amount of the day trying to figure out that tablet of yours."

"Really? How'd it feel? Did it work for you?"

I could hear a vibration in his voice. He was hopeful, but trying to conceal it. I thought of the comic strips, the Adventures of Stanley, the doodles and early sketches of insane apes and other unseemly images, but despite the silliness of what I'd been doing, I felt accomplished.

"It did," I said, looking down at my hands. "I drew for seven hours today."

Stellan reached across the island and squeezed my hand, shaking it. "Are you fucking kidding me?"

I shrugged, but I smiled.

"That's fucking fantastic, F-bomb. Yes!"

"Well, I don't know how great it is. I did a lot of nonsense rather than actual work -"

"You don't owe me shit, woman. It's there for you. Draw whatever you want."

"I did draw up some stuff -" I started, then remembered the various monkeys hovering around that chalkboard, diagramming the scientific trajectory and splatter pattern of well thrown feces. I laughed to myself, but the thought of trying to share it in words stopped me dead. I imagined it funnier if he saw it in drawn form. My stomach turned. Suddenly, I realized telling Stellan opened me up for rejection – rejection of my ideas, at least, if not me. That was enough to give me pause.

"What were you thinking?"

I shook my head. "Nevermind."

"No, woman. I want to know. I *need* to know."

I grabbed a napkin and a pen from the kitchen counter and sketched up a quick image – a chimpanzee throwing a boot, the climbing structure teetering behind him. "There!"

"What is it?"

"It's the barricade you have to destroy," I said.

"Where'd he get the boot?"

I swallowed. "From one of the zookeepers who've been taken hostage by the animals inside the zoo."

He leaned in to look at the napkin closer. "Wait?

What?"

I scribbled brick and mortar and madly gleeful chimpanzee faces above their climbing tower. "The towers – they're the climbing structures – the, like, jungle gyms of a chimpanzee enclosure."

"Oh man."

"And they're in a zoo that's been taken over by primates. You have to infiltrate and take back the zoo."

Stellan stared at me. "Will you draw me Charlton Heston in this shit."

I laughed, imagining how I would hide the Planet of the Apes star in my artwork. "Yes. I promise."

Stellan folded his hands in front of his face, pressing his lips to his knuckles. This was his clear sign of 'I'm thinking.' The smile betrayed his thoughts to be happy. It made me warm.

I sat there with him for several minutes, brainstorming different weapons that could be used against angry chimps. This moment made it very clear that I'd spent a fair share of my life playing, tag teaming, or watching my male friends play video games. My geek flag was flying.

I finished sketching a placated chimp munching on a banana when Stellan spoke. "I love you, you know that right?"

Words almost jumped out of my mouth, but I stopped myself. Suddenly, 'I love you too,' carried too much weight.

He leaned across the table and shook my hand by the wrist again. I met his eyes; they were warm and wide. "I'm so glad you're drawing. You have no idea."

"Well, it's just stupid crap I'm doing, nothing profound -"

"But you're drawing."

I shrugged. "I guess."

I wasn't quite sure where he was going with this.

"It reads on your face."

I raised an eyebrow. "What does?"

"That you're working. That you're doing what you love."

I shook my head. "It was just stupid stuff, Stell. I wasn't working, I was just -"

"- enjoying yourself. I know. You can tell."

I didn't speak. The truth was, even before I'd noticed that email from Dennis Shay, I'd felt lighter. And I suddenly realized that though I'd come running here to share my glorious news, I still hadn't thought to tell him about it. "I think you're just trying to claim responsibility for my good mood."

"Oh please. I'm always responsible for your good mood."

How right he was. He asked me to describe some of my work from the day, and I took him through a few sketches I'd come up with. As I sat there, I compiled and organized in my mind as much of my work from that day as I could remember; thinking of Stanley and his army of obnoxious waiters, or apes and gorillas and bears, oh my. I thought of Stellan's response to seeing the some of the stills and laughed to myself.

He nudged me again. "You have no idea how happy I am to see you like this."

I met his eyes, waiting for an explanation. He just smiled.

"Like what?"

"Like you."

"Well, you can't fault me. I've been going through

some serious crap the past few months -"

He shook his head. "I'm not talking about the past few months, babe."

I waited for an explanation, but he just grinned.

"Then what are you talking about?"

He shrugged. "You just seem more like you tonight than you have – well, in a really long time."

"Well, yeah! I have something to celebrate."

I quickly relayed my news of prospective job, but he brushed it off.

"Oh please. You think the prospect of a job is doing it? If that's the case then I really don't know you at all."

There was something profound in that statement, but I let it slip by. He leaned in, and I tried my best to hide the sudden draw of breath I took at his approach. If he caught it, he paid no mind.

"You laugh -"

"How dare I?"

"- shut up, I'm serious. You've been laughing at your own thoughts," he said. I blushed and started to defend myself, but he continued. "When we were kids you used to do that all the time. We'd be hanging out, and you'd chuckle to yourself and pull out your sketchbook. I'd back off, and ten minutes later you'd hand me a sketch to let me in on the joke."

I let my lips fall open as though I wanted to respond, denounce this declaration of my character, but I was overwhelmed by too many thoughts – he was right, and the thought that someone had paid that close attention – that he did – was enough to ruin me. If I was going to stop thinking of him with desire, he needed to start being a thoughtless asshole, and quick.

I didn't look at him, but I smiled. "I must seem like

a lunatic."

"No, you seem happy. It's been missed."

I shrugged. "No it has not -"

He nodded, and his expression was strange. "I can tell you the exact day it went away -"

"You cannot!"

His brows shot up, and his lips pursed in an almost daring expression. "It was the day before you quit art school."

I stopped short and swallowed. A memory seemed to bubble up and spill over, like a boiling pot of potatoes left untended.

I shook my head, wanting to deny this profound revelation. "You can't be serious."

"I am. Actually, I always wanted to ask you what the hell happened."

"Why I changed majors?"

"And why Faye Jensen, the most creative, punk rock, and funny person I'd ever known, decided she needed to go straight and be a responsible, humorless yuppy at the age of twenty?"

I stared at him drinking his root beer. Before I could even consider the implications of being honest, I knew I would be. Somehow, I was ready to tell a secret I'd kept for a third of my life.

I took a deep breath and watched his face. "My dad came back."

The implications were clear immediately. Stellan's lips parted, but no words came. He stared at me.

My hands grew heavy in my lap, as though someone had sewn thread through my fingernails and tied them to a sinking anchor. I waited for him to speak. The waiting began to burn.

The last time I saw my father – well, the time

before I was twenty – is my earliest memory. He was standing on the third story landing of our old apartment building, sobbing. I remember his voice, pained and high, like a woman's almost. He was begging my mother to let him in, to let him see me. She'd put me to bed hours earlier, but the sound of my father wailing had woken me. I looked outside and saw him, his face contorted so deeply I feared he was in physical pain. His brown hair was sticking up around his unshaved face, his shirt sleeves were tattered where they could be seen at the hem of his jean jacket, and his work boots were untied. As always he had paint spattered all over his jeans. He looked lost somehow, like some stray that had found its way up onto our porch. My mother didn't let him in that night, or ever again. When she finally threatened to call the police, he left. She came back into the dark living room and startled at the sight of me out of bed. Her eyes were so sad, and her face slick from tears. She let me sleep in her bed that night. I found out much later that the initial restraining order wasn't requested until the following day, when while I was at preschool, my father returned to the porch with a baseball bat, screaming to be let in.

"You can't keep her from me, I'm her father," he'd screamed until even the neighbors were calling the cops.

She didn't just threaten him that day.

I was four years old.

My father's name is Charles Winslow Bentley, and he's also a heroin addict.

He's also a genius.

Not like Stellan. From what I gather, my father couldn't solve a math problem with a calculator and a borrowed brain. Yet, when it comes to painting, my father was and is a master. He could recreate any work, any style, to the point of fooling an expert, in just a few days. He is four years younger than my mother, and the two of them fell madly in love at college. My mother was studying Art History. She met this young painter there on full scholarship during one of the student art shows, and that was the end of it. The two of them were together every day after that.

My mother used to tell me how she reveled at my father's talent, watching him paint into the late hours. She loved art, and he literally breathed it. Despite my protests, I've heard how passionately they expressed their love, spending months at a time naked in my father's apartment while he worked. My mother still has dozens of his paintings hidden away. One of them is a portrait of my mother, nude.

I was born shortly after my mother finished college. My dad didn't care much for school and dropped out. My father worked, my mother took care of me, and that was life.

Dad had been using for a year when my mother finally kicked him out. He'd become distant around us, my mother said, acting at times as though he'd come home to strangers. My mother tried to ignore the signs; the strange hours, the calls from his boss wondering where he was, the stuff that went missing around the house. It wasn't until he came home alone one afternoon after taking me to the park that my mother was forced to accept him for what he was.

'Where's the baby?' My mother had asked. When she saw my father's face, she knew.

He'd forgotten me at his dealer's house.

She threw him out that night. He was sobbing on

the porch three nights later.

I don't remember the drug dealer, or his wife, or his kind children who were taking care of me when my mother stormed in, and though I won't defend him, I will say wasn't left at some gun toting pimp's house, by any means. The guy was like my father, selling on the side to support his own habit. (Those two kids were adopted from the foster system after both their parents ended up in jail – or dead. Apparently they grew up on a farm in New Hampshire. Not all drug tales have sad endings.)

Dad disappeared after the restraining order, and we moved in with my Grandmother. My mother told me why when I was much older. We moved when she found the house ransacked, one day. My nicer toys, clothes, my mother's jewelry and our bikes had all been taken. The only thing left behind was my mother's engagement ring, which she'd stopped wearing soon after the restraining order. She kept it in her jewelry box, next to all the other pieces that were long gone.

I don't remember my mother being afraid, though she was. I don't remember her pacing, locking the doors, checking on me a dozen times before bed each night.

I do remember her crying.

Some might call it a sad story, but it was neither sad nor happy to me. It was just a story, and it was mine.

And Stellan knew it well.

"What do you mean he came back?" Stellan asked, his voice low.

I shrugged. "He found me because of some comic strip of mine they published in the Globe. Mass Art student, Faye Tanner Jensen. He hunted me down through the school."

Stellan shifted his weight onto his elbows, leaning closer across the island. "What happened?"

"He took me to lunch."

Stellan glared at me. "Is that all?"

I nodded.

He took a deep breath. "Your whole personality changed overnight because your dad took you to lunch?"

"My whole personality didn't change -"

"Completely," he said, and it was the most powerful whisper I'd ever heard. "Do you realize how worried we were?"

"Who?"

"Me. Evan. Your mother called me constantly. 'Something's wrong with Faye, do you know what happened?' And I didn't. I had no fucking clue. Christ, we thought-"

I waited, watching him scratch the back of his neck. "Thought what?"

By the sound of his voice, it sounded as though I'd come home one day an amputee without explanation. "You don't want to know."

He wouldn't look at me. I waited for him to continue, or to glance my way, but he seemed thoroughly riveted by the knotted grain of the kitchen counter.

"I just changed schools, changed majors. People do that every day."

He shook his head. "You didn't change your major, Faye. *You* changed."

He stood up from the table. I opened my mouth to speak, but nothing came. Was he right? Had he noticed despite my efforts to hide that event from the world?

He stood there a moment, pushing his chair in. The silent was loaded like a rifle. "I can't believe you didn't tell me."

The hurt in his voice left a crack in me, as though someone had taken a chisel to my chest and split it open. "Stellan, come on. I didn't tell anyone."

"I'm not anyone, Faye."

He turned from the table, his eyes nearly closed. I knew this look well.

I moved to speak, to say something, but it was too late and I knew it. "Stell?"

He walked down the hall to the basement door and disappeared downstairs. I knew better than to follow him.

CHAPTER FIVE

Four days passed. Four days of texting empty air, of my leaving messages on his voicemail, four days of trying desperately to distract myself with sketching up ideas for *his* game. Yeah, that didn't help.

I was spending a good part of my day hovering by the kitchen windows, with a cup of tea in one hand and my cell phone in the other. I didn't dare part with it, just in case it went off.

I found myself desperate for distraction on the third day, enthralled with the birds at my grandmother's feeders, standing by her favorite window to watch the sanctuary she created.

My grandmother, Edie Tanner, owned this house with my Grandfather, Terry Jensen. She was a powerful creature – a proper lady in every sense. She went to work when WWII broke out, then refused to stop working when the boys came home. She fell in love with my mechanic Grandfather, but refused to marry him until she finished school. She never left the house without pearls and lipstick, and toward the end, never let anyone see how much pain she was in.

These were her windows waiting for Grampy to come home from the War. Later, she watched her daughter playing from these windows, and held her here when her father died suddenly when she was nineteen. Cancer took Grampy Jensen at forty-five. Grammy never so much as looked at another man.

She once told me she was waiting to die, because then she would be with Grampy again. Dark words to tell a seven year old, but they made it easier to let her go when she did pass.

My mother had trouble recovering from her loss, but in an effort to ease the transition, I tried to adopt some of her habits – the birds, the fires she set on cooler nights, the homemade quilts, folded with lavender packets to help with sleep.

I spent months at this window after she passed, watching the birds, waking with the sun some mornings to catch sight of the Cardinals that only came with the dawn or the snow. My Grandmother had referred to the red and brown birds as 'Mr. and Mrs.,' making me watch as the 'wife' waited patiently for her husband before she would eat. I'd always thought that strange, but Grammy Jensen was too busy fiddling with her binoculars to consider the sexist implications of Cardinal behavior. She would stand there with me, her curved fingers on my shoulder as she pointed out the Purple Finches, or the White Breasted Nuthatches. Her scent would surround me; sweet coffee breath, hairspray, Gold Bond powder, and Gardenia. She taught me the calls of the birds; *Peter-Peter* was the Tufted Titmouse, *Fee-Bee* was the Chickadee, and though I cannot remember what bird makes the sound, *Madge-Madge-Madge-put-on-your-tea-kettle-ettle* was her favorite. As a result it was mine, too, they I never seemed to catch it when she pointed it out. I remember laughing with her, the beaded strand of her glasses cord hanging down her soft, folded throat as she mimicked the sounds to teach me. She said she heard that specific call quite often. I told her she was full of beans.

Over the years since her passing - as a teenager, or a returning adult visiting for Christmas - I'd sometimes find myself sitting here by the kitchen window, listening.

I've still never heard that call.

Meghan sensed the shift in my mood by the fourth day, and she assembled the cavalry. By noon on that day, I was piled in the backseat of Meghan's car, with Jackie sitting quietly in the front, heading for the mall for a 'much needed girl's day.'

Not sure how needed it was, but no one asked me.

"Don't ever tell him I said this, but I kinda see where he's coming from," Meghan said as she pulled off the highway. I grumbled at her, but didn't speak. "Hell, I didn't even know you then, and I'm kinda pissed."

I watched the world pass from the backseat. "It wasn't the end of the world," I said.

Jackie glanced back at me, and I knew she was keeping something to herself.

"Hon, let me be frank – your bat shit crazy, heroin addict father appears wanting to bond and hang out, maybe take you fishing, and you don't think it's worthy of telling anyone? Really?"

Meghan was glancing in her rear view at me. I wished she'd focus on the road and not glaring at me for effect.

Deep down, I didn't begrudge Stellan his upset. Still, not hearing from him for four days was rough to endure. I'd done my best to apologize. I'd done everything shy of dropping by the house. Still, part of me knew I was wrong. All this time, I thought I'd magically hidden the trauma of my father's resurrection like some emotional Houdini.

"I didn't want to worry anybody," I said.

Jackie glanced at me again, but didn't speak.

"What Jackie? Please, just say it."

"Oh please, we both know what she's going to say. You're a jackass. End of story." Meghan was a master of conversation.

I gave an exasperated sigh. "Look, telling Stellan would have been the equivalent of telling my mom. Her knowing good old Bentley was back was the last thing I would ever want. Who knows how she'd take it?"

"It sounds like you worried her anyway," Jackie said finally.

"I know."

I felt the car shift and looked up to see our destination. "Wait, what are we doing here?"

It was the temporary Halloween Superstore that appeared every year somewhere near the mall.

Meghan shot me a piteous look. "We're cramming this tits in every costume that'll fit until I find the one that makes me look like hot sex on legs."

I had a feeling there would be several contenders for that title. Meghan had great tits.

"So what are you going to do?" Meghan asked. I knew damn well she wasn't challenging me to a Halloween costume try on competition.

I shrugged, checking my ever silent cell phone. "I don't know. He won't talk to me."

"Yeah, so what are you going to do?" Meghan liked to get to the point.

"I don't know!"

"You could go talk to him?" Jackie suggested. My stomach tightened. The nerves I felt at the thought of his company had gone from butterflies, to badgers, to the eruption of Mount Vesuvius, bubbling with a violent heat deep in my gut. The thought of being met with disdain, or worse, dislike when I set foot in Stellan's presence was as painful as a shot of rye on an empty stomach. How do I make up for this?

I nodded, finally.

We made our way into the store, and the mood instantly changed.

Meghan was rampaging around the store, collecting costumes and pointing out options she absolutely demanded I try on. I laughed, accepting her challenge of putting on the Tina Turner costume.

Meghan smiled at me. "You seem a little brighter? My winning personality cheering you up?"

I shrugged. "This is me 'trying.'"

"Good for you, honey!"

"Fake it til you make it! That's what they always say, right?" Jackie asked, beaming with a Morticia Addams dress in her hands.

I raised an eyebrow. "I'm not sure. Who is *they*, exactly?"

Meghan pointed at me. "There's the sarcastic bitch I know and love."

I shook my head. "Strange that being called a bitch is supposed to put a smile on my face."

"Hell yeah, it is. Now where the fuck is the sales guy?"

The line outside the changing rooms was four or five people deep, and there was no one in sight, there or near the registers. Meghan's assertive was threatening to come out hard.

Jackie stifled at the language, Meghan having spoken at a volume for sharing. "Meg, quiet down."

"What? Everyone else here is thinking the same

fucking thing, hon. Let's be real."

"She's just spreading joy, Jackie. It's her super power."

Meghan laughed. "Fuck you, Faye. You've been hanging out with Stellan way too much. He's rubbing off."

I chuckled softly to myself. Were either of them telepathic, they'd have heard my commentary on *Stellan* and *rubbing off*. Meghan waved deliberately in the air, calling attention to the sales clerk as he appeared from the back room.

Jackie touched my arm. "What's on *your* mind, missy?"

I looked away, covering my smile.

"Jesus, you'd think retail was fucking rocket science based on that guy. So what are you two talking about?"

Jackie changed the subject to Halloween. Evan's party was just a few days away, and until we veered into the parking lot of the Halloween Superstore, I'd almost completely forgotten. I knew full well that I would be concocting something from my closet if I did decide to go.

Meghan burst out of the changing room in her first costume choice – Wonder Woman.

"God damn, Meghan. You've got some nice legs!" I said, my eyebrows raised in approval.

She smiled. "Hell yeah." She glanced down, framing her crotch with her thumbs and forefingers. "Gonna need a wax first, sweet Jesus."

Both I and a random guy started laughing at this declaration. Clearly Meghan didn't care who knew the state of her pubic region.

Jackie explained that she was freshly shorn, and I

shuddered in my seat.

"I'd never let some overzealous woman with tweezers go near my – regions."

Meghan and Jackie both turned to me with looks of patient disdain.

"It's not that bad. It's a lot easier than doing it at home," Jackie said.

Meghan picked her next costume choice from the massive pile. "You'd love it."

I waved my hands before me. "No, and no. The thought of ripping, and - or yanking anything in that region is just – Christ, no. I'm all set."

Both Meghan and Jackie stared at me a moment, Meghan's lips parted just enough to show disgust. "Wait, do you not wax?"

To hear her, one would think I'd just told Meghan I don't brush my teeth or use toilet paper. I shook my head.

"Then, do you shave?" Jackie asked. I was being tag-teamed on the subject of my nether regions. Fantastic public space conversation, if you ask me.

I shrugged. "If I'm inclined to do anything in that region, really."

"Oh, hell no!" Meghan was up in arms like an Evangelical wife in the face of Satan worship.

"What? It's not like anyone is making the rounds to keep me honest in that department."

"But you don't do it for 'the guy,' Faye!"

I laughed. "Then why would anyone do it?"

"You've got to be kidding me," Meghan said, talking over her shoulder as though she were involving the rest of the room.

Jackie leaned in. "Well, if you want to wear a bathing suit or -"

"Nonononono, don't try to reason with this woman. She's far past it," Meghan said. She glared at me. "What if you want to abuse yourself? Don't you have standards of lawn care, I mean seriously?"

Jackie and I glanced at one another before I shrugged. "I haven't really been in the right – I don't know – state of mind, I guess."

Meghan planted her hands on her hips, and she was more than a little foreboding in her superhero getup. "You're not in the right state of mind, because you're not taking care of business. Take care of business, mind will follow."

Jackie glanced at me with a hint of reluctant agreement. Was I seriously being ordered to shave my hoohah and masturbate by my friends? Is this really my life? This was the greatest 'girl's outing' of all time.

That was sarcasm, in case you missed it.

"I haven't had the motivation to even do laundry in the past two months. You think I'm going to magically -"

"We're not talking about it. It's decided."

I glanced at Jackie for help. "What's decided?"

"Well, to start with, we're buying you some wax."

"Oh no, that doesn't need to happen."

"Don't argue. This isn't Europe. We have fucking *standards*, thank you. Next thing you'll tell me you haven't shaved your pits."

I didn't speak.

"Oh sweet Jesus. No wonder you're not in the right state of mind! Who can think about sex with hairy pits?"

I scoffed loud enough for the gentleman by the last changing room to glance, curiously. "France does all right."

"It really is kind of nice, the way it feels after – you know – all smooth and clean. Kevin likes wax day because I'm always in the mood after," Jackie said, making a point to keep her voice down.

Meghan glared at her. "When are you not in the mood? You're a housewife whore."

I laughed heartily, though Jackie quickly smacked Meghan's arm.

I shook my head. "You're both bat shit insane, you know that right?"

"No, we're right. You do it once, you'll understand."

"Ha! Can we put money on that, cause I could seriously use the dough?"

"No, but I *will* buy you the wax."

With that Meghan disappeared back into the changing room.

I turned to Jackie, half whispering. "Should I be scared, here?"

Jackie smiled. "Looks that way."

"I've clearly offended the crotch gods."

Jackie laughed.

We sat there watching Meghan try on every plus-size costume in the place. Jackie had already chosen her Little Red Riding Hood costume within the first ten minutes. She'd snagged a Big, Bad Wolf for Kevin, as well. Meghan tried on everything from Batgirl to Bank robber, but when she appeared as a German Beer Maid, I practically jumped out of my seat.

"And oddly enough, I already have the jugs for this one," she said, groping her chest. I wasn't the only one in the store laughing with her. I imagined her jostling mugs all over Evan's multimillion dollar home with a fake German accent and demanded she buy it.

We spent a good two hours in that changing room. I kept glancing at my phone, hoping for a response to any of the many texts I'd sent Stellan. I'd drawn, I'd worked, I'd scheduled my interview with Dennis Shay for that Thursday, and I wanted to share these things with him. His absence was a palpable thing and even two of my best friends couldn't fill the void his absence created.

Jesus, how had I gone ten years without daily interaction.

I snorted softly at the thought. *You weren't dreaming of his bum then, Faye.*

When Meghan was back in her dressing room, Jackie leaned into me to speak. She kept her voice low, unlike Meghan.

"Imagine if Stellan hadn't told you about his dad's heart attack."

"That's not the same. I love Stellan's dad."

"And Stellan loves you."

The sound of the words swirled in my chest, casting light wherever they traveled. "It's not the same."

Jackie tilted her head from side to side as she thought. "They're both events that changed your lives. How would you feel if he had kept that from you?"

"I just changed my major – his dad nearly died!"

She rolled her eyes at me. "Faye! He isn't upset about your freaking major."

I didn't want to acknowledge how devastated I would be if Stellan kept something from me. I didn't want to consider how troubled my mother would be knowing my father had tracked me down or more importantly, that the conversation caused an psychological upheaval that threw my entire life in a different direction. Even if I told her about his declarations of clean living, of AA meetings and getting his life together, she might have still lost sleep. I kept it from them to spare them worry. Or maybe, I kept it from them to avoid explaining myself.

By the time we climbed into the car to head home, I'd made the decision to hunt Stellan down. It was Tuesday evening again. I knew where to find him. I took a breath and texted him from the backseat -

Do you still want me to come to class tonight?

After a few moments, my phone buzzed to life. I nearly jumped out of my skin.

Sure. That'd be great. Thanks.

Jackie smiled back at me to hear he'd responded, but I knew Stellan. This wasn't how Stellan spoke to me. This was cordial, 'I'm merely tolerating you' Stellan. I sat silently in the backseat as my companions sang along to Lady Gaga, dreading with each passing mile the evening ahead of me.

I arrived at the dojo just a few minutes early, clad in the same uniform that Stellan had sent me home with last time. Yes, I washed it. I arrived to the other students milling around the front hallway, Daniel being the only one past the arched door. Stellan was nowhere to be seen. I stood at the back of the room, almost afraid to move past the main entrance. It was as though I could feel Stellan in the air, feel him unhappy with me. I did my best not to sigh openly as Candyce approached.

"Couldn't stay away either, I see?" She asked, giving me an eyebrow wiggle.

I nodded, letting the small talk go to the subject of Stellan, his being handsome, how long I've been taking classes, and as a result of my answer, how long Stellan and I have been friends. Before I could answer her, a figure appeared. He glanced over, caught sight of me and quickly turned for the dojo, hollering for everyone to line up. Candyce hurried ahead of me, and I tossed my gym bag into the girl's dressing room before taking my place.

Stellan stood at the front of the room, said something in Japanese, and the room took to their breathing exercises. I did as I was told, feeling taut in his presence, as though some wire had been hung between us and someone was attaching the red end of jumper cables.

When his eyes passed over me, it was as though I wasn't there. My chest deflated, and the strength in my legs quickly diminished, but still I held my stance, letting the burn of my leg muscles be my punishment. When this part of class was done, he ordered everyone to run around the room, stopping with each lap to do pushups or jumping jacks or some other torture of the human body. Candyce had trouble the first time through, and Stellan took a moment with her. I glanced their way and again, Stellan's eyes seemed to look right through me. I felt moisture at my hairline, my breathing heavy, but I hardly felt it over the tightness in my stomach. I caught myself glancing at Stellan every few seconds, just waiting to meet his gaze. We finished laps and were broken into groups for punches. He paired Candyce with Daniel and sent the new kid off with another older student. I stood in the lineup, unpaired, and watched Stellan tell Daniel to head up the class before marching out of the dojo and into his office. Daniel smiled at me.

"How about the two of you pair up for the first few rounds, then I'll -"

"That's all right Daniel. Thank you," I said, and I was off. I didn't know what I would say, or how I would say it, but at that moment I was petrified, and I have never responded well to fear. The only thing I could do was to make Stellan acknowledge me. I stormed into his office.

"What, you're not even going to look at me?"

He glanced up, but still his eyes did not meet mine. "I'll look at you all you want."

I stood there and waited, but he continued to simply slide papers across the desk, as though he was reading them one by one.

My fists clenched at my sides. "Is this how it's going to be? You're never going to talk to me again?"

At this, he looked up. "No, but I think you can begrudge me a couple days to be pissed."

"Who are you to be pissed?"

His lip twitched. "Oh, fucking nobody, apparently."

He rounded the desk and moved to pass me out the door, but I stood my ground, blocking his way. I knew if he wanted to pass he would, but I also knew, or prayed, that he would never physically move me in anger. He stopped in front of me.

My legs were shaking. "I didn't mean it that way, I – I just don't understand why you're so upset with me!"

He looked down at me, meeting my eyes for the first time since I'd sat across from him in his kitchen, and I shrank before him.

"This isn't the time, Faye."

"It *is* the time."

He sighed, running his hand up over his face before rubbing his eyes.

"What do you want me to say? You know why I'm mad. You kept something important from me and put me in a position -"

"I didn't keep anything from you out of spite."

"What does that matter?" He asked and his voice dropped deep into his chest. "Do you realize that for the past ten years I thought you'd been date raped. I thought someone had hurt you, and you didn't tell me because you knew I'd find them and kill them?"

I stared up at him, my mouth going dry. *Oh fuck.*

Again, he didn't look at me.

"I'm sorry, Sensei?"

The voice was soft and wary from behind us. I turned to see Daniel looking in. It was clear that though our words were indecipherable, the fighting tone of our raised voices had carried. Daniel on the other hand, had heard that last part.

Stellan's tone still carried anger. "I'll be right out."

Daniel bowed to him and quickly disappeared. I moved away from the door, leaning against the wall to alleviate the pressure in my legs. Stellan stood where he was, his head down.

"Why did you think that?" I asked finally, fighting to form each word without letting them waver.

"Because you changed. One day you were – I don't know, you - and the next day you weren't."

I swallowed, fighting the knot in my throat. I remembered the heartbreak of every choice I made that day, of the pain of telling my professors I would no longer be in class. Every single minute of it hurt. "I didn't want anyone to know."

He leaned into the doorjamb, and I was painfully

aware of his eyes on me. After all that effort to get him to look at me, now I didn't want him to.

"Know what? Just tell me what fucking happened," he said, crossing his arms across his chest.

"I'm afraid of what you'll say."

"Try me."

I took a deep breath. This was a moment I would have paid to avoid. "He said I was his mirror image. Said I couldn't have followed in his footsteps better if he'd drawn me a map. He spent the whole time telling me how alike we were, how I'd inherited so much of him. How if I kept it up, I'd be-"

My throat grew tight. I'd hated saying every word as much as I'd hated hearing them. Stellan stepped closer to me.

I stepped around the desk to get away from him. "I didn't want to be like him."

"You're not, and you know that," he said.

I laughed softly. "No. I don't."

Stellan didn't know that I'd started losing myself in alcohol almost every night back then, or that I'd taken acid or mescaline five weekends straight when my dad appeared. When my father said I was his mirror image, it was too true for me to hear.

Stellan paused. "That's why you went into marketing – because you didn't want to be like your dad?"

Yes.

I didn't speak.

"I can't believe you didn't tell me."

"I was afraid you'd try to change my mind -"

He stepped toward me. "No, Faye. I would have fucking succeeded."

I grew shrill. "I didn't want to end up some drug

addicted starving artist!"

"That would never happen."

"It was a responsible decision to make, damn it! I made good money!" I said, unsure of whom I was trying to convince. "It's not like I ruined my life or anything."

"No. You just lived someone else's for ten years."

I slumped there like a rag doll, trying to keep my face from contorting in grief. I took another deep breath to steady my voice. The breath shuddered violently. I was losing it. "That's not fair. I did really well -"

"So you tell me."

"Fuck you!" I hollered. I didn't care who heard me.

"You were unhappy. You've been unhappy for years. Tell me I'm fucking wrong!"

He stood close, but I refused to look at him. I shook my head. "I wasn't always miserable?"

It was more a question than a declaration.

We listened to the sound of students whooping and hiya-ing as they practiced their forms.

"If you're so worried about my happiness, then stop being mad at me," I said and despite my efforts, my voice cracked. He moved toward me then, half laughing. He put his arms around me, and I lost it. My lip curled, the tears welled up and over, spilling onto his Gi. I wrapped my arms around his waist and curled my fingers into the fabric of his uniform, fighting to keep my body still despite the urge to openly weep. I could feel those same anchors I'd been tied to for years deciding whether to cut loose and let me float with the current again, or pull me to the bottom. We stood there for a long time, Stellan swaying just so as he held me. I heard Stellan send

Daniel away again and finally pulled free of his arms. I wiped my face, frowning at the sight of the waterlogged clown face on the front of his shirt. This was beginning to feel like an unfortunate pattern.

He bent down to meet my eyes, pinching my chin with his thumb and forefinger. "These are unfair tactics, madam."

I laughed, wiping my face with the sleeve of my uniform. "You mean you're not mad at me anymore? Score. You fell right into my trap."

I smiled despite my state. He gestured for me to take his chair behind the desk and told me to relax until the end of class. He winked at me as he left the office, hollering something about the rest of the class clearly slacking off as he disappeared. I smiled there in his rickety leather office chair, the smell of him still on my clothes, and my breathing steadied.

CHAPTER SIX

Friday morning.

I'd been fretting for days. By the time Friday finally hit, my stomach was churning with a seething hate reserved for Nazis and puppy kickers, and had almost the entire contents of my closet strewn across that cloud top mattress in an attempt to choose an outfit for my interview. I had no luck. I did, however, have a plan for a trip to goodwill with half of the clothes I owned. I tried on a few things, giving my sense of defeat a chance to be proven wrong, and instead ended up down in the kitchen searching for a trash bag to cart upstairs and violently fill with all of my pants.

"A colorful scarf or a nice costume piece - if you go in there dressed like some stuffy old broad, that's exactly what they'll see, and that isn't you, is it Faye Bear?" Mom had suggested on her way out the door. By the time I was heading out, I hadn't come up with any better ideas.

There's something to be said about the mid to late afternoon interview. Sadly, I'd convinced myself that scheduling early in the day would give a good impression.

Look world, I am, in fact, capable of getting up before noon. Hire me!

That kind of initiative has a tendency to backfire when you can't actually get up before noon, but let's pretend that didn't happen. I woke up on what must have been the sixth alarm, having slammed the snooze button in my sleep apparently, and threw myself out of bed. I dove into the shower with such force that not only did I forget to take my socks off when I climbed in, I managed to leave half the conditioner in my hair when I jumped out. No matter! I brushed, I flossed, I smiled wide into the mirror, and I planned my greeting and the caliber of grin I would give to the oncoming horde of potential workmates. And above all, I managed to get my eyeliner on without looking like Tammy Fay Baker. Yet when I returned to my bedroom. I tore through drawers, flipped through hangers and found items for a potential Cyndi Lauper costume for the Halloween Party the next day, but I was pretty sure my future boss wasn't looking to hire Cyndi Lauper.

Well, maybe he was, but probably not some whack job dressed as her. When I finally started up my car, I was running twenty five minutes late, and I was dressed like a stuffy old broad. Pants suit and white blouse to the rescue. I followed my mom's advice last minute and stole one of her scarves from the downstairs closet. I was ten minutes down the road before I realized I was wearing a Monet painting in fabric form around my neck.

"Great Faye, you look like a fucking librarian."

The firm was located in an old brick building in West Concord that housed a Starbucks and the offices of an international weapons company – awesome. Traffic was kind, and I made it with three minutes to spare. Not exactly the sort of entrance I wanted to make, hauling my tired ass up three flights of stairs only to greet the secretary, breathlessly. She smiled from behind horn-rimmed glasses, her lip piercing glinting in the overhead light. I should have taken her appearance as a baseline, but I was too antsy.

"Faye! So great to finally meet you," said a man as he rounded the corner in an untucked white button down shirt and faded blue jeans. He seemed to pause at the sight of me. I could imagine his thoughts.

I gestured to my outfit. "I came straight from my Bridge game, clearly."

Dennis Shay had one of those full bodied laughs, the kind you expect from a man with a bowl full of jelly belly. Yet Mr. Shay was far from jelly. Dennis Shay was a few inches taller than me, his head shaved bald to counter a receding hairline, and his frame betraying an athletic lifestyle. He hooked his thumbs in the belt loops of his jeans and shifted weight from toe to heel as he introduced me to Margarite; the receptionist. He made a point to compliment her on her Bettie Page look, then gestured for me to follow, his smile constant and bright.

We rounded the corner of the front desk wall, and I was greeted with the full expanse of the office.

The room was wide and open, and people milled around desks and printers by the red brick walls. The space was reminiscent of some comic hero newsroom where editors yelled from their corner offices for some seemingly meager paperboy who in his spare time thwarted nuclear catastrophe without wish of credit. I scanned the faces, wondering which one of the lot was secretly allergic to Kryptonite before following Dennis into his office. There was no desk, no separation to declare hierarchy. We sat, and he smiled, leaning in toward me.

I imagined what Stellan would say.

"They sound like a bunch of fucking hippies."

I tried not to laugh at my own thoughts.

Dennis unleashed a slew of affirmative statements, describing my potential place of employment as a 'step outside the box.'

"We try to create a rapport with our clients that makes them comfortable, brings them back to us hopeful and excited."

I nodded. Traveling the country to meet clients, rubbing elbows with potentials, delegating to interns and fellow employees the responsibility of event planning and detail work while I racked up frequent flier miles and sat at expensive lunches, listening to rich people describe how useless their less rich counterparts were and how their career was straining their relationships with wife and/or mistress.

I'd had a few clients attempt to make me their mistress. I wondered how Dennis Shay saw his world differing. I sat across from him feeling like a high school kid in the sensitive counselor's office.

"We don't represent the usual brand of clientele. We shy away from the mainstream. If you're looking for the big beer fest parties, we're not your jam."

Not my jam? He totally just said that. I smiled. "So, I should leave then?"

He laughed, a line of perfect white teeth bared as his eyes shrank to thin slits. I had to be honest, Dennis Shay was a handsome guy. I was sure he'd spent a good amount of time in his life having heart to hearts, convincing people to reach their potential. I feared this job might require hugging - then I thought, what's so wrong with that?

"So what is your passion, Faye? Do you mind 'Faye?' As you may have noticed, we run a pretty casual ship around here."

"Sure, Faye is fine."

"Good, good. So lay it out for me. What drives you – gets you out of bed in the morning?"

I was stumped. The sound of my stomach gurgling, the realization that I reek, the glue at the corners of my eyes hardening to the point that only piping hot water will resurrect my sense of sight? I was sure none of these were the answer he was looking for.

He sensed my trouble. "Let me ask, did you always want to work in marketing?"

I tilted my head to the side like some vapid day dreamer before catching the gesture and scolding myself silently. "No, actually."

"So what was your original purpose in this life, Faye?"

I scratched my head, cautious to admit the fact out loud, especially to a potential employer. Should I say law school? World Hunger? What would Miss America say?

"I originally went to school for – uh, cartoonist. I wanted to be a cartoonist."

Dennis Shay's mouth literally hung open before me a moment as he blatantly searched my face. Woops, wrong answer?

"That's amazing." Maybe not the wrong answer. "Are you serious?"

"Yes?"

"That's amazing! How many people out there are pursuing *that* kind of passion? Not many, I'll tell you what."

I shrugged, and again faulted myself. "Well, one less, apparently," I said, gesturing to myself with two thumbs. "Marketing won!"

"Well, our gain, surely!"

Without another word or a close study of my resume, Dennis carted me around the office, introducing me to each and every person we passed. I met Jarod, the 'paper pusher' as he was called – some form of super hero name given to avoid calling himself mailboy. I met Corrine, who happily displayed a sleeve tattoo from wrist to shoulder blade, peppered with characters from the movie *A Nightmare Before Christmas*. Then finally there was Kathy, the only seemingly stereotypical office staple; a short haired brunette in a peach blouse and pressed black slacks sitting behind a perfectly organized desk. Shortly after shaking her hand and trading niceties, Dennis informed me it was Kathy whom I would be replacing were I to get the position. I tried not to see an *Invasion of the Body Snatchers* type assimilation taking place – get rid of the normal one and make way for the girl who leaves Jackass voicemails. I was more than a little relieved to hear that Kathy was voluntarily leaving the company for greener pastures.

By the time we were back to the front door of the office, I had been given the vote of confidence from everyone in the room, including Kathy, and had yet to actually converse about my credentials or qualifications. As Dennis shook my hand, his wide smile beaming on his smooth, clean face, I felt oddly confident. Does an employer take the time to introduce you to everyone in the room if he's just showing you the door?

I think not. Or, I hope not.

"I'll give you a call, hopefully by the end of the month, and let you know what we've decided."

I shook his hand yet again, smiled and headed out into the hallway. Margarite greeted me by name as I passed her desk. I reached into my purse on the second floor staircase and turned on my phone. Just being in an office, being around the gainfully employed made me feel almost useful. Or perhaps it was the idea of having successfully fooled someone else into believing I was useful. My phone quickly buzzed to life, announcing missed texts.

How'd it go?

Almost the same text from Stellan, Jackie, and my Mom. I responded to Stellan first.

Un-fucking-real.

I'd made it only half way through the response to Jackie's text before he responded.

Damn straight! I'm taking you for tacos before the party, woman! Text when you're home.

I stood by my car, leaning against the open door, smiling. Party?

Oh shit. That's tonight, I thought. All semblance of tranquil self-satisfaction was gone.

"You'll just have to see," Stellan said when I asked of his costume. I didn't confess mine either, given that it was going to be a panicked hodge-podge of my closet's contents. I would rather the outfit be in full effect before declaring my identity as whatever 80's pop star I looked most like. We hung up with the promise of surprise.

I got home and started the thundersacking of my closet all over again. I even called Meghan for help. She offered little. She was completely content with me going as a burlap sack.

"The less competition the better," she'd said, explaining her hope to seduce Evan Lambert – the Billionaire. I could only picture her seducing Evan Lambert – the raging jackass – but that comes from having spent my last three years of high school in his almost constant company.

Stellan, Evan and I had been a trifecta, if you will. They were two of the more asocial oddballs in school, and I fit that description well myself. We spent a good amount of our time holed up in Stellan's basement or my living room. We'd watch TV or play video games, or I'd make them help me with my science or math homework, given their combined IQ was record breaking, I'm sure. We rarely spent time up at Evan's house. Something Evan and I shared; better off absent fathers.

I didn't bother telling Meghan that not only had I spent the better part of three years at Evan's side, but I'd also seen him naked - a side effect of Evan's one-time love affair with hallucinogens, and his tendency to run around the house bare-assed whilst on them. Stellan and I refrained, more enticed by the notion of watching Evan trip his balls off than possibly join him in his screaming nude escapades around the neighborhood. We'd narrowly avoided getting arrested one night in Sleepy Hollow when a cruiser came rolling down into the graves, its spotlight directed on our faces. Stellan and I froze, both whispering to each other frantically over whether or not to yell to Evan that a cop car was approaching. Yet just as the cop opened his car door, a naked blur went whizzing by the front end of the cruiser, screaming "Attica," and the officer's attention was quickly redirected. We made a run for it in the confusion, hauling it back to my house across Bedford Road, and lunging onto the floor of my darkened living room to watch out the window for a sign of Evan. We heard him banging at the back door fifteen minutes later.

That was the night Stellan and I declared ourselves allergic to nudity. Evan agreed never to trip around us again. I'm not sure if he ever dropped acid again after that night, but I do know this – that was the last time I saw Evan Lambert naked.

I found myself standing before the kitchen window, watching the birds. There's something to be said for early risers – they definitely get the better end of bird watching. The female cardinal came and waited, watched her 'husband' eat, then left. She seemed a bit poofy for such a light eater. I imagined her sneaking to the feeders at night after her husband comes home from the bar, gorging herself on suet and cursing his name. I thought of a comic strip and considered heading into the office for a little while to work on some drawings. Instead, I poured cream into my coffee, sweetened it beyond any reasonable measure, and headed upstairs.

I opened my closet door, staring at the rail within, bowed with the weight of too many hangers, all holding more clothes than my old closet could properly contain. My condo's closet had been twice this size. I pushed that thought out of mind and began pulling out the mish mash of items that would hopefully make my evening's outfit – two tank tops of different length, one pink and one black, three separate skirts, all similarly mismatched, a pair of red high top sneakers, and every piece of plastic jewelry I'd ever owned. I searched a moment longer until I found the plastic bag Meghan sent me home with after our Halloween store excursion. I dumped its contents onto the bed. Two strange looking boxes plopped down beside one another; one of bright red hair dye and the other, Bikini Wax - Meghan's orders. I went for the hair dye first.

Time to be a Ginger.

I felt good. I won't deny that the events of the day before may have been helping.

I wrapped myself in a towel when I was done with the dye, my hair too dark while wet to judge how I felt about it. I stood by my bed. The bright blue box seemed to call to me like some perilous siren, begging me to dash myself on the rocks. I opened the box and texted Meghan.

The wax didn't come with strips.

I flipped the box over. A small folded piece of paper fell out as my phone buzzed.

It doesn't need strips, hon. I'll call in a minute.

I sighed openly, realizing the proverbial can of worms I'd just opened.

I stopped at the mirror. My once blonde hair was darker now, but still not betraying its fiery nature. I'd let my hair grow past my shoulders the past few months and I would need to expend two or three canisters of Aqua Net into my hair to get the appropriate Cyndi Lauper caliber updo. I was determined to do Ms. Lauper justice. I rubbed my head in a towel and checked the mirror again. Still too wet to tell. I had hours before I needed to get ready, but I was the kind of person who enjoyed dry runs when the time allowed. I curled up in bed and turned on "Time After Time."

I felt the jab of something hard against my side and

found the box of wax, taunting me with its rocket science. Out of curiosity more than intent, I called Meghan.

"Bitch, are you serious or are you just playin with me?"

"What?" I asked, surprised by the greeting.

"You better be serious about this. If you get my hopes up for nothing I will cut you."

"Get your hopes up? I didn't realize the state of my bikini area had such far reaching effects."

"Get real woman. If I can spread the ways of proper self-care to one hairy bitch, my work is done."

I slewed a few choice words at her before being accosted with further 'pep talks.' Words like 'mess,' 'ripping,' 'yank,' and 'cry' were real sellers for me, yet in the end something she said seemed to settle in my psyche – someplace vulnerable and wrong.

"Nothing beats the way it feels afterward. Do it once and you'll be hooked."

I felt as though someone had successfully convinced me to smoke Crystal Meth. A moment later, I found myself standing in my kitchen, waiting for the microwave to count down.

You're going to flip your shit!

It was Stellan. Before I could respond, the microwave bleeped at me, and I found the wax still as stubbornly immobile as it had been when I opened the thing.

Thirty seconds my ass!

I put it back into the microwave and set it for another minute.

Why? What's up? I responded.

His text came too quickly to have been in response to my question.

You are going to flip your fucking shit! My costume is the stuff of LEGEND!

Again, I didn't have time to answer.

OF LEGEND!

Me - **What is it, damn it? Are you Skeletor?**

His excitement was a beast one couldn't help but ride.

No! But that WOULD be LEGEND. You'll see!

I waited a moment for further texts, the wax taking much longer than thirty seconds to melt completely, but once it was liquefied, I carried it carefully upstairs to my bedroom. I stood there holding the mixture, then finally marched my ass into my nearly forgotten bathroom. I set the container on the sink before dropping trou and gazing at my depantsed self in the bathroom mirror. The room seemed larger than it was due to a two wall mirror that framed the front and side of the sink, something my Grandmother added in my mother's youth. I saw myself from mid-thigh upward, all the brightly illuminated details, ready to be inspected. There was a triangle of light hair where, as Meghan declared, there should be some form of abstract art, and though I saw nothing wrong with it, I was now determined to prune the shit out of it.

Curiosity is a terrible motivation.

I sank down into the dry bathtub, holding my breath against the cold of the porcelain surface. I leaned back, inch by inch, grateful to have the fabric of my shirt shielding me from the slope of the claw foot tub.

I collected the still piping tub of wax, setting it in the bathtub. I had two wooden sticks, a tub of hot goo, sprawled legs, and good intentions. I glanced down at my nether regions and leaned back. The wax dripped everywhere as I moved to apply it; onto the bathtub, onto my leg and God knows where else. It burned like a bastard for the first few seconds. Still, I managed to get the majority of the crap onto the outermost part of my bikini area. This was the area where your leg and torso converge, where some of the bushier feminists I met in college would have what they called 'spider legs.' I smoothed the wax down, the gelatinous ooze pulling with each movement as it hardened. Once it was as smooth as I could potentially get it, I set the stick back into the wax and stared at my groin. I looked like a caulking gun had exploded onto my crotch, but I gritted my teeth and trusted the inner preener that was bat shit crazy enough to do this. I grew impatient and pressed my finger to the goo. The wax had yet to harden, and it stuck to my finger.

"Wait long enough for it to harden, but not too long because then it will just crack and crumble," Meghan had said. With every attempt to reassure and sell this deed, she'd managed to confuse the shit out of me. Honestly, I was probably doing it just as much to shut her up as I was to be hairless. I rolled the wax between my fingers, feeling it harden and pull free of my skin. I let the tiny ball fall to the bathtub surface before checking myself yet again. Not even tacky, really. Oh shit, this is it.

I pulled the edge of the wax upward just to get a finger hold, feeling my skin pulling under it. To say it didn't feel nice would be the understatement of the century.

"What have you fucking done?" I asked aloud.

I arched my back and pressed my fingers against

my skin to hold it taut.

"If you don't hold it taut you're going to fucking destroy yourself. Hold the skin taut, and you'll hardly feel it."

I took a sharp breath and yanked. The wax came free in my hand.

I froze, my eyes wide as the pain registered. The exposed skin where it had been glued was now blindingly hot.

I started laughing like a complete maniac. It was a sardonic, involuntary laughter, the kind that draws the eye of strangers in a crowded room. It deferred to a giggle, and I found the burn had faded to a warm pulsing sensation. I looked down to find my skin pink and smooth.

So unbelievably smooth.

Oh, I can handle this, I thought.

I quickly dipped into the wax, its consistency still thin and liquid, dousing the other side of my 'holy triangle.' I waited, checking the wax impatiently, then tore myself asunder, yet again. This moment reminded me of Dr. Hoar, my biology teacher in high school, who explained to class that the human mind is incapable of remembering pain. This is an evolutionary feat and exists for the sheer purpose of maintaining our species. He said, if a woman could remember the pain of childbirth, there would be no second-borns.

I found the notion intriguing as I pulled the third and largest strip of now hardened wax from the further recesses of my nethers. I was getting to regions that practically required contortionist moves to reach, but with each section, I felt reborn. Even the pain began to feel rudimentary as the flow of the routine smoothed out. I'd managed to de-shag the regions of closest reach, but if I was going to do this, I might as well do it properly. I scooped up another glop of wax, reached blindly downward, and as I watched helplessly, a huge glob of the stuff plopped off the wooden stick and onto my skin. I lunged downward, trying to spread it out before it ran down my ass, but I couldn't find the stuff. Instead, I simply smoothed the wax I still had on the stick, the globs becoming more and more viscous as the moments passed. I leaned forward, returning the stick to the tub and made the decision to trudge downstairs and reheat the stuff after I pulled this bit off. I settled there in the tub, my arms sprawled out along the ridge of the tub as I waited for the wax to reach the appropriate state.

I couldn't help but picture myself there, half naked and brutalizing myself for the pursuit of – well, I wasn't even sure what. I imagined being sprawled out like this at the mercy of the Vietnamese woman Meghan goes to. I chuckled at the thought of Meghan calling me a pussy as I shrieked from behind some salon curtain. A comic strip crossed my mind - Super Crotch, a cartoon version of Meghan whose nether regions were impervious to blows. I laughed loudly, the sound bouncing off the walls of my small bathroom. I let the tip of my finger tap at the wax and found it well hardened. I shifted my body to reach down, only to be met with a flash of white hot pain. I froze, feeling almost frightened. I shifted again, only to be met with the same sharp pain from the furthest recesses of my down below. I slumped back to relieve the pain and stretched the tip of my fingers down as far as I could. The mysterious glob of wax, the one that had lunged at my crotch before I was ready – yeah, that one - it was now hardened and glued to my ass.

Glued to the hair of my ass and the bathtub, to be more specific.

Yes, ladies and gentlemen, I'd glued my ass to the bathtub.

I began to feel a dry panic that one only feels when their pubic area is in jeopardy.

"No. No, no, no," I said, as though somehow the word would make it untrue. I found the edge of the wax that I'd intentionally spread across one side of my private area and with the determination that only comes from the fear of God, I prepared to pull it free. The wax pulled at hair I didn't even know I had, and I couldn't reach down to pull the skin taut without extreme trauma to my glued bum cheek. This was a kamikaze mission. I took a breath, assuring myself that by now, I must've grown at least a little desensitized. Right?

I yanked and every inch of skin, every hair that I'd ever had in that region rallied together in protest. I screamed bloody murder. The wax pulled an inch, then snapped off in my hand.

Oh Jesus. I waited too long!

I tried to pull the edge up, but the wax was further out of reach now, almost impossible to grab onto without pulling at the glob that now held me like concrete to the bathtub surface.

"Only you would fucking glue yourself to the bathtub! Of course!" I hollered at myself.

I had a sudden bout of inspiration. Maybe, if I could heat the wax it might soften enough to pull myself up from the bathtub. I kicked a foot out toward the faucet, hooking my toes on the handles and turning them. The shift in the pipes reverberated through the bathroom wall, then a deluge of frigid water blasted from the faucet, drawing shriek of abject horror from my lips. I frantically kicked my foot at the faucet to shut it off.

Oh yeah, Faye. That's right, the hot water in your shower's broken, remember that?

I growled and tried to reach for the wax again, my lower half now covered in goosebumps and freezing wet. My fingers grazed the edge as the pain shot through my poor hoohah like split second bee stings. I was completely fucked, and I knew it.

I slumped back against the cold bathtub and wiped my watering eyes. Suddenly that crazed waxer didn't seem so scary.

"Suck it up, woman! Suck it up, or you're going to be found here by loved ones in a week, half naked and starved to death. Suck it the fuck UP!"

It was do or die. I wrenched my fingers around the rim of the bathtub, closed my eyes tight, and flung myself forward. I then followed this action with a slew of expletives that even I thought truly inspired. I'd felt a shift under me, but couldn't begin to guess how much I'd freed myself, or if I'd simply managed to flay my tralala in the effort. I reached for the wax between my legs. Though I could only grapple with the very edge, I could reach further than a moment before.

This was joy, this was progress.

This was going to fucking hurt.

At least there was an end in sight - an end that existed on the other side of a football field of hot coals that I apparently had to drag my naked ass across, but in sight nonetheless. I wiped my eyes yet again and braced myself for another tug.

"Fuck your mother cocksucking bitch whore!"

Yeah, something like that.

An inch maybe, a fraction of an inch more likely, but still, progress. I leaned back against the tub, my breath shallow with the effort of constant anxiety. I waited a moment, praying that Dr. Hoar was right and that if I gave myself a minute, I might forget the agony.

The house shook with the force of the front door. I froze, my eyes wide. I listened to the footsteps circle the downstairs. *Fuck, fuck, fuck, fuck, fuck.*

"Faye! Where are you, woman?"

God, if you see fit to give me an aneurysm, please do it now.

I kept silent, listening to Stellan clomp through the house. My bedroom door opened. I held my breath.

"Faye?"

He rapped his knuckles on the bathroom door, his tone urgent and excited.

"Yeah?"

"You decent? I gotta show you -"

The doorknob to my bathroom door twisted, and I must've pulled myself another inch of freedom when I jumped in terror.

"Don't! Don't fucking open the door!"

The knob stopped. This was my fault. Stellan knew I rarely used my bathroom for more than makeup and hair. Downside of having a defunct facility.

"Shit, sorry. Well, come out then!"

I covered my eyes with both hands. "I can't."

"You gotta. You're gonna lose it!"

"I know -"

Stellan was right outside the door, his voice

agitated. "Literally, you're going to fucking freak out!"

"I know, but -"

"Hurry up woman! I can't wait to see the look on your face!"

"I can't, Stellan."

My tone was far more stern than I'd intended – side effect of having your shebang brutalized. There was silence on the other side of the door.

"But I want you to see -" He stopped and tapped a hand to the door. "Are you alright?"

I sighed. "Yes, I just – I'm just indisposed at the moment. Just go home, and I'll see you there."

The hardwood shifted beneath him outside the door. "I thought we were going to go together."

His voice had descended to this soft and almost childish place of honest disappointment.

I cringed to hear him like that. "I know, I'm so sorry, but I'm completely fucked right now, ok?"

"Do you need help?"

Again the doorknob twisted, this time with purpose. I'd clearly concerned him.

"NO! Don't open the — I sweartoGODStellanIwillfuckingstabyou!"

Again the doorknob went still.

"Faye, you're freaking me out here."

"I know. It's alright, just – faaaaaahk!" A sudden tug and the response was involuntary.

"Can I do *anything*?"

"I'm alright," I said. Then inspiration struck. Perhaps there was help to be found. "Actually, do you think you could - like if you literally just open the door enough to stick your hand through, and nothing else – could you throw me my cell phone?"

He moved outside the door before the door

creaked. "Here," he said, holding it just inside the door. It would do me little good five feet away.

"Just throw it toward the bathtub."

"The bathtub? Faye, what the hell are you doing in the bathtub? What's wrong?"

"I'm alright, I'll be alright. Just throw it, please."

"It'll break!"

"I'll catch it! Just throw it, please!"

He disappeared for a moment, then his arm reappeared, and he tossed a bundle of wrapped up fabric into the bathtub. I exhaled gratefully, unwrapping the red CCCP t-shirt I'd loved so much in high school.

"Thank you! I love you! Now please, just go home, and I'll see you later. Please? I'm sorry. Please?"

He sighed heavily. "Alright. Cool."

With that the door closed, and his footsteps shifted outside the door. It was as though I could hear his inner debate through the door. It really was asking a lot of Stellan to expect him to leave when he assumed trauma. Finally, he walked downstairs and out the door. I'd never loved him more than I did at that moment.

"When Karma comes for you, I hope it hurts half as bad as this!" I hollered into the phone when Meghan answered. I relayed my situation to her only to be met with uncontrollable laughter.

"Turn on the hot water, it will loosen the wax."

"Uh, broken shower? Thought of that."

The laughter returned. I cursed her, her name, and the day she was born; she just kept laughing. Finally, she offered to come over. I turned her down outright.

"Yeah, I already had Stellan bangin down my door a minute ago, I'm all set."

"Well, what do you want me to do then?" Meghan asked, breathless.

"Honestly? Suffer like Christ!"

She laughed again, and I explained that as punishment I felt she should be required to listen to my suffering. She agreed to the task.

It took six more outbursts of cursing God before I was detached, then another three minutes of tearing and pulling to get the last chunks of now brittle wax from my region. When I was done, I'd never felt more relieved in my life.

No, I rephrase - I'd never been more thankful to be alive and free to wear pants, in my life.

I ran my hand down across the mound of what I'd once thought of as a sensitive and delicate region. No blood, no torn ligaments or bruises, just baby smooth skin.

Well, on one side. The other side was still a jungle.

"I've managed to give myself a crotch Mohawk."

The piercing cackle carried through the phone for a moment or two.

CHAPTER SEVEN

"I'm not strutting through downtown Concord in these heels, honey," Meghan said, pointing out the pencil thin spike that protruded from the bottom of her boots.

Why Meghan? Why do you always have to make everyone else look like hobos? Seriously.

I was wearing several layers of the puffiest clothing I'd been able to procure from all three remaining clothes closets in the house. My mother's offered little more than some older vintage pieces I might've tried were I going as a member of the Scooby-Doo gang, but I was not. I was going as an 80's icon, and as you've been informed, the 80's are in my DNA. Dishonoring their memory would be a cardinal sin.

My lace gloves were pulled to the elbow, the fingers cut off, my skirts were layered and lace trimmed, pink over black over white. I'd teased my newly rust colored hair out to the moon on one side of my head, leaving the other side combed flat. My lipstick was bright red, my eyeliner as thick as I could smear it, and my bracelets so innumerous that I felt like I was doing bicep curls if I deigned to pick anything up. The final touch felt a little inaccurate, but I had little choice as we were coming down to the wire. My high tops had seen better days, and they fell apart when I tried to put them on. Instead, I'd torn the ever living shit out of a perfectly good pair of black stockings and put on my mother's ancient black cowboy boots. Her feet were at least a size bigger than mine, but I made due with a couple pairs of socks. My feet were still slipping around inside the boots with every step. Ah, what a woman will do for era specific fashion statements.

Meghan gave me another once over. "You look spectacular, lady."

I was almost startled by the compliment. My expression must have betrayed this because Meghan planted her hands on her curvaceous hips. "You have a problem with that?"

"No? Just never really thought of Cyndi Lauper as spectacular."

"Well, whether she was or not, you look fucking fantastic. Seriously, your tits look amazing in that top."

I glanced down self-consciously. The top she spoke of was a collection of lingerie, tank tops, and brassieres, and she was right, there was some serious chest chasm going on. If anyone lost their keys tonight, I knew where to look.

"Is he coming?"

She was talking about Stellan. "I think so? We were supposed to go together, but as you know -"

It was the second shortest drive to a friend's house I'd ever known – the first being Stellan's.

Evan's road was certainly the hardest to climb to, being on the most prestigious hill in downtown. Nashawtuc was one of those roads you brought family members to when they were in town to ogle how the other half live. The houses were each grander than the next, their driveways leading to multiple car garages and million dollar views of the often flooded fields below. Meghan and I decided not to arrive too early, given her love of fashionable arrival. I was more concerned about arriving without Stellan, my buffer. I wasn't entirely weened into the world yet, and the thought of being alone in the house with past peers, or worse, Evan...

I wasn't sure why that thought bothered me.

I checked my phone again. Still no word from Stellan.

Concerned, slightly whiny Me - **Are you alive? Where are you?**

I was beginning to worry. The worst possible outcome here would be for him to not to come at all.

We drove by the mansions, their lit windows looked like the glowing eyes of prosperity on an otherwise dark hillside. Every once in a while, I would catch a glimpse of someone inside, of some pampered child sitting at an Ethan Allen dining room table, his note papers and text books sprawled out before him, or a woman reading on some leather couch. It was almost surreal to see the children of the filthy rich sitting to such mundane tasks as homework or reading. Still, I'd once known one of those kids. Despite the luxurious façade of his life, I knew better. Sometimes inside these houses, there's very little comfort to be had.

The cul-de-sac known as Willith Common was already filled with parked cars on either side of the road. The party was set to begin at eight, and we were pulling in the around nine. Meghan chattered away. I'd been drowning her out with my thoughts when she suddenly mentioned Evan.

"Now you're going to introduce me, right?"

I shrugged. "Sure, if you want."

"Of course I want. And if you feel like dropping the info that I give phenomenal blow jobs -"

I smiled. "We both know you hate giving -"

"Shut up. I was mostly kidding anyway."

I smirked. "Only mostly though."

"Exactly."

We parked a dozen or so car lengths away from the house, walking down the road to the house. It was a mountain of white walls and brick, three garage doors, two of them housing a car worth more than my mother's house (I knew this from my youth, not from a sudden case of X-ray vision, mind you). Meghan was practically shrill as she regaled me with awe. I accused her of wanting to make out with the landscaping, and she quieted down.

There were small lanterns lining the brick path to the side of the house. I knew exactly which entrance we were being led to. Evan's father had built a large sun room onto the back of the house years ago – a monstrous glass room with granite tile floor and leather furniture where he could smoke cigars and remove himself from the family that resided within. Sadly, his intentions to utilize the space were quickly forgotten. When Evan was a teenager, he'd taken over the room, leaving the back door open to friends at all hours of the night.

When Meghan and I rounded the side of the house, the backyard was alight with hundreds of lanterns hanging from trees and lampposts. The sun room door was, as always, wide open. Meghan gasped at the wonderland of his lamp lit backyard that stretched a hundred yards down the slope of the hill. I was too busy scanning the figures through the glass walls of the sun room. I didn't immediately recognize anyone.

I took a deep breath.

The familiar smell of the house was soft beneath the smell of beer and lemon wedges. Still, as I entered the living room, the smell of eucalyptus, something Evan's mother always kept hanging in sconces on the walls, hit me. I felt strangely nostalgic. Again, it was short lived.

"Hey, who are you?"

A tall tawny haired fellow asked over the sound of The Pixies playing through the nearby stereo speakers. His eyes passed over my chest before settling on Meghan's. Though mine might be well displayed, Meghan's was fucking mighty. She smiled wide and introduced us. I didn't return the interest. There were two faces I was searching for – Stellan, and with some trepidation, Evan. The tall fellow offered us his name – Will – and beers. I accepted the plastic cup politely, despite having no intention of drinking it. I was almost startled by the frat party feel of the plastic cup in my hand. I wondered if I might find a rousing game of beer pong if I were to search further into the house. I didn't dare do so without company and by that time, Meghan was fully ensconced in her conversation with Will – how did he know Evan, how charming his costume was; a T-shirt with the word *Costume* written across the chest. I rolled my eyes and took a sip of the beer in my hand. It was sharp and bitter to me, unpalatable, but still it was all I had.

The black leather couches of the living room were as I remembered them, though I was sure they'd been replaced with newer versions. The stone slab fireplace seemed smaller now, a sign of either my having grown, or it simply being surrounded by Lady Gagas and Darth Vadars. Every car parked outside must've carried its maximum capacity. I scanned the werewolves and zombies, the blood covered doctor, his candy striping side kick. I didn't recognize anyone – no old high school friends to hide from. I took my leave of Meghan with the desire for an easier drink. I knew my way around the house.

I wandered into the kitchen to the stainless steel double refrigerator, raising an eyebrow at the array of women dressed in various levels of scanty. Evan's single status was well known. I felt almost ashamed at the presence of my own cleavage.

I loved Evan, to clarify, but we lost touch when my life became marketing and he left for the west. Stellan kept in touch, but I think some part of me assumed Evan and I wouldn't have anything in common anymore. Describing my life would sound the same now as it did in my senior year of high school. I can't imagine that would be of interest to a man who spends his time with Victoria's Secret models on his own island.

I hauled the heavy fridge door open and stared into the recesses of the beast - lines of soda cans, bottled water, condiments, and booze; just as I remembered. I grabbed a water and took a long breathless drink. When I closed the door to the refrigerator, the devil was standing beside me.

"Hey sweet thang."

I nearly dropped the water on the floor. The devil's red suit was tailored perfectly to his slight frame, the small prosthetic horns peeking out from under the dark hair of his still strong hair line. I hacked as quietly as I could, the remnants of aspirated water still tickling my throat. Evan caressed my back the way a parent would to a coughing child, and I desperately tried to catch my breath. When I was finally able to meet his gaze, my eyes were running mascara down my cheeks, and he was beaming at me.

"Dick," I said.

He just smiled wider. "Glad you could make it, *Cyndi*."

Evan held his arms open before me. I faltered only a second and accepted the embrace. It felt warm.

"Hey there, Ev," I said over his shoulder. The hug lasted a while, both of us clasping our wrists behind the other and breathing deeply. He rubbed my back again, and hummed softly before kissing my cheek a couple times as he released me. I could feel female eyes on us with varying degrees of curiosity and outright rage. The Holy Grail seemed to like me. This fact did not bode well with the scantily clad masses, especially when he informed me that my tits looked spectacular.

God, he always did have class.

Evan stood just a little taller than me when we were younger. Now he seemed to have added an inch or so. Still, he was the slight, wily creature I remembered.

He glanced to the plastic cup on the counter beside me before scoffing openly. "What are you drinking?"

"Well, I was trying to drink water, but -"

He grabbed my hand and led me out of the kitchen. We made our way through the living room and the den as people did whatever they could to grab Evan's attention. I felt out of place, not only dressed as I was, but at Evan's side. Seemingly oblivious, he dragged me to the far corner of the house where I found myself across a bar counter from a man in a black vest and white button down shirt. I'd seen another before that moment, but had simply assumed he was in some costume too hip for me to recognize. Instead, I realized he was working the party in a far more direct manner than the rest of the people there.

"Order something," Evan said.

"No, I'm alright."

"Faye, have a drink. You're tense as fuck."

How right he was. I shook my head. "What would my sponsor say?"

Evan laughed. "He'd say nobody likes a quitter!"

I snorted, softly. "You're so sensitive."

I'd just ordered my Rum and Coke when I heard a familiar voice behind me.

"Bitch. You left me with that snaggle-toothed schmuck on purpose."

I turned to find Meghan offering her hand to Evan with the brightest, most catalog model worthy smile I'd ever seen on her beautiful face. Evan smiled back, glancing at me. I introduced them by name rather than blow job preference. The bartender handed me my drink, and I leaned onto the counter to create space between myself and the rest of the party goers. Despite the cathedral ceilings of the main den, the room still felt small with that many people in it. I attempted to scan the faces, leaving Meghan to her conquest without being too blatantly accommodating. After recognizing three people from my high school, I turned back to the bar. I wasn't particularly interested in shooting the shit with complete strangers who might want to pretend we have something to talk about because we went to the same high school. Before I knew I'd even put a dent in my drink, it was gone and the bartender was handing me a new glass.

"Whoa there, Alki," Evan said as he leaned onto the bar beside me and ordered himself two fingers of Black Label. I turned to find Meghan gone.

Evan offered without my asking. "She headed to the bathroom. She seems nice, yeah?"

"Yes, she is."

"Well, who here doesn't?"

I met his gaze and tried to smile. He wrapped an arm around me and squeezed before being called off by some woman in a Black Widow leather catsuit. When Meghan returned, she offered blatant disdain for my letting him leave.

"He's around. If you like you can tranquilize him and tag him before we leave tonight."

She shook her head. "Worst wing man ever."

"I'm not your wing man."

"Apparently not!"

I sipped idly at my drink, feeling warm and large as I listened to Meghan's account of the fireworks she felt between herself and Evan. It was true love, she assured me. She applied a fresh layer of lip gloss.

I was smiling. During her monologue, I'd managed to order myself another drink. Then another.

And we had lift off.

I turned around, leaning my elbows onto the bar behind me and actively watching the crowd. Meghan turned with me, muttering with disgust at the social organism that lay before us. Pockets of conversation would burst at Evan's passing by. Small crowds would congregate around people who'd done so little as recently spoken to the man. It was so strange to see him in this familiar space, but in such a foreign position. It was as though he was some rare and endangered zoo animal, and at any moment he might give birth to the first of his kind in captivity. I began actively lip reading and watching. Women finding reason to relocate, men declaring close personal connection to the host – it was like a school of fish that swims along under the fins of a shark, eating his leftovers, cleaning his gills. I began to contemplate what form of sea creature I would be in this scenario – a barnacle on a rock somewhere perhaps, or a sea urchin, or fire algae; something idly cantankerous.

A figure caught my eye well above the heads of the crowd as he appeared in the kitchen doorway. The man was in a green flight suit, short shorn blonde crew cut and broad shoulders. He had on a pair of Ray Bans that reflected the room around him and perfectly trimmed seventies 'stache. I finally understood the time honored tradition of women moistening at the sight of a man in uniform. He seemed oblivious to the collective focus on Evan, searching for something of his own design.

He stepped into the room as Meghan shifted beside me, murmuring intent for us to relocate to another room in hopes that Evan might be hunted down. The man in camouflage met my gaze and before I could dodge him, he beamed at me. My heart shot into the back of my throat.

Stellan plowed past the masses toward me, stopping for a moment as a man pointed at him and recognizing Stellan's costume as a character from Top Gun, cried, "Pull up, Goose!"

The drunk man in a ketchup bottle costume demanded a high five and a chest bump before he released Stellan to his slow path across the room. When Stellan reached me, my mouth had gone dry.

"You look fucking great, woman," he said, smiling

as I stood there like a slack jawed yokel, staring up at him.

"Holy shit, Ødegård. Not fucking bad," Meghan said. "I even like the stache! You look like a porn star."

Stellan gave an eyebrow wiggle. "How kind of you to notice."

I wanted to say something similar or perhaps something belligerent to her for commenting on the object of my unknown affection - anything really, but instead I just stood there staring.

Finally, he laughed and nudged me. "Is it that bad?"

I shook my head and attempted to speak. I just kept smiling.

When I finally found words, they came out in cracks and whistles. "You cut your mullet."

"I did!" He grabbed my hands, planting them squarely on the top of his head. He waited for me to tousle what was left of his hair. I ran my fingers across the smooth bristle of his blonde hair, then dragged them back upward, letting my fingers fight against the natural current of his hair. I let my fingers fall down the nape of his neck, and then slipped them upward again.

He shivered and stood at full height, smiling. "Do you like it?"

There was childlike expectation in his voice.

I could see the idiotic smile on my face reflected in his aviators. "I'm speechless."

He pumped his fist just slightly in the air. "You better be! Although, the fucking mustache is driving me nuts. Won't stay on for shit."

He began pressing the blond hairpiece into his upper lip, finally grumbling as it fell off in his hand.

He stuffed it into his pocket and took off his shades.

"You look so handsome," I said before the words registered in my brain.

He beamed, yet quickly raised an eyebrow and turned to Meghan. "How many has she had?"

Meghan gave him an exasperated look. "No clue."

"What do you mean no clue?"

"Well, I'm not babysitting her. She wants to get boozed up, she's welcome to it."

Stellan shook his head. "You're a terrible human being, you know that right?"

"Fuck you, Ødegård."

Stellan looks me in the eye as though there might be a 'drunk meter' he could read therein. "What've you been drinkin, lady. Have you seen Evan?"

Stellan turned to scan the crowd, his shoulder pressing against mine gently. My skin felt hyper sensitive to every inch of him. I knew the distance of his leg, his elbow, his cheek, his hip from mine. There was an urge to lean or shift my body in a way that would cause us to touch, but I fought it with purpose. That purpose was translated into turning to the bartender and demanding another drink.

"Hang on there," Stellan said and put a hand out to the bartender. "I'm going to take her for a breather."

The bartender nodded, and Stellan turned me toward the Evan-adoring hordes. It suddenly hit me that I feared walking in these cowboy boots. One foot slips in the boot, and I might tumble. I felt a firm grip around my shoulders. Stellan had hold of me. I leaned into him and looked up, his clean shaven jaw just inches from my nose as he excused himself through the crowd toward the kitchen. He smelled like laundry detergent and shaving cream and soap and home. I giggled up at him, and he smiled back, giving a chuckle as he shook his head at me. By the time we reached the kitchen, the crowd had shifted in an effort to be near Evan. It felt cool in the now empty space. Stellan held me by the shoulders, almost placing me against the kitchen counter before going to the doorway to scan the crowd.

He returned shaking his head. "Jesus, this is fucking intolerable."

"Evan has a lot of people's noses up his bum."

Stellan smiled. "How many did you have, babe?"

I shrugged. "I'm pretty swimmy."

"Yes, you are." He scanned me as he smiled. He pushed one of my nearly deflated bangs out of my face. "I love your hair."

"I love *your* hair."

He almost blushed. "You make a pretty foxy red head, I'm not going to lie."

My lips were on his, and my hands firmly settled on the back of his head before he could finish his thought. I felt his hands settle at my waist, and I stood on my toes to press my lips against his and keep them there. His lips were soft, the grain of his freshly shaved upper lip catching at mine.

Holy shit, I was kissing Stellan.

I can't believe I had the balls to kiss Stellan. I'm kissing Stellan!!

I curled my fingers into the chest pocket of his uniform to pull him closer and let my tongue query at his lips. His hands shifted to my arms, and their pressure grew stronger, gently pushing us apart.

I searched his face, as he pushed me away.

"I think I'd better take you home," he said, smiling. I felt a sharp pain in the center of my chest, as though something jagged and raw had been gouged up under my ribs and twisted there. He brushed my hair back again before telling me to stay put while he said a quick hello to Evan.

He slipped into the crowd and disappeared.

I stood there, like some tired old Jell-O mold, moments from losing shape.

What have I done? What did I just fucking do?

I stood waiting for him to return, aching for him to return, to feel him close to me again. Yet, I remembered only the pressure of his hands, the way he'd pushed me away. Suddenly, I couldn't stomach the thought of seeing his face again.

Before anyone could notice my passage, I snuck behind the crowd and out the sun room door. I turned away from the wonderland of lights and headed past the garage, out onto the dark road. I marched in my cowboy boots past the dozens of parked cars and wobbled down the slope of the hill. I was a mile from home, I'd walked this route a hundred times.

One more time wouldn't kill me, I thought, desperately trying to ignore the heat building at my pinky toe and my heel. I made it down the steepest part of the hill and was getting close to the bridge when my phone buzzed in my bra. My stomach lurched.

Did Stellan realize I was gone?

I pulled the phone out and pressed the button.

Schmuckface - **I'm thinking of you. Call me.**

Seeing the text, seeing his number appear on that tiny bright screen in the middle of that empty road - it chiseled a crack right through me. I set my jaw and began typing.

I ducking hate you!! I fucking hope you catch herpes and it burns a hole thru your dick, you ducking asshole! Go fuck yourself and due Alone!!

SEND!

I stared at the screen for a few seconds, rereading my fury in autocorrected form.

Ducking? Really? Well that just wouldn't do.

I meant fucking! You Asshole!

I pressed the send button with a guttural scream, my voice echoing across the swampy fields by the roadside. I took a few more painful steps. My feet were crumbling into an array of blisters and raw skin, and I wasn't in a state to show a stubbornly brave face. I leveraged the heel of one boot against the toe of the other and pulled.

That's when I nearly bit it. I was too woozy to keep my balance, and the boots were clunky under foot – and clearly hateful. I bent down and gave an angry pull at the boot, but a mix of sweat and old leather seemed to create a vacuum around my foot. I was ready to throw my phone into the river and set fire to my boots. Instead, I dropped to the grass on the side of the road, set my phone aside and double handed, grabbed the first boot, pulled my ankle up to practically my shoulder. I was flashing my crotch (which was almost entirely baby smooth, I'll have you know) to the world - a drunk Cyndi Lauper screaming at her boots on the side of the road.

I felt the skin of my heel tearing against the inside of the boot as I pulled it off. I sat a moment, letting my poor feet cool, dark patches of blood visible on my socks even in the dark. My ass felt cold in the wet grass. Fantastic.

I stuffed my phone back into my brassiere, took a boot in each hand, hoisted myself up, and continued my trek along the bridge.

The headlights appeared behind me as though the car had been following in the dark. I closed my eyes and fought to keep my gait steady. Don't look like a drunk floozy, Faye.

"Where you headed, Jensen?"

I turned to find Evan's ancient silver Jetta pulled up alongside me. I'd been ready to slew profanity at strangers, but seeing a familiar face at that moment startled me a moment. "Home," I said, finally.

He nodded. "Barefoot in the dark?"

I continued to walk without a word.

He rolled alongside me. "Get in the car, Faye."

"I'm fine."

"Get in the car."

"I'm fucking fine!"

"I will forcibly collect you," Evan said, and the familiarity of his tone rattled me somewhere deep.

"I will forcibly kick you in the dick!"

"Sounds fair," he said, and the car stopped. The driver's side door shot open.

I stopped dead where I stood and backed away from him, hollering, "I don't need you to take care of me right now."

The fact that I was near tears when I said it made it totally believable.

"Okay," he said, his hand out in front of him as though he was trying to calm a wild horse. "I'd still like your company."

I growled upward, as though some beast in the sky were challenging me. When that didn't relieve the frustration, I chucked one of my mother's boots at the pavement. It bounced across the road, almost falling into the water on the opposite side.

I watched helpless as Evan sauntered over and picked it up.

He turned to approach me, his red devil suit jacket gone now, leaving his flaming pants to blaze bright in the glow of his headlights. "You ready to get in the car."

I sighed heavily, my breath shaking as I did. Then, without another word, I crossed to the passenger door, and climbed in.

The car smelled familiar – a mix of paper, Febreze, and a sort of dank scent that made the air inside the car feel damp, like its windows were left open to the rain one too many times. The windows were open, and the crisp air tossed my rock solid hair about the top of my head. There was a hint of garage smell to the car, a side effect of being left at Dad's house when Evan ran off to pursue a better life.

Evan drove right past my street. I shifted to look at him, but I didn't say anything.

"Don't worry – just kidnapping you," he said.

I didn't argue. If there was anything one learned from being Evan's friend for any length of time, it was that arguing with him was futile. Unless you planned to physically assault him - he didn't like pain of any kind.

Despite knowing that he would squeal like a frightened cheerleader if I even hinted at nipple tweaking him or twisting his armpit hair, I just wasn't feeling it right then.

We reached St. Bernard's Cemetery, a space of ancient trees towering over old graves. Even in the dark, the leaves across the ground and overhead were vibrant orange as Evan pulled in. I watched the gravestones pass in the glare of his headlights, watching for untold shadows hovering between the graves as I'd always done when I was young and chasing ghosts. This wasn't Sleepy Hollow, where we disappeared to act foolish and be hooligans. This was St. Bernard's; this place was holy to me.

I held my breath as he rounded the familiar corners and pulled the car up to the grass. The headlights flashed across the first few graves before settling on their prize.

I stared bleary eyed at the stone face – *Terrence and Edith Jensen.*

I sat dumbfounded a moment.

Evan had an impeccable memory.

He shut off the car, leaving us in the dark. Despite sitting in a graveyard, I felt safer there than I could express. My phone buzzed in my brassiere, startling me.

I ignored it.

I stared out my open window, listening to the night time movements of animals and leaves rustling, coupled by the rare whoosh of a passing car on Bedford Road. I could have nestled into that corner of the world and faded away if Evan hadn't been there. He ran his fingers up the nape of my neck and gave me a light head scratch. Somehow, despite a decade of not speaking, of not taking nightly trips to this graveyard when I was losing my mind after Stellan left for school – somehow we were still there, still idiot teenagers with fucked up fathers who escaped to graveyards for solace. Sometimes I wondered, between night time graveyard habits or streaks of rabid sexual promiscuity and drug abuse, which one was more disconcerting to a parent. I sat there with Evan rubbing my neck.

"Feel like talking, Cyndi?"

I turned to him and shook my head. I was almost certain I had raccoon eyes, but I didn't care. It was Evan. He let me go back to my window while he fumbled with something in the glove compartment. A moment later, the Flashdance theme was softly playing through the speakers. I planted my palm to my face and laughed quietly.

When I was able to look at him, he was staring at me, bobbing his dark head softly with pursed lips and a look of overwhelming coolness as he jammed along with the stereo.

I shook my head. "Really?"

His eyebrows shot up. "What? I thought this was your theme song!"

I laughed and again shook my head, this time with slow deliberation. "You know, the true shame of this moment is the fact that you had this song at the ready."

"It's true. You can't imagine the crap I have on here because of you."

"What? How is this because of me?"

"Oh, come on. I've got a Faye Playlist on this fucking thing from all the crap you made me listen to. And on repeat if I recall."

I sighed. "It wasn't crap."

He stared at me until I couldn't help but laugh.

"Ok, it wasn't all crap, but you're still the one with it on your phone."

"Blame nostalgia. I was actually going for Time After Time – you know, get some Cyndi going in here - but I couldn't resist."

I looked at Evan for the first time that night – truly looked at him – and saw the same boy I'd spent years of my life with. He'd grown into his looks, the dark hair and eyes, the goofy grin – they'd all combined with a hint of stubble and mature eyes to create a strange Marlboro Man effect, despite his bright red pants. He gave me a queried look, and I smiled.

Evan always carried a 'mark,' as I'd called it – a sadness to his eyes that drove you to want to collect him under your wing and protect him, shield him from something, though you weren't sure what. It was that sadness, that heaviness that seemed faded now.

Evan and I were friends for two years before I discovered the cause of that sadness; the night he showed up on my porch, shirtless and bleeding because his Dad had taken the buckle end of a belt to him for putting a dent in the very car we were sitting in.

I wondered if that kind of mark ever truly faded, or if we carried them like freckles or green eyes. I wondered if he could see mine, if I did indeed have one too.

I was sure I did. How could I not?

"You look good, Evan."

He smiled. "Are you hitting on me?"

I rolled my eyes. "How did I know I would regret saying that?"

"I'm kidding. Thank you," he said and nudged my arm. "I could say the same about you."

I found myself glaring at him. The notion of a male thinking I looked 'good' almost irritated me. I don't like to be patronized. "I highly fucking doubt that."

He furrowed his brow a moment, and I felt a

reprimand coming. Instead his face softened. "It's true. The side Mohawk really works for you."

I laughed, but I felt coddled. Evan had an uncanny ability to say exactly what he was thinking. It'd gotten him in trouble many times. Yet, there in that car, he hadn't said it – whatever it was.

"You have no idea what lengths I went to this afternoon to perfect this."

I shifted in my seat remembering the ordeal of that afternoon. *No, really Evan. You have no idea.*

He paused. "I'm glad you came."

I nodded and leaned my head against the car door, letting the cool air chill my skin. My phone buzzed again, and I retrieved it. There were two people I could think of that might be texting me at that moment. I didn't want to talk to either of them.

I set the phone down on the car seat and continued to stare outside. A moment later, it buzzed again. I didn't care.

"You alright, Jensen?"

It was so weighted, the car felt as though it might collapse in its gravity. He wasn't asking if I was comfortable or cold or in need of sustenance – he was asking far more, and he knew the answer. I shook my head and swallowed hard.

"Is it that douche bag?" He asked.

I laughed sadly.

I bumped my temple against the car frame, as though a jolt of pain might settle this rising misery I felt. "No."

"Ok then," he said. "So what's up?"

I frowned. "I don't even know anymore."

Lie. Yes I did.

He nudged me. "Talk to me."

I shook my head, feeling that hot tension in my throat that betrayed just how close I was to crying. I didn't want him to hear that in my voice. Though honestly, how could he not?

"You know, I know people. I could arrange for an accident of some kind, perhaps with heavy machinery -"

I chuckled. Though it was clear he was kidding, I imagined it wasn't too far off from the truth.

"I prefer karma. It'll be more subtle, I think."

"I don't. I'm all for bloodshed."

I couldn't help but smirk. "Well, I appreciate your love of gore in my time of need, but I don't think it would help at this point."

"Then talk to me. What the hell? All the *Faye* I get these days is through Stellan. You have me here, fucking utilize me."

"Utilize you? How do you want me -"

"Fucking vent. Scream. Punch me, I don't give a fuck. Whatever."

I shifted in my seat. There was a pressure, like air from a punctured tire. I felt close to words, but despite his requests, it felt wrong to subject him to them. "What do you mean you get your *Faye* through Stellan?"

"That's the only way I know what goes on with you."

"He tells you about me?"

He scoffed. "Of course he does. How do you think I knew about the douche bag?"

I'd been too upset to even notice. "You didn't think to ask me yourself?"

"I don't have your number."

I glared at him. "You know people with heavy

machinery and a capacity for murder, but you couldn't find my number? What is the world coming to?"

He paused. "Touché."

"Damn straight, touché."

He forced a smile. "I guess I was afraid you'd…"

"I'd what?"

He took a deep breath and locked his fingers behind his head, leaning back into the seat. When he blew out, it was through pursed lips. "You know, I come back to town more often than anyone knows. Few times a month at least."

I turned at this. Even with our mutual friend, this was news to me. "I thought you were on the West Coast."

"I am for the most part, but I come home. Only person who I really talk to around here is Stell - or the dukes, obviously." I nodded. The Dukes was what he called his parents, in case you wondered. I waited for him to continue. "Do you know what happens when I tell anyone other than Dad or Stellan that I'm coming?"

"No," I said, but I could guess.

"Eighty voice mails, sometimes more - old MIT buddies, people from high school. I fucking heard from Ms. Jameson one time, it was surreal."

Ms. Jameson was our high school Geometry teacher. I watched him drum his fingers on the steering wheel as he searched for words.

"They all wanted to get together; they were so happy for me, proud of me. I said yes, planned parties. A couple times I was truly excited to see a few of them, excited to catch up."

"Yeah?"

"Do you know what they all wanted to talk about?"

I didn't speak.

"Money. 'Oh Ev, let me tell you about this exciting business venture I'm cookin up' – 'Lambert, you crazy son of a bitch, I need a loan.' Every single one of them. Even Ms. Jameson needed money – did you know she had breast cancer?"

I gasped. "She did?"

"It's ok. They got it, she's fine. Almost lost her house trying to pay the bills, but she's fine."

I cringed. Calling what I felt at that moment 'humility' would be an understatement. "Did you -"

"Pay her bills? It's Ms. Jameson. Of course I fucking did."

I reached across the seat of the car and squeezed his hand. He hadn't changed. Somehow, the years since I last saw him, I'd assumed he was different – that money and success had changed him. Yet I sat next to the same punk kid who ran naked through Sleepy Hollow screaming 'Attica' to give Stellan and I a chance to run for it.

"She's the only one though. I was pretty free with the cash at first, but after a while it got – well, let's say I grew fucking tired of it. Starting telling people all my money is tied up in business ventures or real estate."

"Is that true?" I was honestly curious. Here I'd envisioned him swimming in a pool of gold coins like McDuck. "Now I don't tell anyone I'm coming. I move like I'm on reconnaissance, for fuck's sake."

"I'm sorry."

"Psh, don't be sorry. I haven't told you the best part."

"Oh. Ok."

"There are just a couple people in the world I

would literally lay down my life for, as you know. Hire mercenaries, purchase third world countries – I'd do anything for them. Well, I found out this year that one of the elite few had her house foreclosed on and didn't call me."

I opened my mouth, but I didn't speak.

"I know we haven't kept in touch - I'm to blame for that, I realize, but you always have access to me. I didn't magically turn into a raging douche bag because I made some money -"

"I didn't think -"

"- and I know you. You are one of only two, maybe three people in the world who, if you asked me right now, I'd write you a check - not even think twice."

He stopped and seemed to search my face. "But you never would, would you?"

I looked at my hands, inspecting the lines at each knuckle as though the act might make me invisible. I had thought of him a couple times as my world was falling apart – when I needed to come up with four months mortgage payment because they were foreclosing and wouldn't take anything less. I'd thought about how little that amount would be to Evan, thought about the many nights he'd crashed on my couch, or we'd slept in my station wagon because he couldn't bring himself to go home.

I still never asked Stellan for his number.

He smiled. "Yeah. Douche bag doesn't know what he had."

I scoffed. Evan seemed oblivious to the fact that men were practically repelled by me. I tried to brush the thought of Stellan - the pressure of his hands on my shoulders, pushing me away – aside. It wasn't working.

I might have wallowed in my misery another moment, but a strange chant of aggressive rap music was coming from Evan's trousers. He shifted quickly and pulled out his cell phone. He made a face at me and answered it.

"What's up, Brutha?"

Though I couldn't make out words on the other end of the line, I recognized the voice. It was Stellan. He was upset.

"She's fine. I got her."

Stellan grew louder on the other line. I could make out a couple swears, but no actual sentence structure. This was most likely because he'd erupted in Swedish.

"You want to talk to her?"

I flailed my arms around the car in the universal sign of *I'll-fucking-stab-you-if-you-hand-me-the-phone*. Evan made a face at me and found his lie.

"I actually just dropped her off at the house. She's already inside… Yeah, she seemed alright… Would you like me to go stick my head any further up her ass?"

It was my turn to make a face.

"Dude, she's fine. Probably passed out the second she got in the door… Yeah, I can tell. Don't worry about it, I'll catch ya tomorrow. Peace."

Evan set his phone down and raised an eyebrow at me. I did my best not to squirm in his gaze. Then, instead of speaking or demanding details, he snatched my phone up from the seat between us and began examining. He made a tsking sound and turned the phone to face me.

"No wonder," he said and waited for me to look at the screen.

Stellan had tried several times to get me – there

were six texts and a dozen missed calls from Stellan over the course of the half hour that I'd been gone.

Stellan -**Where'd you run off to? I'm back in the kitchen.**

Responsible Stellan - **Faye, where are you?**

Scolding Stellan - **Ignore me after you tell me you're alright.**

Irritated Stellan - **Hello??? I've looked fucking everywhere.**

Guilt trip Stellan - **If you're trying to scare the shit out of me, you've succeeded.**

Enraged Stellan - **PICK UP THE FUCKING PHONE!**

I sighed. Despite my anger at his rejection, I still felt guilty at the thought of making him worry.

No wait, you know what? Fuck him.

"He was worried someone roofied you, and you were being taken advantage of."

Woops. Strike those texts. I'd misread terror as rage.

Ok, maybe I did feel guilty.

"Of course he was," I muttered to myself.

My words betrayed more venom than I'd intended. Evan furrowed his brow and inspected me over the bridge of his nose. "Now what's going on with you two?"

I shook my head. "Nothing. I just did something stupid."

"What's new?"

I smacked him in the arm with more force than was necessary. He flinched. How easily I forget his aversion to pain.

"He sounded seriously fucking terrified. I haven't heard that kid lose his shit in – in a while."

Evan stopped, and I knew exactly what he was thinking.

The tone was rare, I'd only ever heard it once – saved for moments of sheer desperation or fear. The day I heard it, he was calling me from Emerson Hospital, and his Dad was in an operating room with his chest wide open.

Lennart hadn't been feeling well that morning and called in to the office to let them know he'd be staying home, something he never did. Half way through the morning, his work ethic kicked in, and he changed his mind, driving into work. Somewhere along Route 2, Lennart felt unwell, pulled over onto the side of the two lane highway and proceeded to have a massive coronary. No one knows how long he was there before someone stopped. Back before the age of every ten year old having a cell phone, back before help was a button away - had he been any further from the hospital, he might not have made it.

When Stellan called me that afternoon, they still weren't sure he was going to.

My eyes grew heavy remembering it – even moreso to think he cared enough about me to have sounded even close to that concerned now.

There was a knot in my stomach that could only be described as all-encompassing guilt being tied up and beaten by a mildly inebriated sense of justice.

"You should call him when you get home."

I didn't respond. Even if Evan was right, I knew I wouldn't be doing any such thing. Not tonight – and though I hated to admit it, probably not for a while after that.

Jesus Faye, what have you done?

My phone buzzed to life again on the seat between

us, and Evan snatched it up before I could. I didn't mind. I was content to have a mediator between myself and the rest of the world.

"Is he yelling at me?" I asked, bracing.

Evan stared at my phone a minute, glancing at me. "You've received a text from a 'Festering Asshole.'"

Ah, yes. The pseudonym I'd programmed into my phone for Cole a few weeks earlier. I felt an almost burning tension between my breasts.

Oh god, what had I texted Cole? I want your dick to fall off, something like that. This was why I hated saying just what I thought. I hated being on the receiving end of someone else's fighting words. They turned me into someone I'm not proud of.

I held my hand out for the phone. Evan faltered as he handed it to me.

Cockgobbling hobbit - **I deserve that. I know I do. I'm so sorry.**

I squeezed my phone so tightly in my fist, the plastic creaked. Evan gently pulled my fingers open to take the phone from me.

"I take it Festering Asshole is, in fact, douche bag."

I rocked my jaw, my molars grinding against one another as I imagined my fist colliding with the side of Cole's handsome face – imagined myself walking in on him fucking that other girl, his bare ass gyrating in the air, grabbing him by a fistful of hair and dragging him out of the bed to slam my boot heel into his groin. I'd never humored violent thoughts like this, but right now I wanted someone to hurt even half as much as me.

I was too angry to speak. I simply nodded. I didn't bother contemplating how the conversations between Evan and Stellan must have gone for Evan to know of 'Festering Asshole.'

Evan set the phone down on the seat again and rubbed the back of his hand on my arm. I was tempted to swat him away, but I didn't.

The anguished words spilled out before I knew I'd spoken. "Why doesn't anyone want me?"

I immediately turned my face toward the graves outside, refusing to let Evan see more of what must be playing across my face. The tears had pushed through, just a few, and I was now setting my jaw against allowing any more.

Why did you say that? What is wrong with you? Evan doesn't need to hear that! You're pathetic! Shut up, shut up!

Evan shifted angrily in the seat beside me, forcefully shutting down the car and tossing the keys on the seat between us as he faced me. "Are you fucking kidding me?"

I stared at the graves.

He reached into the back of the car and pulled out his jacket, then wrapped the bright red thing around my shoulders. I pulled it tight around me, only then noticing I'd sprouted goosebumps. We were left in complete silence, save for the soft shuffle of leaves overhead in an almost constant flutter and the sound of the engine clanking as it cooled down.

I didn't speak. I pressed my hand to my cheek, as though to hide myself from him. I was so embarrassed. Ten years we'd seen each other maybe twice, and here I was in his car, pouring out more of myself than I'd let even Meghan or Jackie see.

Why did this have to happen now? Why was I loosing the lonely corners of my mind now?

I tried to wipe a tear as inconspicuously as possible.

"Jensen. Just because some fucking asshole – some

Festering Asshole -" He stopped and shook his head, running his hand over his stubbled chin. He was riled up. I couldn't understand why I'd bothered him so much. "He didn't pull a dick move because of you. He's just a dick. Pure and simple. Guy will never find another girl to come close to you -"

I tried to laugh at that, but instead I burbled – a strange mix of snotty chuckle and near sob. Again I pressed my hand to my face. I was embarrassing myself with each passing moment. "I think I need to go home, please?"

He slumped back into his seat again. "Don't let this guy do that to you."

I sat there, my lips curling into themselves as I replayed the moment Stellan pushed me away again and again. If only he knew just how sure I was about this fact – no one wanted me. No one.

But more importantly, Stellan didn't want me.

Evan scratched his head and chuckled. "You have no idea – you know you're the girl who ruined me for other women, right?"

I scowled at him. There'd never been anything more than plutonic love between us. Furiously loyal love, but plutonic nonetheless.

His eyebrows shot up in exasperation. "It's true. I can't find another woman like you to save my fucking life."

I fought past the wet in my throat to speak. "Why would you want to? You could have any woman. That party was practically Vagina Town -" He made a face, but I continued. "Weren't you on some magazine cover as Most Eligible what-fucking-ever?"

He smiled. "You saw that did ya? Fantastic. Hopefully other women like you did too."

"Shut up," I said and tapped him.

"I'm serious woman. Christ, I keep going out with these girls – they're beautiful. I mean gorgeous - from Denmark or Brazil, gorgeous women. They come into my life with a hair flip and a great ass, I fall madly for them, then a few months later they're screaming at me because I'd rather play Call of Duty with Stell than take a trip to Monaco on some fucking yacht. Then boom; they're leaving, and I'm glad to see them go."

"Sounds like you might want to try a different dating pool."

"No shit, right?"

I wiped my face. The smile in his voice was drawing me out. It always did.

He took a deep breath. "Seriously, if I didn't know Stellan would stab me for it, I'd ask you to marry me right now."

I shook my head. "I doubt Stellan would protest."

Evan glared at me, speaking before I could question why. "You're the pipe dream, woman. You're the real deal."

"You've got me mixed up with someone else, guy."

He grabbed at the steering wheel like it was on fire. "Are you kidding me? For fuck's sake, woman. You're perfect."

My mouth fell open at the nonsense of his words. "Yeah, definitely mixed up with -"

"Dude, let's be real. Stellan and I were not cool kids. Biggest fucking tool bags ever. I mean, what did we do with our fucking time? Play video games, blow shit up, tag up the back of Brigham's, hack sites we didn't like, hang out in the woods."

"Yeah, pretty much."

"God, how many days did you spend just watching

us play games for fucking hours?"

I laughed. "Hey, I played."

"Fuck yeah you did."

I searched for a joke to lighten the tone. "I often wonder what I might have done with my life if I'd realized there was more to life than sniping your faces off in *Star Wars: Battlefront.*"

He smiled, but continued through his laughter. "You never complained, or picked on us or left us. You let us be jackasses and kept us company. You laughed at our jokes, made us laugh. Fuck, you showed us up half the time, and when you didn't feel like it, you'd go draw some magnificent thing that I could never in my lifetime come up with, and I'd question the worth of my whole existence."

I shook my head, but he wasn't done.

"You remember the days you'd had enough. You would stand in front of the television and say, 'Let's get out of the house, before I set fire to it.' And we did."

"Yeah, and then we'd end up in a cemetery," I said, gesturing to our location.

He steamrolled right over my joke. "Or Denny's, or driving around. It doesn't fucking matter, what matters is you accepted us. You didn't try to change us. Now, because of you, I have this insane notion that there are other women out there who will love me for exactly who I am - that won't try to change me."

I scoffed. "There are gamer girls all over the world."

"Fuck that! I don't want a gamer girl. I want a woman who games. I want a woman who has her own interests – her own passions. I don't want someone who's only positive is that she's going to fight me for the Xbox, for fuck's sake."

"That's a little -"

"Spoiled? Yeah, your fault."

I smiled and sniffled. "You're full of shit."

He growled softly, smiling. "Let's not fight it any more, Jensen! Marry me! We just won't tell the Swede."

I laughed again. "Nevah!"

He clasped his hand over his heart in feigned despair. "How can you say no?"

"Because I've seen you naked."

Evan burst out laughing with such power, it shook the roof of the car. "Hey, it isn't that bad! Actually, I've heard from several gold-digging models that it's quite nice, in fact!"

"Oh, it's lovely Evan. It's just the fact that I saw it while you were tripping balls, chasing my neighbor's cat and flying ass over tea kettle into my grandmother's lilac bushes. It just doesn't inspire lust, I'm sorry."

He threw up his hands, laughing. "God damn it! I just can't win."

The image of his bare ass in that bush, lit by my back porch light, came blaring back to mind, and I laughed as though I'd just witnessed it.

I remembered Stellan's response when he joined me on the porch – "Ah, my eyes! I can't unsee that, you Dick!"

Evan shot me that show stopping smile of his. He reached over and grabbed me by the neck to pull me over to him. He hugged me and kissed my ear. "I've missed the shit out of you."

I slipped my arms around him and hugged him

back. The comfort was intense. We sat for a few minutes like that. When we separated he threatened to finance a think tank whose sole purpose was to invent a means to wipe my memory so he could propose again. Then he started the car and drove me home.

He parked on my street, took my phone and texted himself from it.

He gave an evil laugh. "Now you can't hide from me."

I took the phone and thanked him for the ride. He grumbled at the thought of returning to his own party as he put the car into drive.

He leaned toward the passenger window and looked up at me. "Text Stellan, you. Don't go to bed til you do."

I drifted up my front steps, watching his car pull away. I still had his jacket draped over my shoulders.

My head was heavy and just about cried out as I draped his jacket over the chair in the corner of my room and slumped onto my bed. I was hardly horizontal when my phone buzzed.

It was Evan. **Sleep well, Cyndi.**

And thanks to alcohol, I did – with my bangs still styled like a hawk's wing over my head.

CHAPTER EIGHT

I didn't just *not* text Stellan that night, I also didn't respond to his texts all the next day.

At noon - **You feeling better?**

At four – **You around?**

At nine that evening – **How long we planning the silent treatment, here?**

Between those texts, I heard from:

Evan – **You stole the shirt off my back, you Minx**.

Jackie – **How was the shindig last night? Did you have fun?**

And finally Meghan. Meghan didn't text though. No, she couldn't have the courtesy to wait and call me after ten in the morning to rip my head off for abandoning her the night before.

"You were supposed to line me up for some hot Evan Lambert action. You whore. I can't believe you left me there."

I explained to the best of my ability without ever mentioning the catastrophe with Stellan or the hour I spent alone in a car with her man of choice. Still, she seemed to soften when I explained I'd had too many and needed to be taken home. She and I were still on the phone when the first text from Stellan came through. I used the phone call as an excuse to not answer. By the third text that day, I had no excuses.

Well, what was I supposed to do? Respond like nothing happened? I just wanted to forget – forget that I'd made a fool of myself, forget that I let myself behave that way, forget that despite all of that, the most damning part was that he hadn't reciprocated. Discussing with Stellan just why he didn't want my tongue in his mouth was the last thing I wanted – today or any other day for that matter.

I fondled my cell that night, chanting and re-chanting in my mind how to talk to him. "Man, remind me never to drink again," or "the rumors were true, I'm the best kisser in town." None of those felt cavalier enough. No matter what I said, my actions had done the talking, and there was no taking it back. I wrote and deleted the same words in various order six or seven times, before I finally just set the phone beside my bed and went to sleep.

I woke to the doorbell and glanced at the clock. It was noon the next day.

I greeted Jackie at the door, my hair and clothes rumpled to an equal degree. She simply set her purse down by the door and hugged me.

Jackie was light itself. The weather could lighten her step in an instant, and from her entrance, I prepared for a truly lovely day outside. She was sunshine, even when she wasn't feeling like sunshine, inside. I was too bedraggled to search her for cracks today. I was one big crack myself.

"Do you want to get dressed?" She asked in an almost pleading tone.

"Why? You weren't planning to spend the day with a wino?"

I turned to the staircase as she assured me that she'd meant no harm. I wouldn't be showering or shampooing the rat's nest of a hairstyle I was sporting that morning, but at least I could clip it into submission.

When I returned to find Jackie on the living room couch reading one of my mother's magazines, I probably didn't look any better. I wore ratty old jeans with tears in the knees that had come from actual wear rather than fashion, and my ancient, yellow Mickey Mouse t-shirt had seen better days. Still, it was well fitted under my bust, so I'd never had the heart to part with it.

I hoped I wore it better now than I did at thirteen when my mother first bought it for me.

"Shoes?" Jackie said.

I raised an eyebrow at her tone. It wasn't stern or pushy in any way, but almost plaintive. I glanced at her, doing my best to read her body language without diving into a line of conversation I might not be mentally capable of upholding. She was agitated – or perhaps energized is a better word.

I pointed to the beat up flip flops by the door and shuffled over. Jackie snatched up her purse and hovered a few feet behind me as I fought to balance and be melancholy at the same time.

No easy feat, that.

"Do you mind walking?" Jackie asked as we reached the curb outside my house.

I looked at her. "Where are we going?"

She shrugged. "I thought we might have lunch downtown. Maybe get something at Sally Ann's or the Boathouse?"

I agreed, knowing full well I had no right to have an opinion given that my jeans' pockets were empty. "Whatever you want."

She froze and watched my face. "Do you not want

to? We can do something else."

"No, no. I'd love to take a walk downtown."

"Oh good. I was thinking we could maybe split a sandwich, then get cannolis over at the Boathouse."

I hummed my approval. Despite knowing full well the best Cannolis were at Mike's in the North End, the Boathouse did their best. Their best cost approximately eight dollars, but what do you expect from downtown Concord?

Jackie seemed to be at a constant clip, just a half step or two ahead of me. I wasn't deliberately meandering, but still, there was a spring to her step I couldn't match. And to be completely honest, as we hit the rotary at Monument Square, the sudden revelation that I was in line of sight from Stell's house gave me pause. I did my best not to stare at it like a David Letterman fanatic.

And just like that, Jackie stopped. "What's going on in your brain right now?"

"What? Nothing."

How does she fucking do that?

"Are you sure? Do you want to go visit Stellan?"

"No, no! I'm fine. Just a little dazed is all."

She stared at me. "What's wrong with you and Stellan?"

God fucking damn it, Jackie. "Nothing. We'll be fine." I hope.

"You *will* be fine? As in, you're not quite fine right now?"

I deliberately continued across the street. She followed, shifting her purse as she matched my pace.

I didn't say anything as we passed the Christian Reading Room and the Hardware Store, but when I glanced up to find her still watching me for a response, I sighed. "We're not talking right now."

If I was hoping for a day spent not talking about it, this wasn't the appropriate way to get it. Jackie wouldn't press. She would never press, but when she searched your face with her sympathetic smile, you couldn't help but share. And, oh boy, did I share.

I practically unleashed. I told her about the Halloween party, about Stellan - and how dare he show up with his hair cut. I told her about the kiss, or the face licking, more aptly, and the resulting push. I managed to get it all out in a huff of exasperation rather than a font of emotion. Crying on Main Street might result in talk. You don't live in Downtown Concord for a good amount of your life and not get to know people.

"You kissed him? And he pushed you away?"

I nodded rather than repeat it out loud. It was hard enough to say it once.

"Why did he push you away?"

I laughed. Sometimes Jackie betrayed a sweeter nature than she wanted the world to believe. "I assume because he wasn't as keen on making out with me as I'd hoped."

"I can't believe you just went for it. I'm so proud."

I stared at her. "Proud? Are you kidding?"

"Yes, I'm proud! You'd been thinking about him for a while. I worried you'd never say anything."

My shoulders slumped. "I wish I'd kept it to myself."

We reached Sally Ann's, and the bell jangled over her head as she entered. I followed her inside, silent. A few minutes later we were walking across the street with a small paper bag and two boxed waters. Jackie decided we should sit amongst the old crumbling gravestones of the South Burying Ground and eat our Turkey Sandwich.

The sandwich was perfect, but I couldn't eat it. My stomach was in knots.

"I still don't understand why he would push you away," she said, finally.

The innocence of her tone was almost grating. Why couldn't she see what I saw? That I was undesirable! He didn't want me! I was sure it was because as far as he was concerned, his sister had tried to make out with him. "He didn't shove me or anything."

"That seems so forward, even for you."

I shrugged. "Well, I did have somewhere around seven rum and cokes beforehand. Nothing like liquid courage."

When she didn't respond, I glanced up to find her watching me.

The corners of her mouth drooped a second, then returned to a smile. "Explains why he pushed you away."

She hopped up, and I faltered a moment.

Finally, I hurried to follow her. "Yeah, he didn't want to make out with me."

We threw our trash away and headed toward the Boathouse. I nearly broke a nail when I pulled on the door handle. It didn't budge.

Jackie's eyes brightened. "I heard a rumor about this."

Before I could ask for explanation, she pointed to a sign, declaring her meaning.

Thank you for Twenty Five great years! – The Boathouse Bakery

I stared, agape. "Are you kidding me? This place has been open since I was little."

"From what I hear, the owners had to choose between maintaining this or their second house."

I frowned. "I'm almost heartbroken. I mean, yeah, their prices were astronomical, but – I mean my Grandmother used to bring me here."

Jackie pouted. "Hopefully it won't stay closed forever?"

I shrugged. "I wonder if Stellan -"

And I stopped. My immediate thought was to tell Stellan, or ask if he knew – share my righteous disappointment and ecstasy at his auburn coffee shrew being out of a job. Then I remembered.

We made our way back toward my house and I vowed that I would not glance toward his house, hoping he might walk outside at just that moment, see me, and come running across the common, arms out, declaring his undying love.

"So when do you think you'll speak to him about it?"

I was almost surprised to hear her return to the subject of Stellan. Almost.

"Never? I was actually considering joining the Peace Corps."

She laughed. "You have to talk to him, Faye."

"Why? Can't I just pretend it never happened? I'd rather not have that conversation." I dropped my voice, doing my best Stellan impression. "'Yeah, thanks Faye, but I'm all set.'"

"You really think that's what he'll say?"

I almost coughed on my ice cream. "What else would he say? He pushed me away."

She stopped, her brow furrowed. "I won't push, you know - but just think about it. Would he be Stellan if he hadn't pushed you away? He thought you were hammered."

"So?"

"So, Stellan doesn't strike me as the kind of guy who would, you know, take advantage."

I stared into my Mint Chocolate Chip ice cream. "Right. What guy doesn't want action when it's offered?"

"If she's drunk? Good ones."

I scowled. I wasn't ready to hear logic, because this brand of logic might give me hope. I couldn't go through having it dashed again. "Fuck that noise."

"Seriously, don't just take it as 'he doesn't like you.' You need to have a conversation. Otherwise, you'll never know, you know?"

Damn it, Jackie. Stop making sense.

We walked home talking about the loss of the Boathouse, the desperate need we both now felt for Cannolis, Jackie's sudden decision to learn to make them herself, and how much we missed college era visits to Mike's in the North End of Boston.

The one thing we didn't mention again was Stellan. Despite not speaking of him, he never left my mind.

By ten that evening I was back in bed, my hair now washed, thankfully, and ready to forget by way of dreams. I'd curled up with my bedside lamp on, reading a recent Charlaine Harris novel about vampires and such when my phone started vibrating again.

To be honest, I was expecting another frustrated text from Stellan, but it wasn't a text.

Festering Asshole Calling...

I felt every muscle from my throat to my groin tighten and shoot up into my mouth. *What do I do? Do*

I answer? What do I say? Hello, Festering Asshole? Oh God, what do I do?

"Hello?"

"Oh wow…you answered."

His voice was as foreign and familiar as the night sky. I swallowed. "I did."

Then I waited.

There was silence on the other end of the phone. I waited for a moment or two, listening to him breathe. It was rhythmic, almost sharp. I let my mouth fall open as though to speak, but a sudden realization caught the words in my throat.

"Cole?"

He was crying. Softly, as though I were listening to him in another room, but certain. Despite everything, the sound made me sad.

God damn it, how dare you call me crying? You've no right. No fucking right!

I didn't say those things. I waited.

Finally, he croaked at me. "I miss you so much."

I covered my eyes as my whole face scrunched up. A flood of accusations, angry questions, even primal screaming all came rushing to the fore.

You coward! You bastard! You're not Stellan! You're not the voice I wanted to hear! Fuck you for that! Fuck you for everything!

These thoughts clamored and fought to be first, tearing at one another like a trampling crowd in this unexpected moment of power. Yet, as they fought, a calmer tone passed them and slipped out.

"I don't know what to say."

His breathing shook again. "What do I have to do? I'll do fucking anything!"

I was startled by the intensity of his tone. "For

what?"

"Can I see you? Would you let me see you?"

I paused. "I don't know if that's -"

He gave a hoarse chuckle. "I drive by your road, you know. More than I want to admit. I went by your house last night, but you weren't there."

I felt my insides twist. What would I have done if I'd come home to find him here? Would I disintegrate into the soil under my mother's petunias, or burst into fiery wrath like some supernova of bitter fury?

I imagined the sight of him, catching a glimpse of him from around a corner, or driving down the road as I reeled from the sensation of having been rejected by Stellan. I'd had the thought in a thousand weak moments over the past few months – of what it would be like to stumble across each other's path, Cole and I. Yet he'd never appeared. Then Stellan wiped away the want of his appearance.

Suddenly, the want of someone's presence, unsatisfied and aching, was leaving me weakened. I knew it, but I didn't hang up.

I started, unsure what I wanted to say, "I'm not -"

"I shouldn't have said that. I'm sorry, I understand if you don't want to ever see me again. I just – I just don't know what to do. I feel like – I just feel like there's too much to say on the phone, you know?"

I searched for words. Finally, one of the brawling thoughts broke free from the group. "Why didn't you call before now?"

Like before I'd started pining for my best friend and had my heart shattered in an instant by a broken kiss.

"I couldn't. I wanted to. Every day I wanted to. I was just so scared you'd tell me to go fuck myself. I was afraid - it would kill me. Then last night -"

His voice cracked again, and he coughed to stifle it. Hearing him in tears or in constant threat of them was supposed to be satisfying, damn it! Instead, it was almost painful.

I thought about the words I'd wished I'd found when I picked up my phone.

Repentant Stellan - **Faye, I love you!**

Love-struck Stellan - **Faye, marry me.**

Lusty, Hard-bodied Stellan - **Faye, I was wrong, I DO want you to eat my face.**

Instead I found myself cornered by the past, wanting to revolt against it, but unable to deny the unfortunate comfort it brought me.

Of Stellan didn't want me, it was nice to know someone did.

Even he sucked donkey balls.

He paused. "Are you free?"

I stood stock still a moment, my feet sinking through the floorboards. "Yes."

***

I plopped down on the stool by the bar, keeping my eyes on the mirror behind the bar at Paparazzi's. My knit hat was slouched back on my head and I'd barely gotten dressed; I was clad in an AC/DC t-shirt and blue jeans.

Despite agreeing to meet, the notion of actually seeing him settled in my stomach like over whipped cream. I'd ordered a drink to steady myself, but by the time I saw his reflection coming in, I hadn't been able to force down a single sip.

He looked as bad as I felt. Well, let's be honest, I

probably looked just as bad, but whatever, I'm talking about him.

He was dressed in his work clothes – the black button down and black pants. His hair was tousled, clearly slept on with product still in it, but his eyes looked like they hadn't seen sleep in days. I didn't move. I wanted to be invisible.

He met my gaze in the mirror, walked up behind me, and waited. He ran his fingers over my shoulder. I shuddered.

After he received no response, he settled onto the bar stool next to me and asked for a drink. It came before either of us said a word.

"You look beautiful," he finally said.

"You trying to sell me something?"

His mouth fell open. "I think you always look beautiful."

I spun on him, turning my full body to face him. "What do you want?"

He didn't speak.

I clenched my fists.

"Faye," he said putting his hand on my knee. I swatted him away, but he continued. "I fucked up. I fucked up so bad. I think about you every day. I miss your face… I miss your laugh."

I turned back to my drink. "I'm sure clit-piercing has a great laugh."

"She was a mistake. I was stupid, and I didn't know what I was fucking doing."

I turned my gaze toward the highest shelf of drinks behind the bar. So she was real. She wasn't just a picture.

Someone kill me, I thought.

"I've heard that infidelity is a symptom of a dying

relationship."

"I didn't even give us a chance to find out. You were spending the night so often, I guess I just started to get scared -"

"I was spending the night too often? Are you fucking kidding me? Mister I-don't-want-you-to-slow-me-down-in-the-morning cocksucker!"

A middle aged man and his young date glanced at us from the other end of the bar. I lifted my glass to them with a shit eating grin.

"I was scared! You lost your place, and you were going to need somewhere to stay, and I knew that it should be with me, and I just freaked out. I didn't think I was ready to move in together."

I thought of the former fantasies I'd managed to collect when we were together, of making him coffee when he was in the shower, or perhaps sneaking in to join him, or the fantasies of us making love before the alarm clock went off despite him pushing me away more than half the time when I wanted him.

I swigged hard on my white Russian. "Well, fucking another girl solved that problem for you, didn't it?"

"I didn't fuck her. Not until after we broke up."

I stopped, staring at him for a long moment. "So what? Just some innocent twat shots?"

"It was texts. That's all. I know that's enough, but -"

"And we never technically broke up, Cole. I sent you that picture and you fucked right off. You didn't even have the courtesy to properly end it."

He pressed his knuckles to his nose and closed his eyes. He hadn't touched his drink. I decided to finish mine off.

"But hey. At least you waited til after I found the

picture to fuck some other girl, right?"

The thought that Twat Shot and Cole did finally consummate their sexting love affair turned my stomach. Should it feel better that he didn't actually cheat on me? Because it didn't. Not at all.

"I would do anything to fix it. Is there anything I can do to fix it? Faye?" He settled his hand on my knee again, and I looked down at his fingers. I didn't push him away this time. "I love you."

Ah, fuck. He'd never been forthcoming with those words before. Hearing the timber of his voice, the waver it carried; he'd meant it. I swallowed hard.

I hated myself in that moment, because despite my righteous indignation, at that moment I felt soother by the knowledge that someone – anyone - loved me.

He leaned in and kissed my shoulder. I shook my shoulder to push him off, but the fervor in me had died. The closeness, the familiar smell, his sad blue eyes – they were all working. I held tight to one phrase I'd heard said from every person in my life. I remembered the person who'd said it with the most conviction, and my throat tightened. "You don't deserve me."

And he cried.

Right there in the middle of the bar, Cole Blanchard cried for the world to see.

I lost the battle right there. I couldn't see him like that; broken and miserable. I tossed the last few dollars I had to my name down on the bar, took him by the hand and led him outside. We stood between his black Infinite convertible and my Santé Fe. After a moment, he teared up again, and I couldn't take it. The sound, the sight of him - I wrapped my arms around him. He clasped his hands into the fabric of my tired old t-shirt and held me as tightly as he could. His body shook, and he gasped softly.

Cole squeezed me in his arms, fighting to get a hold of himself as he did. I thought of things I'd once daydreamed about, some piece of joy I'd held in my heart before that picture on his cell phone, or the ones I held before that Halloween party at Lambert's.

I'd lost those things. I'd lost them, and I couldn't have them back.

The sound of the door opening to the restaurant and the boisterous laughter of the people exiting startled me. I watched them leave with a degree of envy that far passed disdain. I rubbed the back of my hand across my eyes and pulled away. Cole moved slowly, leaning toward me, whispering my name.

I knew what was coming. I didn't stop it.

He kissed me.

I walked into the house at 8:30 the next morning, groggy and confused. My mother was already in the kitchen, shooting me a sideways glance as I sauntered in mid-morning. I hadn't wanted to see her, didn't want to have to explain myself. I was sure there was no one in my life who would rejoice in hearing the words, "I spent the night with Cole." Seeing their faces when I confessed myself did not rank high on my list of most looked forward to moments. I hobbled upstairs and took a shower, then sprawled out on my bed in a towel.

I was sore in certain places, tired in others, and peeing was an interesting experience as well. I actually got up and dressed after a few moments rather than wasting away in bed. I pulled my cell out from my jeans pocket, still dead from the night before, and plugged it in as my mother rapped at my door.

I grumbled in response. She didn't hear, and rapped again.

"Come in!" I growled.

She snuck in through a crack, as though opening the door fully might cause it to bite her.

"Honey, are you and Stellan alright?"

What? I thought. My mother is so adept at reading me that in a quiet afternoon she was able to decipher our rift? Was she a Geiger Meter?

"We're fine, Mom."

"Are you sure?" I lifted my head and glared at her, but she continued. "Because he's sitting on the porch downstairs and won't come inside."

I shot up onto my hands and searched her face for any sign that she was kidding. She wasn't.

"He's downstairs?"

She nodded. "He says he's fine on the porch. I'm worried he's upset, but I have to run out the door."

I muttered some choice words to myself as I got out of bed and began dressing in a panic. Stop it, Faye. It's not like he'll smell Cole on you. Besides, it's not like anything really happened.

You just slept with the asshole.

I descended the stairs and caught Stellan's profile in the living room window. He was sitting in one of the Adirondack chairs, reading.

Faahk!

This wasn't a text message I could avoid. There was no fleeing him here. I scolded myself for forgetting who I was dealing with and patted my hair down atop my head. Then I froze. It was as though my feet were anchored there beneath the floorboards. Part of me wanted to hide in some corner until he went away, avoid him at all costs, but I knew him well – he would wait me out.

I took a deep breath and scolded myself.

Don't be a coward, Faye.

Mom grabbed her bag and turned to search my face. "I'm heading out, honey. Love you."

"Love you too."

She waited a moment, then went out to her car. She kindly left the door wide open, letting the crisp morning air in to tickle at the bare skin of my arms. Still, I couldn't move.

Stellan didn't glance around. He sat reading, tapping his bookmark against the arm of the chair. I could see him clearly, the face I'd been fixated on for a month now; the face I'd last seen staring down at me with confusion, concern, and perhaps even pity. I didn't want to have this conversation. If he wouldn't go crawl under a rock and forget I existed, why wouldn't he let me?

The face I'd been imagining when Cole was on top of me in the dark.

I pulled my legs forward, moving as though I'd grown roots, and stood in the open doorway. He still didn't look up from his book.

"You can come in, you know?"

The tapping of the bookmark grew sharper a moment, then stopped. He placed it in the pages of his tattered copy of *Ender's Game* and stood up, stuffing the book into his back pocket. He stared out to the walk below and buried his hands in his pockets.

He towered there, silent - a column of denim in his ancient jean jacket. "We good?"

His voice was soft, but stern. So stern it startled me to hear it. I'd lost sight of how upset he'd been the night of the party, the sound of his voice on the phone with Evan. I'd caused that worry. I'd caused it, and I'd made no amends, nor attempt at such.

I let myself stare up at his face, something I'd avoided until this moment for fear that he might actually look back at me. His jaw was set, the tendons below his ears bared with tension. I felt a knot growing in my throat.

"Are we?" I asked.

He turned on me, coming to stand like the Colossus of Rhodes over me. The familiar scent of him nearly knocked me over, but I stiffened myself against him.

"I don't know, Faye. Given the fact that I had to come sit on your fucking porch at the butt crack of dawn to get you to even talk to me, I'd say we might not be great."

"It's only been a couple days -"

"Oh, is that all?"

I turned and stormed into the house. He followed on my heels like we'd choreographed it. No one shut the door.

"Where ya goin, Faye?"

His tone was snarky, almost condescending, and I turned back in the kitchen hallway to retaliate. Instead I met with the reality of what read on his face. His forehead furrowed between his brows, and his eyes narrowed. He was hurt. He was hurt, and it was my fault.

"I didn't know what to say to you!"

"So what? Behave like a fucking adult and have some fucking manners when I try to contact you."

"Oh you're one to fucking talk! How many times have you given me the fucking silent -"

"You practically tried to eat my face the other night, and you didn't think we might need to talk about -"

"No, no, no, no! Shut up! Don't fucking say it!"

He stopped and stared at me. I'd lost my ability to speak calmly, and even I had been surprised by how shrill I'd sounded.

I fought to catch my breath before he would speak again. "I didn't know what I was doing. I was fucked up."

"Oh…alright. So is that supposed to explain why you scared the shit out of me – why you didn't speak to -"

"I said I didn't know what to say to you!"

He came back without pause, his volume matching mine. "Anything is better than nothing, Faye!"

I felt the knot pulling and twisting in my throat, but I would not cry. I was done crying. I feared he'd read it as grief, some mourning for a pathetic love affair I'd imagined in my sad, heartbroken mind.

The receiving end of Stellan's righteous anger felt like being shipwrecked.

"I'm sorry!"

He straightened, swallowed hard, and stood there facing the staircase, as though waiting for someone to come down. I watched him and waited for a motion, a word. He glanced back, and his face softened. I almost flinched when he reached a hand toward me, but instead I let him pat my hair down on my head.

He gave a sad smirk. "Ok. We good then?"

I pursed my lips against tears and nodded. I knew the face I was making – the I-just-ate-a-lemon-that's-all-don't-fucking-look-at-me face. I tried to turn my head away, but he saw it. He pulled me into his chest, my face planted against the collar of his shirt, and he kissed the top of my head. There, sheltered under the weight of his long arms, there was no fighting the surge from my tightened throat. I was seconds from losing it in his arms.

No, damn it. No.

I felt a pang of grief. This embrace would never be more than it was. There would never be tenderness here, the kind that could warm my heart and my bed. Still, I assured myself that I would rather have him in this guise, than not have him at all. I fought to keep as still as possible, scolding myself when I shuddered.

I pulled away, thinking, 'get out of his arms, say you need the bathroom and cry there, not here. *Not* here.'

He didn't release me. I pulled harder this time, and he took my arm, turning me to face him so he could inspect my face. I'd managed to hold in the tears, but just barely.

He looked down his nose at me, one eyebrow raised. I waited to know his mind, praying my face didn't betray the shame I felt at having opened myself back up to Cole.

"Wanna get some breakfast?"

I laughed softly and agreed. Stellan was unchanged and in Stellan's world, all roads lead to food. I offered to go put on something other than my penguin pajama pants so that I might look more presentable. He assured me that I was the most beautiful woman to be raised by wolves in the world.

I punched him gently.

He tousled my hair. Like a big brother would.

When I reached my room, I heard the TV switch on downstairs and the sound of Stellan's heavy boots clomping down on the coffee table.

I stood there, just a few yards away from him, shut my bedroom door and slumped down beside my bed. This time I cried without boundary. I keened so hard, I was silent. I was grieving - grieving for something I would never have.

I'd heard of timeless love stories that ended with war widows dying of a broken heart. In their beds, unable to eat, sleep, or live without their husbands. I understood that now.

The next morning, I deleted Stellan's texts. I'd been saving every single one he'd sent me for months. They'd made me smile before, but now, I didn't want to think about them, about how ridiculous I'd been to save them. God, if he'd known…

I continued in the fury of that spirit and deleted every text in my phone. I'd made a habit of deleting Festering Asshole's texts, but Jackie and Meghan received the same treatment. I wiped the phone clean, as though perhaps letting go of the past few weeks would make me forget them.

I didn't change Festering Asshole's name. When I was done, I went for the office.

I stooped under the desk, pulled out the empty trash can and proceeded to dump, crumple and tear every single scrap of doodle covered paper into the bucket. Everything – every comic, every sketch, doodle and design, all shredded in my strange purge. When I was done, I combined it with the kitchen garbage and took the lot outside to await the trash pickup a few days away.

I might not be able to erase the past few days, but I could erase this.

Somehow, this felt better. Somehow, this

masochism felt deserved - righteous. Had I been armed with lighter or matches, I might have set the whole mess on fire.

What would the neighbors think?

These words seemed to come in my Grandmother's voice.

I passed the bird feeders, hanging half full on their metal pole, and stopped. The oak trees were rustling overhead, their leaves having left the backyard a yellow and orange sea of quivering leaves. Every footfall of bird or rodent was announced with their quiet shifts. I listened to the sounds of the neighborhood, smelled the crisp Autumn air. Someone was raking on the next street over, their dog yelping at them in protest from a house window, and far off, the high school marching band was practicing.

I waited for some sound, a declaration that everything was going to be okay. When none came, I slipped back into the house. It even *smelled* empty.

Stellan asked me to stop by that day, to bring by the sketches I had. I thought of the clean office, of setting to work, checking my email for news from Chalice, moving my art files to a flash drive and walking downtown. Neither thought helped the tension in my stomach. Instead I stood in my living room, swaying as though a soft breeze might knock me off my feet.

I couldn't explain my next move. I didn't even see it coming when I turned and strode up the stairs with purpose. I walked through my open bedroom door, took my phone up off my bedside table as though in a trance, and without knowing what I would say or why I was calling, I pulled up the contact in my phone and pressed the call button.

When Evan answered, his voice had the timber of a

man in bed.

I fought to speak, afraid I'd awoken the lumbering entrepreneurial giant and perhaps his wrath. "I'm sorry, I didn't mean to wake you."

"Jensen, hey. Don't even worry about it. What's up?"

I stood there in my room, the phone to my ear, but I didn't speak.

"You alright?" He asked.

Again I didn't speak. Why had I called him? I couldn't decipher a purpose or a word to say. Why would he have any comfort or advice to offer me? There was no sense to the phone call, yet still - "Are you back in L.A.?"

Evan shifted on the other end before he answered. "I am. Why, do you need me?"

I shook my head. Sadly, he couldn't hear it.

"Faye? What's up, goose? What's going on?"

I scratched my cheek, letting my fingertip graze over my skin idly as I stood there, wordless. I didn't know the answer to his question. When I finally opened my mouth, I was surprised by my response. "I think I'm losing my mind."

He shifted again, the sound of a man pulling himself out of bed. He was chuckling softly. "You and me both, dahlin. Why do you think you're losing your mind?"

I sat down on the bed and listened to him getting up. I started talking – told him about the pancakes I couldn't eat, about the undeniable urge to burn everything I'd ever created. He listened to me ramble as he got dressed and made his way into what I could only imagine was a wing in his monstrous house. I never mentioned Cole. I never mentioned Stellan.

Still, Evan and I remained on the phone, a comfortable rapport between us as we both went through the motions of our mornings. He managed to get me talking about the sordid tale of my job loss and then my house loss. He regaled me with tales of his most recent acquisition and the resulting backlash of user protest at their favorite site being 'assimilated.' He called them 'whiny internet bitches,' and I laughed. I felt small in the wake of his problems. Somehow, that smallness was soothing. By the time I became aware of the time, Evan and I had been on the phone for two hours. I offered to let him go when he finally breached a subject I'd have loved to avoid.

"Did you finally talk to Stellan?"

I paused. "I did."

Oh dear God, he must know about my drunken make out attempt. Suddenly the comfort of the conversation was a distant memory.

God, I'm pathetic. Pathetic, pathetic, pathetic.

"Yeah? You two all good? He was fucking intolerable the past couple days."

"He was?" I cringed at the hopeful tone of my voice. He'd been affected. Despite my self-flagellation, my heart leapt at the thought. "Yeah. We're good. We had a bit of a screaming match this morning, but I think we're good."

Evan gave some errands to someone on the other end of the line, and I waited for his attention to return. Suddenly the notion of him having company struck me. "Who was that?"

Evan coughed, as though almost uncomfortable. "That was Louis."

"Who's Louis?"

Evan paused. "He's my assistant."

I called him out. "Do you have a fucking butler?"

"What? No!"

I could tell by the tone that the answer was, in fact, yes. "Are you fucking kidding me? You have a Mr. Belvedere?"

"No! I have a Louis! He's different."

I shook my head, laughing. My mind was suddenly flooded with images of Dudley Moore in Arthur, and placing Evan's face on his tiny, clumsy body. "My whole world is blown."

Evan chuckled. "Shut the fuck up, you."

"Why didn't you bring him to the party? Does he not travel with you?"

Evan coughed again. "No…" I waited for him to continue. "I have staff on the East Coast."

"Blown, I tell you!"

"Don't you fucking judge me, woman!"

"Oh, I'm gonna! Does he actually live with you?"

"No…yes."

I shook my head. "Evan Lambert has a butler. One who butles."

"I believe the correct term is a 'Gentleman's Gentleman,' thank you very much."

I managed to get Evan to admit to a few more regular staff in his household – housekeeper, chef, he even had a clothes shopper, though he assured me they did not live with him.

I mocked him mercilessly the whole time. The truth was, his life sounded beyond blessed, but the notion of naked ass, acid-loving Evan running through his house on mescaline while a man in a vest and tie picked up the clothes trailing behind him made me warm.

Evan expressed a desire to come back home soon

and promised to keep me posted when he would be in town. I assured him I would have my assistant make time in my busy schedule to see him and we hung up.

And somehow, I felt better. Evan was like an island. He was this entity that existed outside of the rest of my life, outside of the drama and the anxiety of my relationships, my job hunt, my failures. Talking to him was like time traveling to days before I saw myself fall.

I glanced at the clock and cringed. I'd woken him up at seven in the morning, his time. Still, he hadn't begrudged me the company. I promised to be considerate of the time difference if the need to call him arose again and headed for the couch. There, I wasted away the day in front of the TV. I never stopped in to see Stellan.

CHAPTER NINE

I could say the month of October barely happened, or perhaps passed with a whimper, but after that morning with Stellan, I hardly interacted with anyone.

By the time Halloween rolled around, I'd seen Stellan maybe twice since that morning he'd camped out on my porch. Yet, somewhere in that span of complete antisocial behavior, I'd started responding to Cole's texts.

I'd also managed to clock several hours on the phone with Evan Lambert.

I couldn't quite express the comfort I felt when he and I spoke. There was solace there, when everything else felt like din. He didn't know my failures unless I told them to him. He still knew me as the bright, shining, glorious version of myself; the one he'd last spent time with before the night of his Halloween party – before I'd learned to be ambitious, before I learned how to succeed at life, before I'd set myself up for complete and utter disaster.

Sure he knew the sordid details of my downfall, in fact it felt almost nice to retell the story to someone who hadn't looked on in pity as it all happened.

Evan and I shared that same ingrained memory, that mark that children of troubled parents have. He could understand why the notion of failing, of falling apart seemed like such a sin. Achieve something, and you're the exception to the rule. Grow up to

236

mediocrity - or less for that matter – and no one will be surprised.

God damn it, I wanted to be a surprise.

Evan often reminded me that I had a long way to go before sucking cock for crack rocks.

I said, "Wait, is that a bad thing?"

Despite the wishes of my inner hermit, Halloween came with a tradition. Every year, Stellan and I sat on my porch handing out candy, and every year we played the Beetlejuice theme, dressed up in matching costumes, and made goofball comments about the little ones' costumes. Or Stellan made snarky comments about how a nineteen year old in a hole ridden t-shirt should by principal, be required to give *him* candy.

"At least put some effort in. Seriously," he'd say.

They never agreed and were learning not to come to my house at all.

Stellan raised an eyebrow when he got to the house and found me in jeans and a black cable knit sweater.

"Don't tell me, let me guess. You're a nihilist?"

I laughed.

"Jehovah's witness? Wait, who doesn't celebrate birthdays?"

I assured him he'd been accurate on the religious reference, but not on my costume. "I couldn't think of anything."

He shrugged. "Suppose it's good I didn't put my zombie makeup on before I came over then. Would have made your nihilism truly frightening, and we have children coming."

I stifled a laugh. "Shut up"

I had trouble looking him in the eye as we meandered into the kitchen. He didn't seem to notice, quickly grabbing the first bag of candy he saw. The pile of bags was bigger than we would need, but given Stellan's habit of eating a good amount of the candy each year, I always made a point to buy extra.

He seemed his usual self. As far as I could tell, he had no sense of the chasm that had opened between us.

"So I hear you and Evan have been talking."

Oh, maybe he did.

"Yeah, it's been nice to catch up with him."

Stellan stuffed the first Reese's Peanut Butter Cup into his mouth, offering me one as he did.

I declined. As expected, my stomach had turned to violent churning the moment he'd walked up to the house. I could no more put that Reese's in my mouth than I could a Mack Truck.

"He seemed pretty chuffed about it."

I smiled. When I glanced at Stellan, he showed the subtle glow of a man in chocolate and peanut butter heaven. He tossed the bag toward me.

"Run, save yourself."

I grabbed the bowl from the cupboard over the sink, a tired old mixing bowl my Grandmother used for making pancakes and stuffing at Thanksgiving. We filled it with Reese's, Snickers, Twix, and Three Musketeers, and made our way out to the porch. Stellan took the chair closer to the stairs, despite not being dressed to terrify. The children would be forced to pass him in pursuit of the bowl of candy. Perhaps his sheer size might give them pause. If not his size, surely his sarcasm would.

Our first visitor was Bethany from across the way. There were a couple younger families on my road, some with kids, some with teenagers. The teenagers brought parties and double-barreled park jobs, but they became rare for one reason – Mr. Hodges did what the rest of the neighborhood was too 'polite' to do and called the cops. Parents were informed, privileges were taken away, and parking equilibrium was restored. Now, it was Mr. Hodges' pride and joy, his eldest great-grandchild, coming up the walk. She was a shy thing, being slowly coaxed toward our steps in her mother's intricately made princess costume. Her sleeves flowed at her sides and her dark hair was framed in a floral wreath.

Bethany froze at the bottom of the steps, glancing back to her parents who stood smiling and urging her on from the sidewalk. The chair beside me lurched, and Stellan was up, the bowl of candy in his hand. Before Bethany could run, Stellan had slipped down the stairs with unnatural grace for a man his size, knelt beside her on the walk, and held the bowl to her with his head bowed.

"M'lady," he said.

She seemed to bloom before him, blushing a deep red. She smiled and hid her face behind her plastic pumpkin.

I feel inclined to say I would have responded the same way. When I caught Caroline's eye, her expression said I wasn't the only one.

Caroline was a playmate of mine when we were very young. She visited on weekends here and there until her weekends were taken over by going to campgrounds with foam weapons and elaborate dresses, beating the hell out of other similar minded people. She'd met her husband at just such an event – Jason, a long haired fellow who roamed the world dressed like a pirate. Though I rarely saw them now, I liked them both. They seemed to feel the same, given that she invited me to their wedding years earlier, which had been one of the strangest events of my life. Fun, but strange. Stellan and I were two of the only people not dressed like employees of Medieval Times. Mr. Hodges had made a face at me from behind a knight, and I'd been reminded of why my Grandmother liked the man so much – why I liked him so much. He didn't take anything too seriously.

Except parking, that is.

Bethany took a piece of candy only to be met with the declaration that "M'lady receives no less than three pieces of candy. Per order of the Queen."

He glanced back at me.

Yep, I was right about that blooming sensation.

I fought not to giggle as I waved magnanimously in their direction.

When Bethany skipped back to her parents, I heard her inform them that Stellan had given her far more than three.

"He's a keeper!" Caroline called back to me as Stellan returned to the porch.

I waved. "Don't I know it!"

Shit! Why did I say that?

I glanced at Stellan, who was making love with his eyes to another Reese's.

Great. Make out with his face? Check. Announce in his company that I think he's a catch? Check. Declare my unrequited and all-encompassing, misguided affection for him? As good as done.

I inspected him out of the corner of my eye. He didn't show any signs of discomfort. He did, however, show an unhealthy affection for those Reese's.

We waited another fifteen minutes, and the flood began. Kids from nearby neighborhoods, kids who came to trick or treat in their grandparents' neighborhood like Bethany - we were one of those lucky parts of the world where you could actually feel Halloween in the air. Rather than deal with traffic, low house participation, or worse, unsafe neighborhoods, people would carpool in to trick or treat in my neighborhood.

We also give the good candy. Though Davis Court wasn't one of the most populated roads in town, we were one or two roads over from the best Halloween streets in town, and we received runoff as a result.

Naturally we had a comment for everyone that came along:

Three year old Spiderman –

Me: *"Holy cow! Spiderman!"*

Stellan: *"Hey Spidey, could you hop up there real quick and clean out my gutters. Thanks pal."*

Five year old Spiderman with full muscle suit, shortly thereafter -

Stellan: *"Whoa! You've been working out since we last saw you?"*

Three year old Spiderman with his mask off –

Me: *"No, Spiderman! Your secret identity!"*

Half assed seventeen year old Jack Sparrow -

Stellan (in pirate voice): *"Arrgh! You can't have me booty!"*

A truly convincing eight year old Jack Sparrow right afterward -

Stellan: *"Arrgh! You CAN have me booty!"*

Spongebob Squarepants -

Me: *"How are you breathing, sir?"*

As the evening wore down, and the crowds

thinned, a twelve year old boy dressed in full drag walked up the steps in slow motion, sideways, staring us both down to the point of near discomfort until he finally spoke.

His English accented lisp was perfect. "Trick or Treat?"

We both sat, dumbfounded be how fierce this kid was.

Stellan: *"Here. No seriously, take all my candy. You deserve ALL my candy."*

I didn't disagree.

The boy-girl gave Stellan a stare down with a cat like meow and left as dramatically as he arrived. We were both speechless for a moment, and down to our last bag of candy.

I checked the clock – quarter to nine. We were well past Trick or Treat hours, and the dwindling sounds in the distance gave evidence to it. Stellan and I shared the glory of the drag princess as though we both thought we'd imagined him. Stellan declared the boy his hero.

Further reason to love my Swede.

It was chilly, and the threat of snow was sharp in the air. I headed inside, but noticed as I reached the kitchen that Stellan wasn't following. I turned to face him, still standing by the open front door.

"Wanna do something?" He asked.

I stared at him blankly. Stellan was the king of 'sit at home and do nothing' if the opportunity arose. I shrugged, letting one side of my baggy sweater droop down my shoulder. It was pretty early for us, but given the empty state of my pockets, I naturally faltered. "Like what?"

"I dunno. You hungry?"

Truthfully, yes. I wouldn't be saying so though, obviously. "I'm alright."

"Liar. You haven't had supper. Come on, let's grab something, go see *What's Under the Bed?* afterward."

What's Under the Bed? was a hokey horror movie I'd been hoping to see since catching the trailer.

I faltered for a moment. Stellan wanted to see *What's Under the Bed?*

I attempted to argue, but Stellan already knew damn well that I was pocket pulling poor. Confessing that wouldn't change his course in the slightest. I pursed my lips, but I nodded and slipped into the kitchen to put the last of the candy into a zip-loc bag for Stellan to devour at the movies. In the living room he shifted, the familiar sounds of my car keys jingling as he grabbed them from the table. I stood frozen, almost petrified to spend time with him – time out in the world.

You stupid cow, I thought.

I grabbed my phone and started texting. By the time I reached him I was finished writing and pressed send.

"Who's that?" He asked.

"Meghan. She's been dying to see *What's Under the Bed?* for weeks."

My phone buzzed as though on cue.

Home alone on Halloween Meghan - **I'm so down. Where we eating?**

Stellan stood in the doorway a second, watching me. He closed his eyes before he spoke. "How delightful."

I laughed, honoring his sarcasm. "But I thought you *loved* Meghan?"

He shook his head with slow deliberation and held

the door for me to pass. I grabbed my purse, knowing how pointless it was, and led the way out to my car.

I'd never been more relieved to see Meghan in my life that night. After a quiet and almost heavy ride, we found Meghan waiting in the parking lot of the restaurant and from that moment on, she never stopped talking. I enjoyed her banter, even laughed a few times when she started yelling at the movie screen – she was in her glory that night.

All would have been perfect save for one glaring detail.

Stellan didn't speak the entire night.

Meghan set him up for insults, jabs and affronts, but he never took the bait. He sat quietly listening, chuckled here and there, but stayed mute. I might have said he was simply in a quiet mood, but there was a clincher.

When we arrived at the theater, Meghan demanded that she buy my ticket, leaving Stellan to pick up his own after us. She paid, collected her purse and ushered me toward the theater.

Stellan's voice stopped us. "Meghan!"

We turned in surprise to find Stellan pointing at the counter. Meghan forgot to take our tickets. She returned, grabbed them, and dragged me toward concessions. I'm not even sure if she noticed it, but I couldn't shake it for the rest of the night.

He'd called her Meghan.

Not Trotsky, not vagrant hobo prostitute - Meghan.

I sense you mocking me, gentle reader.

"What's the big effing deal?" you say?

The big effing deal is that this had never happened before. Stellan has never in his life referred to

Meghan by her first name. Just the idea of it had always been practically an affront to his nature. Since the second hour of their first meeting when their friendly battle began, he'd never called her anything outside of Trotsky, or on a good day, Spawn of Cthulhu. Something wasn't right.

Still, I didn't probe him on the quiet ride home.

Something was definitely wrong, and now it seemed even he was aware of it.

I dropped him off that night and waited as he would for him to get in the front door. Then I drove away.

Damn it Faye, what have you done?

I felt somehow distant from everything. I walked into my house and stood there in the dark for a long while, letting my purse drop to the floor. There was no one to seek for solace, no one to grieve to.

My life long partner in crime had gone straight. I felt like John Dillinger meeting eyes with the lady in the red dress, only to see she is me. The phrase, *I'm so fucking stupid* came to mind a few times.

I sought something to still the thoughts, someone to reach for. Then I did the only thing I could think of to quiet the ache in my chest.

I retrieved my phone from my purse and texted Cole.

When do you want to see me?

In the morning, I found a missed call from Cole. I didn't call him back. Somehow the thought of having such a conversation with the sun up churned my stomach. Instead I called Meghan.

"Dude, he called me Meghan."

Yeah, she'd noticed.

She dropped in on her lunch hour, eating a cobb salad from the grocery store while I feasted on a bologna sandwich. Mayo, mustard, alternating cheese and bologna slices, cut diagonally – that sandwich was delectable. I had to assure Meghan of this several times while we sat at my kitchen counter.

Meghan took a generous bite before she spoke. "So I gotta say it – I think it's finally happened."

"What?"

"He finally realizes he wants my shit."

I laughed, given the glob of salad dressing and egg stuck to her chin. "He *did* call you Meghan."

"I know, right?"

I grabbed the bread down from the cupboard, ready to make a second sandwich. I wasn't kidding when I said it was delectable. "It's just that latent sexual tension that finally got to him."

She scowled at me. "Bitch, do the two of you wiseasses share a brain or some shit?"

I shrugged. "Could be."

She poured the rest of her salad dressing packet into her food. "It was inevitable. No one can resist my womanly charms forever. They fight it and fight it, but then Bam -"

"-they're calling you Meghan?"

"It's unfair really. He never had a chance."

I smiled, ignoring her glare as I slathered mayonnaise on my bread. I slapped on the bologna and cheese as she watched.

"So, any clue what's really up with him?"

I shrugged. I wasn't ready to tell her. Unlike Jackie, this woman would pull no punches. Well, not that Jackie had either, but – never mind. "No clue."

She slammed her fork onto the counter. "You lying

bitch."

"What?"

"Jackie fucking told me, you slut."

I slumped onto the counter. "She's dead to me."

"I can't believe you were just going to sit here and not tell me."

My phone buzzed in my jeans, and I pulled it out, grateful for a distraction. "It's not something I really run my mouth about -"

"Run your mouth? You whore. You owe me for last night. That was fucking awkward as hell. Thank God Jackie told me, otherwise I might have said something."

I glanced at my phone as a reprieve from her scolding. Though I hated having to defend myself, the realization that she had known and still came along drew both my gratitude and affection. I nodded as she regaled me. Still, I couldn't help but laugh when I read Evan's text.

Unnaturally charming Evan - **My spider senses tell me you desperately need to hear my voice.**

Meghan noticed the chuckle and demanded to know who was texting me. My answer resulted in a two minute wrestling match as she tried to steal my phone for Evan's number.

"You whore! How can you deliberately try to keep me from my soul mate?"

"A second ago I thought Stellan was your soul mate."

She lunged for my phone again "No, that obnoxious fuck just wants my shit. Evan and I are in love!"

I laughed and fought until I was shrieking at her. I finally pried it away. "I'll let him know."

"You better!" She said, straightening her perfectly pressed button down shirt.

She made her point with a purposefully angry bite of her salad, letting half of it fall down her chin. I laughed and responded to Evan's text.

Me - **It's true. You should fight crime.**

He texted back sometime before Meghan left, letting me know he'd be calling that evening. I looked forward to it.

Meghan was an adept woman - she caught me texting and assured me before she left that she'd destroy me if I so much as imagined Evan naked. I assured her right back that though I didn't need to imagine, she had nothing to worry about.

And with that she threatened my life and left.

I ended up in front of the TV, as per usual. I was happy to remain there. I could have gone for a walk, brought a book out to Sleepy Hollow and read by the three brother's tomb, but what is it they say about an object at rest?

I'm not sure. Stellan would know.

The phone rang right as I was wiping tears away after watching the most recent episode of the Biggest Loser, and I hopped up to answer it.

"No matter what I say during this conversation, you are hereby ordered to refuse," Evan said.

I was startled by the opener, but not enough to show it. "Okay? Drama queen."

"Promise."

I rolled my eyes. "Fine. I mean, I refuse."

"Good. So, I've seen the early stages of 'Gorilla Warfare' and as a business man, I'm required to offer to buy your artistic rights to the game."

My eyebrows shot up. "What you talkin' bout,

Willis?"

The boards I'd done were apparently animated into game form, and Evan proceeded to regale me with his 'unmitigated adulation' in the form of attempted 'hostile takeover.'

"Why would I refuse that? I could use the money."

"You just refuse," he said. "You fucking promised."

"Well, it would depend on how much you offer – And why the hell would you tell me to refuse?"

"No, no it doesn't matter how much I offer, and I'm not prepared to make an offer now, I'm waiting for beta."

Beta meant an early, playable version of the finished game, sent to early testers to find and hash out any glitches. The thought of something I was working on being unleashed on actual testers stopped me in my tracks. "How close is it?"

Evan went quiet a moment. "Stellan isn't keeping you updated?"

I couldn't help but pause myself. I tried to gauge how telling my answer would be. "No. I sketch, he programs. And really, I'm just sketching what he tells me to."

"That's not what he says."

I paused. "Why, what does he say?"

The phone beeped into my ear, and I looked to find an incoming call.

Cole.

I didn't want to answer, but I'd put it off long enough. "Evan… I've got another call, can I talk to you later?"

"You ok, Jensen?"

How did he know? "Yeah, why?"

"Who's calling?"

"Nobody important."

Evan paused. "Take care of yourself, goose. Love ya."

"Love you too."

I pressed the accept button. Cole had hung up.

I stared at the phone a moment, waiting – no voicemail.

I felt like a coward. I fretted over the manner in which I would answer, planning my phone voice – soft, calm, but perhaps a little deeper.

No, no Faye, we don't want to sound sultry. Just "Sorry, I was in another room," will suffice.

I didn't call back. The prospect of that phone call felt like the trigger to some quiet bomb. In an attempt to distract myself, I settled at my drawing table.

Having cleared the remnants of all my doodles, I created the blankest space in the house, like fresh paper or a wet chalkboard. I picked up my pen, turned to the shelves where the sketchpads were now waiting, and set my hand on the pile – a pile my mother and Stellan provided against my requests.

I didn't open the notebook, I didn't fiddle with my pen to get it settled in just the right nook of my thumb and forefinger. No, I turned to my computer, opened my email, and began to write.

Dear Dennis,

I am just dropping a quick note to check in with you. How are things at Chalice? Any news on the position?

I hope you're all well, and I hope to hear from you soon.

-Faye

It was breezy, right?

Wait, was it? Was it too breezy? Aah, fuck life.

The next move of the evening was a choice – ignore Cole, call him back, wait on the chance that he might try again, or play Words with Friends on my phone with a complete stranger and cheat like a toothless sailor.

I did none of the above. I chose not to decide.

Yet, when Cole called an hour later, I'd been so lost in unpleasant thoughts about Stellan, Cole felt like a better alternative. I grabbed my coat and snuck out of the house.

Cole opened the door before I had a chance to knock. He wasn't wearing a shirt. I found it odd, but let him kiss me on the cheek as I walked in.

Cole's apartment was a bachelor pad in every sense, given its masculine leather furniture, the browns and grays and the lack of bright colors, the massive TV, which seemed to be a staple of all the men I knew these days, and the constant supply of Corona and lime he kept in the fridge. He offered me one of said Corona's, but I refused.

One might think after all this time that he'd remember I don't drink Corona. He dropped down on the couch beside me, still without a shirt. He'd grabbed himself a drink and sat with his body twisted toward me, the Corona resting on his knee as he took a few sips. I watched the television. The football game was on. The Patriots weren't playing. I felt something wet and slippery graze the nape of my neck. I squealed and turned to find Cole running his now cold, wet fingers over my skin.

I swatted him away. "What are you doing?"

He tried to touch me again, a smirk on his face. This time he went for the skin at my throat and down. "Do you like it?"

I pushed his hand away again. "No."

He made a pouty expression for a flash, then simply slid down the couch closer to me, slipping the back of his hand across my breast as he leaned in to kiss my shoulder, his knuckles deliberately grazing my nipple under my sweater. I shuddered.

Jesus, I just got here Cole!

I took his hand and held it in my lap, turning back to the TV. I hoped he'd get the message.

No such luck.

He took it as an invitation to move southward, pushing his hand between my legs. I physically lunged across the couch to get away from him. The movement startled even me.

He muttered his surprise, and when I looked over at him, shirtless and clearly agitated by the shape at the front of his pants, the look was one of clear offense.

"I'm sorry, I'm – I haven't had the best few days. Do you mind if we just watch TV?"

He furrowed his brow at me, picked up his Corona off the coffee table and took a long swallow. Then he tightened his lips and looked at me, as though he was holding back bile.

I waited, almost excited to hear what he might say.

Give me one reason, Cole. Say something. I fucking dare you. What about all the times I turned to you, literally begged you to touch me, and you wouldn't? Told me I was 'obsessed with sex,' that you weren't an object, and now I'm not in the mood for the first time in my entire life, and you act affronted. Well, fuck you, Boyo! Put on a fucking shirt.

A moment later, he did just that. He returned to the couch with clear indignation, as far from me as was possible. Given my mood, I appreciated the distance.

After fifteen minutes of heavy silence, he spoke, offering to put on a movie. I agreed, and we settled in to watch Thor, which I only partially regretted given the hour and a half I had to spend ogling handsome Scandinavian men.

God damn it.

I offered conversation a few times, asking about his week, his Thanksgiving. He kept it to one word answers, shrugs, and nods. This was the Cole I remembered. Though the silence was meant as punishment, I didn't mind it. It's easier to hold your tongue when your mouth is closed.

The movie ended around nine, and my eyes were heavy. I rose from the couch and grabbed my jacket. I turned to face him, offering a hug. He remained on the couch, with his most recent beer in hand.

He looked up at me, exasperated. "You're not going to stay?"

I was startled. "It's Sunday. You work in the morning."

"So?"

I stared at him. "I've never stayed on a -"

"You did the other day."

"Yes, but I didn't realize -"

He shrugged, taking an swig as though to drive home his indifference. "That's fine, you don't want to stay. Drive safe."

He hopped up and walked past me to the kitchen, dumping his empty bottle in the recycling. I had so many words that wanted to come out, so many spiteful, angry, venomous things I wanted to say – but

I didn't. I held them in and waited for him to emerge from the kitchen. When he did, he stopped and glared at me with his palms out at his sides. "What are you waiting for? Have a nice night."

"Why are you being like this?"

"Oh, I don't know. Maybe because I haven't seen my girlfriend in days, she's barely responded to my texts, and now she refuses to even touch me."

I realized at that moment that he'd been hoping I'd be easier to cajole into sex if I was lying in his bed. I probably would be. It's easier to close your eyes and disappear when you're on your back in a dark room, but making out on a couch like a teenager when the sensation of touch feels like slivers from a twine rope left under your skin – that's another matter. I understood his upset; I'd lived it.

"I'm sorry, Cole, but – maybe it's just too soon - too fast, I don't know."

His arms fell to his sides, and his expression changed. He crossed to me and put his hands on my arms, squeezing tenderly. I did my best not to shirk at the sensation.

His voice was soft, suddenly repentant. "I know. I know, you're right. I'm sorry."

I shifted my coat in my hands. "It's alright, I just can't st -"

"You don't need to explain. I know. I need to be patient. It's just hard – when I know what I have."

There was a compliment there, but I couldn't receive it. He pulled me to him and hugged me, running his hands up and down my back. I let him do it, resting my head on his shoulder. I caught a trace of his cologne, subtle enough to be from another day. I'd hated that cologne when he first wore it, but when

I was heartbroken, just the hint of it in a department store or on a man walking by would send me into fits of longing. I remembered when I loved it, because it reminded me of him.

I didn't love it anymore.

My cell sounded a familiar ringtone from the recesses of my coat. I jumped, shaking Cole free as I did. He looked down at my coat, expectantly waiting for me to check the text. Unlike past days when Stellan's texts would draw his chagrin, he seemed content. I feared the text, what it might say, the affect it might have on me, especially with having Cole watching my every twitch. I reached for my pocket, felt the phone in my fingers, and my stomach turned. Why did I dread messages from Stellan now? What had I done to deserve such a shift in the world? I had to escape this feeling of loss.

I leaned into Cole, and I kissed him. He received me with a hum of intention.

I didn't go home that night.

I'm heading to the store after work. Are you doing dessert on Thursday? Need me to pick up anything?

The text came in just as I was climbing into my car the next morning. Oh my fucking god, I thought. It was Thanksgiving. How had November already gone by? Stellan and I hadn't been speaking, and I'd managed to wallow through three weeks of near silence. Three weeks.

I felt like I'd been punched.

Dessert on Thanksgiving was a Jensen tradition. Supper itself was always a family affair – unless my mother had a boyfriend at the time, which had happened once or twice when I was young. Yet, after supper the doors opened and neighbors and friends would come, and my Grandmother would lay out her best works. Pecan Chocolate Pie, Swedish Apple Pie, sometimes a Strawberry Rhubarb or a Pumpkin Pie. Many years she left one of the staples for someone else to bring, an act of kindness she thought, given they were the easiest to run down to the supermarket and purchase last minute. I'd spent many years at her side in this kitchen, helping her roll out pie crust or smashing pecans or slicing apples. Over the years, as her fingers bent and shook, I took over little by little. When she passed, I continued this alchemy for her - my way of communing, perhaps.

I texted back the ingredients for the mainstays. I'd do Chocolate Pecan and Apple. I swiftly turned to the project of reminders, informing the usual suspects that they were all invited to the Jensen Family Thanksgiving Dessert, err, shindig thing. I stood texting away for the next half hour as I sipped a cup of tea and watched the bird feeders out the kitchen window. I cajoled Jackie into bringing cannolis.

I came to Stellan and paused.

Then I thought of Cole, but the decision was quick. No, clearly. He has never set foot in the house or met my friends and family, and what happened between us was far too new – wait.

Are we new?

The thought stopped me cold. I'd slept with him – something that in my past had always meant 'relationship,' but did it mean that to him? And if it did, was I happy?

I stared at Stellan's name. I knew my answer.

I opened a new text message and typed.

Breezy 'Let's-Pretend-It-Hasn't-Been-Super-Weird-For-Three-Weeks' Me - **Is the Ødegård brood coming for dessert Thursday? Anything specific you want?**

Then like a trained rat pulling a lever, I sat there staring at my phone, waiting for a response. I'd say five minutes passed before I realized my tea was getting cold, and my arm was falling asleep from leaning on the windowsill. I turned for the sink and the phone fired off in my hand; Stellan's ringtone. The sound of it made my heart pound.

Swedish Apple. Always.

Done, I responded and set the phone down. I wiped my hand across my eyes and watched the birds.

CHAPTER TEN

Jackie came by on Wednesday night to help me with the baking. Despite her culinary prowess, we had a long understanding that when it came to my baking, she was NOT to interfere. No helping unless asked, no advice, no suggestions, just sit there and look pretty and keep me company while I work. The one year she tried to step in and advise me on my pie crusts, I snapped at her that my Grandmother had done a fine job of teaching me once, I didn't need to be taught again. She never overstepped again.

"So is he coming tomorrow?"

I tossed flour across the counter to roll out another crust. "No. I didn't invite him."

"But you've seen him again, yes?"

I nodded. She was referring to Cole.

My phone buzzed on the counter. Jackie glanced at it and raised an eyebrow. It was Cole. Again. He'd been texting all day.

"He's a chatty guy these days, I see," she said.

I shrugged. He was. He was at work, calling me sweetheart and such. I responded as often as I had reason, but being elbows deep in pie crust made the act a little inconvenient at the moment.

"Are you two officially back together then?"

I pushed the rolling pin across the dough one last

time and paused. I feared the response. "Yes. A kinda trial thing."

Jackie drew her finger through the flour on the counter drawing a heart, and smiled at me. "That's wonderful."

I felt small in her gaze, like a patronized child showing terrible artwork. She continued to search my face; I kept my eyes to the crust.

"It sounds like he is making a sincere effort. That's a good sign."

It was. It was a big difference from the aloof way he'd been before. Now, I was the one being aloof. I didn't mean to be, but I simply didn't have a response to his texts about the man in traffic talking to himself, or the bar customer who left his dentures in the bathroom. Part of me felt unkind, given that I had once been the one to send these random texts in search of connection, but I simply didn't have anything to say. I was giving myself time.

It was going to take time.

I shaped the crust into the pie pan, mixed and poured the pecans and corn syrup, then tossed in chocolate chips, eating more of them than I would like to admit. I tossed it in the oven while 'letting' Jackie cut apples to help with the second pie. I hated cutting apples. It made my teeth sweat.

I started the Kitchenaid Mixer whirring away at the batter for the Swedish Apple Pie and took a moment to respond to Cole. Instead, the phone buzzed in my hand, followed by a familiar, but rarely heard ringtone - Stellan.

Two guesses how my stomach reacted.

You getting your Swedish on?

I smiled with every inch of my being.

Me - **Not as well as you.**

I stood there clutching my phone, the mixer grinding away at the now whipped concoction of butter, flour and sugar.

Jackie set the apple wheel cutter on the counter with a firm thonk and said, "What now?"

I met her gaze. Her brow was furrowed, but she was smirking. I set the phone down, shut off the mixer and returned to my work. With every moment that passed, my stomach tightened.

Stellan wasn't responding. He wasn't responding. He still wasn't responding.

This naturally translated into - He hates you. It was a mistext, he can't stand you. He's ignoring you.

I flustered with the mixer, trying to yank the beater free to wash it.

The phone buzzed – Cole.

My heart sank.

Yeah, it was going to take time.

My mother and I cooked a small bird, mashed potatoes, corn, and stuffing, and I made my grandmother's green bean casserole and gravy. We sat and chatted about things, mainly museum news, details about a current student exhibition with a painting she was contemplating splurging on by a young man named Bertrand Fuller. She mentioned how his technique and pallet and eye for light reminded her so much of my father's work, and I shut down completely. I let her go on, I even nodded and mhm-ed a couple times to be an active listener, but I didn't hear a word of it.

We finished around 2:30PM, just enough time to clear the table, start the coffee and set out the dessert plates and utensils. The Hodges would always be first, and they would bring the brownie tree from the Concord Bakery; then the Fallons would come from up the road, potentially bringing a teenager or two with them; the Merle-Witts had RSVP'd this year, a first since the two women had moved in next door; and finally Jackie and Kevin and the Ødegårds, who walked down from their house in the center. At 2:55PM the doorbell rang, and I wiped my hands on a kitchen towel and dashed down the hall to answer it, still in my grandmother's blue striped apron.

"What up, sexy?"

I gasped at the sight of him. Evan stood on the doorstep in a black pea coat, navy blue scarf and a pair of, I could only assume, five thousand dollar leather shoes. He had a bottle of dessert wine in his hand and his collar up against the light flurries of snow that had started coming down. I launched myself at him, throwing my arms around his neck and kissing his ear. He locked his wrists behind my back and squeezed.

Behind me I could hear my mother preening at the sight of him as well. She hadn't seen him in at least ten years, so I could understand her being a little star struck to have him back at the house. Evan came in and kissed my mother on the cheek and let me take his coat. Before I could steal him away to the kitchen for asinine conversation, the doorbell rang again, and the Hodges family filtered in with Caroline sending Bethany running to the chairside cabinet where my grandmother kept coloring books and crayons. My mother once suggested turning it into a magazine cabinet, but I refused. Even if only used one day a year, it stayed as Grammy left it.

I gathered coats and took orders for coffee. I quickly introduced Evan to Caroline and Jason, who realized the developer of their favorite game was in the room. This led to Mr. Hodges swooping in for a long talk on investments. That was before the Merle-Witts arrived, leaving their daughter Chloe with Bethany at the cabinet of coloring books and insisting they follow me into the kitchen to help retrieve desserts. I sent them into the living room with the pecan and last minute blueberry pie I'd whipped up.

They were off in the living room when I heard further entries, the stomping of feet on the porch and the tell tale giggling of young teenage girls betrayed the arrivals of the Fallons.

I grabbed the ice cream out of the freezer and retrieved the Swedish Apple from the oven. There was a cool draft coming from the front door as I hit the living room. I stalled halfway down the hallway.

Stellan held the door for his parents as he leaned down to kiss my mother on the cheek. He slipped his ski cap off to show his recently buzzed hair was growing out, and unzipped his jacket. He noticed me then and smiled, then raised his eyebrows appreciatively at what I had in my hands. It took every ounce of will I had to take a step forward.

He met me at the table, reached for the Casserole dish in my hands to help me, but when I relinquished it, he hunched down and tip toed a few feet toward my office as though to hunker down with the whole pie by himself. I knew him well, he would if I let him. He flashed me a big grin before returning the pie to the dessert table, and I did my best to stifle some strange burble of longing.

What was I, fourteen?

No, but I'd missed him. I'd missed the shit out of him.

I fled back into the kitchen, giving a quick hello to Linda and Lennart. I'd used the excuse of checking the coffee, but really I just couldn't be near Stellan. He made my heart race.

God, how would I get through today?

I heard a few more stomping feet and the guilt of being a bad host began to set in. I grabbed the last of the dessert plates and brought them to the table. Jackie was there with her cannolis, setting them beside the big fruit display of chocolate dipped strawberries and melons that the Merle-Witts provided. I felt a presence at my shoulder as Stellan leaned toward my ear.

"So that's what lesbians eat?"

I snorted.

Evan appeared on my right. "Among other things. Know what I'm sayin? Knoohohooow what I'm sayin?"

Stellan and Evan bumped fists as I turned to smack them. I was grateful to have them both rather than attempt a Stellan encounter solo. Evan was wearing a blue button down shirt with a fresh wine spot just below his collar. I kept Evan's gaze, working up the courage to meet Stellan's and not betray how miniscule I felt. The clank of plates drew them both away with a low groan of "Foooood."

"Anyone want tea or milk or coffee?" I asked the room, receiving a few orders in response. I sauntered off into the kitchen happy for the open space.

There was nothing quite like a gathering in an old house like this. The sound of conversation and laughter and silverware hitting plates – it was one of those moments when people who might otherwise never speak to one another suddenly have endless amounts to talk about. I loved seeing Mr. Hodges talking to Lennart, or Caroline and Terry Merle-Witt (the short-haired, wire rim glasses wearing lesbian with salt and pepper hair) sharing tales of Chloe's adoption from Korea and Bethany's 36 hour birth.

I set the coffee and tea pots on the table and scanned to find everyone eating, some on the couch or in chairs, others standing. I followed familiar voices to find Jackie and Kevin had snuck into the dining room with Stellan and Evan.

Stellan looked up to see me and groaned his appreciation. Evan nodded and grumbled in agreement as I sat down.

"You going to have some?" Jackie asked. I noticed both Evan and Stellan's piled up plates were both void of cannolis, one of which Jackie now pushed toward me on her plate.

I shook my head. "I'm waiting for a little while."

Kevin tapped his fork to his plate. "This Apple Pie is phenomenal, Faye. I've never had this kind before."

I beamed at him. "It's Swedish."

"Which makes it exceptional," Stellan said with a mouthful.

I snorted. "Yes, which makes it exceptional."

"Would you mind my taking a slice to my parents? We head there after this."

Stellan grunted like a caveman and hammered his fist on the table.

Kevin gave me a sheepish look. "Just a small slice?"

"Hush up, Stell. There's plenty for you to take home."

He grunted again, glared at Kevin who smiled back,

then returned to his plate. Evan quickly punctuated the moment by grabbing the can of whipped cream on the table and spraying it directly into his mouth. Stellan gestured for Evan to hit him next, but I jumped up from the table and took the can away before they could continue.

The conversation picked up, and I left them to it, giving a quick run through the living room to make sure everyone was fed, hydrated and comfortable. There I ended up settling in for a good talk with Jill Merle-Witt about the age of my house and the architecture of the neighborhood.

A moment later, Mr. Hodges was telling me how nice it was to see me around again.

Finally Linda wanted me to know how impressed she was with my sketches. She'd always thought I was so very talented, she said.

It was a lovely thing to hear, but not the easiest. I can't say I am at my best when someone showers me with praise. I turn into a bit of a gargoyle – frozen in some awkward facial expression.

Conversation has a way of passing time – well, good conversation. The first group to head out was Caroline and Jason, taking Bethany home before the munchkin got too tired. Then Jackie and Kevin followed with a plate full of pie and a glaring Stellan watching them out the door. I expected Evan to head out, but he assured me he had no intention of spending more time with his family than was absolutely necessary. He was soon sitting with my mother on the couch drinking wine, listening to her acclaim for the same Bertrand Fuller she'd been so happy to regale me with earlier.

I started my rounds of the living room, taking

empty plates and drink cups to the kitchen. As I walked down the hallway, I found someone following close behind – Stellan, with a pile of plates himself. We silently filled the dishwasher and piled the excess into the sink, his arm brushing mine a few times. Believe me, I was well aware of each time. Finally, the last round was done, and I said farewell to the Fallons as their teenage daughter and her friends wordlessly lead the way out the door.

I gathered the last few mugs and brought them into the kitchen to find Stellan standing at the sink, the sleeves of his red flannel shirt rolled up, and the water running. He was washing dishes.

That bastard.

I put my hand on his arm. "Stell, let me do that."

He shook his head. "You did the cooking, woman. Relax a bit."

I stood at his side a moment, knowing that further protest could result in him grunting at me, spraying the sink hose at me, or worse, he'd once picked me up and relocated me to another part of the house when I argued, though that was before I'd gained twenty pounds.

I futzed around, organizing and wiping down the counters, piling the dirty dishes neatly by the sink for him, and tucking leftovers in the fridge. We worked in silence, but I was trying not to dwell on that. Still, it became more apparent now that the sink was off.

I couldn't take it.

"So how are you?"

Nicely done, Faye. As smooth as it comes.

"Pretty good. A little depressed though," he said.

I was honestly startled by this declaration. "No, why?"

He gestured to the empty pie pan on the counter. "Because there's no more Apple Pie for me to take home and eat for breakfast the rest of the weekend. That's why."

I smiled. "Aaah, I thought you knew me better than that."

He leaned back against the sink as I snuck passed him. I opened the fridge and pulled out a half size casserole dish before turning like a model on *The Price is Right* so he could see his prize.

His grinned from ear to ear. "You're fucking kidding me."

"Nope! Feel special?"

"Marry me," he said, taking the pie and lowering his face so he could make inappropriate tongue movements towards it. I leaned against the counter across from him, the gentle murmur of conversation drifting in from the living room. He set the pie down and leaned back on the counter, crossing his arms. His flannel was open at the top, showing a gray tank top underneath, and his sleeves were still rolled up, displaying his forearms. God, he looked nice.

I did my best not to noticeably look down in disdain at my own ragamuffin appearance.

"So how have you been?" He asked.

I shrugged. "Alright, I guess."

"Any word on the job front?"

I shook my head. "No. How bout you? How's the game coming?"

"Stellar. Has Evan tried to buy you out yet?"

I smiled. "Yes actually!"

"What a prick."

I laughed, and there was a pause in the conversation. I searched for something to say. Silence had never been a problem with us before, but now it felt unbearable.

He crossed his ankles and leaned back. "So, I hear you and Cole are talking again?"

Fuck. You. Jackie.

I swallowed. "Yeah."

He nodded. "How's that working out?"

"I don't know, pretty good I guess."

"Really?"

I paused. "Yeah?"

He pursed his lips in an exaggerated frown. "Have you ever thought of putting yourself out there more?"

I stared at him. "What? What does that mean?"

"You know, like dating wise. Maybe try some dating web sites or some shit."

"Why on earth would I do that?"

His hands flailed out in a gesture of mild exasperation. "To meet people, get out there and maybe find someone worth your while."

"Stellan -"

"I'm just saying. I mean, are you giving Cole the time of day because you're lonely and bored, or -"

Because I can't have you, I thought. I shook my head violently, as though I could shake the thought free. "Whatever reason I'm giving Cole the time of day is my business." I paused. "And 'putting myself out there' isn't going to do anything for me anyway."

"Sure it will."

I felt my volume rising. "What do you expect to happen? I put my chubby face up on some site and say, 'Hey fellas, look no further! Desperate and sexually frustrated thirty something who needs to lose thirty pounds. Now, you'll need to pay for everything because she has no job and therefore no money,

AND she lives with mom, so when she does drop her panties, you get to have awkward sex in the childhood bedroom of her mother's house.' Seriously, I'm a fucking prize. I'm surprised they're not banging down my door, right fucking now."

Stellan stared at me a moment, mouth open. "Is that really how you see yourself?"

"That's how anyone else would see me."

"Bull shit."

I fought to keep my eyes as wide as I could, knowing that if I blinked, tears might roll down. "It's true. I'm painfully aware of it, Stell. Fucking painfully aware of it."

Stellan shifted his arms and set his jaw. "You know how I feel about that prick -"

"Yeah, everybody else feels the same fucking way, but it's my decision."

His lip twitched in a half snarl. "Of course it is. But you deserve better."

"Yeah, hard to believe when 'better' doesn't want me!"

Jesus, Faye! Watch what you say right now! Watch what you fucking say!

It was his turn to get louder. "That's fucking bull shit."

"I'm a fucking mess, Stellan. Nobody wants this!"

He moved so quickly, I didn't have time to jump. I felt warmth and pressure at my sides, then at my chest as he closed the distance between us, locked his arms around me, and kissed me. He held me tight, gripping the fabric of my shirt and pulling me away from the counter.

His kiss was soft, but his arms were strong. Every inch of him pressed into every inch of me as his kiss lightened, then returned with double the force. I shivered, reaching up to his shoulders, locking my fingers into the folds of his flannel. My body had melted the instant he touched, and I was holding onto him to stay upright as much as to pull him closer. He lightened his kiss again, and I whimpered as he slipped his tongue past my lips and darted it against mine. The response was involuntary, and I almost crumpled against him. I gripped him, pulled at him, and he reciprocated, the two of us shifting against the counter until I was almost lifted completely onto it. I moved my hands to his back, my mouth open, my tongue seeking his. He hoisted me onto the counter and slid his hand up my back, folding his fingers in my hair.

"Have you guys seen my keys?"

We parted instantly, Stellan turning for the fridge, his hand to his lips to hide a smile. Jackie stormed in from the dining room to find me sitting on the counter, my hair probably knotted at the back of my head, and I could feel the afterburn of his stubble against my chin.

I swallowed, staring at her. She glanced at me, then at Stellan, then back at me.

I shrank under her gaze.

You're a whore. You're a whore. You're a whore. You're no better than Cole.

"What's going on in here?" She asked, her tone jovial and teasing, but I was up and heading down the hallway toward the stairs.

I bounded up and away, up and free of what had just happened, away from the glaring reality of my fuck up.

I turned to shut the door to my room.

Stellan was there. "What's wrong?"

I growled. "Why now?"

"What?"

"I wanted you so bad! I practically threw myself at you."

He raised his eyebrows. "When?"

My voice was shaking. "At Evan's party! You pushed me away."

He shook his head. "You were drunk as a fucking skunk, Faye."

"I wasn't that drunk!"

"You were fucking steaming. What kind of man do you think I am?"

I gasped for breath, trying to settle my voice as I spoke. "But now I'm not free anymore. Why did you have to do this now? Why couldn't you want me before -"

"What? I've always wanted you. And what do you mean you're not free?"

I put my hands to my face. I was an instant from weeping, openly bawling on the floor. I fought it, feeling my throat clench and burn. "I'm with Cole."

He shook his head like I'd slapped him. "So fucking what?! Break it off. He's a cocksucking fuck bag!"

"I can't do that!"

Stellan stood there, his face changing slowly. "Why not?"

I searched for an answer. Why couldn't I? Why couldn't I simply tell the man who collapsed in my arms weeping at Paparazzi that he should go fuck himself? "I can't just hop from one bed to the next -"

His expression hardened. "Are you serious? Is that what you think this is?"

We stared at each other. He held my gaze, and I trembled. Then he was gone, and his absence felt like drowning. I pressed my hand against the door and gently pushed it shut.

CHAPTER ELEVEN

No one heard from me for days. Even my mother attempted to breach the sanctity of my room and was met with Troll-under-the-bridge worthy disdain. I'd even let my phone die as I tried to avoid whatever might be happening with Cole.

So he hadn't cheated on me.

So he wanted to be friends - maybe more.

Not even going to think about it.

The newly charged battery resulted in a near extinction level event of my phone blowing the hell up. Every ringtone I had on the damn thing sounded off, one after another after another, cutting each other off like they were all stumbling to be heard; Cole, Meghan, Jackie, Evan, Mom, and yes - Stellan.

I stared at the phone, imagining what the text might say – all the caring, even loving things he might say that would make my heart feel better.

Rather than acknowledge this thought, I picked up my phone, scanned the inbox, ignoring all other texts and opened Stellan's.

I need the last of the sketches you were working on, if you have them. Thanks.

Natural reaction? I cried. Clearly that wasn't the heartwarming message I'd been hoping for.

But it's such a simple message, what's the problem you basket case? You ask.

He said, 'Thanks.'

Thanks. Not "Thank you," not "You're a Doll," not... well whatever, he said Thanks! It may seem the simplest thing, but I knew him well. He had the manners of some juggernaut of chivalric purpose. He held the door open for everyone, he called men 'sir' and women 'dear,' and he himself was the person who'd solidified my stance on the words used to express gratitude.

If you mean it, you say Thank YOU. If you don't – well, you're a dick so hopefully nobody does anything for you, but that's not the point! Damn it, I clearly wasn't thinking straight.

I texted back.

Cavalier 'I'm-not-sobbing-right-now' Me - **I might have a few strays. Nothing major. When do you need them?**

I scanned through my other texts, responding to Cole's many random notes that had culminated in a somewhat brisk declaration of my silence being rude and undeserved. I told him I'd had a few bad days and wasn't in the greatest mood – and that my phone had died – but as I was typing, I started spewing my thoughts of how, given his previous behavior, I could stab a fork in his eye, and he'd still have no right to call me rude.

I gave Jackie and Meghan blanket statements, and ignored Evans' text completely. They all wanted to know how I was, or in Meghan's case, whether she should try going redhead as well. By the time I breached the downstairs for the first time in 72 hours, Stellan's ringtone sang from my phone, firing off a strange pressure in my stomach - like someone bracing themselves for bad news.

Stellan - **Not to be a brat, but can you rework a**

couple stills for me? I've emailed you the files and the details. Thanks.

I saw the 'Thanks' again and almost threw my phone.

Thanks. Thanks? I'll show you what 'Thanks' will get ya!

I know what you're thinking. That I broke out in a rendition of "Sobbing on the Kitchen Floor," but I didn't. The sense of indignation I felt at Cole's texts was still with me. I paced around the downstairs looking for something - anything to do that would give me a solid excuse not to check my email and respond to his request. After some tea, a shower, and an attempt to read two pages of the same god awful book I had waiting to punch me in the face with stupid, I caved.

Fucker.

The email consisted of seventeen sketches and notes on detail, color. Some stills he wanted me to sketch in a couple specific chimps; a gorilla here, a couple startled capuchins there. Others he wanted me to redo the whole thing *without* any animals in it.

I grumbled and swore at the screen, reading his email out loud with additional f-bombs until I heard the front door open. Mom called for me, and I declared myself, turning my chair to face the door. She leaned in, dressed in full work regalia.

"Hey hon. How are you feel – oh, I'm sorry. I'll let you work." And she disappeared again.

"No, Mom. I haven't started yet."

She returned to the door with a strange smile on her face and hovered with electricity.

"What you forget?" I asked.

She sighed heavily. "What didn't I forget? Just one of those mornings."

She took a step into the office and leaned in to inspect the screen. Clearly her glasses were one of the forgotten items. She chuckled. "What on earth is that about?"

I shook my head. "It's just a few panels for Stellan's game."

She raised a curious eyebrow, but was in too much of a rush to delve further. "Well, I'm off like a herd of turtles. You can tell me about it later, maybe?"

She slipped out of the office, and I began my response email.

Stellan,

I don't know how you want me to rework these sketches. I don't have the fancy sketch pad anymore. Do you want whole new paper sketches?

Oh, I was being a bitch. I opened the panels side by side and began scanning through what I needed to do, when I felt a gentle pressure on the top of my head. I looked to find my mother had snuck back in to kiss the top of my head before she headed out.

I felt like I was twelve years old all over again. I didn't mind it.

She smiled at me. "I'm so happy to see you drawing."

And she was gone.

I sat there staring at the screen trying not to be a blubbering asshole while I waited for Stellan to respond. Twenty five minutes later, boots stomped up my front steps and the doorbell rang.

It was Stellan, returning the fancy doodad. Stellan trudged in the front door, his hair growing out, and his face flushed. He was wearing a quintessentially Swedish sweater, its high collar framing his jawline.

He always looked good in Swede.

Really? Really?! You couldn't just send me a snide email back, you had to make me see you with your tussled hair and your sexy - You son of a -

"When do you need them by?" I asked.

He met my gaze with unwavering intent. "As soon as you can. I'm on the final stretch so it would be nice to get them soon."

I nodded, staring him down. "I'll see what I can do."

"Thanks," he said. "Let me know if you need anything."

Then he turned and stomped back down my porch steps and up Davis Court. I stood in the doorway a while, the cold air creeping in. My grandmother would have screamed from the kitchen by now, and I'd have shut the door, but for now, I just watched him walk up the street and out of sight.

I plugged in the pad, went for another cup of tea, a quick snack from the cupboard, then settled in to work. Perhaps it was the chill in the air after leaving the door open so long, but instead of holing up in my tiny little office, I pulled my laptop out into the living room, plugged it in by my favorite chair, set my tea in the windowsill and pulled on my snow boots. I headed out the back door to the wood pile and grabbed as many logs as I could carry. I dumped them on the floor in front of the fireplace and sat cross legged on the hardwood. A few moments later, I had a roaring fire.

My grandmother always told me I should have been a girl scout.

I settled into my chair with my pad, my laptop, my tea, and over a dozen sketches. When I finally called it a night, I'd burned through as many logs as sketches, and it was almost midnight.

Stellan actually broke his emotionless streak when I emailed him that all the sketches were ready, and I could drop them off the next day. I didn't receive the boisterous '*You're fucking wonderful*' email until the next morning, but it was appreciated nonetheless. Appreciated, and painful. I didn't respond.

The next day, I packed up the pad and the flash drive, which contained several unsolicited sketches that the muse had demanded alongside those Stellan had. I tossed on my coat and scarf and headed out the door. I was feeling surprisingly light that morning. I'd fallen asleep thinking of Stanley's comic strip, or the poo flinging Howler monkey with the joyously bulging eyes. The images spilled over into each other like boiling water. It wasn't until halfway to Stellan's house that I realized I hadn't looked at my feet once.

The weather had shifted with purpose. I grumbled in the cold, not because the insides of my nostrils were freezing – though they were - but because I was determined to be as put out as humanly possible. How dare he ask me to just drop everything in my busy life and cater to his basement programmer hobbies? Yes, I could have driven, and yes if I'd stayed home I would probably be perfecting my rendition of "Sobbing on the Kitchen Floor," but that isn't the point. The point is – whatever.

I caught sight of Stellan's house and the tail end of a rather slick looking black sedan in the driveway. I stomped up the steps onto the porch, and unlike any other visit in my life, rang the damn doorbell.

With derision!

A Mazda 3 came barreling into his driveway,

blocking in the black sedan. I didn't recognize it, and naturally imagined some new, vapid girlfriend I might be forced to meet and be made miserable by.

Oh, so this is the kind of girl you *do* want to make out with? I hate her.

Then the driver hopped out of the car.

Patty Hannity looked just as button worthy cute in her yoga pants and boat necked shirt as she did in her Ranger uniform. I stopped and watched her.

Her energy wasn't right.

She caught on her seat belt, struggled with the keys, muttered some swears to herself, glanced at her cell phone, slammed the car door when she finally got out and started patting her pockets as she stood there a moment. I stood at the front walkway and waited for her to notice me. She hustled to the back door of her car and pulled a strange bucket out of the back seat. She turned, saw me, and I smiled.

She did not.

She glanced awkwardly toward the bucket in her hand, and forced a wave. "Hey Faye, what are you up to?"

I took a few steps toward her, waiting for her to actually meet my gaze. "Just visiting Stellan. How bout you?"

She gave one of those smiles that consists of frowning, but fighting to keep the corners of your mouth up. She took a moment, shrugged, and closed her eyes. "Working."

It was then that Patty Hannity broke into a cover rendition of Faye Jensen's mega hit single, 'Sobbing on the Sidewalk."

Well shit.

I stood there frozen a second, the way any person

does when random people explode in untold misery before their very eyes. Yet, that second passed quickly, and I crossed the front lawn and hugged her. She wrapped her free hand around me and apologized into my coat, but she didn't stop crying. I squeezed her and released her enough to look at her. She didn't meet my gaze, but she wiped her eyes and apologized again.

"Do you want to talk about it?" I asked.

She shrugged. "What is there to talk about? My life's falling apart, that's all -"

And she was off again, tears streaming down her fairy princess worthy face. I hugged her as tightly as I could and said, "Welcome to the club."

She stifled a sob. "I'm sorry! I don't know why I'm crying so hard."

"Because that's what all the cool kids are doing." She stifled a laugh. "You wanna go for a walk?"

She glanced to the front door. "I have two more houses to clean this afternoon, so -" She pressed her thumb to the spot between her eyebrows and closed her eyes, fighting off another bout of tears.

I rubbed her arm. This was the strangest sensation in the world, to be on the giving end of comfort for a change. It almost felt – I don't know – liberating? As though offering her my shoulder somehow lifted my own troubles. I wanted to hear her vent, to know what could bring the incomparably perky Patty down – and in that desire, there wasn't a shred of satisfaction in knowing she was suffering. This must be progress.

Finally, she dropped the bucket on the front steps and turned back with a sudden air of dignity and an air of 'I do what I damn well want.'

"Yes, I think I'd like that," she said.

We headed for Main Street, keeping a snail's pace as Patty opened up. Perhaps that isn't the right word, exploded more like. Tears quickly gave way to a righteous indignation as she described the last six months of her life.

"So, you know we were living with my folks, yes?" She started.

"No!" I said with a little more fervor than I'd intended. It was out of a sudden inexplicable sense of camaraderie, but I didn't expect her to know that.

Thankfully she didn't take offense. "Oh yeah. They sold their house and moved in with us last year. So six months ago Geoffrey loses his job, right? Got *laid off*, he said. So, he starts looking for something else, and I try picking up extra hours at work. And you know how it is, three months pass - no job. So that leaves the mortgage to me and my parents - my *retired* parents. You can only imagine how that went over. So I picked up some work cleaning houses -"

And again she trailed off.

"Honey, there's nothing wrong with cleaning houses."

She jumped. "No! I know! I know there isn't, it's just – I just didn't want anyone to know, you know? I mean, this is fucking Concord, for fuck's sake."

The sound of Patty's Glee Club caliber voice swearing across Main Street was more than a little awesome, to tell the truth, but she quickly settled herself. "But then things got so bad, I had to take Stell's house on – he's the first client I have that I know, you know? I mean, I went to high school with, you know?"

"And that bothers you?"

She tilted her head. "Well, yeah. It really kinda does."

"And yet, he's living in his parent's basement. No offense to him."

She seemed to mull that over a moment. "I don't know. I mean, he's friends with you, with Evan, who knows who else?"

I laughed. "No one else, I promise. Liking people isn't one of Stellan's virtues."

She nodded and started walking again. "He pays me more than he needs to, too. Seriously, I think Linda Ødegård repels dirt or something. Their house is always fucking spotless."

I glanced back at her, her eyes on the ground. "Is that what's bothering you? Just cleaning Stellan's house?"

She looked back at me sheepishly, and frowned. "No."

We'd gone two blocks when Patty's tears returned, but this time, she powered through them with an explosion of words. "Three weeks ago, I heard about a contracting job from Peter at the Visitor Center. He said to give Geoff the information - and I did! Geoff said he had an interview with the guy the next day and was gone all afternoon. He came home saying it went great, right? Really great! So a couple days later I ask Peter if he's heard anything from his friend about the interview and - he looked at me like I'd sprouted horns, Faye! Geoffrey never went to the fucking interview! He'd never even called the guy!"

I made exasperated noises to show I was listening, but she was off.

"So I checked his credit card for that afternoon, you know to see if he'd gone anywhere while he was out living a damn lie. He'd been at the bar. That day and I can't even count how many others. Days that he told me he was out looking for work. He was drinking! The fucker was getting wasted on money I was earning scrubbing fucking toilets! He was having a few pints down the pub! Why I didn't smell it on him, I don't know."

We'd drawn some attention there on the street corner, but I simply glared back at any disapproving faces, and they moved right along.

"I confronted him, of course. And he denies it, so I show him the credit card statement, and he accuses *me* of being conniving! Like I'd committed some great crime by pointing out that he was a lying sack of shit!"

"Did you kill him?"

The tears overcame the tirade, and she put her face in her hands. "No. He left me."

I grabbed her like she was on fire, and she bawled on my shoulder. The passing faces of disapproval shifted now, and instead the looks were those of honest kindness. I waved at a couple of silver haired ladies who mouthed things like, 'Is she alright? Does she need anything?' People who didn't know either of us. I nodded them away with my thanks and held Patty for several moments.

She recuperated and glanced around in embarrassment, only to find an older woman in a long black coat waiting at her side with a handkerchief. Patty took it and smiled through tears before the woman walked away.

This was why I still loved my hometown.

We crossed the street as though Patty didn't want the same store front to hear the rest of the story. "He said he'd been unhappy since my parents moved in. Said he didn't want to live like that anymore. That he'd been planning it for a while, but didn't know how to tell me."

"Planning what?"

She sniffled. "Leaving. His whole family knew. I've talked to his mother on the phone so many times the past few months, and she knew…"

I shook my head. "Knew that he was a douche bag? Would be nice if she mentioned that, right?"

Yeah, the words just came out, sorry. I didn't know what to say.

"He packed up and went home to Edinburgh last Thursday. I don't know what to do."

I hooked my arm with hers, and we continued to walk. It seemed she'd spent the more powerful tears by now, and what was left was a soft sorrow that read like age on her beautiful face.

"I'd give my friend Meghan's advice and say fuck anything that moves, but that won't help." I know from experience.

She forced a smile and shook her head. "I don't know if I could let anyone touch me, even if I wanted them to."

God, I felt her in my damn bones. I was angry for her, angry that someone would bring pain to her door, to a woman who had never so much as frowned at a stranger. The notion of her huge cocked Scotsman turning out to be such a disappointment just rocked my whole idea of Patty – of huge cocked Scotsmen in general. Her wonderland of a perfect life that I'd resented her for had been a lie.

There was a lesson in that somewhere. I was too messed up to catch it, but it was there.

We rounded the corner back onto Central Square and something struck me. I couldn't tell you where it came from – a desire to help, maybe even to step out of the cave I'd been in and spend time with another human being, but the words were out before I knew I'd said them. "I'm actually planning on having a get-together, Christmas dinner party sort of thing – and I'd love to have you come."

She smiled at me, and for the first time that day, it was a true smile. "Really? When is it?"

I searched my nonexistent schedule and picked a day. "Next Saturday actually."

She hemmed and hawed a second about her own schedule, but the tone was clear. She accepted. Suddenly, I had a dinner party to plan.

I forgot to ring the doorbell at Stellan's and simply walked in out of habit. It's hard to remember to behave indignantly all the time, friends. We found Stellan in the living room. He launched out of the chair, heading straight for me. He must have heard us outside earlier and was waiting anxiously for what I carried under my arm.

When he had a project to work on, he didn't like to be kept waiting. Stellan was patient as Job - unless it really mattered. Then whatever it was couldn't come soon enough.

I handed the satchel over to a solid and sincere, 'Thank you.'

I actually smiled at him.

Patty tried to scoot past us in the front hallway, but Stellan stopped her. "Hey, here lady."

He handed her an envelope and turned for the basement door. I glanced her way, trying to decipher if I was meant to follow Stell.

She stifled a strange noise. "What is this?"

There was a shrillness to her voice, like she was holding something hot in her mouth.

"Today was tuition day at Ninpo, so I thought I'd take care of a couple months in one go while I had the cash."

He waved to me, and I hustled to catch up as Patty protested from the living room, her voice still shaky. I shot her a look, silently asking what was up.

Her face crinkled in a strange, happy frown. "This is more than two months' worth, Ste -"

"Three months then, whatever it will cover."

He was on the basement steps and gone before she could protest. She shook her head at me, her mouth open, but no words came out. I watched her plop down into a chair and press the envelope to her forehead to cover her face.

I left Patty to her thoughts.

I followed Stellan downstairs.

"What up, Jensen?"

I was greeted at the bottom of the basement stairs by Evan's distracted How-Do-You-Do? He was splayed out on Stellan's disheveled bed. Stellan hustled over to his 'wall of screens.' I stood at the edge of the Persian rug and kicked at the tassels.

Why did Evan have to be there? And why did Stellan have to be so sweet to Patty? I'd deflated completely!

Stellan's room was a basement, ladies and gentlemen. No one ever claimed differently, but it was nice. The walls were still cinderblock on two sides, but the floor was finished. The door to the bathroom was at the foot of the bed. There was a separate, unseen section of the basement for storage and robotics circuitry when Stellan felt inclined.

I mentioned he was a genius, yes?

He'd made the space a home – art on the walls, a fleet of technological wizardry in the form of three separate monitors on his work desk. There was a flat screen the size of an industrial fridge on the wall with bookshelves and an entertainment center he built himself. He had every video game console known to man, every movie he'd ever liked, but those were all stored away behind the wooden cabinet doors.

Stellan was no slob. There wasn't an item of garbage in sight, and there were plenty of comfy seats available, had I chosen to take one. I stood a few moments, feeling like a complete asshole. I was close to turning and walking out the door when Evan suddenly exploded.

"Aw fuck! Are you serious?"

"What's up?" Stellan asked.

"They just threw shit at me! Shit?! Jensen, you drew this? Those dirty, shit throwing bastards."

Stellan smiled. He'd ignored me since I came downstairs, but I knew why. I didn't forget how lost in work he could get, I'd chosen to ignore it and silently judge him. He gestured toward a chair, but I shook my head and handed him the flash drive.

"There's not much on it, just some backdrop stuff."

"Anything you have is good -"

Evan burst into laughter. "Jensen, you're a fucking genius!"

Stellan and I turned to him. I raised an eyebrow.

Evan wiggled his iPhone at me and the image of the chimps gathered around a chalkboard with bulging eyes and expressions of manic glee flashed on the screen. "Beta testing, bitches!"

"Really? It's that far along?" I directed my question to Stellan, but he didn't have a chance to answer.

Evan sat up, staring intently at his phone. "This is fucking hilarious."

"Lemme see!"

Evan shifted to make room on the bed. "Oh my fuck! I'm addicted."

Stellan slid his chair between myself and Evan. "No, she can't see it yet."

I stopped, but Evan asked on my behalf. "Why not? Let the woman see her baby!"

Stellan shook his head. "It's not done."

I sat on the bed. "Oh, I don't care."

He pointed at Evan and glared. "I said no."

Evan shrugged at me and went back to playing.

I searched Stellan's face. He just turned back to his screens, and the room fell back to silence.

Stellan went back to his screens, and I plopped right onto his bed. I'd left the house in a grump, but something about that walk with Patty, that full day of sketching, and hearing Evan playing the very game I'd been drawing for - it all left me feeling almost incapable of disdain. I mean, I had it. I definitely could muster it if the troops needed to be rallied, but by default, I was just sort of there.

Stellan brought up the files on his screen and chuckled at the first panel he opened. "You're a fucking machine, woman."

I shrugged on the bed, slumping back against the wall. "Naw, just kinda fell into a rhythm."

"Well, I love your rhythm."

Evan made an inappropriate comment, and I

laughed.

Stellan started working, inspecting each panel as he opened them. I listened like a child at the top of the staircase after bed time, hoping to catch a sharper inhale or a chuckle with every one he opened. Of the twenty two panels, I got at least a dozen chuckles and one 'Fuck Yeah!' I was content.

"You need me for anything specific?" I asked, finally.

He shook his head. "No, why? You leaving?"

When he turned to look at me, I was struck by the disappointment on his face. I'd fixated so thoroughly on the tension between us since Evan's party, that I never thought he might still want my company as a friend. "Well, I don't have to. Just figured if you were working, I might leave you to it."

He spun his chair halfway back and then shifted there a minute. "Well, it's up to you. I guess I will be preoccupied."

Despite that, he didn't spin the chair the rest of the way. He was waiting for my decision. I remembered the comfort we'd once shared, the capacity to do separate nothings, together. It was something I missed every day.

"Ok, I'll hang out for a while. Can I please see the game now?"

Evan shot me a smile, but Stellan turned back to his screens. "Negatory."

I groaned at him. "What the hell, man?"

He flashed a grin over his shoulder. "It isn't done, damn it. Slow your roll!"

"I don't want to slow my roll!"

He turned back to his screens. "Hush up. Daddy's working."

I laughed. Kitchen cupboards rattled upstairs, and I remembered Patty. "Oh, hey. So I'm apparently having a Christmas party."

The click clack of his fingers hitting keys stopped. "What's this now?"

Evan made a soft humming sound.

I shrugged. "Yeah, seriously. Not sure what I was thinking, but I guess I'm having a dinner party next Saturday night."

"You animal," Stellan said.

I chuckled. "I know, right? Get some thirty-somethings together with some red wine and reindeer sweaters and see what debauchery unfolds. Right up your alley."

"No doubt."

I shifted forward on the bed, resting my weight on my knees. "Will you come?"

Without hesitation. "Of course."

I nodded, muttering my approval and grabbed the remote for the talking wall, finding an episode of *Spaced* on Netflix. I then pulled my phone from my pocket, shooting a mass text to the usual suspects.

Don't call the cops or anything, but I'm having a Christmas Party next Saturday. Seven sharp. Reindeer sweaters optional, booze is not.

I sent the text off to Jackie and Meghan, then added Evan, given he couldn't take his eyes off his phone. I knew it was a shot in the dark to invite him, but even if he's busier than Hades, a girl could hope. I sat there letting Simon Pegg's accent work its sultry magic on me until I made the decision to copy the text to another contact – Cole.

This was trying, right?

By midafternoon, I'd watched half the season of

Spaced and said maybe seven words to Stellan. He was working, but still the time felt well spent. I'd forgotten how easily the three of us could just be. During that time, I heard Patty finishing upstairs and finally decided to head out.

I finally stood to leave, offering a quick wave to each of them.

"Hold up! Did you walk?"

I tossed my answer over my shoulder to Evan. "Yep."

"Alright, I'll walk you home."

"If you value your life, you will not show her the game," Stellan said, his tone rumbling in his chest.

Evan grabbed his red scarf from the bed. "I know, dick. God, you're such a diva."

I felt almost strange at the thought of walking through town with my old friend. Still, it felt nice to have someone want my company.

Once we hit the sidewalk, he wrapped his scarf around his neck and glanced back at the Ødegård front door. "So, what the fuck was that?"

I startled. "What do you mean? I thought that went pretty well!"

He gave me an exasperated staredown. "Are you serious? That vibe was awkward as hell!"

It was? Fuck!

I turned and stormed off down the sidewalk. The thought that someone else could feel tension between us pained me. This bastard was not going to see me upset again, damn it.

He caught up and matched my pace. "Babe, you don't have to tell me what's going on, but – are you doin okay?"

I managed to shake my head. He hooked his arm in

mine and walked me across the street. The closeness - and the silence – was appreciated.

We made it as far as the town hall before he spoke again. "I've never understood the two of you."

I glanced up at him, too startled to care how red my eyes were. He stopped walking when he saw my face and grabbed me, squeezing me against him, the thick fabric of our coats and scarves leaving the embrace to feel like that of a sleeping bag more than a man. God fucking damn it Evan, you give good hugs.

He shook his head as he squeezed me. "I swear to god, the two of you are on the same cycle or something."

I punched him from the confines of his long arms.

"What? I'm serious! Stell's been weird for weeks. Fucking mopey, snippy bastards, the both of you."

"He didn't seem mopey -"

Evan snorted. "Yeah well, he put on a brave face when you got there, didn't he?"

I stopped and stared down the street. Did the idea of Stellan being upset too make me feel better? It didn't change the fact that he didn't want to make out with me, but –

Fuck. That thought ruined my mood all over again.

My phone chimed in my pocket – Cole. I frowned, struggling with the notion of giving Cole 'a chance' all while pining for a man who doesn't want me back. A part of me felt guilty for a moment. Sure, I didn't have pictures of Stellan's junk on my phone.

That thought made me frown. I would love to have a picture of Stellan's junk on my phone. How fucked up was that?

I didn't share any of this with Evan, of course.

We turned and started walking back toward my

house when Evan said, "I have to ask. Do you know what's up with Stellan?"

I opened my mouth, but no words came. I shrugged.

"Do you think it's because you two had sex?"

I stopped dead in my tracks and stared at him wild eyed. "What! We did not! We just made out!"

"Boom!" He punched the air and started pacing, muttering 'I knew it! I fucking knew it!'

I punched his arm with all the fury I had. "You fuck bag!"

"What!? It's about fucking time! God, I'm good! "

I gaped at him.

He furrowed his brow like I'd asked what color the sky was. "The two of you should have been making out in high school as far as I'm concerned. God, that fucking explains it! I always wondered why he kept dating the most vapid, boring girls -"

"You don't date much better!"

"Yeah, but I've learned my lesson. He hasn't."

He continued to pace and silently celebrate this great revelation. I grabbed him by the sleeve of his coat and made him look at me.

He threw his hands up. I realized the two of us were making quite a scene for downtown Concord, but I didn't care. I was a basket case, and he was a billionaire. We could do what we damn well pleased.

"Well, he's holding out for you, isn't he?"

I openly scoffed at this notion, but he flailed his hands a few more times in celebration. "It's true! And what, did you reject him? Jensen! You fucking didn't?"

I frowned. And they call this kid a genius.

"I didn't! He rejected -" The words stalled in my

throat. I couldn't say them. They made me too sad. "I tried to instigate things with him at your house and -"

"WHAT?! Where was I?"

My face contorted in frustration. "It was your Halloween party. He didn't -"

"Bull shit! Really?"

"Yes, and he didn't exactly react -"

Evan lunged toward me, ready for juicy details. "What do you mean? How'd he react?"

I glared at him. Evan was impossible to communicate with when he was excited. He displayed his palms in apology, and I continued. "He pushed me away. Then on Thanksgiving -"

Evan punched the air again. "I KNEW it!!"

"Will you shut up?"

"Sorry, sorry! So, what? On Thanksgiving, you pushed *him* away? What, to get back at him?"

"NO!" It was my turn to lose my cool. The thought of Evan thinking I would ever deliberately hurt Stellan was an insult to my very being.

He could tell. He apologized again. "So what then?"

"Well, Cole and I -"

His eyes went wide. "Cole? Who the fuck is Cole? Oh! You mean Festering Asshole. Yeah, fuck that guy. In the ass, if you don't mind me saying so."

I started to speak, to defend or harangue, but instead I stood silent. What was it? Why had I pushed Stellan away? Because I couldn't stoop to Cole's level? Because I couldn't hurt someone after they'd poured their heart out to me and convinced me to take them back? Because I really wanted to try to work on things with Cole? Or was it something else?

Evan waited a moment, his face softening.

I stared across Monument Square.

"It's ok, hon. You don't have to tell me."

I stood there a moment, my mouth going dry. Evan put his hand on the top of my head, patting my hair down gently before grabbing me by the back of the neck and kissing my cheek. Then he held his arm out to me and walked me home in silence.

CHAPTER TWELVE

Evan came in to sit with my mother for a few minutes. Pam puffed up like a proud peacock to see him. They sat chit chatting about the museum, his most recent projects, and an upcoming exhibit at the school that included an artist my mother had been fawning over for a few weeks – Bertrand Fuller.

I managed to sit and be pleasant, but I was preoccupied. Evan knew about Stellan and I. The thought worried me.

Before he left for the afternoon, I pulled him aside.

"Please don't say anything to Stellan, ok?"

He gave me a snarky raised eyebrow, as though to say 'Do you really need to ask?' then was on his way.

Three days later, I woke up to find my mother staring at the front wall from behind the couch, smiling and preening. I turned to see what she was fawning over. The painting was impossible to miss – an impressionist landscape of gold, green and blue now taking up almost the entirety of the front wall. I was impressed at its size as much as its skill. It was spectacular. I inspected the signature at the corner.

Mom beamed at me. "My first Bertrand Fuller."

I took it in, appreciatively. "Holy crap. You weren't kidding, it's gorgeous."

She stood behind the couch, taking a few more steps back into the hallway, all the while staring at the painting. "It's just a masterpiece, isn't it?"

I joined her. "I'm very impressed."

"He has such a gift. I have to call the insurance agency this afternoon to see about having someone come down."

At this I furrowed my brow and turned to her. "Really? You have to insure it? How much did it cost?"

She didn't miss a beat. "Forty grand."

My jaw dropped. "Holy fuck."

"I know!"

I shook my head as though I was shooing off a fly. "You spent forty grand on a painting? Where the hell did you get forty grand, mom!?"

She smiled and shot me a sneaky glance before turning her eyes back to the painting.

She handed me a small note card. I flipped it open to find a familiar scrawl. I'd received many inappropriate notes in this very handwriting throughout Chemistry class, junior year.

Pamela,
I couldn't agree more. His work is exceptional. As I recall, this was your favorite.
Take care,
Evan

"Are you fucking kidding me?"

My mom beamed. "I know!"
"Excuse me."

I turned for the kitchen and despite my mother's jovial protests from the living room, called to harangue Evan. He answered on the second ring.

I had two words for him. "You dick!"

"My secret identity! Who told?"

"I'm so mad at you."

"I swear I didn't say a word to Stellan!"

"Not that!"

He laughed. "Then, what did I do?"

I took a few minutes to berate him, demand he buy me a small island if he wants to throw his money around, then quickly had to convince him I was kidding, please don't buy me a small island. The conversation settled onto the subject of my impromptu dinner party.

Evan was in full sarcastic glory today. "Very exciting news. I'll get to enjoy that awkward silence between you and Stell again. Looking forward to it."

"Damn it, I didn't think it was that bad!"

Evan sighed. "Seriously, you're both idiots."

"Screw you!"

"So what shall I bring to this gala? Other than my devastating good looks."

I chuckled. "Humility. And I don't know, whatever you can grab – or can have one of your minions grab."

"Yes, yes. My minions." Evan let out as maniacal a laugh as he could before yelling off to some imaginary servant. "Dance monkey! Dance!"

I was always a little unnerved by how well Evan could laugh maniacally. If there were ever a comic book caliber super villain waiting to happen, Evan had the right stuff. I suddenly had an idea for a comic strip of a billionaire super villain whose idea of evil was to redesign Facebook - again. I wondered whether Evan would be honored or insulted. He made further demands of the imaginary minion, and I decided the answer was honored.

My mother slipped into the kitchen past me.

"What's he bringing to what?"

I turned into the phone. "I gotta go nut job, but I'll see you Saturday."

"Fuck yeah you will. Kisses."

I laughed and made a puckering sound before putting down the phone. My mother ogled me a moment, appraising the innocent gesture between old friends. I shook my head at her. "I actually decided to have a get together. Bit of a dinner party."

"Oh, isn't that nice? You haven't done that in a long while."

"I know. Trying to remember how I used to go about it."

She scoffed. "Oh, you're a master at that sort of thing. You take after Grammy."

My phone buzzed on the counter – Cole. I ignored it for the moment, but was surprised to find my mother apparently knew his ringtone. "So you and Cole are on speaking terms again?"

I grew tense, instantly. "Yes."

She pulled a mug out of the cupboard and began filling the kettle. "Well, that's nice."

I didn't move or speak for a long moment. When the spell broke, I shrugged.

She glanced toward me, but did not make eye contact. We discussed dishes I might make for the party, and she laughed when I asked if she still had any puff paint style Christmas sweatshirts from the eighties. She assured me she did not and headed upstairs to read. I finally ventured toward my phone.

Cole - **I might be willing to do that. Are you free tonight?**

I glanced around the kitchen, trying to decide if I had prior engagements. Or more aptly, was there a movie on cable I might enjoy watching alone. I decided there was.

By Friday afternoon, Stellan had gotten me to work on a few more sketches, told me I was a genius a few times, and threatened to send pictures of his bowel movements when I didn't accept the compliment.

I was meandering through Crosby's Supermarket during just one such conversation when my phone went off with an alert I'd almost forgotten – my work email. It fired off in the produce section, and I was so startled by it, I almost dropped a bag of Cortland Apples.

I scrambled to my pocket for my phone and found the alert text – Dennis Shay.

I leaned against the counter with my heart pounding against my ribs.

Ms. Jensen,

My apologies for the delay, but I'm sure you know how these things can get. I have an early Christmas present for you. The position has officially opened, which gives me the opportunity (finally) to offer it to you. If you accept, you'd start the second week of the New Year.

Please get back to me as soon as you can to let me know if you're still interested.

We're so looking forward to having you join the group – and thank you for your patience.

Dennis Shay
Head of Marketing, Chalice Enterprises

I stared at that email with the stem of an apple pushing a divot into my left butt cheek for at least five minutes, reading the words over and over again. I didn't move until an older woman excused herself to reach past me for a Fuji.

I was in shock. I'd been disappointed for so long, this felt like someone popped a brown paper bag next to my ear to cure hiccups. I paid for my groceries with my mother's bank card and proceeded to sit in a catatonic state in the driver's seat of my car for another twenty minutes.

I didn't call anyone, text anyone, nothing. I just sat there.

It wasn't until I pulled into my driveway that I finally called Dennis and accepted the position.

I decided to save the announcement for my party – turn the shindig into a celebration of sorts. I could tell everyone, we could toast, maybe get plastered, play a few games, and all would be right with the world. Keeping it to myself made sleep just about impossible that night, so I spent much of it cooking. It was similar to Thanksgiving – pies and more pies, my usual suspects. For Christmas, though, I switched it up - gingerbread whoopee pies with pumpkin frosting, and my own version of fruitcake, made with lemons, blueberries, and a sugar glaze. I wasn't messing around, ladies and gentlemen. I also whipped up three batches of my grandmother's chocolate chip cookies and placed them with red tissue paper into holiday tins to be given as prizes.

Yes, prizes.

Yes, I have games at my parties, is that a problem? What? You don't like fun?

I knew my friends well – Stellan would most likely

bring Sam Adams and then devour the entire Swedish Apple Pie by himself, Evan would bring whiskey, Meghan would bring wine, and Jackie would bring some extravagant baked good to shame mine by appearance alone, but I'd love her for it. Patty and Cole were the only wild cards. I couldn't imagine them bringing a grand array of savory dishes, so I'd accepted that responsibility as well – French bread, brie and grapes, a platter of bruschetta with basil I kept growing in the kitchen window, and tuna croquettes.

Yes, I said croquettes, whatever. And I said it in my best Julia Child impersonation, I assure you.

I finally rounded out the pretentious spread with a bowl of lays chips and a big ol' tub of onion dip. I'd most likely drown myself in that bad boy before the end of the night.

I spent Saturday finishing up the last few dishes, stuffing the fridge with prepared platters, setting out the table in the living room and decorating it. Then I spent the late afternoon preparing the games, with sporadic last minute cleaning spurts in between.

My mother made comment of how lovely the house looked just before heading out for the evening – a dinner date with a college friend. I knew she'd made the plan deliberately in order to leave me the house for the evening, and though I would have loved her company, I appreciated it.

Jackie, as expected, was the first to arrive, offering my favorite chocolate raspberry porte at the door. Kevin carried an industrial sized cake carrier in behind her. I took the bottle to the kitchen while she started setting up. I came back to the living room to find Jackie's baking proclivities had veered into cake decorating. She was unveiling a three tier Christmas tree cake on the table. It was immaculate, with fondant ornaments and rice crispy treat presents frosted and tied with bows.

I naturally called her a whore.

She beamed at me. "I've been trying."

I glared at her. "Trying my ass, it's gorgeous!"

She shrugged. "My first attempts weren't great -"

"They were delicious!" Kevin called from the kitchen.

"-but I think I'm getting there."

Not long thereafter, Meghan arrived with the expected bottle of Merlot, barreling past me to toss her coat into the closet and demand I appraise her outfit. She was wearing a fitted red dress that one might expect on Marilyn Monroe, a flower in her hair to match. She looked almost as stunning as Jackie's cake.

I'm pretty sure I called her a whore, too.

She wagged her finger at me. "Honey, I'm wearing no less than three pairs of Spanx right now. Beauty is pain."

Jackie joined me in the kitchen to start relocating platters to the table when I heard the front door open, coupled with a new male voice. I spotted Cole from the hallway, offering yet another bottle of wine to whoever would take it. He spotted me and grinned. I kissed his cheek and took his jacket, suddenly aware that I'd half expected him not to come. I introduced him to Kevin, and he gave a polite nod and a hand shake, despite Meghan's greeting being a few muttered expletives that he surely could have made out if he tried.

A new set of feet stomped away the snow on the

porch. I hustled to the door and found Patty waiting in a white knee length wool trench coat, her hair hidden under a green knit hat.

She looked fucking adorable.

She smiled at me, and her nose crinkled as she handed me a brown paper box, tied with string.

"What is this?" I asked.

She shrugged off her coat, smiling. "It's – um, goose liver pate, actually."

If I glared at the box, I swear I didn't mean to.

"No, I swear, it's really good! You eat it on crackers or bread. You have to try it. And hey, what's more Christmassy than goose, right?"

A voice startled her from outside. "Fuckin A, right! That's what I've been sayin for years."

Evan smiled at her when she turned.

Evan and Stellan traipsed up the steps together. I should have heard their guffawing from up the street, but I was too busy trying to beam at Patty. This whole damn shindig was, in essence, for her. She'd never know that though. I'd never tell her.

She almost hopped in place when she recognized him. "Evan Lambert? Oh my god!"

Evan leaned into her and gave her a kiss on the cheek and a one arm embrace as he tried to hand me the bottle of Glennfiddich. "Hello Patricia. How are you doing, my dear?"

She glanced at me, smiling. "I'm good. I'm good. How are you?"

Evan gestured to Stellan coming up behind him. "Miserable. This fucker followed me here."

Stellan kicked his boots against the door jam a few more times before entering. As expected, he had a case of Sam's. I glared at it, shook my head and muttered, "predictable" loud enough for him to hear me.

"What? It's winter lager, woman! Drink up while you can!"

He then shifted his weight and pulled a small six pack of Magners into view. This he handed to me with a grin. I smiled up at him. A good hard cider wasn't the easiest thing to find around here. One had to hit a specialty shop or drive to east bum for Magners. Apparently, Stellan had taken the time. Magners was my favorite.

Evan tried to hand me his coat, and I called him a jackass, pointing to the closet. He made comment about 'being unable to find good help these days' and walked his ass over to the closet himself, taking Patty's coat as well.

Patty mouthed her surprise when his back was turned. I smiled. I heard Meghan introducing herself by the coat closet and chose to distract myself in the kitchen. A quick glass of ice and I was sipping away at my Magners.

The wine and whiskey was open and flowing. I listened to Patty delight over the Christmas cake, and Meghan flirting with Evan. Kevin filtered into the kitchen with Stellan, and I watched his body language as he gestured to the case of Sam Adams and gave Stellan a nod. "Mind horribly if I grab one of those?"

Stellan hauled the case up onto the counter and ripped the top open. "Hell yeah, man. Dig in. It's actually pretty damn cold, too."

Kevin grabbed a bottle and groaned his approval. Cole filtered in from the dining room and leaned against the counter. I settled with my back to the sink and searched for words to fill the silence.

Kevin beat me to it. "What you drinking there, Faye?"

I lifted my glass as though startled to find it in my hand. "Oh, it's a Magners."

"What's that?" He asked.

Stellan coughed and looked at him. "Philistine!"

I smiled. "It's a hard cider. Guinness makes it."

He approached the center island and inspected the small Magners case. "Really?"

"Yeah, feel free to try one," I said.

"Is it like Woodchuck?" Kevin asked.

Stellan and I shook our heads, but Cole answered. "Yeah, it's the same thing."

"No way. Magners is the way to go," I said.

Stellan swallowed quickly. "Unless you can get Scrumpy."

I moaned. "Och, Scrumpy! Yes, please."

Cole swallowed quickly in order to speak. "Have you even had Woodchuck? It's the same thing and a lot easier to get your hands on."

Before I could answer, Stellan did for me. "She hates Woodchuck."

Kevin gestured to Stellan who quickly produced a metal bottle opener from his pocket.

Cole made a face. "I'm a bartender; I might know something about it. If you like Magners, Woodchuck is the same thing."

Stellan shook his head, but I answered. "I just really don't care for Woodchuck."

"It's fucking foul," Stellan said.

Cole scoffed. "They make more than one kind. Maybe you just need to try a different one."

I shrugged before taking a sip of my Magners. I didn't want to continue the conversation. "Ok," I said.

"Faye! Oh my god, I *love* this painting!" Patty called from the living room.

I bounded down the hall, happy to get out of the kitchen. "Yeah, about that. Seriously?"

I delivered the words and the accompanying glare directly to Evan.

He flashed me a grin. "Your mother is a wonderful lady."

I didn't argue. Given that my mother had once cut a key to our front door for him because of the many nights we'd found him passed out on our front porch chairs because he was kicked out of the house or too afraid to go home, I knew exactly what inspired the generosity.

Patty turned to Evan who was cornered on the couch by a puma – also known as Meghan. "Did you buy this?"

It suddenly struck me that I hadn't completed the set up for the party. I snuck over to the stereo and turned on the playlist of Christmas songs I'd collected for the night - Bing Crosby and Old Blue Eyes crooning away. I let the music play and slipped out the back door to grab firewood. When I snuck back in, Stellan lunged at me, demanding I let him take the burden. He made quick work of building the fire. Moments later, it was crackling away, and I was blissfully people watching in my own living room.

I took in the space – Stellan and Kevin were chatting about Fallout 4, Jackie was by the office with Cole discussing the restaurant business, and both Patty and Meghan were hanging on Evan's every word. It felt comfortable to be in this space, and not need to talk to anyone. I felt like the conductor of an impromptu orchestra. Kevin and Stellan glommed onto one another at get-togethers in the past, but seeing Cole and Patty settle into the dynamic was nice.

I watched Patty from the fireplace. She was sitting at the edge of her chair, a glass of wine in her hand. She was smiling. She was laughing. I was glad, despite the 'Patty is such a cock block' conversation that would surely come from Meghan by the end of the night.

I felt a hand graze my lower back and jumped. Cole smiled at me before pointing at the pieces of paper on the walls. "What's this?"

I beamed. "Everybody grab a piece of paper and a pen from the table. We're gonna play a game."

"What kind of game?" Cole asked.

"It's a riddle game."

Jackie and Patty were heading for table.

"And did I mention that the prize for winning is a batch of Grammy Jensen's Chocolate Chip Cookies?"

News of cookies sent Stellan and Evan surging past the others. Everyone else milled where they were, Meghan going so far as to grumble. I explained the first game – there were six pieces of paper on the walls throughout the downstairs, each paper contained four riddles. The person with the most right answers, wins. Patty was ready to go, walking down the hallway toward the first piece of paper. Jackie headed into the kitchen. Evan and Stellan nearly tackled each other as they followed Patty, calling each other 'ball bag' and 'homosexual,' to which Meghan hollered her disapproval.

I laughed, and beamed with love for both of them. I was sure it read on my face.

Truth be told, this was not a fair game on my part. The first game was riddles, the second was a sheet of anagrams, all containing the first letter of each word in the title of a Christmas song. Despite some blatant cheating between the laypersons, Stellan and Evan both tied for first in each game. They were openly accused of cheating by Patty, given their 'superior intellect.' Evan said, "Why thank you," and Stellan said, "Where's my cookies?"

Yet, there was one riddle that stumped the brainiacs.

My voice is Tender, my waist is slender, and I'm often invited to play. Yet wherever I go, I must take my bow, or else I have nothing to say. What am I?

"A violin?" Patty said.

Both Evan and Stellan threw their pens and groaned loudly.

Patty just beamed.

I gave her a small half tin of cookies for having shown up the genius twins, and she took the tin from me as though I'd just given her an Oscar. After the games, we broke into the desserts and the porte. Patty followed me into the kitchen to offer help cleaning, and though I naturally refused, she began filling the dishwasher. Once she finished, we sat sipping porte and talking. She was a couple drinks in and in a good mood. Geoffrey came up, a declaration that he would have hated the evening and made her go home early.

"Really?" I asked.

"Oh, god yeah. He's never gotten along with any of my – err – friends."

I nodded quickly to assure her that this word was applicable. She smiled and continued. "I mean, I wouldn't have minded that so much – not all personality types get along, you know? But the past few months, he wasn't even making an effort with me. We spent most of our evenings in silence."

"Well, that's not always bad."

"True!" She said with such a bright flourish I began to wonder if I should cut her off from the wine. "But there's a difference between being able to just be with someone and not talk, and silence being like another person in the room."

I frowned at her. I wasn't sure why.

"And, really – oh my god, Faye I'm going to be so honest with you!"

I smiled as she leaned in toward me. "Yeah?"

"We hadn't had sex in almost a year."

I widened my eyes to offer an expression of surprise. I wasn't surprised. Before Twat Shot, Cole and I were well on our way. "No!"

"Right? A freakin year, Faye. I don't care if my parents are in the house or not, you've got a penis; it works!"

I laughed as her volume rose. "Preach, sister."

"I mean, what did I marry you for, anyway?"

I raised my glass to that. "Damn straight! I'll be honest right back, I've always been a little jealous of you."

She stopped dead, her eyes wide. "Really? Why on earth?"

"You had my ideal life."

She scoffed and a tiny spray of red wine appeared between us. She blushed, covering her mouth. "You're joking, right?"

"Nope. School in Edinburgh, marry a huge cocked Scotsman, be gorgeous and adorable and perky."

She shook her head with a slow deliberation. "Oh

honey, you had it all wrong."

"What do you mean? That accent -"

Before I could finish my sentence she held her hand up with her thumb and forefinger a couple centimeters apart and hung her head low.

I gasped. "Really?"

"Such a shame. The accent really is so sexy at first, but then the main event was just, well - And that's when he wasn't too drunk to keep it up."

I grabbed her wrist and squeezed in a gesture of solidarity. Oh honey, how I knew. "Oh my god!"

In the living room, there was a bit of ruckus. It had been going on a while before the sound traveled toward us. Kevin and Cole came into the kitchen followed by Stellan, a satisfied smile on his handsome face.

"Honey, you drew this shit?" Cole asked, holding an iPhone in the air.

I glared at Stellan. "Wait, they can see it, but I can't?"

He shook his head, gesturing to Cole to hand me the phone. Cole instead stood beside me and let me watch over his shoulder as he continued to play, doing his best to dodge and block various objects being thrown from the branches of a tree. I recognized the vines, the elephant trunks appearing over the walls, the bulgy eyed monkeys that appeared within the trees. I even recognized the various objects being thrown – after a moment, shit was included.

Cole dodged poorly, took a splatter to the face and physically curled up in grossed out chagrin. Despite the gross out factor, he was laughing. The sound effects, the wacky crazed monkey sounds, the one liners of the brave zookeepers had all been added without my involvement, but everything came together.

I felt almost overwhelmed. Those were my drawings, and they were alive.

I stared at Stellan, speaking too softly to be heard. "You're amazing."

"That's just one level, dude," Evan called from the living room.

Kevin held his hands out to Cole who, by rule of the video game gods, needed to hand off now that he'd died.

Cole forked over the phone reluctantly and chuckled again. "Is it done?"

Stellan took a swig of his beer. "Not yet. Getting mighty close though."

I smiled at Stellan. He winked at me.

Patty leaned in to the iPhone as Kevin played and turned to me with her mouth open. "You drew all of that?"

I shook my head. "I sketched some stuff up -"

"It's all her. I compiled her stills and gave it sound effects, but everything you see was from her brain."

Patty got almost teary eyed when she spoke again. I knew then she'd had enough to drink. "That's so wonderful, Faye. I always thought you were so talented when we were in school."

I started to react as I always did when receiving a compliment – attempt to deny it. Stellan cut me off. "She's fucking brilliant."

"I had no idea you could draw, honey."

I turned to Cole and shrugged. "I don't really do it anymore."

"It was what she went to college for." Evan called.

Cole raised an eyebrow. "Really?"

"Originally," I said.

Cole laughed. "Must have been a quick phase, then."

Stellan chuckled softly as he cracked another bottle of Sam.

Kevin growled, then fist pumped the air in celebration. Apparently it was just a *near* death experience. He then started laughing and showed me the blackboard, shit trajectory panel. "Faye, this is you?"

I nodded and chuckled to myself. There's nothing quite like hearing people laugh at your work - at least when you were trying to be funny.

Patty beamed at me. "I can't believe you didn't stay in art school. You'd be famous by now."

I attempted to scoff at such a notion, but was overshadowed by Cole doing it for me. "Who becomes famous for drawing?"

"It's animation," Evan called again, followed by a softer, 'you twat,' quiet enough for only Stell and I to recognize. For someone in the next room, he was certainly paying close attention to our conversation.

"Even so. I'd say it was a pretty sensible choice. Marketing you might actually make money at. Animators don't make money."

It was Stellan's turn to scoff. "Walt. Fucking. Disney."

Cole laughed, but before he could say anything, I spoke up. "Or what about Matt Groening? Stephen Hillenburg? Trey Parker?"

Cole made a face. "My point exactly. Haven't heard of a single one of them."

Stellan grumbled, and Evan hollered the animated series each had created – The Simpson, Spongebob

313

Squarepants, South Park. He then added a few more expletives each of them growing louder. I suddenly noticed my hands were getting sweaty.

I spoke to cover the sound. "Matt Groening is worth like $500 million or some crazy thing."

"If not more!" Evan yelled.

"Who is Matt Groening?" Cole asked, half rolling his eyes in his bottle of Sam.

Stellan stared at his beer. "Creator of the Simpsons."

Cole chuckled. "Well, it's not like you created *The Simpsons* here, hon."

Evan exploded in the living room, and the front door slammed. I heard Meghan follow him out.

I searched for words. "No, but Charles Schulz was worth like $35 million, and he was a comic strip artist."

Cole shook his head. "What? No comic strip artist is worth that much."

Stellan swallowed hard. "Bill Watterson is worth almost as much as Matt Groening."

"Who the hell is Bill Watterson? I swear you're making these names up."

Again Stellan spoke, still not looking up from his beer. "*Calvin and Hobbes.*"

"Oh please, there is no way in hell -"

My turn. "It's true!"

Cole shook his head and made a duck face at me. "No way."

I frowned at him. "Why don't you believe me?"

"Because it's not possible. You're blatantly making it up to try to prove some point, which I don't understand why you feel the need. It's not like you draw anymore, so what's the point? It *is* a funny game, but trying to pretend that you know the bank accounts of all these obscure people is just nonsense. Seriously, why would you know that?"

"Because it's what I wanted to be."

Cole blinked at me. "Sure, when you were seventeen."

I stood silent. I didn't want to say that I'd looked up these numbers just the day before as I tried to make it through the day without telling anyone about my job offer.

Suddenly, Kevin looked up from the game. "Maybe it's not *the Simpsons,* but you might have an *Angry Birds* on your hands. Those guys are billionaires."

I exhaled, only then realizing I'd been holding my breath. Suddenly, I loved Kevin with all my being.

Cole laughed and pulled a cigarette out of his pocket. "Oh my god, you guys are living in a dream world. I'm going out for a smoke."

He pecked me on the cheek before sneaking down the hall. I hoped that Evan would remember his manners out on the porch.

Kevin looked up from his game and glanced around in the silence.

Jackie came in to offer me a slice of her amazing cake, but I didn't feel like eating. Stellan saw the slice of cake and took off for the living room. Patty and Kevin both accepted happily, moaning their appreciation with every bite.

I refused to be rude and forced one forkful into my mouth while Jackie, love that she is, did her best to lighten the mood.

"It's lemon with a raspberry mousse center for yours, honey. I remember you liked that one."

I smiled at her, feeling guilty that I would have

given anything at that moment to spit out the only bite I'd taken. She leaned on the counter next to me, close enough for our arms to touch. I knew this was a form of comforting, but she was keeping it surreptitious. Patty turned to further regale Jackie with her love of cake when the sound of the front door bursting open startled us all, shaking the front end of the house. High heeled shoes clomped across the living room floor toward the kitchen.

Meghan appeared in the hallway and stared at me a moment. "I so almost don't want to tell you this, but Stellan is outside, and he's about to kill your asshole boyfriend. Just so you know."

"What?!"

The entire population of the kitchen lunged down the hallway and out onto the porch. Stellan stood on the sidewalk in just his t-shirt and jeans, all his weight settled into his back leg, his arms loose at his sides.

Cole stood in front of him, at least a foot shorter, but his chest out. "What you gonna do, guy? Hit me?"

Stellan exhaled through his nose in a half laugh. "No, guy. I'm going to end you."

I bounded down the steps in a panic. "Stellan, stop!"

Cole gestured to Evan, who was standing just a few steps into the street. "Go ahead, I've got witnesses to attest to the fact that you're a fucking psycho."

Evan glared at him. "Fuck you, dude. I could make you disappear."

I got physically between them, and Cole pushed forward, as though my sudden presence was invitation to accept the challenge, jostling me into Stellan.

I pressed my hands against both their chests. "Both

of you, stop it!"

Cole hollered in my ear. "What have I been saying? You see what I fucking mean now, Faye? And you hang out with this guy?"

"That's enough!" I said as sternly as I could.

Stellan stood perfectly still. "Keep talkin, asshole."

Evan bit his knuckles. "Stell, I will straight up pay you to make him eat his own teeth."

I glared at him. "Shut the fuck up, Evan!"

There were some words called from the porch, but I couldn't decipher them. Cole tried to pull me aside, knocking me off balance. Stellan grabbed me before I fell over the curb, and I held onto him.

I straightened, looking up at him. "Stellan, you need to go home."

He stared at me a moment. "What?"

"You need to leave."

He paused. "Are you seriously telling me -"

I nodded. "Yes! Please."

He searched my face, his eyes growing brighter in the streetlights. Then he stormed off down the snow covered street in nothing more than a t-shirt.

"Stellan!" I called, but he was gone. "Evan, don't let him go alone. Please."

Evan gave me a look to match Stellan's and hustled after him.

Cole hollered something after them, and I hauled out and punched him in the chest.

He pressed his hand to the sore spot. "What the fuck?"

"You leave, too!"

He furrowed his brow, doubling his chin as he gave me a look of half disgust at this suggestion. "You're kidding, right?"

"No! Go home."

By now, Mr. Hodges was at his front door. Before he could attempt to walk in the snow, I called my apology over to him, assuring him that the party was done for the night.

I stormed up my front steps and back into my living room. The act of speech was too much, so I didn't bother speaking to anyone as they collected their coats and serving dishes and headed out. Cole tried to sneak in for a kiss on his way out, but I swatted him away so fiercely, I almost backhanded him.

He left in a huff.

I gave my hugs in silence, one by one, until it was just Patty and I in the living room.

She stopped in the doorway, her adorable green hat back on her head. "Are you going to be alright?"

I forced a smile, but still no words.

She took my hand and gave a sad smile. "I'll be honest, I'm jealous of you. I'd give anything to have friends that loved me that much."

And the bomb detonated. I let Patty literally hold me up while I sobbed.

CHAPTER THIRTEEN

I texted Stellan a few times that night to no response. Evan explained he'd been dismissed at the door of Stellan's house when they got there, and he didn't hear further.

Cole texted me, dancing between righteous indignation and penitence, but I did not respond. I crawled into my bed with a pillow in my arms, holding it close, weeping into it when I needed and sleeping upon it when I could.

By morning, I had little sleep to speak of and a knot in my stomach. I snatched up the phone and asked Evan if he'd heard anything. Still no.

God, we were doing so much better too! Why did it need to get clusterfucked again? I slumped back into the bed, contemplating another month of not seeing him, not hearing his ringtone go off on my phone, knowing he was just a walk away and feeling as though some imaginary installation of razor wire would certainly eviscerate me if I were to attempt a closer approach.

To distract myself, I thought about starting work in a few weeks. My stomach turned. At least it would keep me busy. I wouldn't have time to miss him. Wouldn't have time to do much of anything. I pondered how long they'd have me get accustomed to the client base before I'd end up flying into whatever god awful city the companies hailed from. I searched the unpacked boxes in my mind, remembering where my carry-on was settled, still half packed, in the upper corners of the attic.

I wrote Stellan a new text.

Please talk to me.

I didn't expect a response. Whatever repairs had been done to the bridge between us, his sad eyes spoke volumes of its burning. At that moment, I damn well wanted a hug.

The **'Let me take you to breakfast?'** text was from Cole.

I begrudgingly accepted and got dressed. My mother greeted me as I came downstairs, still in her bathrobe, despite planning to spend the day in at the museum. Cole pulled up along the curb, and I hustled outside to hop into the car. The thought of asking him in to visit my mother as she was drearily brewing coffee didn't even cross my mind.

He reached across the car to kiss me. It wasn't going to be that kind of a kiss.

"You look beautiful," he said.

I can't deny that my eyebrow shot up, but I didn't say anything. It was a quiet drive.

He snuck me a smile as he unbuckled his seatbelt in the parking lot of Bickford's, watching me do the same before leaning in for another kiss. He may have been hoping for it to take a romantic turn, but he was sadly mistaken.

I wasn't particularly hungry, but I let Cole order us both Mimosas and Waffles.

"So that was an interesting night, huh?"

I nodded.

"Would you say he'd had too much to drink maybe?"

I furrowed my brow. "No."

Cole thanked the waitress for his drink. "Didn't realize he had such a temper."

I chuckled. "He does."

The table vibrated, and I went for my phone. It was still. I looked up to watch Cole read something on his phone and smile. He took a sip of his drink. "I was surprised to see Evan getting involved."

"Oh he's always 'involved.'"

Cole didn't look up from his phone, his thumbs flailing over its surface as he typed. "You'd think with his success he'd have more sense than that."

"Would you?"

Cole nodded vehemently. "We're lucky you didn't have to call the cops."

I played with my straw, swirling the ice cubes in the water. "I seem to remember you being pretty involved as well."

Cole displayed his palms. "What could I do? The guy came at me. He was off his nut. Now we know, don't criticize his video games, clearly."

Cole laughed.

I smiled up at the waitress as she set my waffle in front of me. Cole glanced at his phone again, smiling.

I watched him a moment, the waffle before looking as appetizing as licking a 9 volt battery. "Who you talking to?"

He glanced at his phone and shrugged. "Just Matt from work."

Cole took my hand and brought it up to his face, kissing the back of my hand. I let him.

"Faye, I'm sorry. I shouldn't have let them get to me, but – I don't know, I think I felt a bit cornered, you know? It's your house, your friends, the only other sane one was – what's his name – Jackie's guy there?"

"Kevin."

"Yes, and he was no where to be found, and Meghan is a right bitch. You know how I feel about her." He took a sip of his drink. "I never got to hear what your big news was."

"No one did."

He gestured for me to continue.

I shrugged. "I got the job at Chalice."

He clapped his hands together and leaned across the table to touch my arm. "That's amazing!"

I smiled. "Yeah, I was pretty floored."

"Fantastic!" He was up from his seat and leaned into me to kiss me a few times, his big, bright smile and brown eyes in their full glory just inches from my nose. "When do you start?"

"Second week in January."

The table buzzed and despite the pattern, I still went for my phone.

I sat staring at my blank screen and my waffle. "Why is Matt texting you on a Sunday morning?"

Cole raised an eyebrow and settled back into his seat. "Just work stuff. He's covering brunch and relaying the nightmare as it unfolds. That's such great news, sweetheart. I'm sorry you didn't get to celebrate last night."

"I didn't know you guys were so close."

Cole set his phone down. "What? Matt and I? I wouldn't say we're close." He paused. "It's just Matt."

"Ok."

He stared at me a moment, and when he spoke, each word dripped with snark. "You want to look through my phone, Faye? Would that make you feel

322

better?"

I met his gaze over the table. It was a hard look.

"No."

We sat silent a moment. Finally, I grabbed my phone and stood up. "I'm gonna hit the bathroom. Be right back."

I snuck away with my phone clutched in my hand like some brown bellied eagle with a salmon. I intended to work my Stephen King worthy mind powers on it in the bathroom stall. I sat there with my jeans around my knees and my phone in my hands, typing, deleting, and retyping a message to Stellan over and over, hoping that when I was done, it would be the magic amalgam of words that needed to be said for him to respond, to forgive me, to just acknowledge my existence.

By the time I resigned myself to not speak at all, I'd settled red lines into my thigh from the toilet seat.

Classy, Faye.

I was going for toilet paper when the buzz startled me so badly, I nearly dropped my phone onto the white tile floor.

Stellan - **There's nothing to say.**

My chest pounded.

Well, fuck that!

I didn't use soap when I washed my hands, I admit that right now. I hauled my ass out of that bathroom, sat down across from Cole and leaned in.

"I do."

He looked at me sideways. "What's that?"

"I do want to look through your phone."

He leaned back and glared at me a moment. I expected a fight, an argument, but he shrugged and went for his pocket.

"No, Cole! I don't actually want to look through your phone."

He furrowed his brow. "I'm confused."

"I mean, I do, but I'm not going to."

"Faye, honestly - you can if you want, I have nothing to-"

"Yes, but you did once. I get the creeps every time you smile at your phone because I'm thinking of what girl might be sending you pictures of her twat."

"Faye -"

"And that's on me. I said I wanted to give this another try, and I swear to you I truly did, but now that we're here - there's too much noise."

He was silent a moment. "I understand that, sweetheart. And I'm willing to give it time if you are - "

"I know you are. I just don't think time is going to make a difference."

He reached across the table and took my hand.

It hurt to say it, but it was as true as my name. "I hate being in your apartment with you because I see her on every surface. I hate watching you get texts because even if you are texting Matt, I know once upon a time you were texting her. Maybe even while I was sitting across from you, just like this."

He cringed. "Honey, please -"

"I'm sorry, Cole. I wish I could shut off the noise. I know I said I wanted to move past it, but - I just can't."

He squeezed my hand. After a moment, I squeezed back.

His eyes welled up just as the waitress returned to fill our drinks. I waved her away with a polite "we're all set."

There were more words milling about in my mind, but I wouldn't say them. I just couldn't be his. Not anymore.

We asked for the check, which Cole quickly paid.

The drive back to my house was silent, punctuated by a very soft kiss in the car before I climbed out to stand on the curb. He waved through the passenger window, his eyes heavy, and drove away. It hurt me to see him so sad. Despite everything he had done to me, all the nights I'd wept over him - I had loved him once. His car disappeared at the end of Davis Court, and I turned to my front door, pulling my coat tight around my jaw. Mom brought home a purple and gold wreath the day before to add her own festive touch to my complete failure of a party, and I now stared at it from the bottom of my steps. I considered the warmth inside, the house I'd known my whole life, the one I considered home even when my condo was filled with IKEA furniture and good intentions. This was the haven I ran to when the storms brought me to harbor.

Right now, this wasn't the harbor I sought.

I turned and took off running. The road was dry, a path of white salt and gravel. My boots clomped over the ground with an even and purposeful rhythm. I knew where I was headed, and I would not be slowed. I rounded the end of Davis Court with clouds of steam pumping from my chest, and the cold biting at my throat. I barreled toward the center of town. I was a beast, I was purpose incarnate, I was – out of breath. Fuck running.

I hustled as best I could across Central Square and onto Lowell Road, watching Stellan's house as though I might burn through that invisible razor wire with my Stephen King worthy mind powers. Out of stubbornness as much as haste, I ran the last thirty feet to his doorstep, trudged up the steps as loudly as I could, to clear my feet of snow as much as announce my damn presence, and plowed into the foyer like I was being chased.

There was no one to greet me. The house was dark. I made for the basement door and opened it, hearing the familiar hum of electronics downstairs. As always, Stellan was perched at his wall of screens.

I went for him. "There's nothing to fucking say?"

He sat silent, staring at his computer screen.

"How dare you fucking say that to me, you shit?"

At this, he calmly leaned back in his chair and turned, crossing his arms over his chest. "I'm sorry, are we in an argument I was unaware of?"

"Fuck you! Yes, we are!"

He nodded, rubbed his chin, then stood up. I swallowed hard as he took a couple steps toward me.

"Alright, then let's get clear on who was wronged here."

"I didn't wrong you!" I said, and let's be honest it was irritatingly shrill.

"You chose that fucking prick when you threw me out of your house!"

"No I didn't! I would never throw you out of my house! And I didn't choose -"

"Bull shit! That's exactly what you did! Threw me out to make way for that cock gobbling hobbit of a boyfriend of yours!"

"I didn't! I didn't want you to get in trouble!" And with that he laughed in my face. "Don't you fucking laugh at me!"

"Oh I'm gonna! What? You think you were

protecting me?"

"Yes!"

"From what? I could pick my teeth with that fucker, and there ain't a soul who would say otherwise."

I frowned. "He would have pressed charges."

"Let him. Big man. It'd be hard to tell the cops what happened with his jaw wired shut."

"I'm serious!"

He surged toward me. "So am I! It would have been fucking worth it! Fucker needed to taste his own blood."

He was yelling at me in a whisper, and my fervor was collapsing. I coughed back a tightness in my throat. The effort caused the words to come softer than I intended. "You can't get in a fight!"

Stellan tilted his head to the side. "What?"

"Assault with a deadly weapon. You would have gone to jail."

He furrowed his brow and shook his head as though shooing off a fly. "What are you saying?"

"I know him, he would have pressed charges, and you had to register -"

He cracked a smile, and the thought of him mocking me again was too much.

I covered my face. "I hate you! Don't laugh at me!"

His hands were at my elbows, then at my hands, trying to pull them away so he could see my face. I fought with a couple swats.

"What are you talking about, F-bomb? You're not making any sense."

I flailed my hands away from his, stepping out of his reach. "You're a fucking black belt. If you get into a fight you could go to jail. I didn't want you to go to jail."

And like any other day that year, tears rolled down my cheeks.

He chuckled and pulled me to him, put his arms around me and rested his chin on the top of my head as I tried to hit him.

He held me to him too tightly to put up much of a fight. "Oh Älskling. Where did you hear that?"

I tensed in his arms. "One of the ninjas from your school."

He laughed again and swayed.

I didn't like his laughter, but I liked the sway, so I let him continue. "Is it not true?"

He cupped the back of my head and rubbed. "No, it can be. I don't think I was going to get quite that rowdy." He released me, pinched my chin between his thumb and forefinger and smirked at me. "You never know though."

He took my head in his hands and kissed my forehead, before whispering "I'm sorry."

Fuck, how those words carry power. Especially when he wasn't in the wrong.

His phone rang on the desk, and his arms loosened. When he let go I almost fell to the floor.

He crossed back to his chair, checked the phone.

"Who's that?" I asked. I imagined the auburn girl from the now defunct Boathouse Bakery, and my chest ached.

He smiled. "Evan. He's been haranguing me to talk to you all morning. I'm telling him you booted my door in like a crazy person."

I wiped my eyes. "You love it."

He smiled and went back to typing on his phone a moment, set it back on the desk, and leaned against the wall. He looked so relaxed in his Monty Python t-shirt and jeans, his legs crossed at the ankles. I stared at him, my mind racing through words too fast to say any of them.

He snorted softly. "It's official, though. Your boyfriend sucks cock. If I ever hear him talk to you like that again -"

"He's not my boyfriend."

Stellan raised an eyebrow. "Do tell."

My mouth went dry instantly as I felt the words rise in my throat. "What if we fuck this up?"

Stellan shifted his weight and paused. "Interesting segue."

"I'm serious!"

"What are we talking about here?"

My throat was still tight, a tension inspired by both fear and a sense of a dam cracking in the wake of a flood. "You know what I'm talking about. Last night. You and me. What if we fuck this – us - up?"

He raised his eyebrows and nodded. "We really having this conversation right now? Cause if so, I'd say that's not the most positive way to start it off."

"We have to! I've missed you. I fucking missed you every day!" He tried to speak, but I wasn't done. "I can't do that again. I can't sit there wanting to talk to you and feeling like I can't. I felt fucking trapped every day we weren't talking."

"You never need to feel like that, ever."

I took a shaky inhale. "You didn't talk to me!"

"You didn't talk to me either!"

We were getting loud.

"What if we end up bitter exes who never speak because we can't stand the sight of one another?"

He scoffed. "You really think that would happen?"

"I don't know!" I stopped and watched him as he scratched the heel of one socked foot with the toes of the other. "What if we hurt each other and break each other's hearts? You're the one I want when I'm sad. You're the one I want hugs from, and I know now how hard it is when I can't have them."

He came at me then. "You should never have felt that way."

"You weren't talking to me!"

"You weren't talking to *me either*!"

He came close enough for me to touch, so I hit him.

I'm such a grown-up, I know.

He smiled and moved closer. His breath had changed, his energy. When he stepped into me it was as though there was a bubble, a membrane between us that I felt him break as he closed the distance.

He stood before me, turning my hands palm up so he could look at them as he spoke. "I don't have all the answers. But I'll say this - I'd rather get it wrong with you than never get it right, because you and I were too chicken shit to try."

I stared at my hands. "I'm not chicken shit."

He chuckled and pulled my hand up to his face. He kissed the pad of my thumb. The distance closed between us another inch as he leaned in.

My breath caught in my throat as he leaned down to me. I couldn't have moved if my life depended on it. Oh god, he was going to kiss me again.

He breathed in at my cheek, then said something –– in Swedish.

I shivered against him, unable to lift my face to his. "No Swedish. Swedish is cheating."

"Oh you're getting plenty of Swedish. **Jag vill ha dig**

så mycket."

I curled into myself smiling, turning my face away, as though his lips would burn me. "Shut up."

He smiled and gently lifted my chin. "Jag slår vad om att du låter trevligt."

I squirmed. "Unfair."

He touched his nose to mine. "Älskling."

I waited for him to meet my eyes. "You're killing me, Smalls." He laughed. I swallowed. "What does that mean?"

"What part?"

"All of it. Or just - Elsking?"

He grabbed hold of my coat lapel and pulled me toward him, his smile turning wicked. Then, he said the word into my mouth. "Darling."

He pressed his lips to mine and breathed in. The energy surged between us. I touched my fingers to the bare skin of his arm, and he pressed forward, pushing me back a step. I wrapped my arms around him to hold on, and he responded by touching his hands to my lower back, letting one hand drift down my backside. My body tensed to feel his hand move in such a way.

Sweet Jesus, I approve!

His kisses remained surface, slow presses of the lips, his breath hot, his mouth open. I pulled away to speak. He stilled me quickly, taking the invitation of my open mouth to pierce me with his tongue. I whimpered in response.

He pulled me into him, walking backward toward his bed. He dropped down on it, pulling me between his knees, my chest at eye level. He looked up at me, making eye contact as he slid his hand up under my breasts. I shivered and cried out at the electricity his touch seemed to cause. I almost grabbed him by the hair to recover from my giddy behavior and slammed his face into my tatas just to see the response. That was sexy vixen-like, wasn't it? I didn't do it. However well I knew this man, seeing this side was strange, almost frightening. This was the one piece of Stellan I truly didn't know.

Instead he grabbed my jacket. "Damn it, take this off!"

I let it fall to the floor. My voice cracked when I spoke, like a nervous teenager. "Are we really doing this?"

His hands slid up under my arms, his breath warm against my nipples even through my clothes. "We better fucking be. I can't wait to get my hands on these gorgeous tits of yours."

I giggled against him and tried to pull away as he palmed my ass with both hands and scooped me over him onto the bed. He propped himself above me on all fours, smiling down between leaning in to kiss my neck, my collarbone, and my ear. I shivered with each new touch, running my hands up the back of his neck and letting my fingers run over the soft bristle of his hair. He lowered himself nose to nose with me and smiled against my lips. Then he pressed himself between my legs so I could feel him through his jeans. I drew a sharp breath and stifled a cry.

He seemed to like the sound, because he growled. Then he kissed me, roughly.

That kiss opened the gates. Something about the way he took hold of me, pressed his full weight on me - it made me desperate. I wrapped my legs around him, dragging my nails up under his shirt as I pressed my teeth against his shoulder and bit him. He growled again and began to move against me, a slow but deliberate rhythm.

We're all adults here, so I'm just going to say it. Dear god, my pussy ached.

He whispered something in Swedish, and I grabbed his ass and pulled him against me, kissing him deeply. If he kept moving like that, I'd be having my first orgasm before either of us took off a single article of clothing. He pulled away, lifting himself to his knees and pulling his shirt off before me. He hovered there a moment, running his hands over my knees and down my thighs and smiling wickedly. I took a moment to stare up at him – at every contour of his body, faltering as I reached up to touch his bare chest, as though his skin might burn me. The sight of his body, solid from years of martial arts, stirred something primal in me.

"Are you hungry, Gullebit? I'm making your father some lunch if you want to come up."

We both froze at his mother's voice. She'd opened the basement door and called down, but we almost scattered from the bed like middle schoolers.

"Thank you hon, no. I'm all set," Stellan called back.

She accepted and shut the basement door.

Stellan shook his head and stared at the mattress beneath us, laughing softly to himself. He patted my knee before running his hands over his head and slumping over on the bed. "Did that really just happen?"

I smiled and sat up, gesturing for him to kiss me. He did, and he smiled, reaching down to the front of his pants to reposition himself, grumbling. The moment, the momentum, the tension of the air deflated. Still, I longed for his warmth.

He exhaled, heavily. "I'm two seconds from walking you across the street to the Colonial Inn and getting a god damn room."

I swallowed, feeling shy as I spoke. "My mom is out for the day?"

He turned and glared at me, silent. Then without a word, he grabbed his shirt, my jacket, and yanked me toward the stairs. His shirt wasn't on until we reached the front door.

I wondered what his mother must've thought as we barreled past the kitchen and out of the house.

I reached the front path and felt his hands squeezing my back side as he passed me toward the driveway.

"Where are you going?" I asked, looking back at him as he unlocked the doors to the jeep. "It's a five minute walk, if that."

"Exactly. It's a whole five minute walk. Get that sexy ass in this car, right now."

My face burned as I buried it into the collar of my jacket, hiding my smile. I climbed into the passenger seat, and he grabbed me before I could buckle myself, slipping his tongue into my mouth and his hand between my thighs. I squealed and gripped his wrist before he could get anywhere dangerous and demanded that he drive. He obliged, with a little less concern for traffic laws than one would expect from a Virgo.

We were parked at my curb within sixty seconds, and I was hustling to get out of the jeep and into the house. He beat me to it and was in my living room, shirtless and shoeless before I even reached the door. He grabbed me at the threshold, kicking the door shut behind me as he pulled me in. His skin was hot even through the fabric of my shirt, and his body was solid.

I suddenly felt so very soft. He kissed my ear and whispered something in Swedish. His hands finally moved with purpose under my jacket, up my waist, and onto my breasts, squeezing them gently, but forcefully. I gasped and pulled away. I was suddenly so aware of what was happening, what was about to happen that I couldn't go further.

Not yet.

He felt the apprehension and softened. "What's wrong?"

I took three breaths, then swallowed. "You're going to hate me."

He gave me a gentle look, without expectation. His embrace remained firm, but his hands settled in a neutral zone. "What's up?"

"I need a second – to shower. I'm gross as hell."

"You are not, you smell like sunshine." He ran his lips over my jaw to my ear. "I can't wait to taste you."

That was it. I pulled free, giggling nervously. "I do. I need to take a minute."

He let me step away, still smiling. "Ok. Go take a shower - woman."

I protested the stereotype, and he kissed my forehead before gently pushing me toward the stairs, smacking my ass as I hit the first step. I scurried into my bedroom, cast off my jacket and shoes before making a ridiculous ditch effort to collect scattered clothes from the foot of the bed and toss them into the closet. I went to the bathroom and turned on the water, listening to him downstairs. I brushed my teeth and went pee before suddenly freezing on the bath mat as the room filled with steam. For a moment, I couldn't get undressed - as though he might feel my nudity through the floorboards. I scolded myself, stripping down and climbing into the claw foot tub, letting the water pour down my throat.

I stood there, slowly leaning into the water, staring down at my legs, my stomach, my breasts. I saw every soft inch of my body — the white lines at my breasts, the crease across my stomach when I bent at the middle, the softness at my inner thighs. Every inch of me now felt like a betrayal against my inner porn star. This was the body of a woman who had only ever had sex in the dark, under the covers. It was daylight, there were no curtains in the world dark enough to cover what I now saw. I fought to drown out the self-flagellating voice, hastily grabbing shower gel and shaving my legs, under my arms - hell, even my nether regions got a once over. Somehow my brain had decided I could potentially groom myself to a slender version of myself, but no matter how clean shaven and smooth my legs were, I still felt like cottage cheese squeezed into a sausage casing.

Fuck. Fuck.

He's an Adonis, and you're frumpy as hell.

Fuck.

I was so busy wishing I could use my Schick to shave off twenty pounds of rolly polly that I almost didn't hear the bathroom door open. I froze, unable to even mutter his name as the shower curtain pulled aside, and Stellan stepped in behind me.

He groaned at the sight of me, but I kept my face forward, my eyes closed tight, as though I could will myself invisible. His energy was palpable in the small steamy space. I was exposed, unprotected. His body moved in behind mine, pulling me against his chest, as one hand slid across my stomach and the other ran over my hip and down my thigh.

Well, there's no hiding now. He's just managed to caress every flaw you have.

He pulled me into him, and I felt him hard against my backside. Flawed or no, his body didn't seem to mind my rolly polly half as much as I did. He kissed my ear and slid his hands down the length of my arms to take the shower gel from me.

I swallowed hard.

He turned me to him. "Come here, beautiful."

I pressed myself against him, shielding my body from view. He leaned in to kiss me before running his hands down my back. They were slick and soapy, finding their way down the back of my legs before he snuck one up between my cheeks. I squealed and wriggled away from his hand, but he just gave a wicked laugh and smiled, running his hands over my stomach and my breasts, watching his hands as he squeezed them.

"What? I'm just helping you get clean. That's all."

I sighed at the sensation, letting him walk me back under the water to rinse off. As the soap cleared away, he suddenly stooped down to take my nipple in his mouth. I gasped, running my hand up the back of his neck. He suddenly switched to the other breast. I cried out. Nothing had ever felt so good.

He groaned and rose to kiss me deeply. He grabbed my ass and pulled me against him. I let my hands rest at his chest, feeling the smooth skin and the small mound of his nipples, slippery under the running water. Without taking his tongue from my mouth, he grabbed my hand, moving it down. Oh my sweet

Jesus, every inch of him was perfect – and hard, ladies and gentlemen. I grabbed him like I was playing Atari and let my hand move with gentle rhythm. He growled into my mouth and forcefully slipped his hand between my legs. I bent at the waist, trying to escape his touch without relinquishing my own. He wouldn't let me, grabbing me and pulling me against him so I couldn't squirm free. His fingers slipped into the wet that had gathered there and grazed against me in such a way that I simply gave in. Anything he might do at that moment, I would have welcomed. He slid his fingertips further down, and I ached to feel them inside me, but instead he pulled his hand away and before I could protest, slipped his fingers into his mouth to taste them.

I shrieked and grabbed at his hand, but he just smiled wide and pulled me away from the water. He turned the shower off before brushing the curtain aside. The light from the bathroom now bright on my wet skin, I shirked for but an instant before Stellan pulled me onto the bathmat and wrapped a towel around us. Shyly, I turned from him once, but he seemed oblivious, running the towel over every inch of me, taking moments to kiss my shoulder and my mouth before rubbing the towel against my hair, roughly.

I laughed and watched him make a quick pass over his own body. I reached out for it to cover myself, but he simply tossed it back onto the bathroom door. Then he leaned down to hook his forearms under my ass and lifted me up. I clung to him, crying for him to put me down, that I was too heavy, but he simply hooked my legs around his waist, the prize of both our bodies now pressed together, and walked me down the hall to my bedroom. He knelt onto my bed and let me fall back. I tried to hold onto him, keep him close, but he pulled away to kneel over me, smiling.

I'd never felt so naked – and I'd never seen anything so beautiful. He groaned at the sight of my breasts and lowered his mouth to them again, sucking as my breath caught in my throat. He flicked his tongue against my nipples and pulled me toward the edge of the bed. He dropped to his knees on the floor, and. I shot up, meeting him at eye level before he could do anything further. He kissed me, smiling and despite my protests, slid his hand between my thighs. His body was between my legs, there was no shielding myself from his fingers. They pressed against me as his tongue slid into my mouth, stifling my cries. I braced my hands on the bed behind me as his fingers moved, his lips breaking from mine to look down at his work. He groaned appreciatively, sucking at my nipples and speaking in Swedish. I squeezed my legs around him as his fingers slipped lower, teasing me. He returned them to my clitoris and glanced at my legs before grinning at me. A moment later, he was spewing the sexiest shit one can imagine in a language I couldn't understand.

I whined.

He smiled. "What's wrong?"

"I can't understand you."

He smiled. "Is that bad?"

I gasped as his fingers moved faster. "No -"

He threatened again, slipping his fingers low and then back to their same rhythm. I growled, softly.

"I know what's wrong. You want to understand the nasty shit I'm saying to you, don't you?"

I blushed, covering my face, and he started to kiss down the length of my torso, his intentions clear. I pulled at him, trying to keep him at eye level. He let me, kissing me before tugging me to the edge of the bed. He could move me like some weightless thing. He would do what he wanted, but I was too timid to let him without protest.

He smiled up at me. "You trying to fight me?"

I whined again. "Yes."

"You sure you want to do that?"

My brow furrowed in fear as I bit my lip. "Yes?"

He leaned against me, pushing me back onto the bed and taking one of my breasts in his mouth. He tried to move lower again, kissing my stomach, but I pulled at him.

He chuckled. "Ok then."

With those words he slid his fingers inside me and began moving them with such speed and purpose that I screamed. My screaming seemed to only urge him on faster and harder. My legs buckled against the sensation, and my body curled into itself. I reached down to grab hold of his wrist, to slow him, but it was useless. He continued to drive his fingers into me as I screamed "Please!"

He growled, watching me writhe. "Please what? You gonna be a good girl?"

I gasped to hear such words come from his lips. "Yes!"

"Alright then." He pulled his fingers from inside me and slapped my ass. "Get up on that bed then."

I took a breath and crawled up to the pillows as he stood up, looming over me at full height. The sight of him inspired a new mischief, and I quickly settled on my knees, reaching for him. He leaned into my touch, watching as I took hold of him with both hands, and began stroking him. He ran his hand over my hair and my ear, smiling down at me. I languished in the way he felt, his cock hard and smooth in my hands. I leaned in and ran the smooth skin of him against my lips.

He shuddered, violently.

I let one hand cup under him, cradling him as I took him in my mouth. His head fell back. Watching his eyes close like that excited me, and I grabbed his hands, pulling him down onto the bed. He tried to climb on me, but I wouldn't let him, making him lie on the bed beside me as I propped myself over him, kissing his mouth, his chest, flitting my tongue over his perfect nipples, his stomach, and soon the ridge at his hip. I shifted myself down to kiss his thighs and run my tongue up the inner side. He shivered as I slid my tongue over the sensitive skin of his balls, and I let my open mouth trail up the length of him, breathing in as I moved. His flesh jumped in response.

Hearing his breath catch, his soft groans, made me feel powerful, excited. I wanted to make him whimper. I took him as fully as I could in one movement, sucking deeply. He buckled under me, his hand taking grip in my hair. He sighed and muttered to me in Swedish as I moved my mouth up and down, sucking and flitting my tongue at him. He reached down to feel my breasts, a sensation I loved. He succumbed to the sighs my mouth caused him. He whispered again in Swedish, and I stopped just long enough to speak.

"English. I want to hear you."

"Yeah? You want to hear how good your mouth

feels on my cock?"

I growled at him and returned to work. He reached over and smacked my ass, hard. The sound of words like that coming from him, in that tone, that sexy tone he sometimes used to talk to pizza or to make me uncomfortable, now made me quiver and melt. I sucked deeper in response. He chuckled and growled wickedly.

I shifted again on the bed, settling on my knees so he could watch me. He groaned, his hips moving with my mouth. He brushed my hair away from my face and slapped my ass again.

I looked up to find him watching me and smiled.

He glared at me, and before I could laugh or ask 'what?' he sat up, hooked his arm around my thigh and yanked my lower half toward him. I cried out in surprise and protest, but he dragged me up over his shoulders and centered me there over his face, helpless. I tried to pull from him, but he simply locked his arms around my hips and pressed his open mouth against me.

I screamed so loud, I'm sure Mr. Hodges heard me.

Stellan's mouth was searing hot against me, and his tongue was hard and quick. He pressed firmly, letting his tongue slip from side to side. I wriggled to pull free, unable to simply let him please me. God it felt so good. I couldn't focus on anything, but the sensation. He responded to my fight with a hard smack of my ass. If he expected me to continue my work on him, he chose a poor approach. He pressed his mouth against me and began sucking at me, turning his head from side to side.

That was it, I started moving on him, pressing my hands onto his stomach as I rode his mouth. He groaned in appreciation.

I let my hands work on him as best I could, but I was useless. Dear god, he's good at everything he does. He pulled me down onto him, building the pressure of his tongue and his mouth, and I was a constant stream of moans and choice obscenities. I think I called him a motherfucker a couple times, but all in affection.

I finally pulled from him, too determined to be stopped, and I shifted on the bed. I was ready, I needed him. I grabbed at him, pulling him toward me, and he obliged, rising over me to kneel between my splayed legs. He ran his fingers across his lips and then over the head of his perfection before leaning over me and directing himself. I held my breath, and he pressed himself against me. He slid inside me, groaning as my body yielded to him. I felt a twinge of pain as he pushed deep, moving my legs so I could take him. I couldn't barely breath as I waited for him to push all the way inside.

With a shift of his weight, he began thrusting into me, holding himself above me as he moved. I watched every inch of his body – his shoulders, his forearms, the contours of his hips, his thighs, the dark tuft of hair at his groin. He blew air out through his pursed lips and sped up. I was a whimpering, gasping mess. After a moment of finding our rhythm, he spoke.

"You like that?"

It's amazing what a simple question in the right tone can do. I gasped. "Yes!"

"Yeah? You want it faster?" He lowered himself onto his elbows and began to plow me into the mattress, the bed shifting and creaking with every thrust. I lifted my legs high behind his back, and grabbed his ass, pulling him into me. He let his weight press into me and kept his rhythm – oh god, he was going to succeed, and quick.

He groaned. "Holy fuck, Älskling, you feel so fucking good."

My body began to tense. "I love it when you talk to me."

"Mmm, I noticed."

I gasped. "Keep talking."

He laughed. "You like that?"

"Oh my fuck." I pressed both hands to his ass and pulled him, the warmth of friction getting stronger. I pressed my cheek to his shoulder.

"You going to come for me?"

"Oh my god, don't stop!"

"Yeah? You gonna come for me, sweetheart?"

I tried to form words, but I was losing the skill. "Yes! Please!"

His movements grew bigger, the bed shaking louder and louder beneath us. "Yeah?"

"Please don't stop!"

"You like that cock pounding your pus -"

"Oh my fuck! Don't stop!"

He moved his hands under my head and shifted me. "Look at me."

I tried to turn away, to hide my face. "No!"

Despite the labor in his breathing, his tone was both stern and pleading. "Look at me, Faye."

I turned my eyes to his, warm and blue. I felt exposed, seen in a moment when I'd never wanted to be seen before. Yet in this moment, the blind reality of what was happening hit me fully. Stellan was making love to me. My massive, Swedish confidante was above me, inside me, watching my every gesture. I fought the urge to look away, but before I could lose the battle, he kissed me.

"Come for me, Faye."

I closed my eyes. "Oh god."

His voice trailed to a whisper. "Come for me."

I let my whole body tense, my mouth fall open, and my fingers clutch at his shoulders. No matter how tightly I pulled, his movements kept rhythm. I held my breath as he continued to whisper, "Come. Come for me, Älskling."

I did. I quivered against him and under him. I exhaled in a desperate wail that trailed and peaked with each thrust of his hips. His movements drove deeper, more intense, and his breathing grew sharper until he grunted and pulled from inside me, kneeling on the mattress, holding himself.

I sat up swiftly, grabbed him in my hands, and took him in my mouth before he could protest. He whimpered as I sucked at him, finishing him in my mouth. A moment later, he whimpered again with the sensitivity of my touch.

I released him, feeling the taste of him, light on my tongue.

He sighed, and called me amazing.

I slumped back onto the bed and pulled him onto me as we caught our breath. I felt his chest rise and fall in my arms, the pressure of his body on me. He felt warm, safe. He kissed my collar bone, my ear, letting soft, satisfied groans escape every few breaths.

I ran my hands up over his shoulders and back, clutching him, feeling his smooth skin and wanting to literally absorb him. I couldn't pull him close enough to me to be sated. My Stellan was here with me, holding me, looking at me in a way I never thought someone could.

Suddenly, my breath shortened, and my throat grew tight. I covered my face in my hand as I realized what was happening. I turned my head away, but there was no hiding this. He would know.

"Stell?"

He shifted, but I fought to hold him against me. "Yes, love?"

"How weird would it be if I cried right now?"

And with the last word, my chin quivered and tears welled in my eyes. He squeezed me tight and whispered into my ear. "Oh, F-Bomb."

I shook there against him, clutching him and letting tears pour down onto his arm as he held me. There wasn't an ounce of sadness in my heart at that moment, yet still they came.

I couldn't explain it, but they felt like release – like divine release.

Stellan held me until I stopped, cooing to me softly.

Finally we separated, and he stood up, his skin damp and warm. I watched him putting on his jeans and listened to him head downstairs to make coffee. I remained there in my bed, my hair still wet from the shower, my skin still damp, now coupled by our sweat. My sex throbbed from my orgasm, my body bared to the open air. I had no desire to cover up.

I listened to the birds outside the window, the coffee grinder whirring away in the kitchen below. I wiped my eyes and forced myself out of bed.

I reached the kitchen hallway and watched him. Stellan stood at the sink, his bare back to me, silhouetted by the light of the kitchen windows. He filled the coffee pot with water, his head bowed as he leaned his weight against the counter. I felt his distance like shackles at that moment, despite his only being a couple yards away.

He shut off the faucet and turned, smiling when he spotted me.

The words came as though someone pulled them from my throat.

"I love you," I said.

I held my breath.

He smirked, set the coffee pot on the counter and crossed the kitchen toward me. He leaned down, locked his arms around me and lifted me again. "You better."

Stellan then walked me down the hallway and back upstairs.

CHAPTER FOURTEEN

For the next couple weeks, Stellan and I discovered we were dirty fucking perverts.

Seriously.

We spent every free moment at my house while my mother was out, then nights in his basement apartment where we were two floors from his parents. We shagged multiple times a day, in every position, on every surface. No room, nor space was sacred. If he ran his hands over my ass while I stood at my fridge, I'd have my hand down his pants before he could exhale. If I snuck up behind him and put my arms around his chest, his tongue would be in my mouth before a word could form.

I texted while he was working, informing him of the debauchery he could expect when he was done, and I'm not afraid to admit it – Stellan definitely had a twat shot on his phone.

I'm not afraid to admit I had a couple cock shots on mine, too.

We fucked like porn stars; I called him Daddy, he called me his dirty little slut. He smacked my ass, I slapped his face and demanded he chase me down and force himself on me, or bang me like an episode of wild kingdom, with him crouched over me, his legs burning from the effort. He was equipped for some of the marathon sessions we engaged in. I was not so in shape, and after long stints of bouncing up and down on his couch, I would wobble and fall when I tried to get up, my legs exhausted.

Two weeks in, I'd lost seven pounds. When we did find the need for food, we made out in the produce aisle of Crosby's, or I gave him a blow job in his jeep outside the Chinese restaurant.

He was a spoiled guy, it's true. He spoiled me right back.

Save for programming work, or Ninjitsu classes, Stellan and I spent almost no time apart, and had no intentions of starting to. Stellan brought up my going back to work once or twice in those hours. I was silently counting the days.

A few days before Christmas we spent the night at my house. I woke to him hooking his fingers at my hip to pull me against him, his breath against my shoulder, his body and his erection pressed against me. We didn't really need words by then. I laughed on the mornings when he woke me by climbing on me and saying, "Sorry honey, this will only take a minute," or "brace yourself." Some mornings, I woke him with my mouth, just to hear the happy startled sounds he made.

I listened to the familiar sound of my mother collecting her keys and heading out the door downstairs. We were safe for the day. Stellan reached down between my legs and whispered in my ear. I opened to him – we were long past timidity now. I was wet from the night before, and he groaned when he touched me. I rolled onto my back to receive him, but he didn't move. Instead he grabbed my hands and pulled me onto him.

I dutifully got into position, grumbling. "Damn it, I can't get off in this position."

He stared at me with feigned shock. "What? Challenge accepted."

I laughed. "You'll be disappointed, handsome."

He shot me an evil grin. "Not possible."

I loved any position, really, but I grumbled, disappointed I wouldn't get to enjoy lazy-lie-on-my-back-and-grab-his-ass sex.

I suppose it was his turn.

He shifted under me, licking his fingers before running them over his erection. I centered myself and slowly lowered down onto him, gasping at the initial soreness of weeks of sex.

He groaned and hummed as he watched me.

I started moving on him, using the full range of motion in my legs. He held my hips, lifting me in rhythm as I moved. I pressed my hands on his chest for leverage.

He pulled my hands upward. "Come down here. I want those 'tiddays' bouncing in my face."

I giggled and grabbed him by the head, firmly planting my tits onto his face, smothering him. He growled and laughed, kissing every spot he could get to before I released him.

"You're such a dirty old man."

He chuckled. "Hey, I'm only a year older than you, young lady. And who fucking wouldn't be with this sex goddess bouncing on their cock?"

I laughed again and bounced harder. I was nowhere close to having an orgasm. He felt good, amazing really, but it was amazing in an arousing and enjoyable way, not a body convulsing, muscle spasm kind of way. I could do this a while and be moaning and shrieking the whole time, but I wouldn't have an orgasm.

Oddly enough, I didn't mind. I loved the act itself with him – the orgasm wasn't as important as simply feeling him close. And being on top was powerful, I could call him names and watch him sigh and remain in control of myself - mostly - at least until my legs gave out.

Let's be real, it wouldn't be long. Even with weeks of sex, I was still out of shape.

"God, I love watching you," he said.

I ran my hand over his face, covering his eyes for a moment. "Don't say that, you'll make me all shy."

He groaned and thrust himself up into me. I gasped.

"Don't you dare get shy. I want you in all your fuck slut glory."

"Did you just call me a fuck slut?"

He thrust up into me again, and I cried out.

He made his point with a hard smack on my backside. "I did. What are you going to do about it?"

I stopped moving for a moment and leaned as though I would get off of him. He grabbed me around the waist and held me there. "Where do you think you're going?"

He sat up enough to kiss me, his tongue piercing my mouth, wetting my lips. I squirmed on him, and he growled at me. Then, he dropped back onto the bed and locked his wrists behind my lower back.

"Alright, enough fuckin around. You say you can't get off like this? Let's put that to the test, shall we?"

I smiled, but quickly realized the seriousness of his pursuit. He shifted under me, planting his feet into the mattress, the pressure of his hands on my back forcing me down against his chest. I held myself up to watch his face, but a moment later, there was no seeing anything.

He pinned me against him and thrust up into me with purpose. I shrieked and grabbed the pillow under his head. He was moving so fast and forcefully that if he wasn't holding on, I'd have been bucked off.

He spoke low, but forcefully. "Does Daddy's little slut like getting fucked hard?"

I'm sorry, I don't care if your sensibilities are compromised here, but I fucking love it when he talks like that. My words wobbled and undulated with his rhythm as I drew out each word "Oh my god!"

"Yeah?"

And I did. The friction of his body against mine, his cock hitting all the right places – it felt amazing. My muscles tightened around him, and I whined as the sensation grew more intense. "Holy shit, don't stop!"

"Oh, I'm not gonna stop!"

"Please, fuck! Oh god, Stell! Do it! Do it!"

His words were getting labored with the exertion. He was annihilating me. "Yeah, I knew you'd fucking love this?"

"Oh god! Fuck me!"

He obliged, almost lifting me off the bed with every few thrusts. The bed shook beneath us, the headboard tapping against the wall in rhythm. I clutched him, my face in the crook of his neck and my hands locked onto his shoulders. He squeezed me tighter and growled loudly, a sign of his effort to keep pace and keep from losing it. I curled into him, my middle tight, and my legs squeezing around him.

He whispered into my ear with approval. "That's my good girl."

I came in waves, shuddering there against him as he moved, melting onto him like warm syrup. He kept moving, a rule we had after the one time he slowed in the middle of my orgasm.

Never stop until I say so!

I sighed and shook there, my legs exhausted despite having seemingly done so little. He slowed his movements finally.

I kissed him before smiling down at him. "Want to bend me over now?"

His eyes went wide, and he was up and pulling my backside to the edge of the bed before I could respond. He took me from behind while I yelled porn worthy obscenities at him about his sexual prowess. He drove deeper in this position, and I couldn't help but cry out as he moved in me. When he was ready, I turned on the bed and took him in my mouth, finishing him there. He whimpered, a sound I loved to hear him make, and held his fingers tight in my hair. I slowed my movements before his sensitivity got to be too much, and swallowed everything he gave me.

When I rose to my knees, my legs were completely useless. He caught me and held me against him, leaning down to kiss me. I teased him with light touches to his now overly sensitive sex.

"You spoil me, Älskling."

I smiled against his lips. "You love it."

I grabbed his bare bum and squeezed before dropping back onto the bed. He stood there before me, naked and beautiful, and I told him so.

He responded by planting his hands on his hips and doing his best Superman pose. I laughed as he got dressed.

"You want some tea, beautiful?"

I pursed my lips and considered. "Yes. I'd love some."

I lied there quiet, my body sore in all the right places from weeks of soul satisfying love making with a man who seemed to have been sexually made for me - a man whom I loved with fearless abandon.

I heard the soft pat of footsteps coming back up the stairs. I was surprised by the speed of their return. He snuck in, closed the door behind him and stood there staring at the floor. He looked troubled, hovering shirtless and silent – beautiful, but troubled. He finally shot me a glance, then turned his eyes back to the floor and reached down to grab his shirt.

"What is it, baby?" I asked, finally.

He took a deep breath. "Pam's downstairs."

And I died inside.

Stellan pulled his shirt on and slumped down onto the edge of the bed, pinning me under the blankets. He rubbed the back of his head and his neck. I scratched his back, trying to soothe him while fighting a violent cringe that was pulsating in my chest.

"What did she say?"

He shook his head. "'Good morning?' Fuck. Your mom is never going to look at me the same, again."

I shut my eyes. I was thinking the same thing. I wanted to crawl in a hole and die, but I made Stellan get up and let me toss on some clothes. We forced a smile at one another, before venturing downstairs. Mom was milling around the kitchen, a large collection of canvas bags filled with art books by the door.

"Hey Mom."

She smiled at me as I rounded the refrigerator.

"Good morning!"

Jesus, if that's how she said it to Stellan, no wonder he was upset. The tone was shrill it was so pleasant.

Yeah, she'd definitely heard us.

"Whatcha up to?"

I tried to make it sound as nonchalant as possible – not "What the hell are you doing home?" or "Get the hell out"-y.

"Oh, I promised Kelly I'd bring these in for her. Some fund raising thing they're doing at the school. Didn't realize how much I still had, as you can tell."

She stooped to grab one of the satchels and Stellan stepped in, scooping up two per forearm and chivalrously hauling them out the back door to her car. If he thought I wouldn't spot the desertion for exactly what it was, he wasn't the genius I thought him to be.

I stood in the kitchen with my mother.

"I'm hoping they go to good use. There's some really great stuff in there."

I buried my hands in my jeans pockets and leaned against the fridge. "You ok parting with them?"

She nodded. "Yes. I never actually look at them. If I had some palatial estate with a library, I might keep them, but as it is, they're just taking up space in my closet. I say let them take up space where someone might read them."

I fought with the idea. Should I apologize? Acknowledge what she heard, that I'd had loud, porn worthy sex in my childhood bedroom with her just a floor away? Her tone and her busy movements made me question whether she wanted such an apology. Still, this was her house.

Stellan slipped inside to grab the last two bags and

was gone again.

Mom smiled. "He's a wonderful man, Faye."

I glanced up at her. She was standing at the kitchen sink, watching out the windows. A moment later, she waved to him and turned to collect her keys.

I couldn't stay silent. "Mom – I'm wicked sorry."

She looked at me and shook her head. "You deserve a wonderful man, honey. You always did. I'll get out of your hair now."

She crossed the kitchen to give me a quick peck on the cheek, then turned and left. I stood dumbfounded and a little ashamed. When Stellan came back inside, he closed the kitchen door and waited for me to speak.

"Dick."

He grinned. "What? Those were heavy bags, woman!"

"You're not getting another blow job for the rest of the day."

He came at me, grabbing me around the waist, whining. "Don't say that!"

I smiled. "Nope, you're cut off. And you promised me tea."

His hands slipped down my backside, and his tone shifted as he moved me down the hallway. "Well, now that you mentioned blow jobs, I'm all excited over here."

"You're not getting one! Damn it, I'm humiliated, can't you think of anything else?"

He smiled and nuzzled the crook of my neck, kissing me. "Nope!"

I didn't fight him, and he knew I wouldn't. We practically didn't make it upstairs.

My mother was the first to know about Stellan and I. His parents might have suspected, given how much time we were spending together, but they were accustomed to him being incognito in the basement, so whether they were even aware of my presence, I wasn't sure. Meghan was completely oblivious to anything, save for the fact that Cole and I were no longer, and that I'd acquired a sudden inability to respond to a text or phone call in a reasonable amount of time.

We weren't trying to keep anything secret, we simply didn't talk to anyone. I thought the oblivion would remain universal until I received an early morning text from Evan. He was concerned that Stellan had disappeared off the face of the earth.

Have you heard from him? I'm close to flying into town to track the homo down.

I turned to Stellan in bed and showed him the text. He grumbled, grabbed his phone and responded to whatever message waited.

Evan texted me two minutes later.

Smug Bastard - **I fucking knew it!! God, I'm good!! Thanks, sexy. You may commence with your flagrant shaggery.**

"That dick!"

Stellan chuckled.

Jackie already knew. She texted to ask how I was, and I didn't respond for three days. Given how I'd looked after the Christmas party, she followed up, worried.

I finally texted back. **Sorry, I've been with Stellan.**

Smug Bastardess - **Is that so?**

Nymphomaniac Me - **Yes.**

Does that mean…?
Shrilly Excited Nymphomaniac Me - **Yes.**

I threw in a smiley face - or seven. She responded in kind. I knew that unlike Meghan, this would be enough for now. We would talk when I was ready. We would talk when time allowed.

The official 'coming out,' was at Christmas. We slept at my house and had breakfast and presents with my mother before walking over to the Ødegård manor.

Lennart was already in his chair when we arrived, and he hopped up to greet us. Linda rushed out from the kitchen as well. I was hugged and kissed by both before being led into the front room and offered Lennart's chair. I refused of course and sat by the windows. They'd clearly been told.

Lennart spoke loud enough to be heard in the kitchen. "I can't imagine you're hungry yet, so Linda says we have to do presents first."

Linda told him to quit whining, and Stellan hollered something in Swedish.

I smiled and tried to apologize, but Lennart simply smiled before yelling back, also in Swedish. I was used to this, but today it almost made me nervous. Suddenly, I wanted to make a good impression. Suddenly, I needed to be on my best behavior. I wasn't Stellan's goofball friend anymore, I was his girlfriend.

Wow. Even just saying that feels earth shattering.

I nestled in with Lennart and let him regale me with tales, many of which I'd already heard once or twice. Linda came in carrying a tray of Pâté, cheese and crackers, which Lennart quickly jumped on. Lennart spoke between – or perhaps in the midst of – crunchy bites. He explained the finer workings of the recent stock market behavior, and seemed to be in a good mood. I took this to mean his investments were doing well. Still, investments was all he was doing since retirement, and he said the futility of retired life was setting in.

I looked up just in time to see Stellan follow his mother into the room with mulled wine and a few glasses. He was wearing a tall pointy red hat and a fake white beard. Linda turned and feigned surprise. "Tomte! Tomte's here!"

Stellan flashed me a smile as he settled on the floor beside the tree.

I'd asked Stellan about the immortal Tomte when we were younger, and I'd spotted a little bearded figuring on their mantel in the weeks before Christmas. Apparently, Tomte was the slightly unkempt, tiny gnome like Swedish version of a Santa Claus who may or may not kill your livestock if he thinks you're rude.

I told him Sweden was so fucking metal.

This was the first time I'd witness the great Tomte tradition in person. It was endearing as all hell.

I leaned close enough so he and only he could hear me. "I'd still bang you."

His eyes betrayed a smile hidden under his nonsensical beard. "Good to know, I'll bring the beard to bed later."

I returned to Lennart, and Stellan rubbed his knuckles against my ankle as he spoke to his mother.

Presents were passed out, many of them between Lennart and Linda. Stellan gave his mother a set of Creuset cookware, and I practically drooled. It was purple for Christ's sake! He gave Lennart a few new tools for their joint workshop and then a couple little items here and there. Lennart and Linda jointly gave me a beautiful little vase, a set of pens that Stellan had clearly advised on (they were my favorite), and then as the rest of the presents were all passed out, Stellan pushed me a large wrapped shape from behind the tree.

I lifted it up into my lap as the room grew quiet, and I shrank to half my size. I tore at the paper as gently as I could, pulling it back to see worn wood finish underneath. I lifted the wooden box out of the paper and let the wrapping fall to Stellan before setting the box in my lap. It was old, the top slanted toward me with a hinged cover, and the corners were worn lighter than the rest of the stain. I lifted the top of the box to find a small sketchpad inside. I looked up at the faces of the room, searching for the source of the gift, the person whose inspiration could be blamed.

Linda leaned in. "I know you're an artist, so a writer's box might not be quite appropriate, but I thought you might be able to use it for your sketching too?"

I nodded. I could. I certainly could, and I had no words. I ran my hand over the top of the box, feeling the nicks and knots along its edges. I felt Stellan's hand run up my calf and squeeze as I put my hand to my mouth.

Linda hopped up and coaxed me to turn the box over. I did.

"Here, Lennart thought this was the best part."

I saw it. In perfect penmanship, a name was carved into the bottom of the box. Some other soul had loved this box enough to mark it as hers. "Providence

Merle Fields – 1862"

My mouth fell open. I did my best to hide the emotion, keeping my head down as I inspected the name, traced my fingers over this ancient thing.

Maintain your cool, damn it.

Despite my best efforts, my eyes welled too quickly and a tear fell onto the wood. Before I could wipe it away, Stellan kissed my knee.

I couldn't quite explain why it moved me so much – the fact that Lennart had been involved in the choosing of a gift for me? The fact that Stellan's family had enveloped me with such warmth, finding such a thoughtful gift in the mere two and a half weeks since their son and myself had become a couple?

I'd never had a Christmas outside my mother's home, and that was simple enough since Grammy Jensen died. My mother was a lot of things, but a rabid Christian observer of the holy day of Christ's birth? Not so much.

Linda reached over and patted the back of my hand.

For future reference, when someone is clearly trying to keep their shit together, don't make it harder by being all loving, damn it.

I swallowed hard and whispered. "Thank you so much."

We ate dinner early; a smorgasbord. No really, an actual smorgasbord. Dessert was a sweet porridge that Linda assured me was a Swedish tradition. She passed out the bowls as Lennart grumbled about how he'd take one of my apple pies over this any day.

I smiled.

I dug into my bowl of Swedish rice pudding only to

discover a hard object in my mouth after the third bite. I pulled it out to look at it.

"Oh oh! Faye found the almond! Everybody, Faye found the almond! Looks like somebody is going to be getting married next year, hmmm?"

The tone was so syrupy that I couldn't help but laugh. Lennart and Stellan called Linda out, accusing her of having planted the almond in my Risgryngrot. She feigned complete ignorance, winking at me over the table.

Stellan and Lennart assured me that it meant I got a wish, not a marriage proposal.

"Well, what if I wish for a marriage proposal?"

I stared Stellan down with a wicked smile on my face.

He smiled back and raised an eyebrow. "Better wish hard then."

His mother swatted at him, and he smiled, taking my hand and kissing it.

I held the almond in my hand and made my wish.

We spent the evening with my mother, a good amount of it spent in the living room while she and Stellan conversed. I watched.

There's a strange pride to watching your partner engage in easy conversation, but all the moreso when it is with your people – your tribe.

I don't know how else to phrase that.

Your family doesn't quite cut it – your kindred, perhaps. Seeing the one you choose fit seamlessly into the clan you come from – it validates your choice. After hours of him making my mother smile, I was ready to eat him alive, I was so fond of him.

I brought the writing box upstairs to my room and settled it into an open spot on my bookshelves.

Stellan followed me up and snuck up behind me, wrapping his arms around my waist. I went to squeeze his arms into my belly and found a present in his hands.

Thus far that day, he'd given me a few little things; candy, a wind up robot that did backflips, and an iPhone case with *Calvin and Hobbes* on it. Ownership of the digital sketchpad had been unceremoniously transferred to me a day or two earlier with the words, "Call it a Christmas Present. It's not like I'm using it." It was now plugged into my laptop in the office. And above all, that morning he'd given me an original still from the Goofy cartoon, *How to Ski*. In case I didn't mention this by now, Walt Disney is my hero. One can imagine I was rather pleased with that gift.

Still, here he was handing me yet another present. Baked goods were the extent of my broke ass gift giving that year – baked goods and blow job coupons - so I felt almost bad to see he'd gotten me something more.

I turned to him and he smiled, waiting for me to take it. I sat on the edge of the bed and opened it.

"I was going to save it for when you start your job - "

It was an iPad. I shook my head as I opened the box and found it already charged and in a purple case. He sat beside me, and I turned to him and smiled.

He leaned in, excited to show me the gadget. "Here, look."

The screen lit up and as Stellan's fingers danced over the surface, I saw many familiar images peppered into the foreign shapes and squares. "I downloaded you a few comic strip compilations; *Far Side* and stuff. And I signed you into my Netflix account so you can watch whenever you want to."

"Oh, you know I'd be watching it with you."

He gave a half smile. "Well, this is for when you're on the road. I know you're not sure when you'll start traveling again, but I wanted you to have something, you know, when you do. I figure airports have Wi-Fi and most hotels these days, but the LTE -"

He was off.

My Stellan and his gadgets.

His fingers continued to dance, showing me *Gorilla Warfare* ready to play, but he'd lost me. I couldn't hear him over the sound of my own thoughts.

Fourteen days.

I went back to work in fourteen days.

I kissed Stellan's shoulder and said, "Thank you, baby."

Stellan and I curled up into bed, my bare chest pressed against his back and my arms locked tightly around him. He made a lovey dovey sound when I squeezed him, turning to me in bed to kiss me. The kiss quickly shifted to him moving onto me and making love to me as quietly as we could. I locked my hands behind his back, held my legs at his sides and let him move against me, the way he now knew I liked. When we were both spent, he collapsed onto me, settling his head into the crook of my neck. I kept my hands locked behind his back, holding him as tightly to me as I could. Had I the ability, I'd have sewn us together to keep him close.

He didn't fight the embrace.

When we woke the next morning, we hadn't moved.

CHAPTER FIFTEEN

Despite the quiet of the Christmas holiday, I did receive well-wishing texts from everyone I knew. Meghan's included the word 'slut,' and Evan's made reference to Stellan's penis, but I responded with "Merry Christmas to you too," nonetheless.

Jackie's Christmas texts included a proclamation that I would be spending my New Year with her. I prepared to argue, still quite content at the notion of being holed up by a fireplace, cuddling with my Swede.

She insisted.

When New Year's arrived, Meghan, Jackie and Kevin all stomped their way up my porch steps around nine. Stellan was plopped into my living room couch with a laptop, silent. Stellan was grumpy at the news that our evening wouldn't involve complete, naked alone time, but after some grumbling and a promise of a languid blow job, he'd agreed to do whatever it was I was being suckered into.

"Happy New Year, slut! Glad to see you're alive," Meghan said as she entered.

I hugged her, fawning at the sight of her. She was yet again dressed to the nines in a short black dress with silver sequins across the low cut breast. Jackie came in her simple tweed trench and scarf, with Kevin in a similar get up behind her. She carried a cardboard box that looked to be from a bakery. I leaned in to look, but she quickly shifted to keep it hidden.

When I was able to shut the door behind them, Stellan and Meghan were already well into berating one another.

"So are we heading out right away? Where are we going?" I asked.

Stellan was standing in the living room, having set the laptop aside to exasperate "Trotsky."

Jackie beamed at me. "We can go whenever you guys are ready."

I turned to find Meghan glaring at me. "Why do you hang out with this asshole?"

Stellan gave me a shit eating grin. "Yes, Faye. Why do you hang out with this asshole?"

"Both of you shut it."

I tossed Stellan his jacket, and he pulled a black ski hat out of the pocket, pulling it down onto his head. I bundled up in a coat and scarf, eyeing Meghan with some trepidation. A part of me felt like I'd almost failed the man I loved by not getting gussied up for the evening. Given that we'd had sex a half hour before everyone arrived, I was strapped for time. I settled for Jeans and one of Stellan's Bruins shirts. I'd just pulled my boots on as Stellan made comment about Meghan's dress.

"I love that dress, Trotsky. You're going to be the classiest hooker out tonight!"

She threw her keys at him. "Die slowly."

He caught them without flinching. "Love you too."

We milled out onto the porch, puffing and groaning against the cold. It was snow weather, and I could smell it coming in the air. I shifted over to be by Stellan, forcing him to give Meghan her keys. We followed Jackie down the stairs, ready to suggest a driving plan that included Stell and I driving alone, but instead Jackie walked through the parked cars and headed up the street.

I hustled to follow, Meghan's heels clacking against the pavement behind me, yelling her disdain.

I met Jackie's stride. "Where we heading, lady?"

She simply smiled and looked up the road. Wherever we were going, it made her happy.

I hoped it wasn't too far.

Stellan caught up to me, kicking the back of my heel with his foot as I tried to step down. I stumbled, but he had his arm around me before I could call him names. We rounded the corner and headed for the center of town.

"If I knew we were going for a fucking hike, I'd have worn different shoes," Meghan said, her heels clacking on the sidewalk.

Stellan glanced back at her. "Lift your skirt when the next car passes, maybe you'll get a ride."

"Shut up, waste of skin."

"What?! I thought that was helpful!"

"Faye, I hate your friend," Meghan said, groaning.

"Oh, Trotsky. That hurts. And I was always so fond of you."

Meghan glared at us. "I want your balls in a jar."

Stellan gave an impressed nod. "And I want to smoke bath salts and eat your face."

I fought through laughter to holler at them. "Both of you are intolerable!"

Meghan passed us to catch up to Jackie and Kevin. "Blame the primate. Jackie, we better be getting close, my feet are killing me."

With Meghan in front of us, I swiftly reached down

and cupped Stellan's balls through his jeans. He shifted and squeezed at my nipple under my shirt. I tried to get away without squealing too loudly, but he whispered softly. "Mmm, careful or I'll throw you in the bushes and have my way with you."

I laughed, and grabbed his collar to kiss him. He smacked my ass, feigning ignorance when Meghan turned to ask what the sound was. We hit Main Street, and Jackie's pace picked up, much to Meghan's chagrin. Stellan and I walked with our arms around one another behind the pack, our footsteps matched. I fondled him a couple more times before we caught up.

Jackie was hovering just outside the now dark and defunct Boathouse Bakery, fidgeting with her coat pocket. Before I could ask, she pulled out a set of keys and unlocked the front door, stepping aside to let us all in. My eyebrows nearly flew off my forehead, and I met her gaze, searching for explanation.

She just smiled.

The chairs were settled atop the tables as they'd been left the day the place closed. The glass cases in the counter were empty, the trays disheveled and in some cases missing. Still, there was a warmth to the place when Jackie turned on the light. The wood stain of the counters and floors, the metal of the shelves and mirrors behind the counter – it almost gave the vibe of an old western saloon, like at any time, one of the thin framed chairs would be put to use, shattered over the back of some cheating gambler.

Kevin set up a few chairs as Jackie busied herself behind the counter. Meghan plopped down in the first chair Kevin offered and quickly removed her shoes to rub her feet.

I approached the counter. "What's going on Jack?"

I turned to meet Meghan's eyes, and after a quick shrug back, I knew I wasn't the only one oblivious.

Meghan said something from far behind the counter. Whatever she was up to, she was in a tizzy. Kevin disappeared into the back to join his wife.

Stellan smiled at me and patted the seat beside him in offering. Before I could accept, Meghan propped her feet up on it, oblivious.

Stellan's expression was priceless, and I instantly burst into laughter.

Before he could make comment, I sat in his lap. He nuzzled my chest and wrapped his arms around my hips, holding me on him.

"What the fuck?"

Stellan and I both turned to find Meghan with a traumatized look on her face.

I inhaled sharply at the realization. I still hadn't told Meghan.

I wasn't eloquent in my delivery. "Oh shit! Yeah."

"Are you fucking kidding me? Tell me this is just some new friendly cuddling Swede thing, and you two are not, actually, fucking."

"Oh we are definitely fucking, Trotsky."

I gasped, swatting at him. "Stellan!"

"What? Am I lying?" He asked, giving me an eyebrow wiggle.

Meghan shuddered. "I think I just threw up in my mouth a little."

Stellan laughed. "Did it taste like semen coming up, too?"

I gave him a shocked expression. Did he *want* to die?

Stellan threw up his hands. "What? Alright, I'm

sorry. It was just too good –"

Meghan went for him. "Ødegård, I'm going to fucking kill you!"

A warm glow behind the counter distracted us from further banter. Jackie had appeared carrying an exact replica of the Boathouse Bakery in cake form.

Stellan was awestruck. "Did you make that?"

Jackie beamed at us as she set it on the table. The roof was shingled with a tiny brick chimney, and the side stairs to the second floor were each perfectly painted in wood grain. We all stood to get a closer look when she finally stepped away from the table.

Stellan pulled out his iPhone and crouched next to the table to get a good picture. I caught Jackie smiling as she watched him. Meghan leaned over Stellan to get a shot as well, the two of them hovering with their phones.

They insulted each other for getting in the way or blocking the light.

"Suck a dick, Ødegård."

"Why, Trotsky? Are you giving lessons?"

Stellan leaned in close to the cake, trying to make out tiny words. "Thoreau-ly Baked?"

I stepped in to see. On the tiny awning, there was a perfect silhouette of Henry David Thoreau with the words just under him.

Jackie bit her lip, frowning at me sheepishly. "You don't mind my stealing your idea, do you? You've always been the one oozing brilliance. I couldn't come up with anything better."

I shook my head.

Stellan chuckled. "I don't think anybody could. Why? Whose idea was it?"

"It was Faye's brilliance, not mine," Jackie said,

shrugging at me. "I'd actually half hoped you come be my – I don't know – wingman, but then you got the job at Chalice."

"Wait," I said. Dawn was breaking on Marblehead. "You bought the bakery?"

Jackie hopped up and down a little where she stood.

I stared at her ecstatic face. It was so huge, so big – the risk, the jump, the dream itself – and she'd just up and fucking did it.

I searched for words to encompass what I was feeling. "You're so brave," I said.

Jackie's face fell, but Meghan rounded the table to give Jackie a hug and take a selfie of the two of them with the cake. I stood there staring at it. The skill it took to make it, the time she'd taken to learn to do this very thing, wiling away the hours in her beautiful kitchen. Now here she was, stepping outside that beautiful kitchen, and if the sheer cool factor of that little sign had any say, she was going to do well.

I know I'd order my cakes from a place called "Thoreau-ly Baked."

I wanted to feel honored to have had a hand in its naming. I'm not sure what I felt.

Jackie pulled a tray down from the top of the glass case and set it alongside the cake. Cannolis. "And I brought these!"

Meghan was on them without pause. They were small, half-sized and perfect, with chocolate chips on either end. I moved closer to look at the cake, inspecting every little detail. Jackie was an architect with fondant.

Meghan spoke as she picked crumbs out of her sequins. "I can just see this window with your cakes in it."

"I'm hoping to branch out from just the sweets and stuff. You know, keep the Cannoli alive, but charge a lot less. Maybe do sandwiches or soups and stuff. I don't know, I'm still a little – I haven't decided." She laughed nervously.

Stellan ran his hand up my back. "That sounds boss. We'll come patronize the shit out of you."

Jackie laughed. "Yes, please!"

I stood with my back against the front window, watching my friends eat Cannolis and laugh. I felt somewhere far away, like I was watching the scene from behind a window, like a ghost that they couldn't see. Kevin snuck behind the counter and produced a bottle of champagne, popping the cork into the back recesses of the bakery.

We sat there for some time talking and drinking, Stellan at my side, interjecting as though on my behalf. I wondered if he knew how far away I was - if he could feel it. I did my best to engage in the conversation, finding my comments to consist mostly of how beautiful the place was going to look, or how fat I would get having her so close to home.

After a while, Meghan and Kevin finally demanded cake. The tiny bakery was carved into, cleaving the front window in twain. Stellan handed me a piece and pulled up a chair for me to sit in. I took my fork and poked the cake, but my stomach warned against a bite. The Champagne didn't settle well either.

I shifted in my seat.

"You alright, dove?"

I touched my hand to my stomach. "I don't know."

He set his hand on my stomach too, rubbing me softly. "You feeling sick?"

I shook my head. "No, no. I'm fine."

He leaned in to me. "You haven't touched your cake, and I finished your drink. What's up? Do you need me to take you home?"

He rubbed my stomach again and when I didn't answer, turned to the room. "Hey, I'm gonna run Faye home. She's not feeling well."

Jackie fawned, and Meghan called me a quitter, given that it was only ten forty five, but I didn't protest.

Stellan wrapped my coat around my shoulders and opened his hand to Meghan.

She glared at him. "What?"

"Give me your keys, Trotsky. I'll run your car down so you don't have to walk back."

Meghan's gaze softened a moment as she stared at him. After a moment of speechlessness, she did as she was asked. "I'm still gonna hate you though."

He took the keys. "I wouldn't have it any other way, twat."

"Fucktard."

Being curled up in my bed away from cakes and cannolis sounded ideal at that moment, so I let him hustle our exit without complaint. I made a round of hugs, taking a moment to tell Jackie how proud of her I was. She teared up when I said it, and I felt even more determined to get the hell out of that building.

Maybe if I was alone I could understand why I felt so wrong in that space, why I was so incapable of – of being happy for her.

Stell said 'Thank you' and walked me out into the cold, pulling his hat on outside. He hooked his arm with mine, and we walked.

"What's wrong, baby?"

I shook my head. "I don't know. I just feel off."

"I know. Bit worried actually."

I frowned. "I know."

It worried me, too.

Stellan did as he promised, putting me to bed and delivering Meghan's car to the center. He threatened to go drive it into the quarry and suffer the cold walk home simply to see her face when he told her. I curled into my covers and sheets, and nestled into the mountain of pillows. When Stellan got back, I listened to him kick off his boots downstairs. He slipped into bed beside me and wrapped an arm around me.

I pretended to be asleep.

That was the first night that Stellan and I did not make love.

CHAPTER SIXTEEN

If someone doesn't get drunk or stay up all night, how the hell do they spend New Year's Day morning?

I woke late to the smell of Stellan cooking breakfast and my mother chatting away downstairs. I shimmied out of bed to join them.

Apple Pancakes with Maple Bacon and eggs – I sat at the kitchen counter as Stellan put a plate in front of me. I took one bite and called him a slut. They were phenomenal.

My mother moaned over her plate beside me and took a few more bites before she spoke. "So, any plans for today?"

I shrugged, but Stellan answered. "I've got a little work I need to get done at home, but otherwise, not a damn thing."

He sat across from me, digging into his own breakfast. God damn, those were good pancakes. Still, my stomach began to shift around the third or fourth bite.

What on earth was wrong with me?

My mother leaned onto the counter. "Working on New Year's Day, Stellan? What has the world come to?"

He smiled. "Believe me, I've been blowing work off a lot, lately."

I pushed my food around. "What do you need to do?" I asked.

"Something Evan's been pestering me for. Told him to 'stuff it' one too many times, so I'm afraid he'll show up to 'motivate' me."

He shot my mother a smile.

She shook her head. "I didn't realize you worked with Evan."

Stell nodded and stuffed another bite in his mouth. "Off and on."

"Taught the man everything he knows," I said.

Stellan blew me a kiss.

Stellan headed home after breakfast, despite hemming and hawing at my bedroom door over whether he should have his way with me before he left. I urged him to go get his work done, and I would follow after a shower. I spent that unabashedly long shower sitting in the bathtub, thinking.

My mind went everywhere — to what I might want to read on my iPad when traveling, to Jackie's bakery, to *Gorilla Warfare*, to Stellan and I not having sex the night before, to Jackie's bakery, to how many months of paychecks I'd need to get out of my mother's house – to Jackie's bakery.

I considered having a claim to responsible adulthood again. In a few days, I'd officially be working. In a few days, I would no longer be wiling away the hours curled up on couches or in beds with the man I love. I would be working; I would be making a living and a good one at that, doing what I'm so very good at. I would be traveling all over the country within a few months, seeing cities I loved, staying at my usual hotels, seeing old friends. I thought about actually using my frequent flier miles to pay for Stellan and I to travel somewhere warm and spend the hours curled up in beds or on couches in tiki huts or bungalows with margaritas. I smiled at the thought and vowed to do just that in several months - when I could afford to take time off of work.

It was snowing when I went downstairs. I bundled up and headed over to Stell's. Downtown was quiet, all the shops closed up tight. I was the only person in sight when I crossed the snow covered square.

Linda was folding laundry at the dining room table, flashing me a smile as I came in. I said a quick hello before heading downstairs. Stellan was at his wall of screens, talking away on a headset. I thought for a moment that he'd tricked me and was busy playing Battlefield, then I heard that language – the inexplicable drone of programming.

I mentally shut right the hell down.

He squeezed my legs as I bent down to kiss his neck. He whispered that he'd be done soon. Though I loved his company, I wasn't sure how long he'd be, and Linda was alone upstairs.

I enjoyed chatting with Linda immensely. She was like a second mother, at times, and given the strict sex schedule Stellan and I had, I'd missed a few weeks' worth of her interrogation that I loved so much.

She smiled and greeted me as I came in and sat down. She finished folding one load and set it aside before starting on another. I offered to help, but she naturally refused.

"So how was your New Year's? Stellan said it was quiet."

I nodded. "I slept through it, actually."

"Yes, he said you weren't feeling well."

I spotted a t-shirt I knew well – *Hoverboards don't work on water*. She was folding Stellan's laundry.

"How was yours?" I asked.

"Wonderful. Lenn and I actually went out for once. Did one of those parties down at the Sheraton. Apparently they do them every year. You rent a room and party all night. Lots of drinking and dancing – wonderful food."

"Wow, that sounds amazing."

"Lennart had a blast. Loved it. I literally had to drag him by his toenails to get him there, but once I got a drink in his hand, he loved every second of it."

I laughed. I could imagine the tone I would get from Stellan if I ever asked him to go to such an event. I could also see the big smile on his face after actually getting him there. God, he's a pain in the ass, but he's *my* pain in the ass.

Linda leaned across the table to touch my hand. "So I hear you start your new job soon?"

I answered faster than I'd intended. "Yeah. Next Monday."

"Isn't that a blessing? I know you were looking for a long time."

"I certainly was."

She shook out another t-shirt, a picture of the Dude with the word; *Abide.* "You must be excited."

I said "Mhmm" as quickly as the breath would leave my lips. "It'll be nice to get out of my mother's house."

"Yes, of course. I've tried to convince Stellan of how much happier he would be in his own space."

I chuckled. "I don't know about that. He has it pretty good over here if you ask me."

She smiled, but the look was strange. I gestured to the laundry and she laughed. "Well, it's the least I can do."

It was my turn to look quizzically. "No Linda, you

really do spoil him. I just hope I can keep up with it if we ever move in together. I have trouble even taking care of myself, sometimes."

She smiled and shook her head. "As far as I'm concerned, he could ask for the moon, and I would find a way to give it to him."

She folded with a far off look for a moment and glanced at my face. "I'd like to see him in his own place with you. I think that would make him truly happy."

I smiled and rested my face in my hand. "I'd like that, too. Might get a little lonely while I'm traveling, but I'd love to come home to him."

She leaned in. "Well, maybe we can both go to work on our stubborn men and make that happen."

I raised an eyebrow. "Do you mean Lennart?"

She nodded. "He is wonderful, but Lennart is a very proud man."

I watched her, my brow furrowing. "What do you mean?"

She spoke in a hushed tone, as though the walls might tell Lennart when he got home. "Well, he doesn't like to accept help — now does he? Stellan's rent is the only thing keeping us afloat much of the time, and it almost took a fist fight between the two of them for Len to accept even that."

"His son lives in his basement, and Lennart wouldn't accept rent? Really?"

Linda stopped folding the *Knights Who Say Ni* shirt in her hands and searched my face. Something seemed to dawn in her expression, and she frowned in the gentlest way. "Faye, Stellan owns this house."

If someone had shoved a cherry bomb down the back of my pants, I don't think I could have been more surprised.

Linda could tell, it seemed. She pushed the basket aside and sat across from me. She then proceeded to tell me a story.

After Lennart's heart attack, Stellan came home to tend to the house and work back at the Dojo until Lennart was well enough. Stellan went back to school after a few years, and all seemed well. Then Lennart started having anxiety attacks, episodes that at times felt like little heart attacks, always striking when Lennart was in the office or on his way.

Lennart did tell anyone. He simply stopped going to work.

He kept it so well hidden that she only discovered what was happening when someone delivered a certified letter to the house, announcing the foreclosure process had started.

"Lennart begged me not to tell Stellan, wanted me to tell him some story about how we were *choosing* to leave, that we didn't need the space, but my baby is a smart boy. He could tell we were lying."

I swallowed. "That's why he left MIT, again? Because you were losing the house?"

She nodded. "The next day, Stellan made me take him to the bank, and he paid the mortgage. In one swoop, just paid the whole thing."

I stared at her. "Where did he get the money?"

Linda shrugged. "I don't know. I know he makes a bit of money from those little telephone things he does, but I didn't know he made that much."

iPhone apps? Stellan paid for a house in Concord fucking Massachusetts with iPhone apps? Are you fucking kidding me? "But he pays rent."

She smiled. "It's the only way he can get Lennart to

accept money. I can't believe you didn't know all this. God, he is just like his father."

I planted my head in my hands and stared at the table.

"Don't tell him I told you then, please. I trust your discretion."

She stood and went back to folding the last couple pieces of Stellan's laundry. I sat there, fighting with something I couldn't describe. My stomach was churning, my heart was racing, and my throat had tightened beyond the ability to speak. I forced a smile and shook my head in disbelief, but I didn't say a word.

I was relieved when she finished folding and accepted my offer to take the basket downstairs. Yet, when I reached the basement door, I suddenly didn't want to go down anymore.

Stellan was silent at his wall of screens and for a moment, I thought he might be done. A sudden burst of laughter and a few expletives, and I knew otherwise. He smiled at me, gesturing to the basket with an appreciative grin. I walked behind him and set the basket on his bed. He reached behind his chair to grab my leg, but missed me. I pretended not to see.

I slumped down on the couch, listening, but making neither heads nor tales of his conversation. I was sure it was Evan on the other end.

I stared at the wall, growing impatient,/ kicking at the edge of the carpet as a means to self soothe.

"Hey, I'm gonna cut out here in a sec. You cool?" Stellan said.

Stellan's exchange lasted another minute or so before he pulled the headset off and tossed it onto the desk. He leaned back in his swivel chair and turned from side to side with his hands behind his head. He blew a long breath out and tussled his own hair before hopping up and heading toward me. He bent over the couch to wrap his arms around me and kiss my jaw. I let him.

Then I betrayed Linda completely. "Why didn't you tell me you own your parents' house?"

Stellan stood to full height and yelled through the floor to his mother. His tone was relaxed, but scolding. I heard her in the distance, cooing back.

He grabbed my shoulders and started rubbing me. I pulled away, standing to face him. When I met his gaze, it was clear he hadn't realized my upset.

"Baby, what's up?"

"You own your house. You've always been living in your parents' basement, but now I find out it's your parents living in your upstairs?"

"No, no. This is their house."

"How could you not tell me something like that?"

He was taken aback, watching me a moment. "Faye, Älskling, why are you so upset?"

I shifted away from him when he rounded the couch toward me. I felt small, miniscule. If he got close enough to touch me, he could pull me in whether I wanted him to or not.

"Because I feel lied to."

He startled, his brow furrowing. "What? Don't you think that's being a little dramatic?"

I grabbed my coat and went for the door. He shifted quickly to get in my way. "Why are you so upset, F-bomb. Please calm down and talk to me."

"What is there to say?"

"What? Oh no, don't you act all cavalier like that."

"I'm not being cavalier. I'm trying to consider the

mountain of shit you might also *not* be telling me."

He reached for me, and I backed away.

"Faye -"

"How much money do you make from those apps you do?"

He raised an eyebrow. "I do alright."

"Is that code for I have more money than God?"

"No!"

"How the fuck could you afford to buy your parents' house then?"

He stood silent a moment, his eyes wide. I moved to pass him, and he blocked me again. "I sold my fucking soul to Evan. There, do you feel in the loop now?"

I stared at him.

He groaned. "Evan loaned me the money. I've been doing work for him to pay it back, ever since."

"Bull shit! Evan would have easily just given it to you."

"I wasn't looking for a fucking hand out, thank you very much."

I rolled my eyes, half growling. I couldn't believe what I was hearing. "He's your best friend!"

"Exactly, and I'm better than that."

"Better than asking for help?"

It was his turn to roll his eyes. "Oh Jesus. No, I asked for help. It was a loan. I agreed to work it off on his stupid fucking projects."

"For three years?"

He shrugged. "He may be a genius, but he can't program for shit."

I growled. "He would have just given it to you!"

"I didn't want a fucking hand out!"

We stared at each other.

I took a deep breath. "You're not serious."

He chuckled sadly. "Wish I wasn't. Fucker, practically owns me - for another three months, anyway."

I stared at him. Evan always proclaimed Stellan to be the smarter half of the genius brigade, but I'd always thought he was just being kind.

I watched Stellan's face fall, wanted to touch him and shower him with my warmth, but this fire in my belly was growing. He bailed out Lennart, was a self-inflicted indentured servant to Evan –

"Anything else I should know?"

He came toward me. "God damn it, Faye! I love you. Please stop."

"Don't! Just answer the question."

He blew air out through pursed lips. "What do you want me to say?"

"Why didn't you tell me?"

He jerked back at the question like I'd flicked a lit cigarette at him. "You know my Dad. He'd fucking kill himself if that got around town. Jesus, what do you care? You weren't even around when it happened –"

I threw my coat at him. "No, but it might have come up in conversation recently in between the many times you had your dick inside me!"

Pardon my language, but I was furious.

"Faye!"

"I can't fucking believe this."

"What? What!? You want to know the fucking details? How my father almost fucking disowned me when I came home from the bank? How the neighbors called the cops because we were fighting in the fucking driveway, and he practically head-butt me? What do you need from me to make you happy right now, because you're being irrational?"

I fought a tightness in my throat. Hearing him yell, hearing him describe an event that seemed so life changing, so intense - and he was right, I hadn't been around. I'd been on the other side of the world, as far as he was concerned.

"I can't believe you didn't tell me," I said, almost inaudibly.

"Baby, I didn't tell anyone."

I brushed my knuckle under my eye and laughed. "Yeah, well – I'm not 'anyone' now am I, Stell?"

His face fell, and we stood there, silent. Finally, I snatched my coat up from the floor and walked past him as he reached for me. I dodged him and ran up the stairs, blowing past Linda as I careened through the house.

My body was wound tight as I stepped out into the cold. I half expected Stellan to chase me, but as I hit Central Square, I didn't hear footsteps behind me. I shuffled in the snow, barely watching for cars as I steamed home.

The streets had been plowed since I arrived at Stell's, but the snow was quickly accumulating over the asphalt. I glanced back as I crossed the square and saw no blonde giant tailing me. It hurt that he didn't follow.

I reached my porch and barreled through the door, not even bothering to kick off the snow I'd collected. I wanted to go inside, settle into some corner of the world and fade away. When I closed the door behind me, I found my mother standing behind the couch in her robe, sipping a cup of coffee and holding a plate of cheese and crackers. She looked surprised.

I couldn't hold her gaze. She'd see right fucking through me.

Damn it Faye, run. Don't let her see this. God, what the fuck is this?!

I failed. I dropped to my knees on the living room floor and curled over into myself, and I wailed.

My mother was on me, instantly. "Sweetheart. What's wrong? What happened?"

I shook my head. I couldn't answer this. I couldn't explain.

"Is it Stellan, sweetie?"

I shook my head again, vehemently this time.

She settled onto the floor beside me, her arms tight around my shoulders as I shook against her. "Come on, sweetheart. Talk to me."

I didn't want to tell her, I didn't want to admit it out loud, as though keeping it silent could make it untrue. She whispered that whatever it was, we would figure it out.

When I finally opened my mouth, the words came between hacking sobs, but they came nonetheless.

I couldn't have stopped it if I tried. "I don't want to go back, Mom. I hated it. I hate it! I felt so lonely all the time." She squeezed me tighter and pressed her forehead to my hair. "I was alone all the time. I couldn't even have a cat because I was never home!"

I curled up tighter and opened my mouth, letting myself scream silently. "I won't see Stellan, I won't see you -"

She shooshed softly. "Then don't go."

I growled at the almost naïve simplicity of my mother's response. "Like I have a fucking choice!"

"You always have a choice."

"It's this or continue being a fucking failure -"

She pulled away to look at me. "You're not a failure!"

I frowned, looking around the room. "I'm pathetic, Mom. I'm a burden to you, to my friends -"

She shifted with purpose. "No you are not! You are the love of my life. I'd have you here the rest of my days if I could. Don't you ever say that. You are *not* a burden."

I felt muscles in my face pulling and twisting as misery tried to etch itself across my face. I was still trying to hide it from her. God, if she'd knew how sad I'd been – how sad I still was. My life was about to be perfect – great job, gorgeous man at my side.

I'd tried to pretend I didn't know why my stomach still hurt all the time. I knew exactly why. My stomach hurt day and day out for ten fucking years. I knew exactly why I was so unhappy.

Her eyes were watery, but there was a serenity there that couldn't be argued with. "You are not a burden to me, sweet girl." She brushed my hair behind my ear, staring at my face. She'd always had a magic touch for moments like these. No wonder I'd tried to hide from it for so many months.

"I feel like one, Mom."

She shook her head. "Never feel that way. Never. I'd rather you here and happy than somewhere far away and miserable."

I took a deep, shuddering breath.

"I want you to be happy."

I shut my eyes so tight, my head almost hurt. "Happy doesn't pay bills, Mom."

"Bull shit. You give it a try, then tell me that."

I laughed, nearly dripping snot all over the floor as I did. "No one's going to pay me to eat like a walrus and draw cartoons all day, but that might make me happy."

She chuckled. "Why wouldn't they? The cartoons part anyway."

"It's a pipe dream, Mom. Nobody makes a living drawing car -"

"Walt Disney. Isn't that what you used to say?"

That was my answer. That had always been my answer – back before I'd become the biggest critic of my own dreams. "I'm a thirty four, mom. People who do what I want to do start when they're like fifteen."

"That is when you started."

I rolled my eyes. "Yeah, but then they don't stop for ten years in the middle."

"Then be the first of your kind, lady. Why are you so adamant to quell this creative spark of yours? There are millions of people who would give anything to have a fraction of your talent. Myself included."

I stared at the floor. "I don't want to turn out like Dad."

"What? What do you mean?"

My face contorted, but I got hold of myself before tears could take hold. "I've redirected every single goal I ever had to avoid it."

She inspected my face a moment, then she gave a sad sigh. "That's why? Because of your father?"

I nodded, sucking on my lower lip to steady myself.

"There are worse things in this life than being like your father," she said, then she paused. "That's why you walked away from art school?"

I nodded and inhaled a harsh sob. Hearing her phrase it like that resurrected every pang of guilt and regret and lost hope I'd been forced to contend with as I said goodbye to my professors.

Leaving my dreams behind was the worst heartbreak I'd ever known. Give me another Cole. Hell, give me a thousand Coles – Cole I could handle again. The anguish of that choice I made when I was nineteen made Cole look like a hangnail in comparison. I wouldn't wish it anyone.

Yet I'd been wallowing in it for weeks, feeling that pain all over again at every mention of the job at Chalice.

She squeezed me. "Damn it Chuck, I told you to keep it light."

"What?"

She took a slow breath. "When he came to see you, he promised he'd –"

I pulled from her. "You knew?"

She nodded, giving me an almost piteous smile.

I shook my head as though I might be able to loose the thoughts. "You talked to him?"

She touched my hair. "Honey, I've always been talking to him."

If the earth had split beneath me at that moment, I would have happily let it swallow me. I glared at her. "What? You've just been grabbing coffee with a known drug addict who just so happens to be the source of my genetic material, and you didn't think to share that information?"

"He *is* an addict, no one would say otherwise. He'll tell you that himself, but he has been clean for fifteen years now."

"Fantastic! That just makes him a deadbeat, absentee father! When did you start talking to him again?"

She touched her face. "You were eight."

"What?! What about those years that you couldn't

sleep because you thought he was going to show up in the night and take me or something?"

She settled back onto her hip, curling her legs under her. "I was scared for a while. He was a different man when he was using. When he started to get clean, we started talking. Your grandmother almost killed me for it."

I clenched my fists, took a deep breath, and paused. The words I wanted to ask were dragging through my throat like hot coals. "Why didn't he come see me?"

She frowned. "He didn't want to take the chance of disappointing you."

I laughed. "Yeah, because not having a father wasn't a disappointment in and of itself."

She wiped her eyes, and I thought to rein in my snide, but there was no guarantee it could be curtailed. I felt certain that anger was the righteous response to this news, but somehow instead of angering me, it deflated me.

She touched my arm. "He didn't want you to get attached and then fail you if he relapsed. And he did. Many times."

"So he waited until I was fucking nineteen?"

She nodded. "It took that long for him to feel sure he wouldn't relapse again."

I scratched my head roughly.

"He tried to convince me so many times it was his fault. That he'd caused your – your crisis. Said he shouldn't have sprung on you like that, but I thought you would have told me if –"

"I thought it would upset you!"

She shook her head. "I wish I'd known. He's stayed away ever since because he felt he'd done you harm. I've tried to convince him that wasn't the case, but now - I don't know what I would have done to change your mind, but – I just wish I'd known."

We sat quietly for a moment.

"You still talk?" I asked, finally.

She nodded.

"Where is he?"

She smiled and gestured to the painting on the wall. "He teaches at Mass Art. Fuller is one of his."

I turned toward the painting, suddenly seeing it anew. Part of me wanted to rally against the painting, as though it were some interloper sneaking into my otherwise perfect world. The other part of me wanted to soak it in with new eyes.

My dad taught this painter. My dad.

"Is he still married to that lady? Have you met her?"

She had a far off look for a moment, but she smiled. "Oh no, that intolerable woman – she's long gone. And I never met her, thank god."

"Why 'thank god?'"

She gave me a half smile, signifying that she expected me to know the answer to this question.

I did.

"Because I love him, Faye. Always have."

At that, I began to sniffle again. I wiped my hand across my nose. Gross, I know, but better than letting it drip down my face.

"I don't know what to do, Mom."

She ran her hand over my hair "Yes you do. And anything beyond that, we can figure out later."

Familiar footsteps clomped up the porch steps, and the door opened. Stellan crouched right down beside us.

I glanced at him, but kept my eyes down. I wasn't

angry at him anymore. Not sure I ever really was. Mom said something about clouds lifting and shifted out of the way so he could collect me and move me to the couch. After a moment of him snuggling me into the crook of his neck, softly whispering how much he cherished me, my mother returned from the kitchen with a cup of tea and tissues. She set them next to the crackers and cheese on the table.

"Tell me you'll call them tomorrow. Promise me that," she said, hovering by the arm of the couch.

I felt like a child being given permission to come home from a miserable week at camp – freed and protected, not a desperately stumbling adult about to blow off the best job prospect she'd seen in a year.

I stared at my hands in my lap, watched as Stellan interlaced his fingers with mine. Could I do it, could I choose just the possibility of something better over a paycheck? Could I say I had enough hope?

She offered me a cracker with cheese. I took it, and I nodded.

We ate Brie and Butter Crackers, sipped tea, and spent the afternoon on the couch watching a Monty Python marathon on PBS as the snow fell outside. And we laughed.

Stellan and I woke the next day to another snowy morning. Mom left for work, taking my Santé Fe with four wheel drive to battle against the snow. I had nowhere to go that day, and there was no way she wasn't going in to work. She had curating to do.

After breakfast, and a couple hours of internal struggle, I finally called Chalice. Dennis seemed sincerely disappointed when I broke the news, even tried to change my mind. Somehow, my mother's words had given me permission to say no.

"I've decided to pursue something else," I said. Felt like a complete jackass when he asked me what that was and I answered, "I haven't actually figured that out yet."

Oddly enough, he seemed to respect it. He left the door open, saying to check in with him if I ever changed my mind.

I smiled. I knew that such a day would never come. Even if I decided to work at Arby's, I knew I'd be happier.

As I sat there with the phone in my hand, I felt a sudden inspiration.

I pulled up a blank message for Jackie. **Think you might still like some help down at the bakery? Looks like my calendar just opened up, and I'm told I make a mean Swedish Apple.**

Jackie responded within seconds, a million exclamation points to declare her pure elation. She promised to call after dinner. I smiled and searched for the words to send my mother, telling her the deed was done.

Yet, before I could press send, my phone lit up – incoming phone call from the 617 - Boston. I stared at it a moment, contemplating letting it go to voicemail. Was my mother calling me from a museum phone to celebrate the momentous joy of my life as a mooch?

I made my way down the hall toward the living room, watching my phone. I finally answered.

"Hello?"

"Is this Faye?"

The man's voice was soft, almost cautious.

"Yes?" I said.

"Hey, Fayebell."

I froze by the fireplace holding the phone to my ear.

I swallowed. "Hi, Dad."

Stellan moved on the couch, closing his laptop and turning toward me. I leaned against the fireplace for support, letting it warm my legs.

"Your mother tells me you've decided not to go back to that marketing job."

Wow, they really do talk.

I pressed my finger to my other ear as though there was some cacophony I was trying to drown out. Hard to do when the din is in your own head, ladies and gents. "Well, it's not the same job, but yeah – yeah."

He mumbled something to someone on the other line, then shuffled a moment. "Well, I talked to a couple people and – I hope you don't mind your mother talking to me about it. You can tell me to fuck right off."

Before I could say anything, my phone buzzed again – Evan was calling. I ignored the call. "No. No, it's okay."

He whistled, softly. "Okay – uh. Okay. Well, I talked to a few people and, if you had the notion, you could always come take a few classes. Get back into the swing, maybe."

My mouth fell open, but it took a moment to speak. Whose idea was this, and why did it feel like I could fly? "I can't afford them."

"Honey -" He paused. "That's not an issue. I know you're more into the cartoon side of it all, so my classes might not be your cup of tea, but Jerry would love to have you back. And you might not know this, but your Dad works here so – there's that whole free tuition thing. I know your Dad's a flaming asshole, but why not milk nepotism for all it's worth, right?"

I laughed. I really laughed.

He heard me and chuckled back. "I'll send home a schedule with your mother. You can have a look and decide. No pressure, ok?"

I nodded. "Okay."

"Alright. Alright, yeah. Okay, kiddo. Alright. You be good."

I swallowed. Did I have more to say? Did I have a million things I wanted to say? "Okay," was all I could manage.

He was gone, and I was left with the phone to my ear like a toddler on an imaginary call with Big Bird.

I knew the Jerry he spoke of – Jerry Hallowell. He'd been a teacher of mine, and one of the professors I found hardest to say goodbye to. We shared many of the same heroes, and in some cases, my heroes shared drinks with Jerry Hallowell. He was head of his department now.

I stared at the wall, finally taking the phone away from my ear.

I turned and smiled at Stellan, who had been perched on the edge of the couch, watching me for the duration of the conversation, as though readying himself to run across the room and catch me.

I didn't move. Instead I pulled up Evan's number and pressed send. I needed to talk to someone who didn't know about the bomb that had just gone off in my chest before acknowledging the look on Stellan's face.

There were no pleasantries when Evan answered. "Do you think Patty would mind if I called her?"

I laughed. "Well, hello to you to. No, I'm sure she

would love that."

"Fantastic."

"You hoping to catch up, or you hoping to maybe make out?"

He scoffed. "Definitely make out."

"Nice! How'd you get her number?"

Evan coughed. "You were about to give it to me."

"Oh, you dick!"

He laughed. "Hey, how are sales? Any news from Stell?"

I glanced across the room. "I don't know. He hasn't said anything."

"What haven't I said?"

I relayed the message to Stellan. He assured me he was just about to check the stats again.

Gorilla Warfare had gone live at midnight the night before. With Evan agreeing to a marketing blitz for just ten percent equity, Stellan had seemed rather disappointed when only fourteen sales were registering when we woke up.

"Sometimes there's a delay," he'd said as I brewed coffee that morning, and it sounded as though he was trying to assure himself as much as me. He was proud of his game, and I wanted to see him succeed. Though I stood to benefit from its success, I was far more terrified than proud. I hadn't put artwork out into the world since publishing a comic strip when I was nineteen. Still, if my marketing savvy was any judge, there would have to be *some* kind of response. Maybe not millions of dollars' worth, by any means, but something. Right?

I informed Evan of the lackluster response that morning.

He scoffed, making a 'psh' sound. "Yeah, just you

fucking wait. Those monkeys have been in front of a million eyes by now. Just you fucking wait."

The notion of that many eyes seeing my work terrified me. What had I gotten myself into?

I hung up, texted Evan her contact info, and finally turned to face my honey.

"You alright?" He asked as I approached.

I thought a moment.

Yes. I was.

I nodded.

"Do you want to talk about it?"

I took a deep breath. I'm sure he was worried that call from Dad might trigger another complete mental breakdown, and I'd be living in an ashram with a shaved head by Thursday, but I shrugged.

I took a moment, mulling over what it was I was feeling. "Not yet, if that's okay?"

He nodded and gestured for me to come to him.

I did, getting pulled down for a few kisses and a long, deliberate hug. I snuggled into him and grumbled from the folds of his shirt that he forgot deodorant that morning. He then proceeded to try mashing my face in his arm pit as I screamed.

Ah, l'amour.

I pulled free of him, and he grabbed my hand, tugging me back down for a kiss.

I let him return to his laptop.

"Anything coming up?" I asked.

He made a face. "Still loading. Cross your fingers, will ya?"

Money or no, I was ready to say I'd made something, and though cash money would be a nice thing to have, oddly enough, I wasn't so worried about that anymore.

I tried to find something to distract myself from waiting. The fire called to me. I settled down into my favorite chair and reached for something to read on the side table. I spotted a dog-eared page, picked up the book, and began reading.

I was three pages in before I realized what I was reading. I tossed the book onto the floor.

Stellan looked up from his laptop. He looked as exasperated as me. "What's up?"

I grumbled. "*Pussy, King of the* God damn *Pirates*, that's what's up. I swear to God, this book is mocking me."

He raised an eyebrow, and I reminded him of the absolute derision I felt for the brain cell melting power of its pages. "I feel like I get stupider every time I read it."

"Did you just say 'stupider?'"

"See?!"

He laughed. "Write that in comic form, please?"

I grinned at him and bent down to pick up the book from the floor. "I will."

"And burn the book."

I was enticed, turning to the fireplace with a wicked grin. Yet, I didn't throw it in. "Still can't do it. Feels sacrilegious."

"Pussy."

I flipped him the bird. He blew me a kiss.

I turned the book over in my hands, skimming the back cover before deciding that despite my seething hatred for every page, it might be someone else's Keats. And even if not, I just couldn't burn it.

I then remembered that my mom had a stock pile of books to donate in her trunk. Perfect.

I headed toward the back door, glancing back at

Stellan. "Any luck? Are you working once you check the stats?"

"No, I can stop. Why?"

"Cause I'm gonna fuck your brains out when I get back in."

I headed toward the kitchen.

He called after me. "I fucking love you, you know that right?"

"You bettah! Now take off your pants!"

My slippered feet hit the snowy deck, and I pulled my sweater tight against the flurries. The birds were riled by my appearance, but not enough to scatter from the feeders. I cracked mom's trunk and tossed the book into one of the bags, stuffing it under a book on Monet so no one would mistake my mother for one who would read such 'Avant garbage.' I shut the trunk softly to avoid upsetting the birds.

The birds flitted in a snow inspired tizzy. This was Grammy Jensen's favorite time to watch them, when the snow was falling. I gasped at a flash of red and watched the male Cardinal peck through the seed. He was joined by his Missus, their colors bright against the crowd of brown and black sparrows. I watched a moment, enjoying the chaos. At this rate, the feeders would need to be refilled by the end of the day.

"F-Bomb!" Stellan called from inside. "Baby! Get in here!"

I called over my shoulder, still watching the birds. "What is it?"

"Come see! Holy shit! You're not going to believe this! I gotta call Ev!"

The birds startled by Stellan's excited tone. Even I felt like flitting through the snow, my heart was racing to hear him so excited. I turned back toward the stairs and stopped. A small brown and black bird landed on the railing between me and the door.

"Jesus! The number just keeps climbing. Where the fuck are you, hot pants! Come look!"

The bird tilted his head to the side, watching me. I didn't dare disturb him from his perch. For some reason, I felt as though he had something to tell, too. Stellan called out to me again, disturbing all the birds save for one. The little bird hopped once on the railing, looked at me with ruffled feathers, and sang.

Madge-Madge-Madge-put-on-your-tea-kettle-ettle.

He stared at me, waiting for a response.

I smiled.

ABOUT THE AUTHOR

Michaela Wright is an American author with a 'bordering on unhealthy' relationship with Deep Fried Mars Bars, Scottish Accents, Iced Caramel Lattes, and commas. Her long standing love of history and ghost stories (and a staunch belief in soul mates) has resulted in many a randy love story, often told over the backdrop of some of the darkest moments in history. These interests have inspired a Google search history that has most likely resulted in an FBI dossier on her, but that's neither here nor there.

Author of WRITING MR RIGHT, and the Gothic Mystery Series, THE NAMESAKEN, Michaela lives in Chelmsford, Massachusetts with her daughter and a cat named Chapter. When she isn't writing, she's performing aerial silks in her backyard or hula hooping, and on some occasions, sipping a Cider with friends until her own fake Scottish Accent comes out.

Sign up below for Michaela's Newsletter, bringing you the latest on New Releases and Freebies directly from the author.
http://eepurl.com/bUQ3pf
For more information, please visit michaelawrightauthor.com

Also from Michaela Wright

WRITING MR RIGHT
The VILLAIN Trilogy (Coming Soon)

From THE NAMESAKEN Series

WILLING
HYSTERIA

Watch for the next title in
THE NAMESAKEN Series
by Michaela Wright.

HEARTLESS
(Coming SPRING 2016)

Find Michaela online at:
www.michaelawrightauthor.com

Made in the USA
Columbia, SC
26 November 2017